HELLSING ③
ヘルシング

平野耕太
KOHTA HIRANO

translation
DUANE JOHNSON

lettering
WILBERT LACUNA

DARK HORSE MANGA

DMP
Digital Manga Publishing

publishers
MIKE RICHARDSON and HIKARU SASAHARA

editors
TIM ERVIN-GORE and FRED LUI

collection designer
DAVID NESTELLE

English-language version produced by
DARK HORSE COMICS and DIGITAL MANGA PUBLISHING

HELLSING VOL.3

T 251336

published by
Dark Horse Manga
a division of Dark Horse Comics, Inc.
10956 S.E. Main Street
Milwaukie, OR 97222

www.darkhorse.com

Digital Manga Publishing
1123 Dominguez Street, unit K
Carson, CA 90746

www.dmpbooks.com

To find a comics shop in your area, call the
Comic Shop Locator Service toll-free at 1-888-266-4226

First edition: May 2004
ISBN: 1-59307-202-3

3 5 7 9 10 8 6 4

Printed in Canada

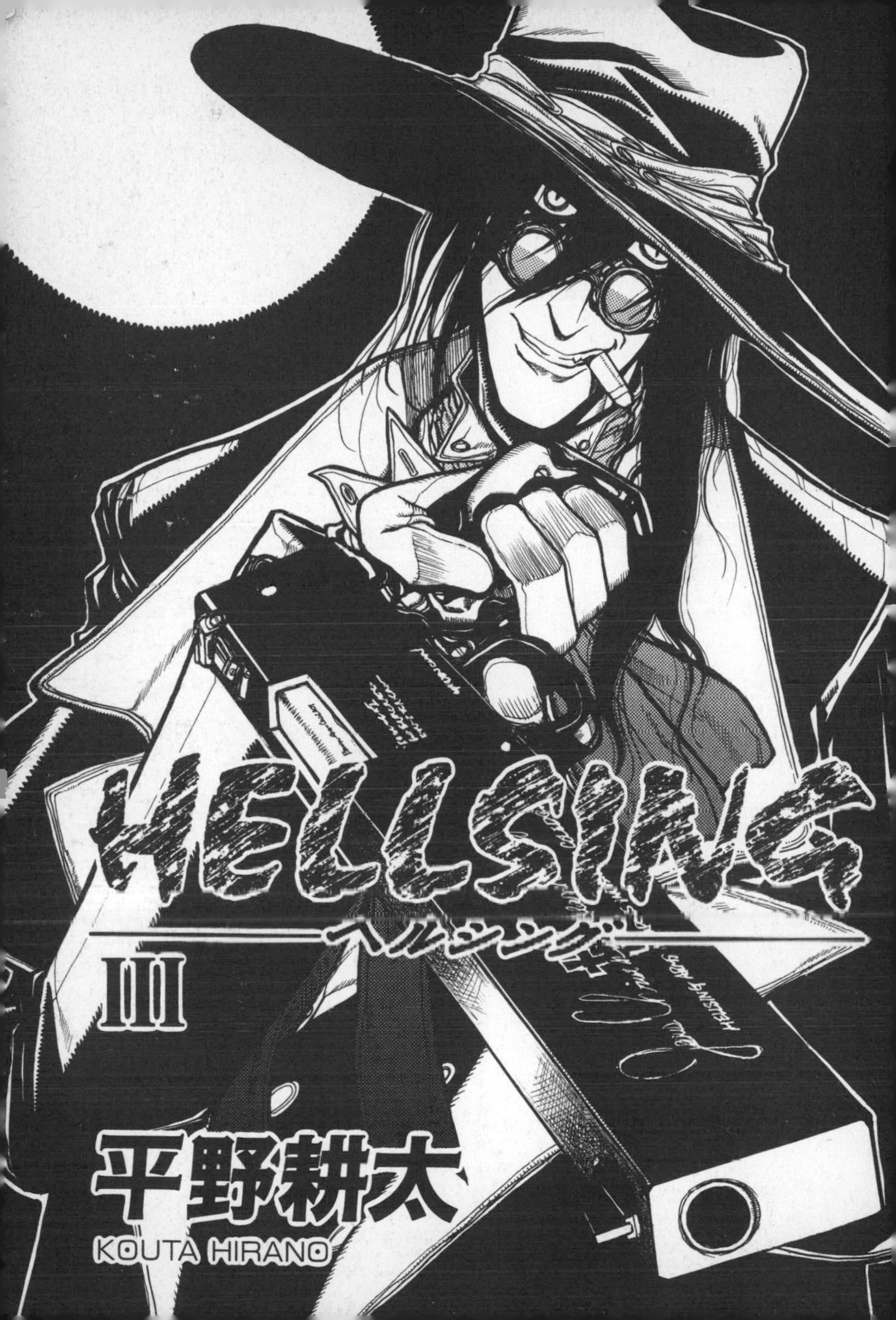
HELLSING
ヘルシング
III
平野耕太
KOUTA HIRANO

HELLSING ③

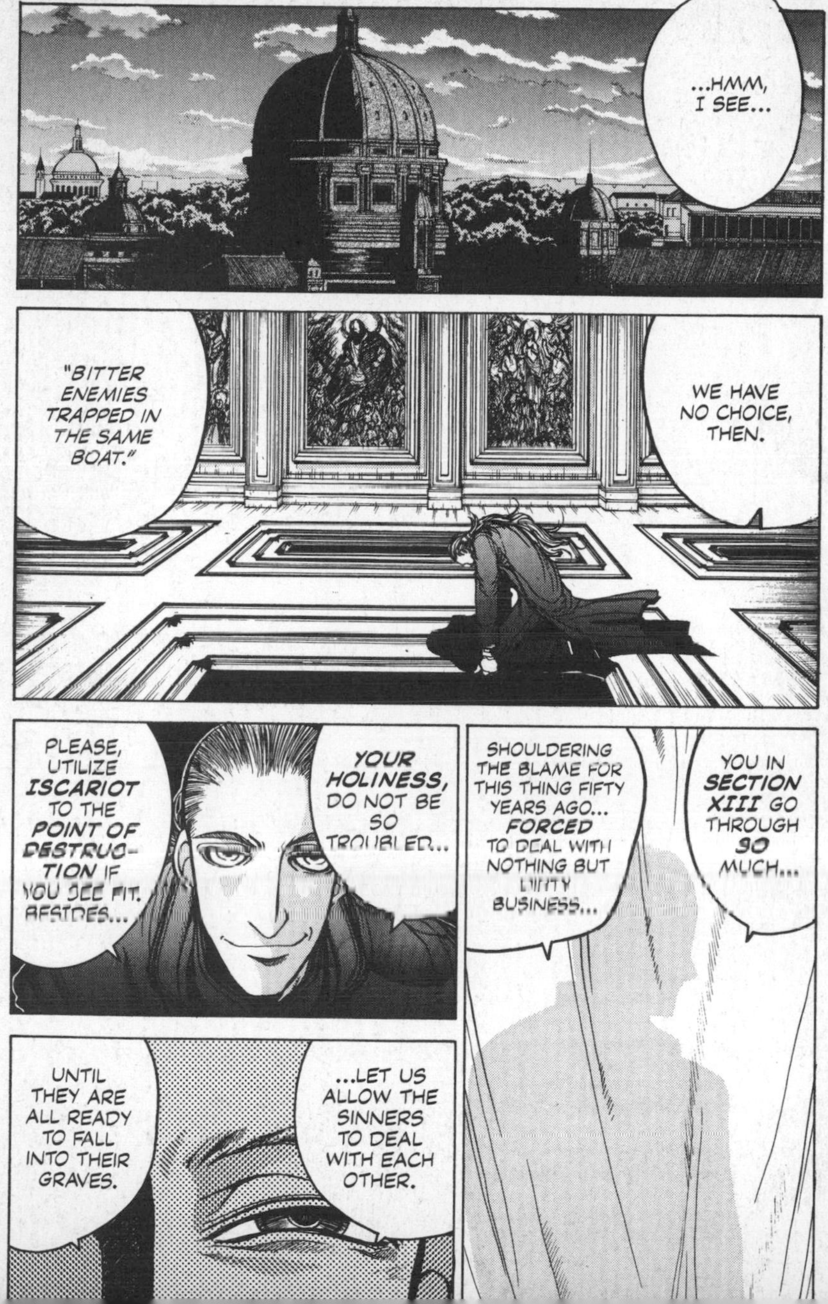
...HMM, I SEE...
WE HAVE NO CHOICE, THEN.
"BITTER ENEMIES TRAPPED IN THE SAME BOAT."
YOU IN SECTION XIII GO THROUGH SO MUCH...
SHOULDERING THE BLAME FOR THIS THING FIFTY YEARS AGO... FORCED TO DEAL WITH NOTHING BUT DIRTY BUSINESS...
YOUR HOLINESS, DO NOT BE SO TROUBLED...
PLEASE, UTILIZE ISCARIOT TO THE POINT OF DESTRUCTION IF YOU SEE FIT. BESIDES...
...LET US ALLOW THE SINNERS TO DEAL WITH EACH OTHER.
UNTIL THEY ARE ALL READY TO FALL INTO THEIR GRAVES.

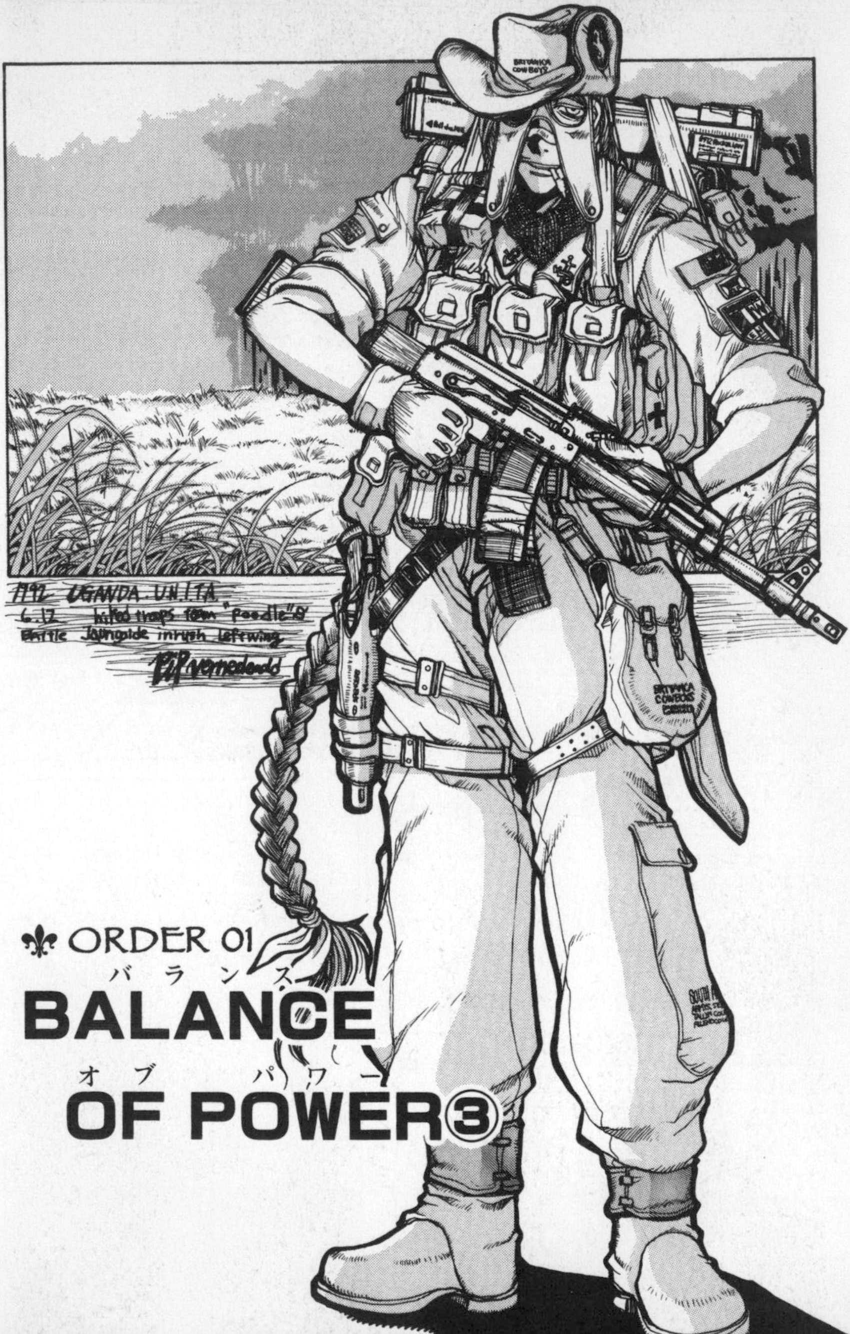
1992 UGANDA.U.N.I.T.A.
6.12 hired troops team "poodle"
Battle jungside inrush leftwing
BRITANICA COWBOYS

ORDER 01

バランス BALANCE オブ パワー OF POWER③

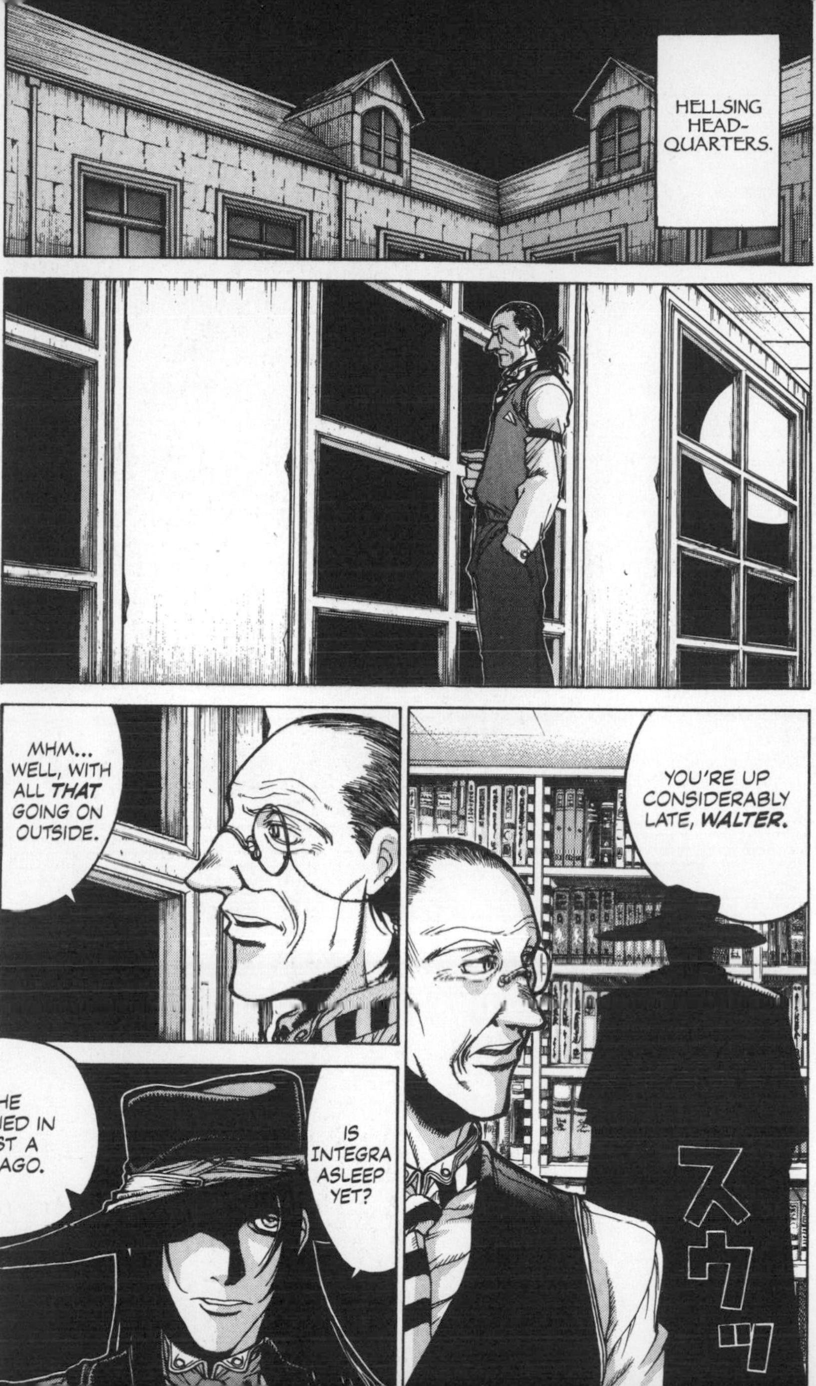
HELLSING HEAD-QUARTERS.
YOU'RE UP CONSIDERABLY LATE, WALTER.
スウッ
MHM... WELL, WITH ALL THAT GOING ON OUTSIDE.
IS INTEGRA ASLEEP YET?
SHE TURNED IN JUST A BIT AGO.

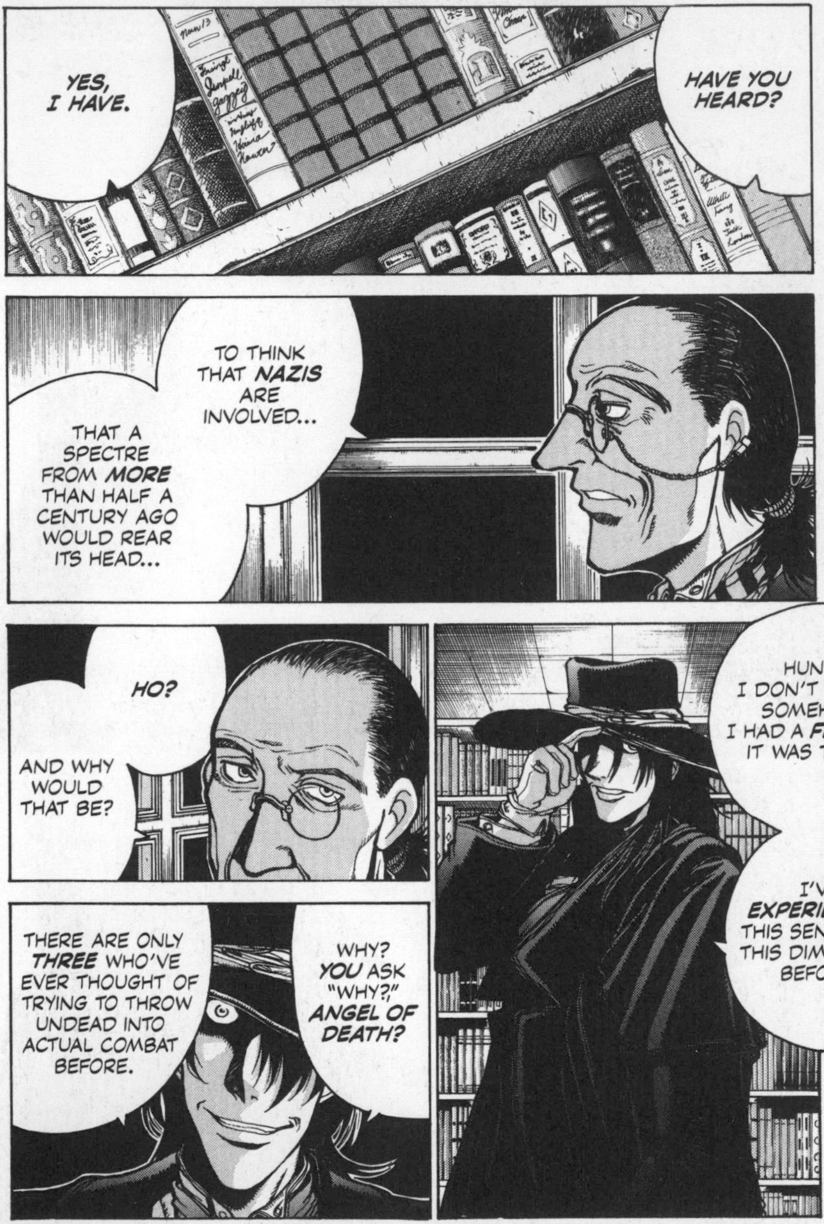
HAVE YOU HEARD?
YES, I HAVE.
TO THINK THAT NAZIS ARE INVOLVED...
THAT A SPECTRE FROM MORE THAN HALF A CENTURY AGO WOULD REAR ITS HEAD...
HUNH. I DON'T KNOW. SOMEHOW, I HAD A FEELING IT WAS THEM.
I'VE EXPERIENCED THIS SENSATION, THIS DIM SENSE, BEFORE.
HO?
AND WHY WOULD THAT BE?
WHY? YOU ASK "WHY?," ANGEL OF DEATH?
THERE ARE ONLY THREE WHO'VE EVER THOUGHT OF TRYING TO THROW UNDEAD INTO ACTUAL COMBAT BEFORE.

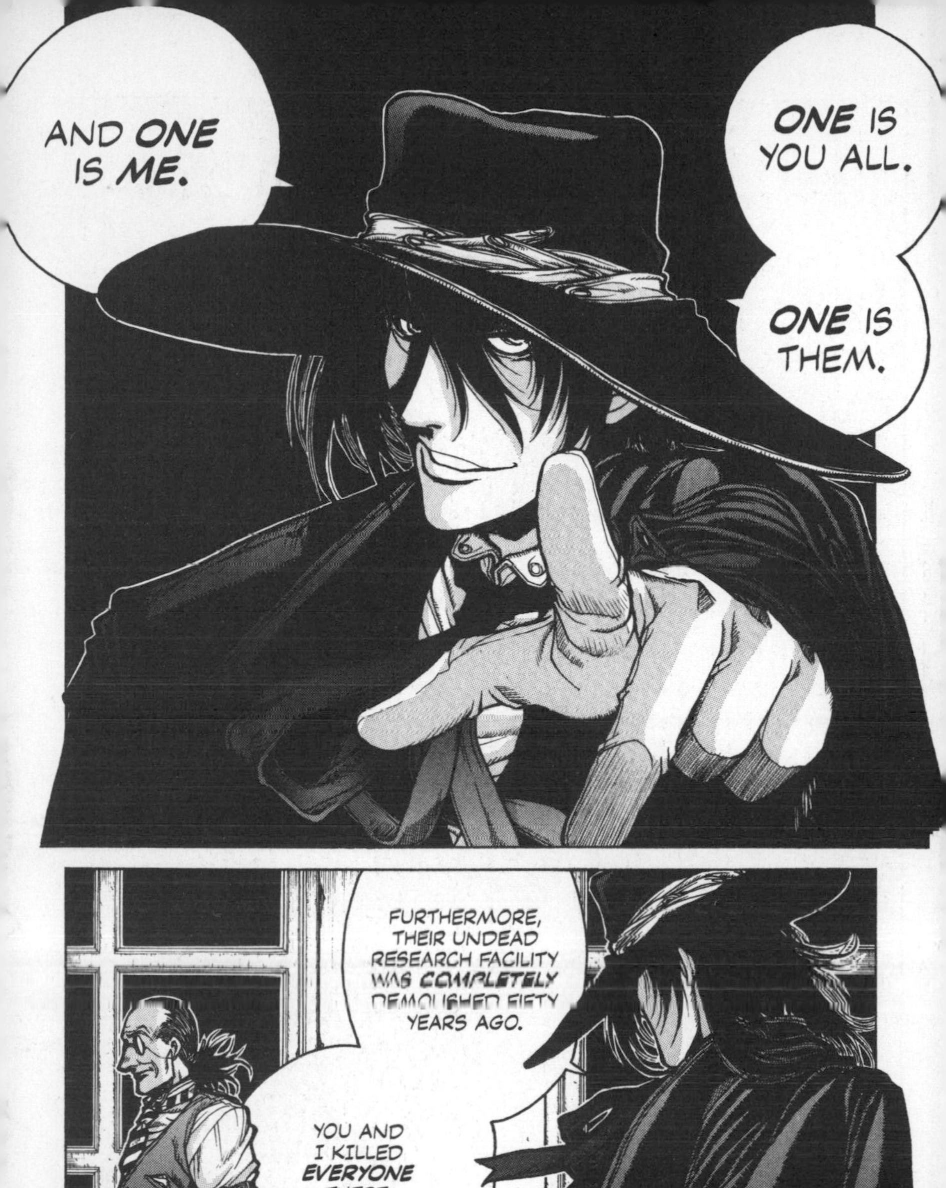
ONE IS YOU ALL.
ONE IS THEM.
AND ONE IS ME.
FURTHERMORE, THEIR UNDEAD RESEARCH FACILITY WAS COMPLETELY DEMOLISHED FIFTY YEARS AGO.
YOU AND I KILLED EVERYONE THERE, DIDN'T WE?

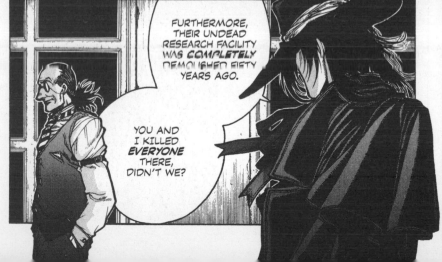

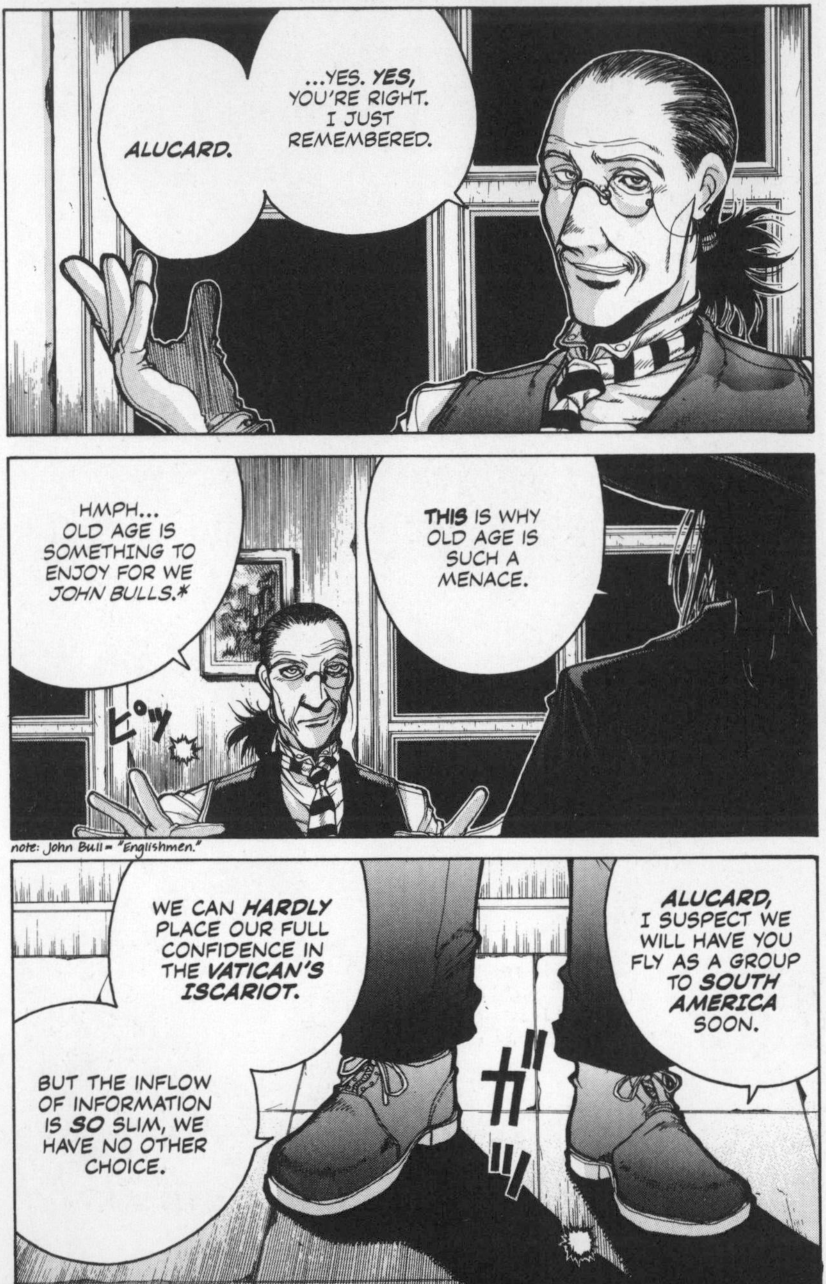
...YES. YES, YOU'RE RIGHT. I JUST REMEMBERED.
ALUCARD.
THIS IS WHY OLD AGE IS SUCH A MENACE.
HMPH... OLD AGE IS SOMETHING TO ENJOY FOR WE JOHN BULLS.*
note: John Bull = "Englishmen."
ALUCARD, I SUSPECT WE WILL HAVE YOU FLY AS A GROUP TO SOUTH AMERICA SOON.
WE CAN HARDLY PLACE OUR FULL CONFIDENCE IN THE VATICAN'S ISCARIOT.
BUT THE INFLOW OF INFORMATION IS SO SLIM, WE HAVE NO OTHER CHOICE.

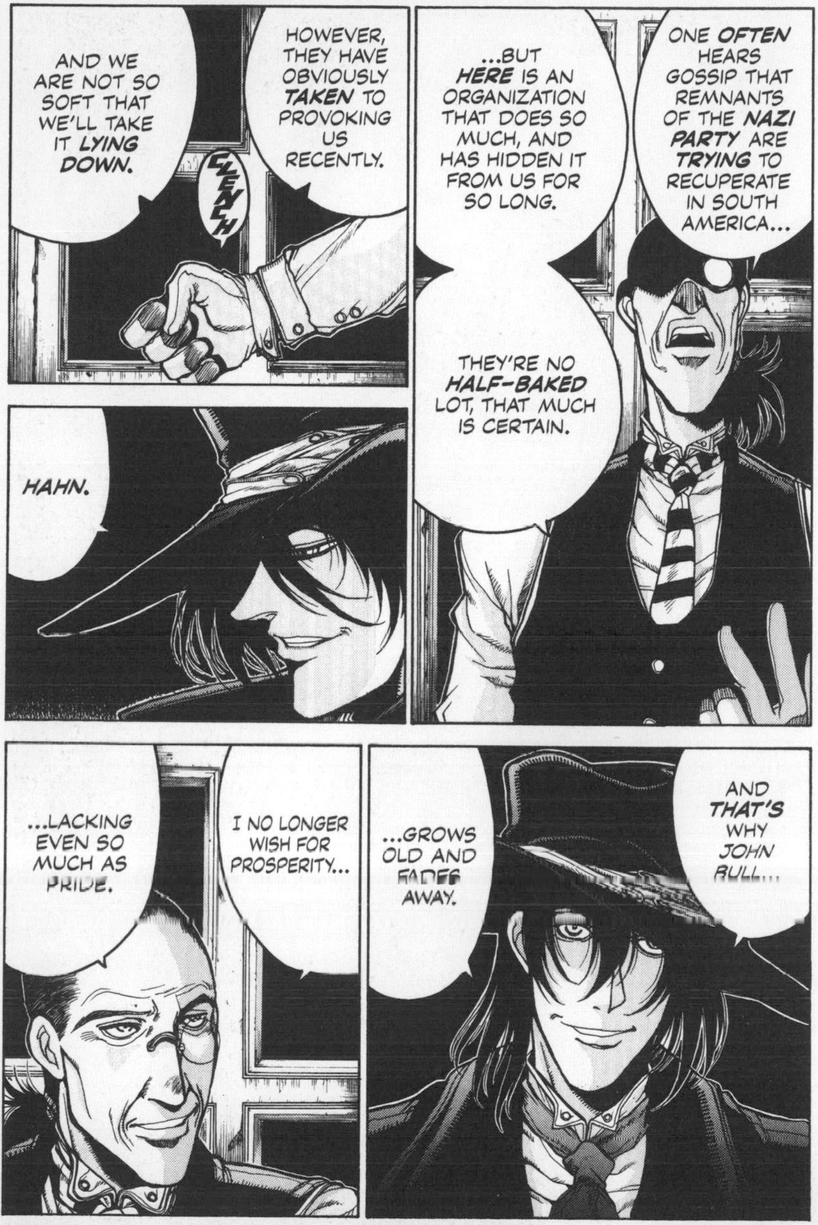
ONE OFTEN HEARS GOSSIP THAT REMNANTS OF THE NAZI PARTY ARE TRYING TO RECUPERATE IN SOUTH AMERICA...
...BUT HERE IS AN ORGANIZATION THAT DOES SO MUCH, AND HAS HIDDEN IT FROM US FOR SO LONG.
THEY'RE NO HALF-BAKED LOT, THAT MUCH IS CERTAIN.
HOWEVER, THEY HAVE OBVIOUSLY TAKEN TO PROVOKING US RECENTLY.
CLENCH
AND WE ARE NOT SO SOFT THAT WE'LL TAKE IT LYING DOWN.
HAHN.
AND THAT'S WHY JOHN BULL...
...GROWS OLD AND FADES AWAY.
I NO LONGER WISH FOR PROSPERITY...
...LACKING EVEN SO MUCH AS PRIDE.

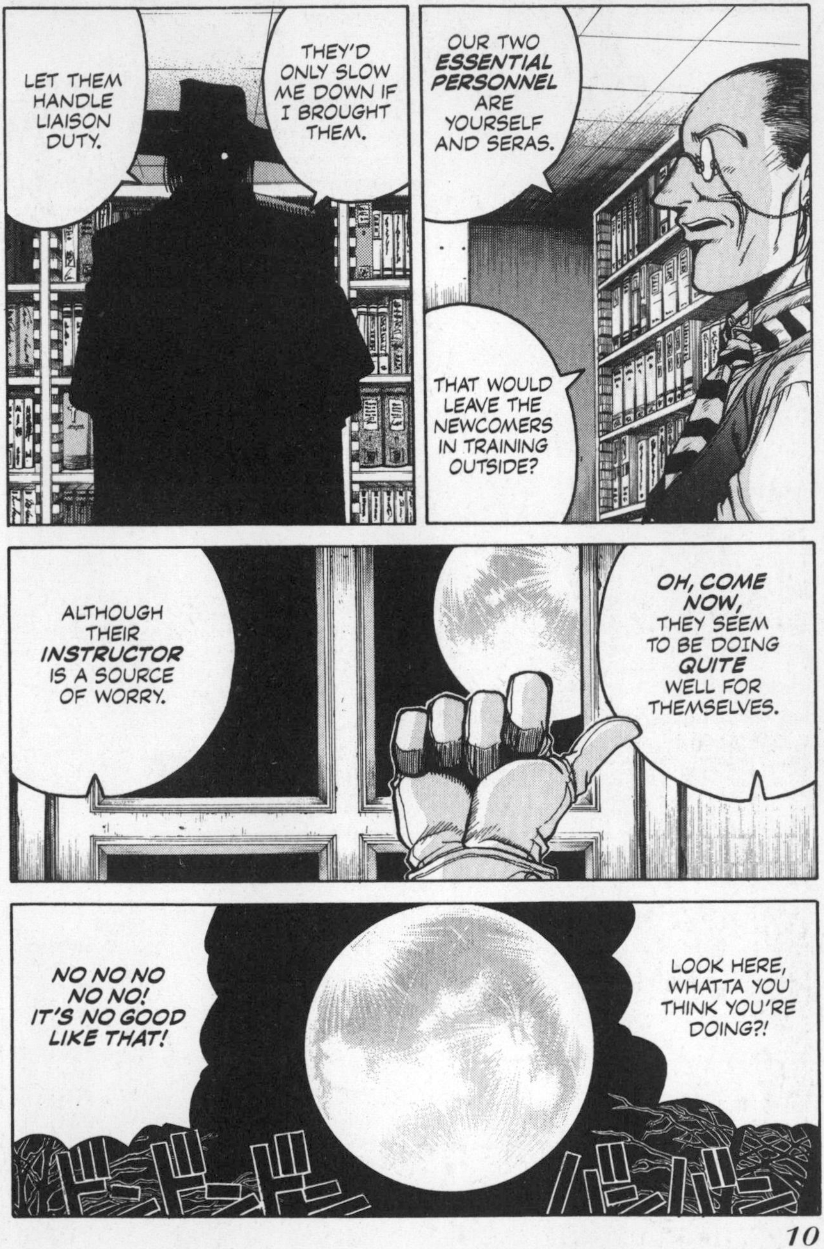
OUR TWO ESSENTIAL PERSONNEL ARE YOURSELF AND SERAS.
THAT WOULD LEAVE THE NEWCOMERS IN TRAINING OUTSIDE?
THEY'D ONLY SLOW ME DOWN IF I BROUGHT THEM.
LET THEM HANDLE LIAISON DUTY.
OH, COME NOW, THEY SEEM TO BE DOING QUITE WELL FOR THEMSELVES.
ALTHOUGH THEIR INSTRUCTOR IS A SOURCE OF WORRY.
LOOK HERE, WHATTA YOU THINK YOU'RE DOING?!
NO NO NO NO NO! IT'S NO GOOD LIKE THAT!

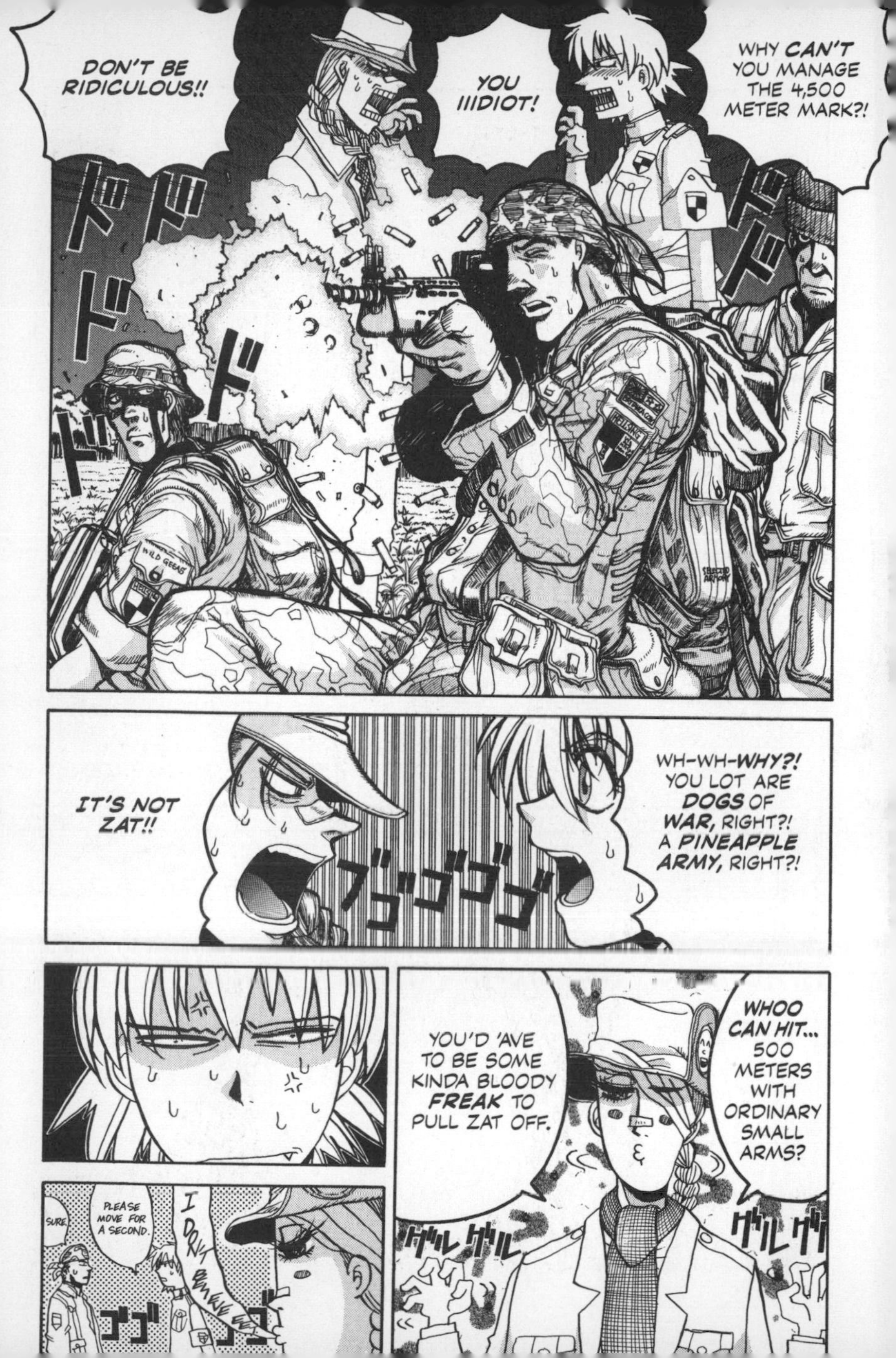
WHY CAN'T YOU MANAGE THE 4,500 METER MARK?!
YOU IIIDIOT!
DON'T BE RIDICULOUS!!
ドドド
ドド
ドド
ドドド
WH-WH-WHY?! YOU LOT ARE DOGS OF WAR, RIGHT?! A PINEAPPLE ARMY, RIGHT?!
IT'S NOT ZAT!!
ゴゴゴゴゴ
WHOO CAN HIT... 500 METERS WITH ORDINARY SMALL ARMS?
YOU'D 'AVE TO BE SOME KINDA BLOODY FREAK TO PULL ZAT OFF.
グルグル
グルグル
PLEASE MOVE FOR A SECOND.
SURE.
ゴゴゴ

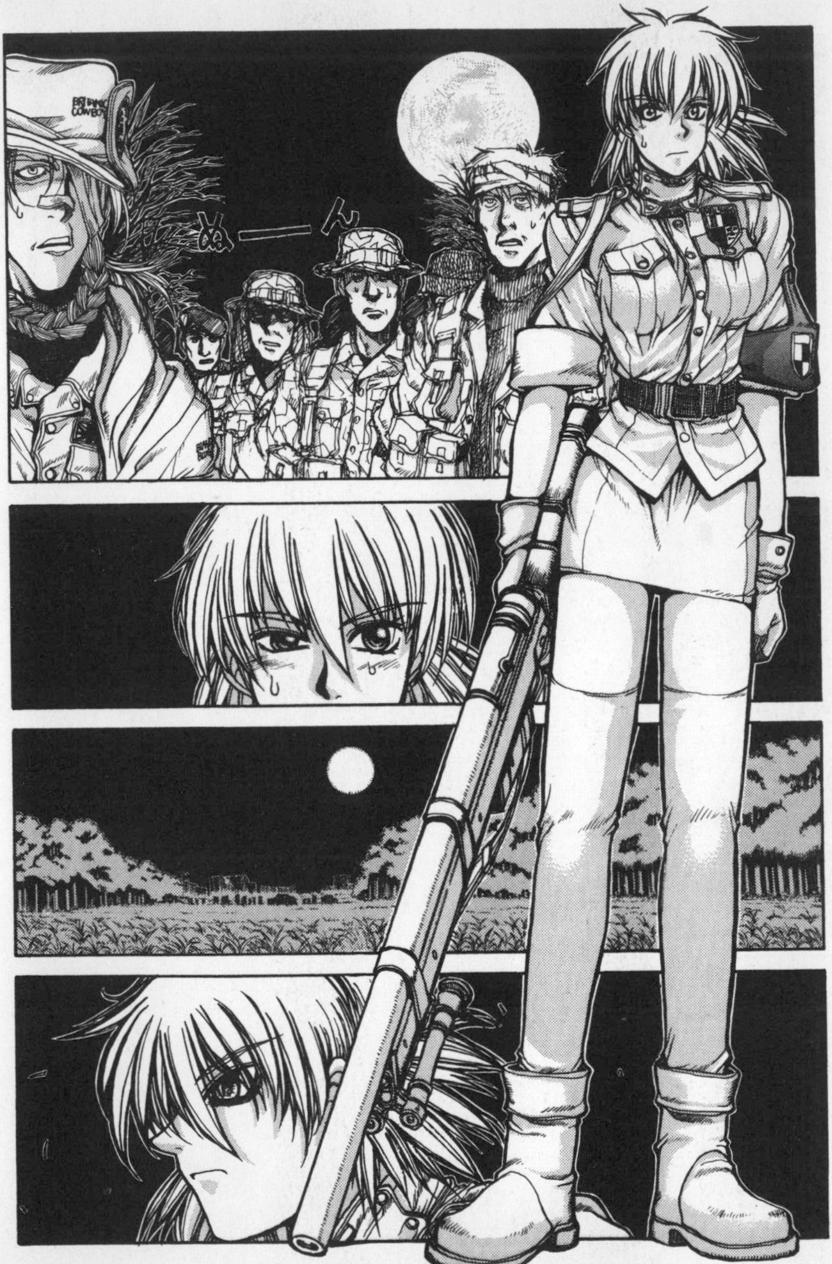
ぬーーーん

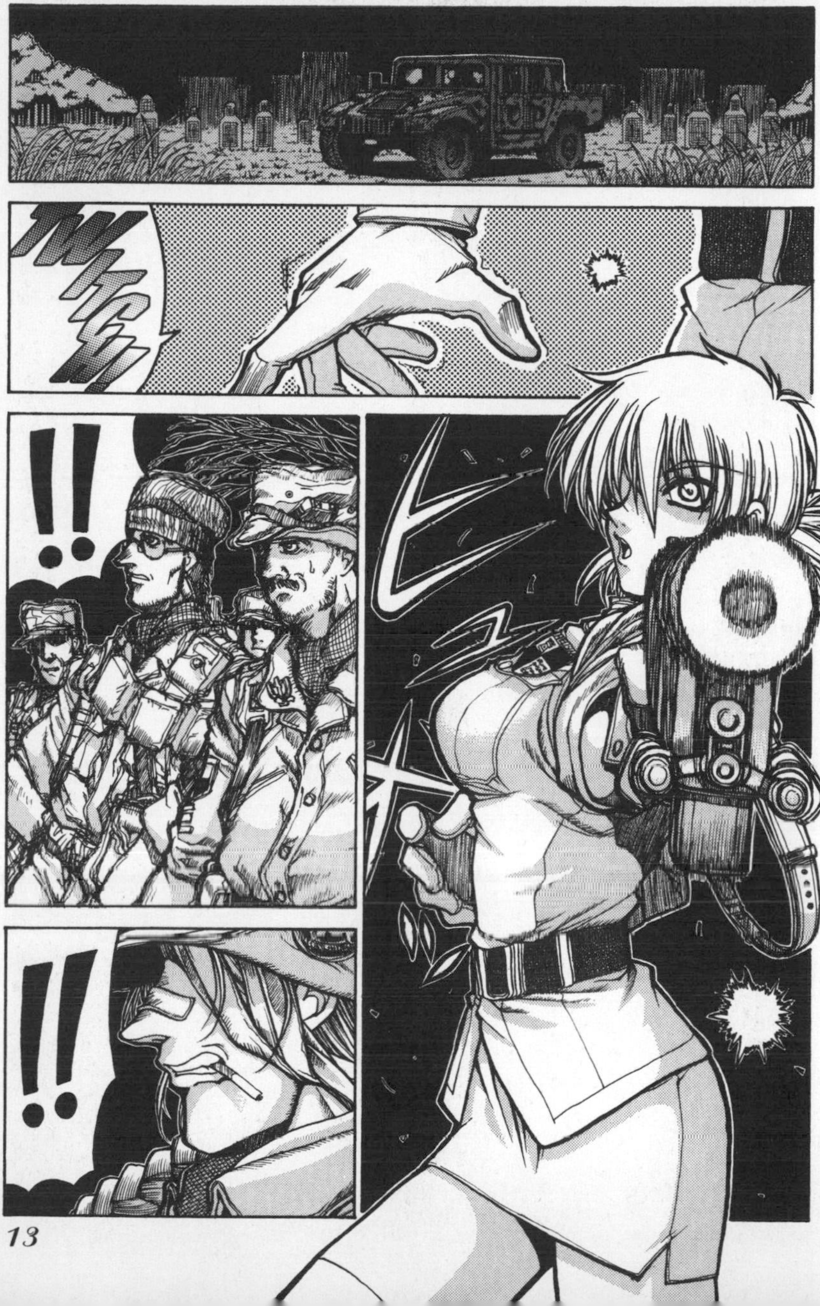
TWITCH!
!!
!!

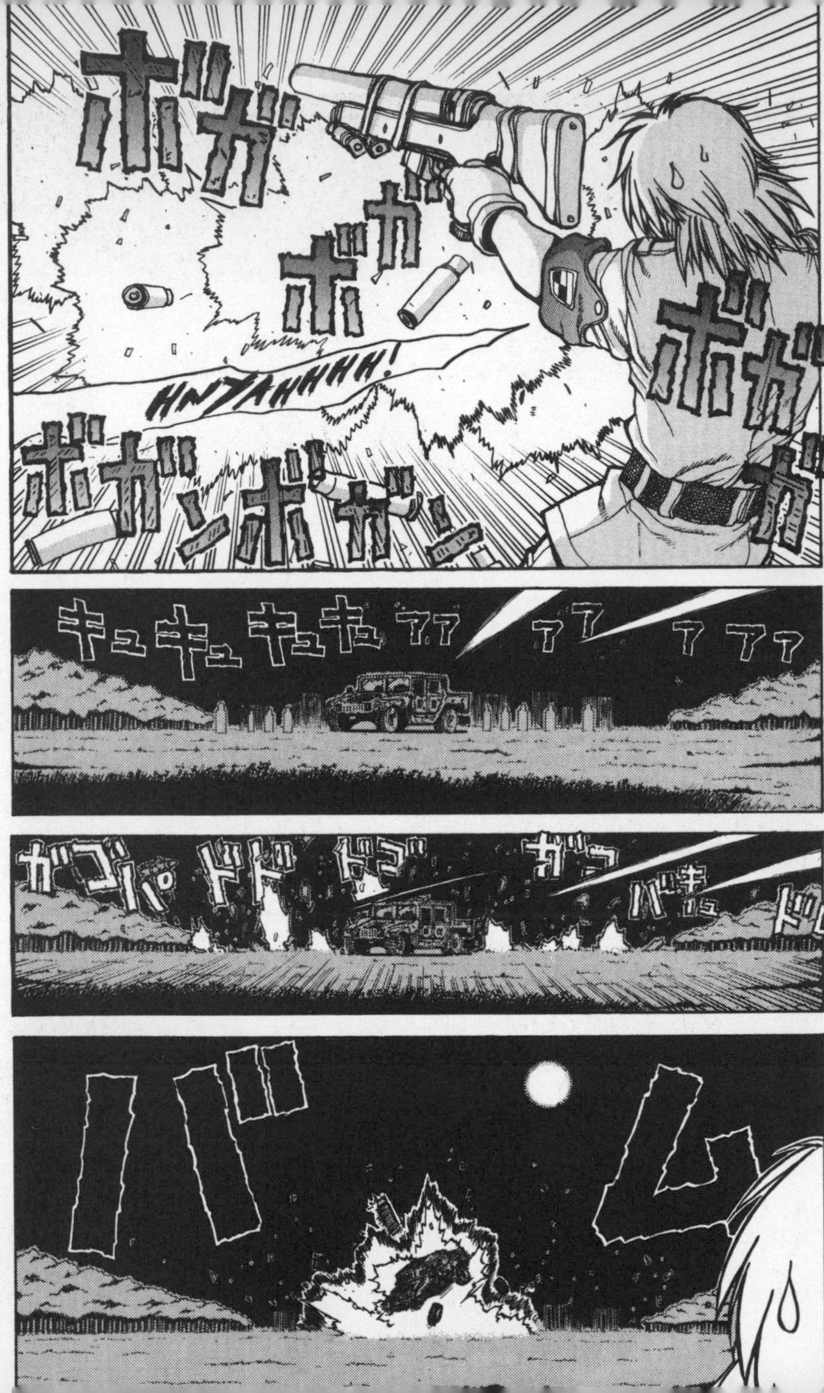

ボガボガ
ボガ
ボガ
HNYAHHHHH!
ボガンボガン
キュキュキュキュアァァァァァ
ガゴパドドドドゴガッバキュドム
バム

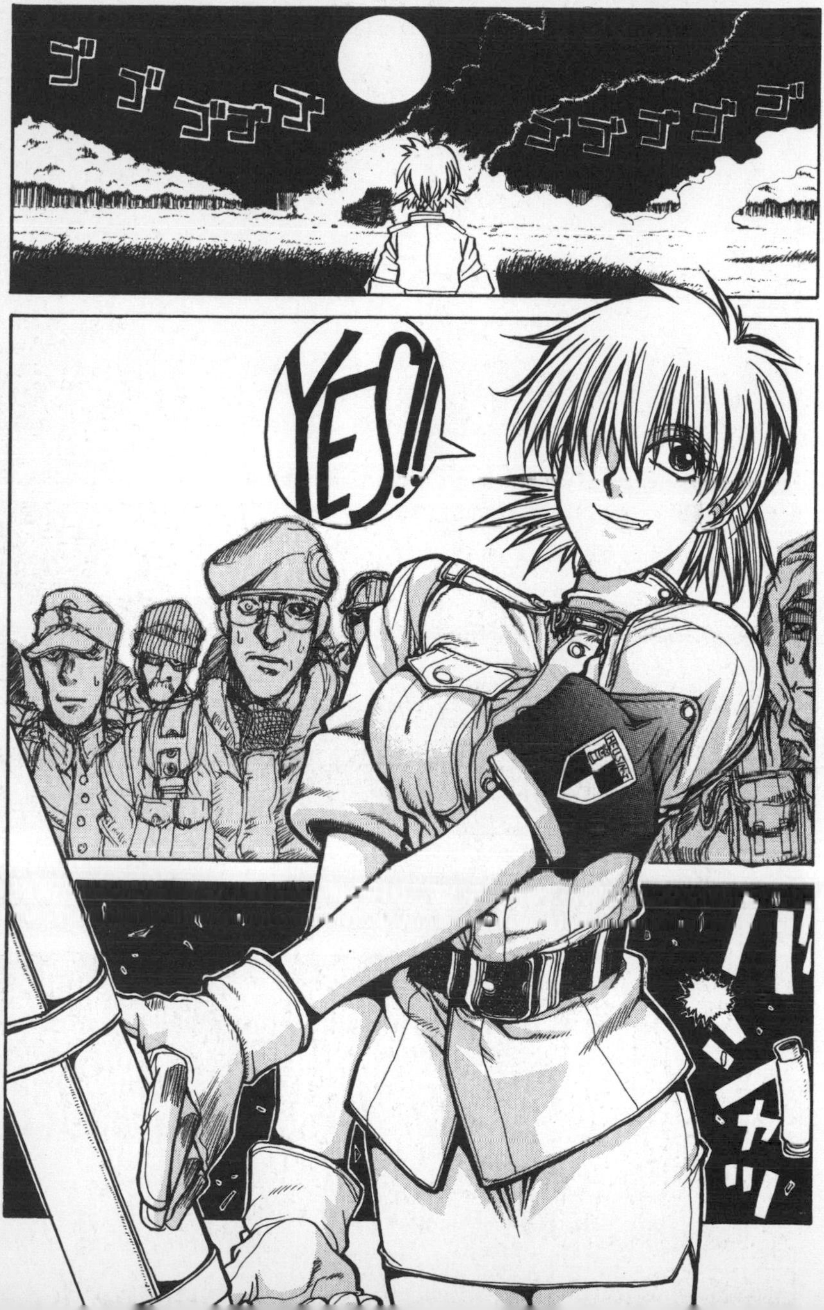
ゴゴゴゴゴ
ゴゴゴゴゴ
YES!!
バシャッ

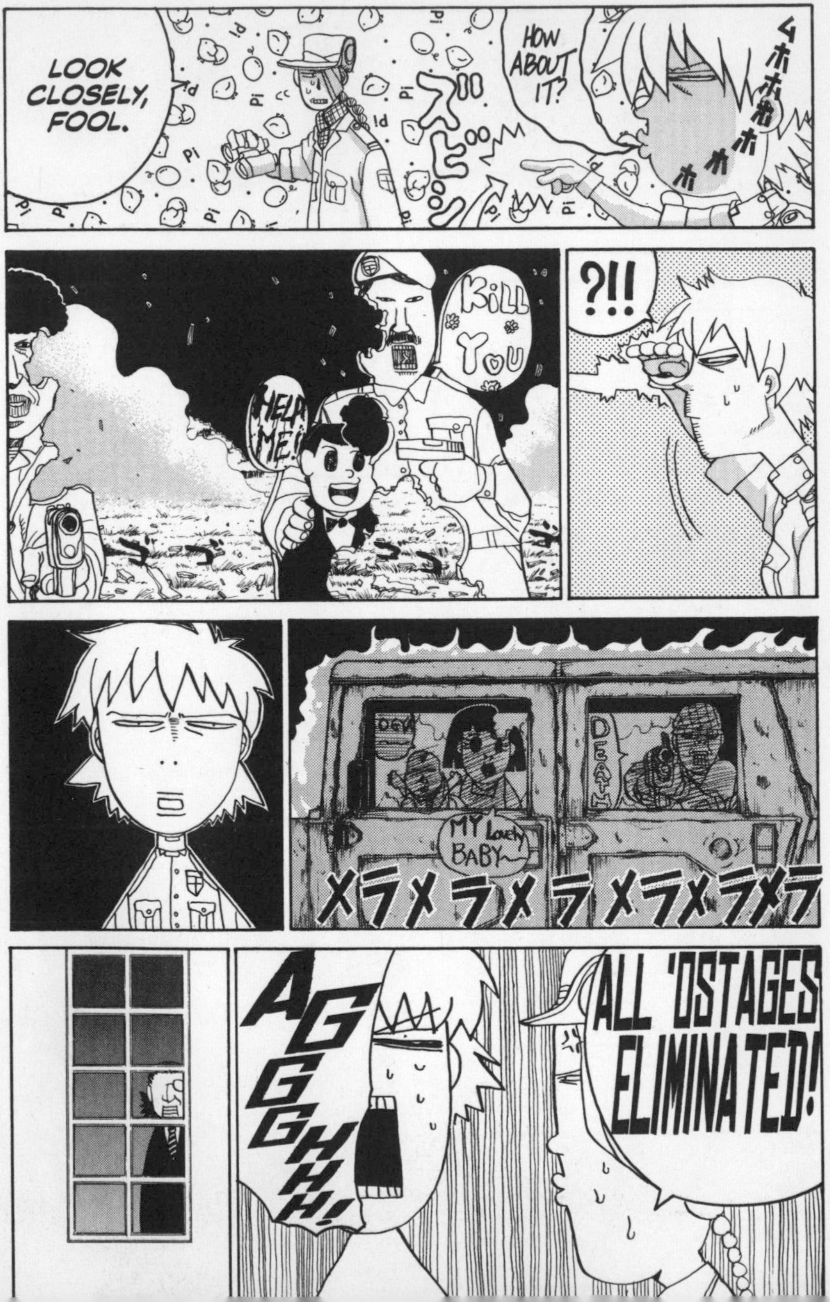
HOW ABOUT IT?
LOOK CLOSELY, FOOL.
?!!
KILL YOU
HELP ME!
MY Lovely BABY~
DEATH
メラメラメラメラメラメラ
ALL 'OSTAGES ELIMINATED!
AGGGHHH!

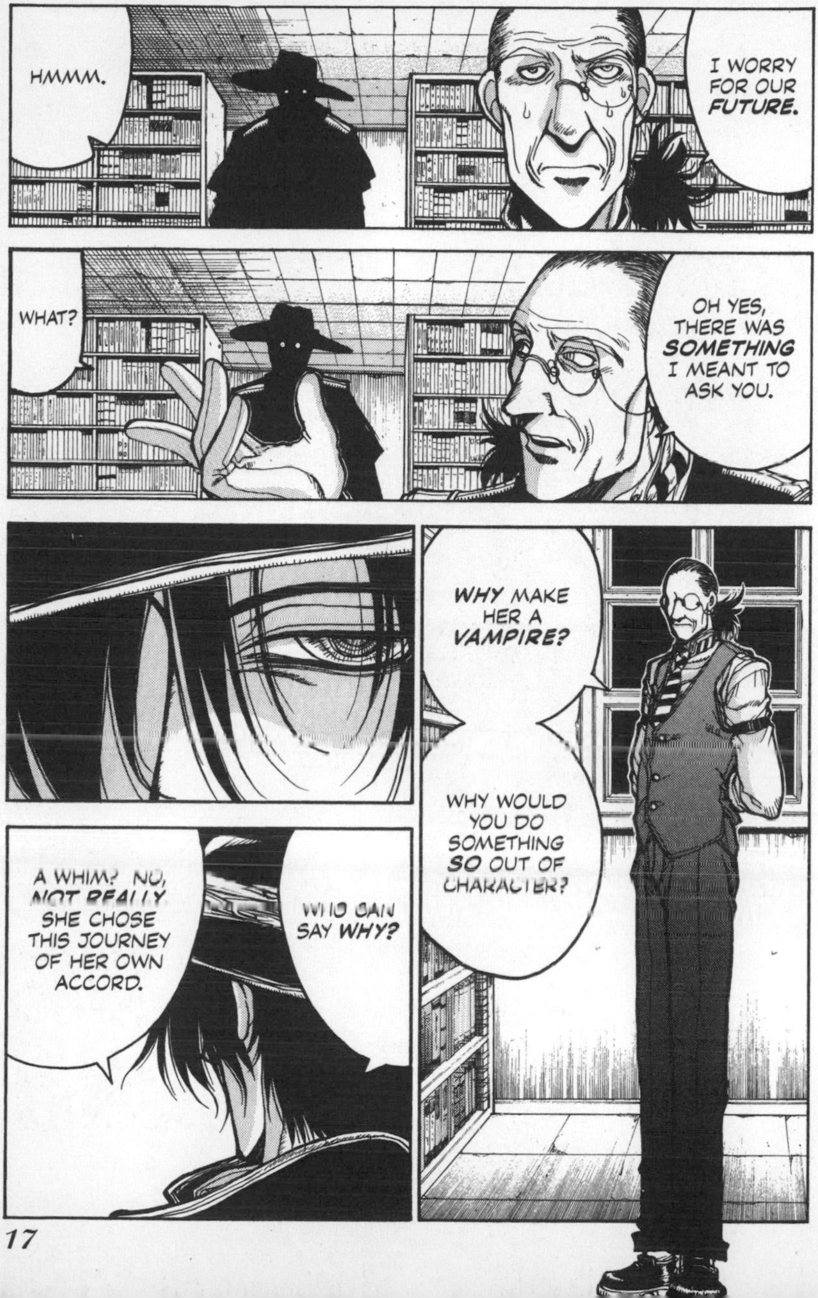
I WORRY FOR OUR FUTURE.
HMMM.
OH YES, THERE WAS SOMETHING I MEANT TO ASK YOU.
WHAT?
WHY MAKE HER A VAMPIRE?
WHY WOULD YOU DO SOMETHING SO OUT OF CHARACTER?
WHO CAN SAY WHY?
A WHIM? NO, NOT REALLY. SHE CHOSE THIS JOURNEY OF HER OWN ACCORD.

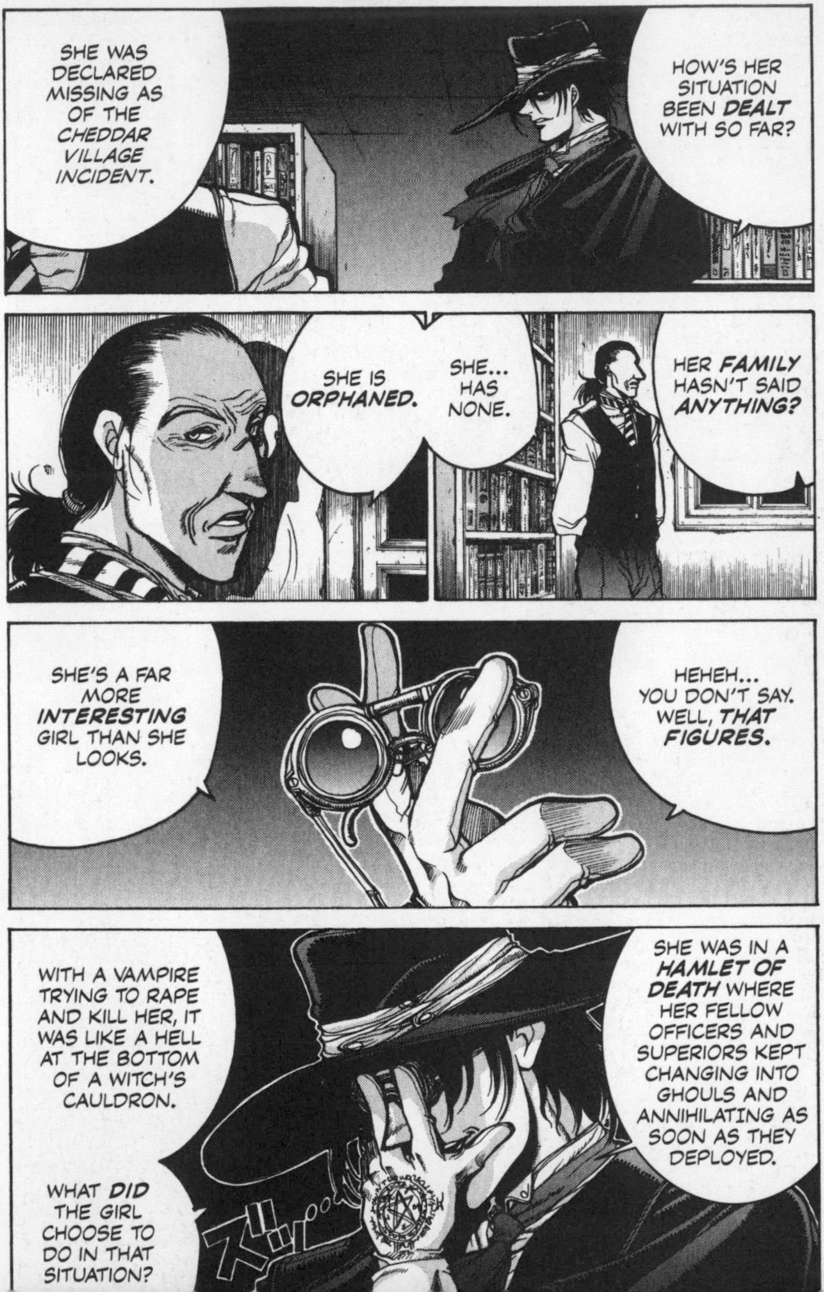

HOW'S HER SITUATION BEEN DEALT WITH SO FAR?
SHE WAS DECLARED MISSING AS OF THE CHEDDAR VILLAGE INCIDENT.
HER FAMILY HASN'T SAID ANYTHING?
SHE... HAS NONE.
SHE IS ORPHANED.
HEHEH... YOU DON'T SAY. WELL, THAT FIGURES.
SHE'S A FAR MORE INTERESTING GIRL THAN SHE LOOKS.
SHE WAS IN A HAMLET OF DEATH WHERE HER FELLOW OFFICERS AND SUPERIORS KEPT CHANGING INTO GHOULS AND ANNIHILATING AS SOON AS THEY DEPLOYED.
WITH A VAMPIRE TRYING TO RAPE AND KILL HER, IT WAS LIKE A HELL AT THE BOTTOM OF A WITCH'S CAULDRON.
WHAT DID THE GIRL CHOOSE TO DO IN THAT SITUATION?

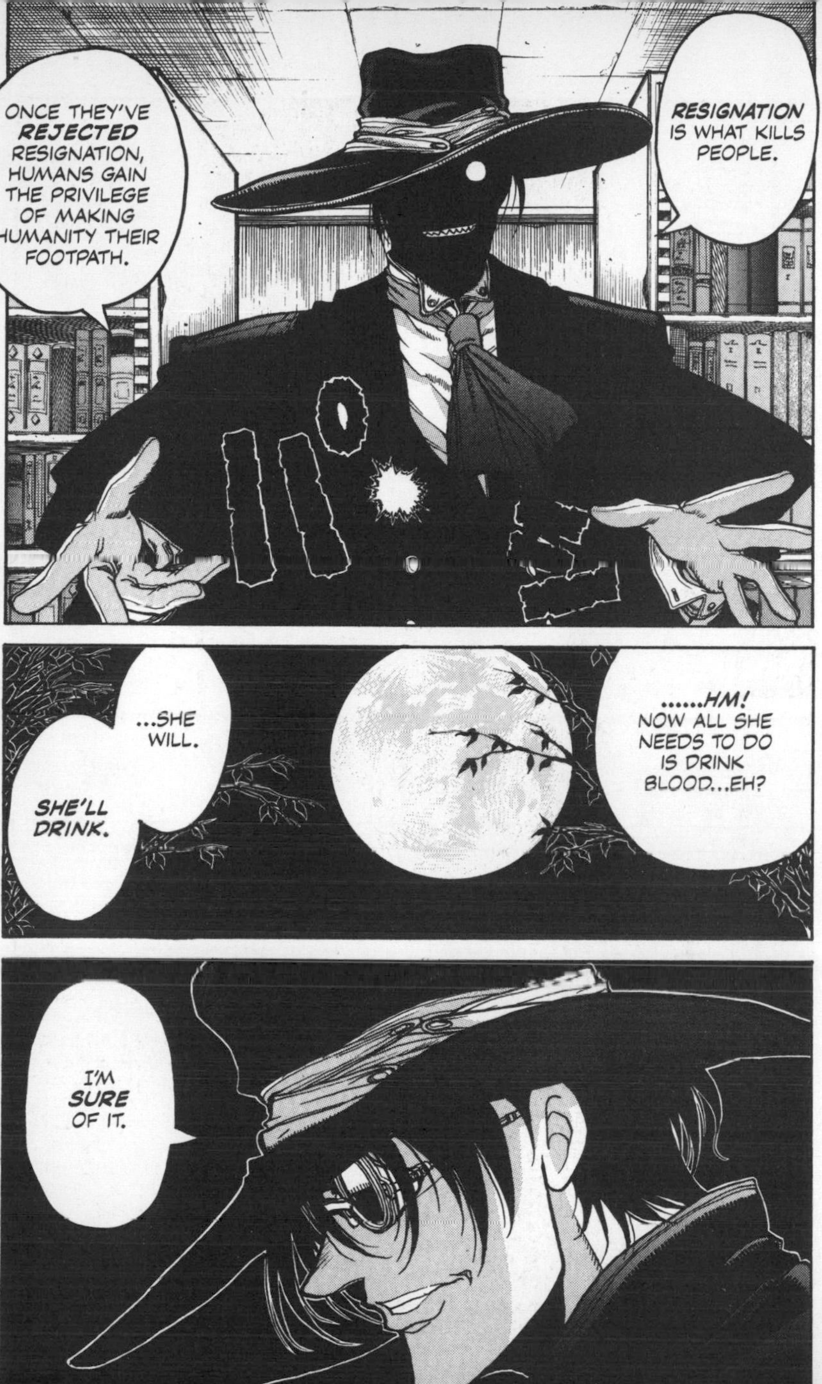
RESIGNATION IS WHAT KILLS PEOPLE.
ONCE THEY'VE REJECTED RESIGNATION, HUMANS GAIN THE PRIVILEGE OF MAKING HUMANITY THEIR FOOTPATH.
......HM! NOW ALL SHE NEEDS TO DO IS DRINK BLOOD...EH?
...SHE WILL.
SHE'LL DRINK.
I'M SURE OF IT.

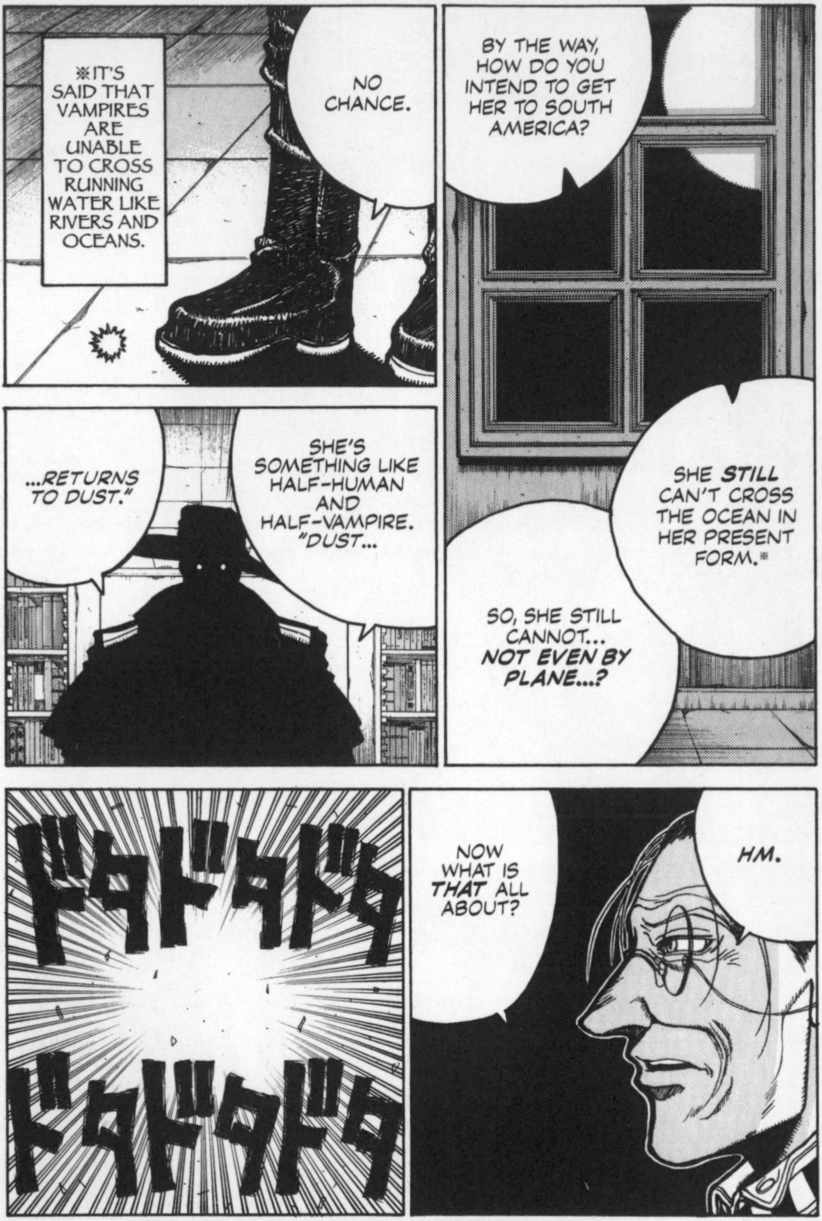
BY THE WAY, HOW DO YOU INTEND TO GET HER TO SOUTH AMERICA?
SHE STILL CAN'T CROSS THE OCEAN IN HER PRESENT FORM.※
SO, SHE STILL CANNOT... NOT EVEN BY PLANE...?
NO CHANCE.
※IT'S SAID THAT VAMPIRES ARE UNABLE TO CROSS RUNNING WATER LIKE RIVERS AND OCEANS.
SHE'S SOMETHING LIKE HALF-HUMAN AND HALF-VAMPIRE. "DUST...
...RETURNS TO DUST."
HM.
NOW WHAT IS THAT ALL ABOUT?

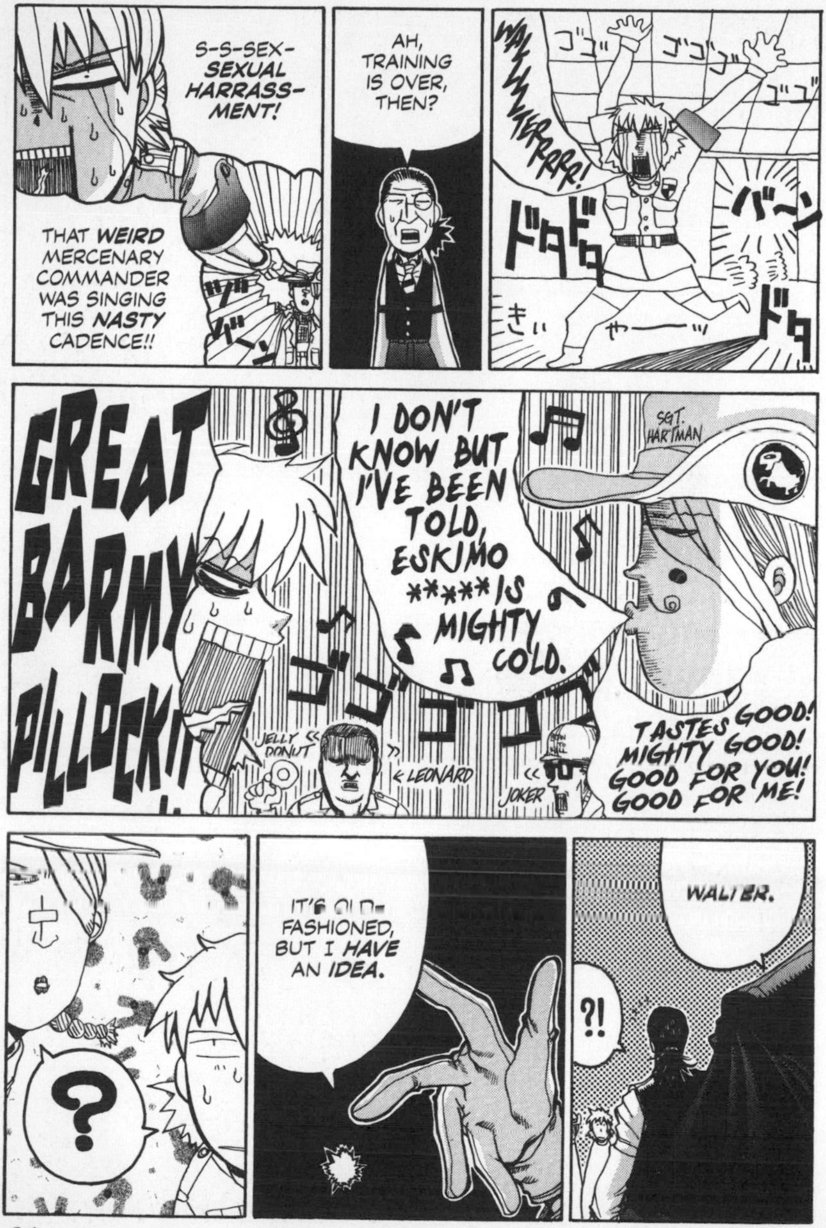
ドタドタ
バーン
ドタ
きぃ
やーーッ
AH, TRAINING IS OVER, THEN?
S-S-SEX-SEXUAL HARRASSMENT!
THAT WEIRD MERCENARY COMMANDER WAS SINGING THIS NASTY CADENCE!!
SGT. HARTMAN
TASTES GOOD! MIGHTY GOOD! GOOD FOR YOU! GOOD FOR ME!
I DON'T KNOW BUT I'VE BEEN TOLD, ESKIMO *****IS MIGHTY COLD.
JOKER
LEONARD
JELLY DONUT
GREAT BARMY PILLOCK!!
WALTER.
?!
IT'S OLD-FASHIONED, BUT I HAVE AN IDEA.
?

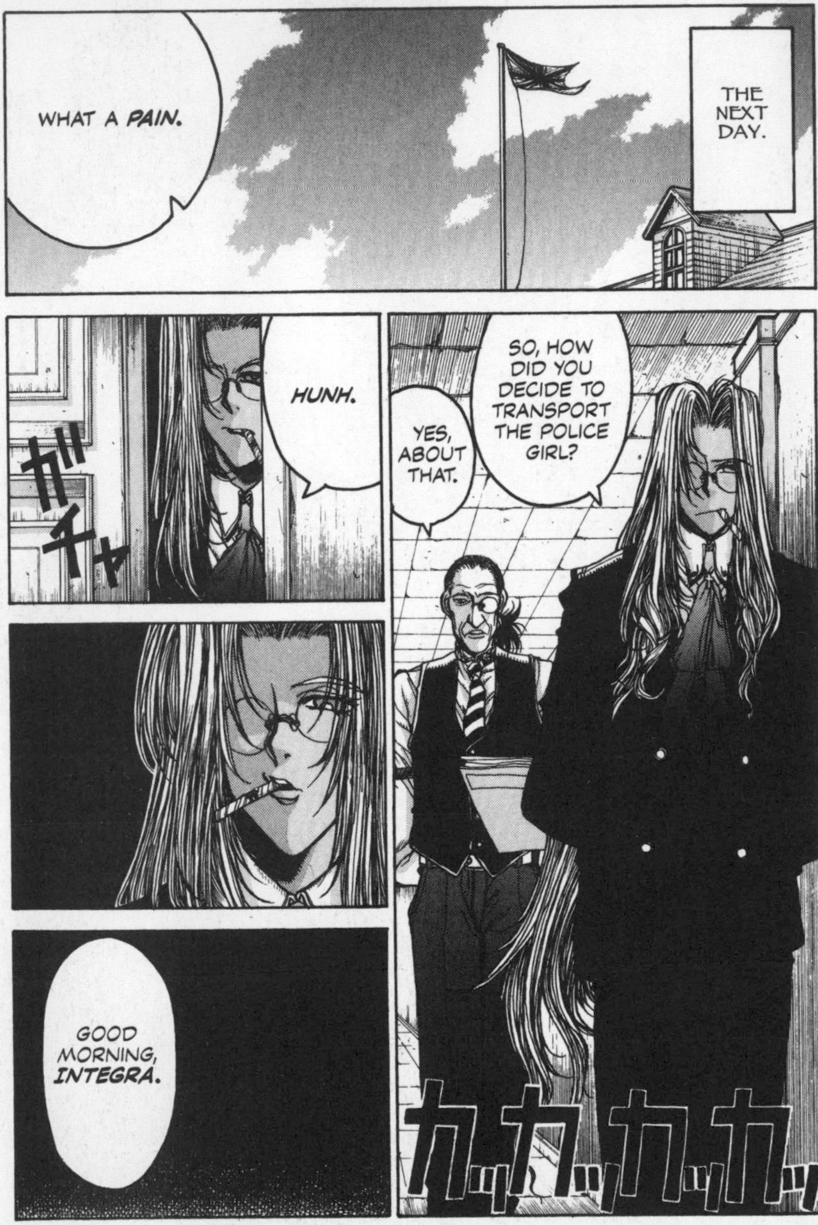
THE NEXT DAY.
WHAT A PAIN.
SO, HOW DID YOU DECIDE TO TRANSPORT THE POLICE GIRL?
YES, ABOUT THAT.
カッカッカッカッ
HUNH.
ガチャ
GOOD MORNING, INTEGRA.

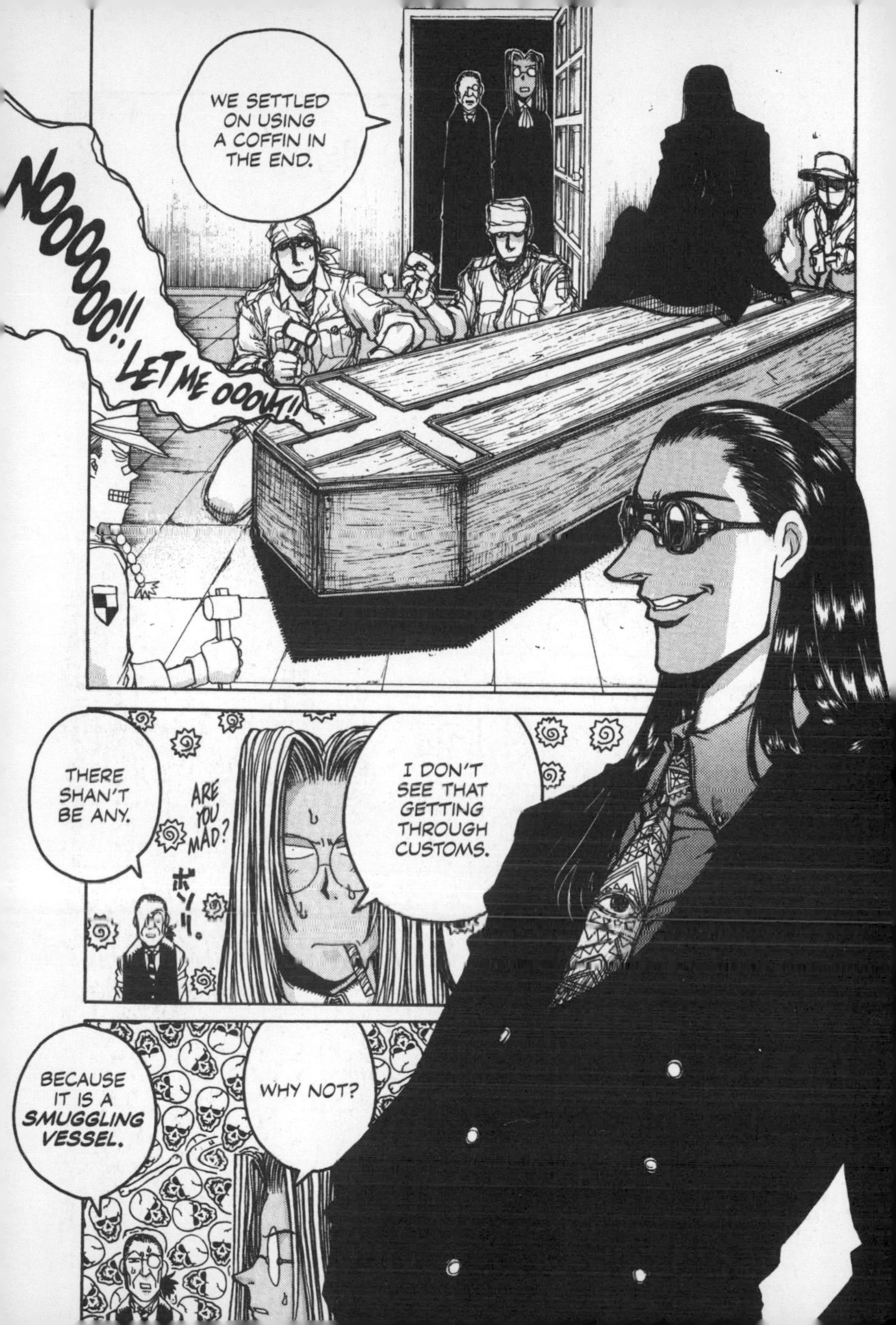
WE SETTLED ON USING A COFFIN IN THE END.
NOOOOOO!! LET ME OOOUT!!
I DON'T SEE THAT GETTING THROUGH CUSTOMS.
ARE YOU MAD?
THERE SHAN'T BE ANY.
ボソリ。
WHY NOT?
BECAUSE IT IS A *SMUGGLING VESSEL.*

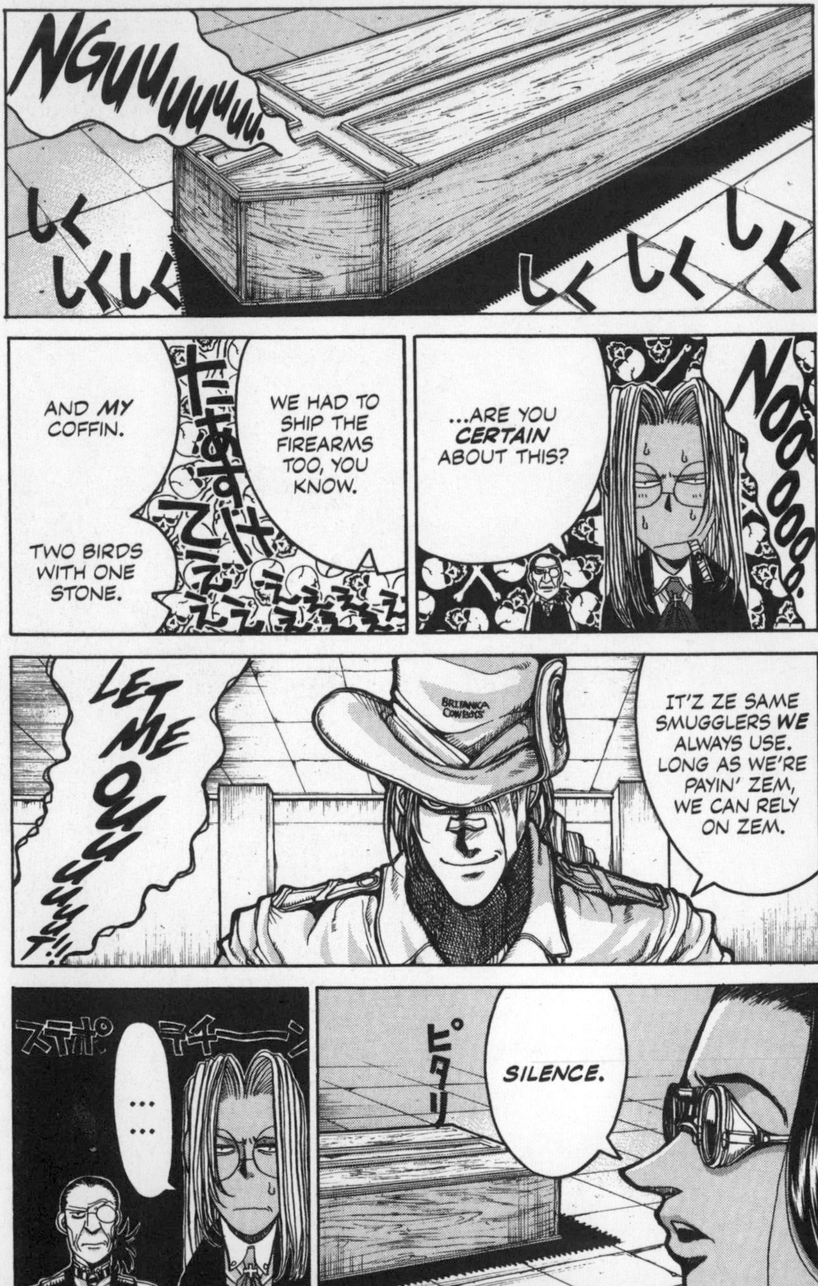
NGUUUUUUUU.
しく しく しく
しく しくしく
NOOOOOOOO...
...ARE YOU CERTAIN ABOUT THIS?
WE HAD TO SHIP THE FIREARMS TOO, YOU KNOW.
AND MY COFFIN.
TWO BIRDS WITH ONE STONE.
IT'Z ZE SAME SMUGGLERS WE ALWAYS USE. LONG AS WE'RE PAYIN' ZEM, WE CAN RELY ON ZEM.
BRITANICA COWBOYS
LET ME OUUUUUUT!!
SILENCE.
ピタッ
... ...

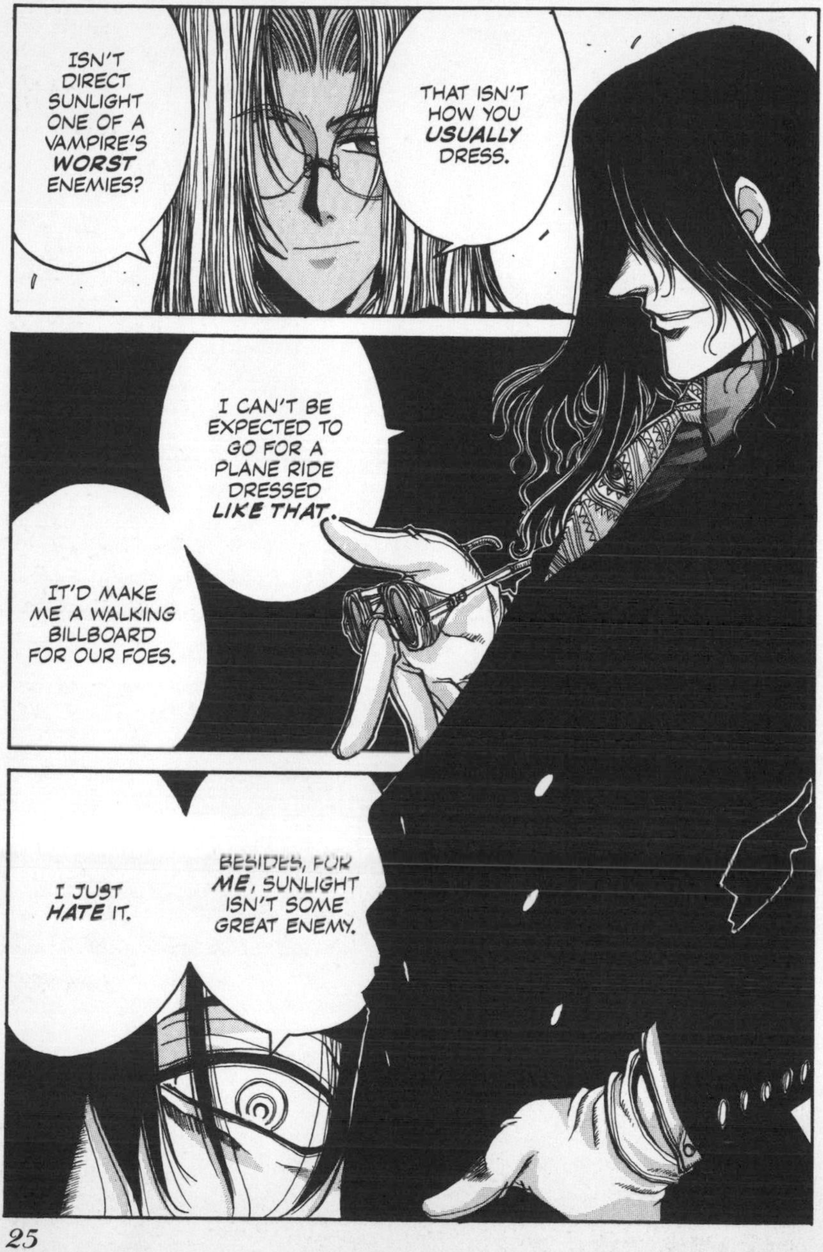
THAT ISN'T HOW YOU USUALLY DRESS.
ISN'T DIRECT SUNLIGHT ONE OF A VAMPIRE'S WORST ENEMIES?
I CAN'T BE EXPECTED TO GO FOR A PLANE RIDE DRESSED LIKE THAT.
IT'D MAKE ME A WALKING BILLBOARD FOR OUR FOES.
BESIDES, FOR ME, SUNLIGHT ISN'T SOME GREAT ENEMY.
I JUST HATE IT.

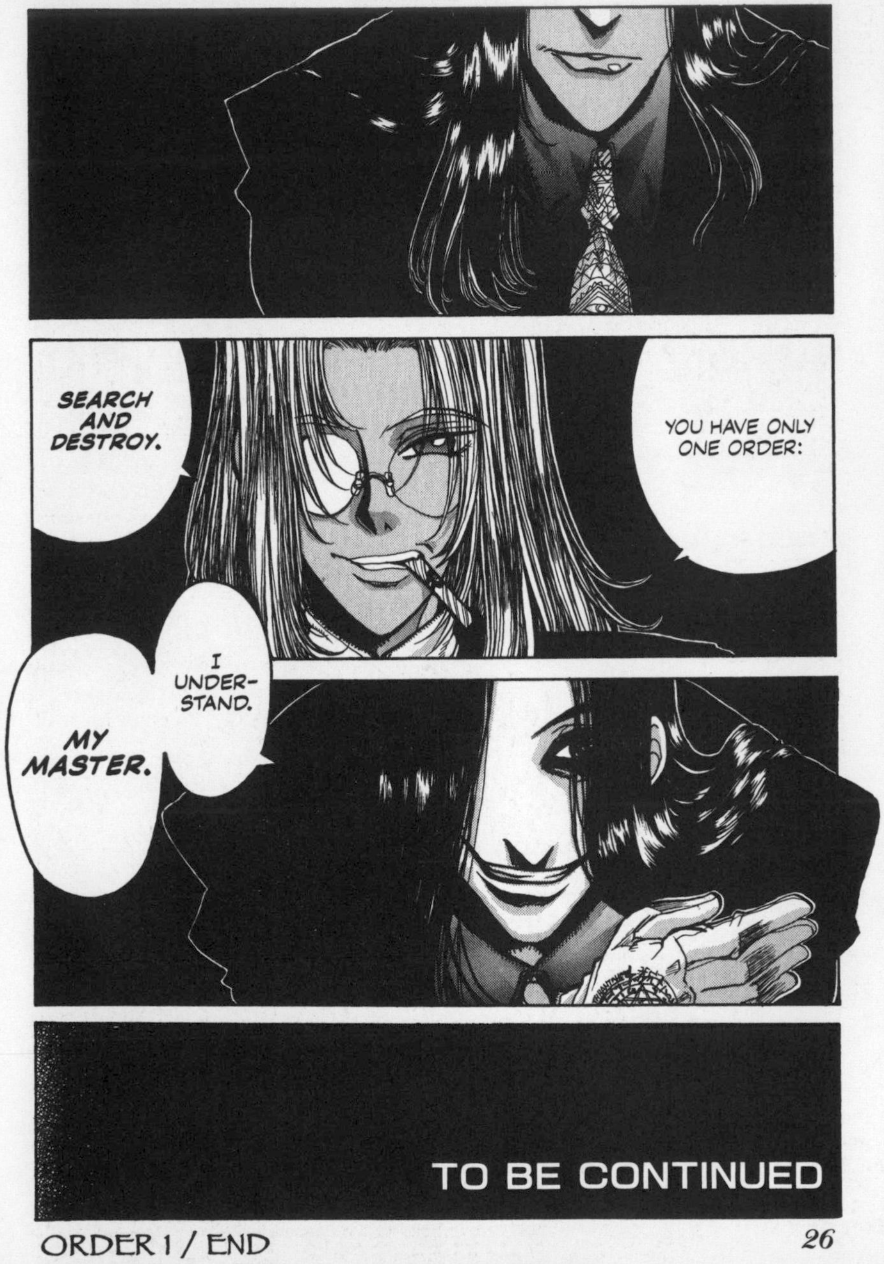
YOU HAVE ONLY ONE ORDER:
SEARCH AND DESTROY.
I UNDER-STAND.
MY MASTER.
TO BE CONTINUED

ORDER 1 / END

ORDER 2

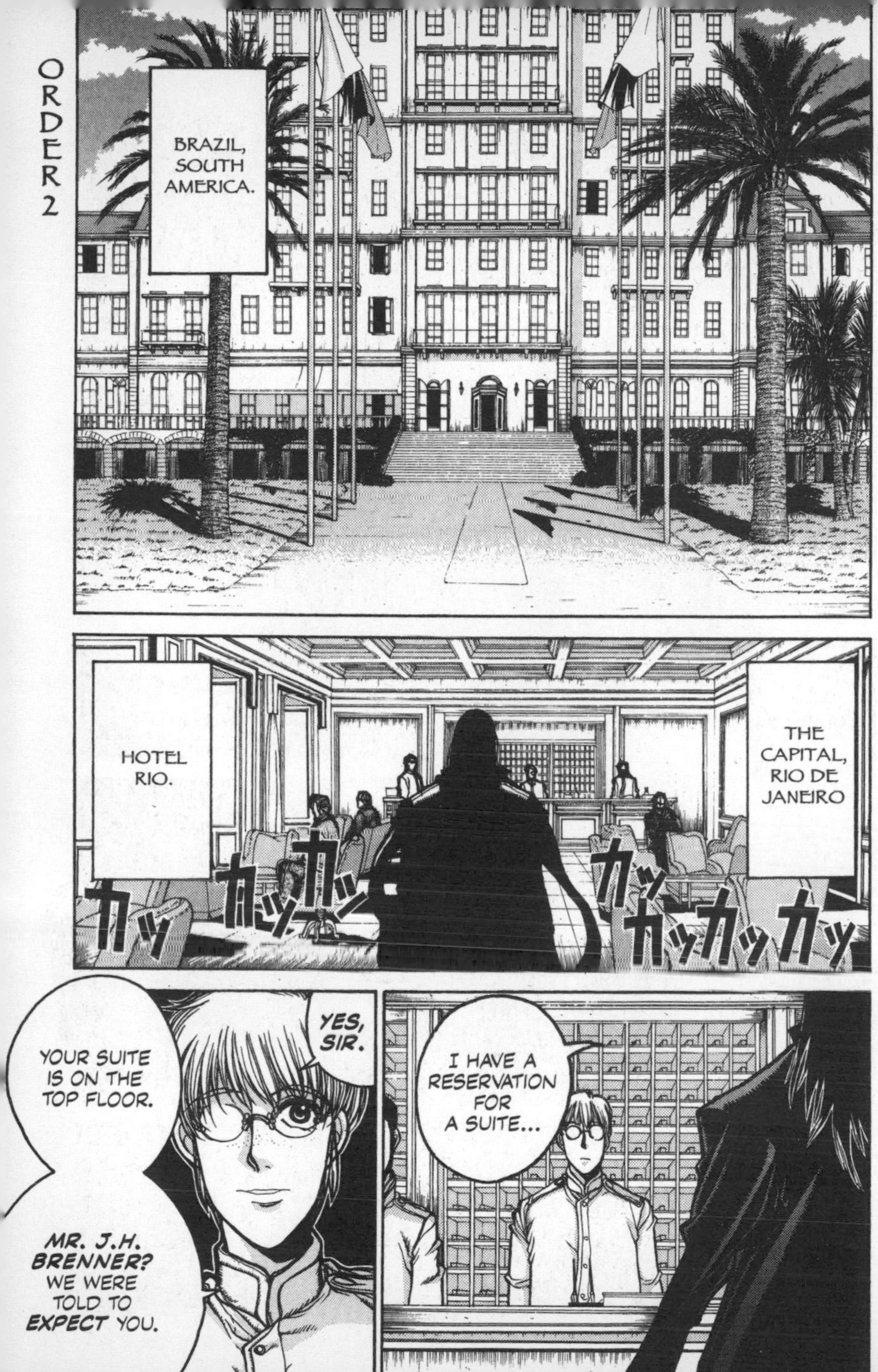
BRAZIL, SOUTH AMERICA.
THE CAPITAL, RIO DE JANEIRO
HOTEL RIO.
カッ
カッカッカッカッ
カッカッカッ
カッ
I HAVE A RESERVATION FOR A SUITE...
YES, SIR.
YOUR SUITE IS ON THE TOP FLOOR.
MR. J.H. BRENNER? WE WERE TOLD TO EXPECT YOU.

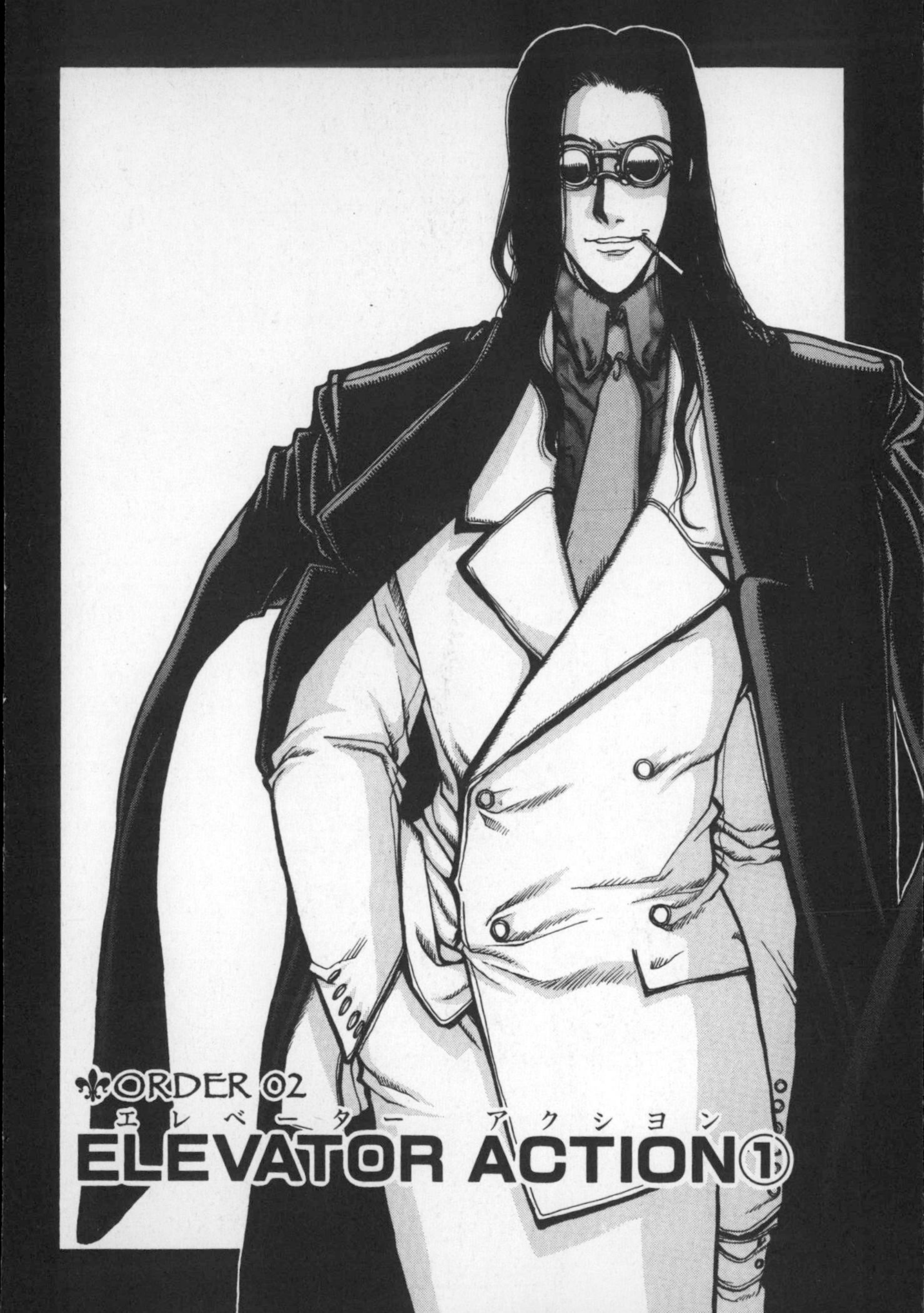
ORDER 02
エレベーター アクション
ELEVATOR ACTION①

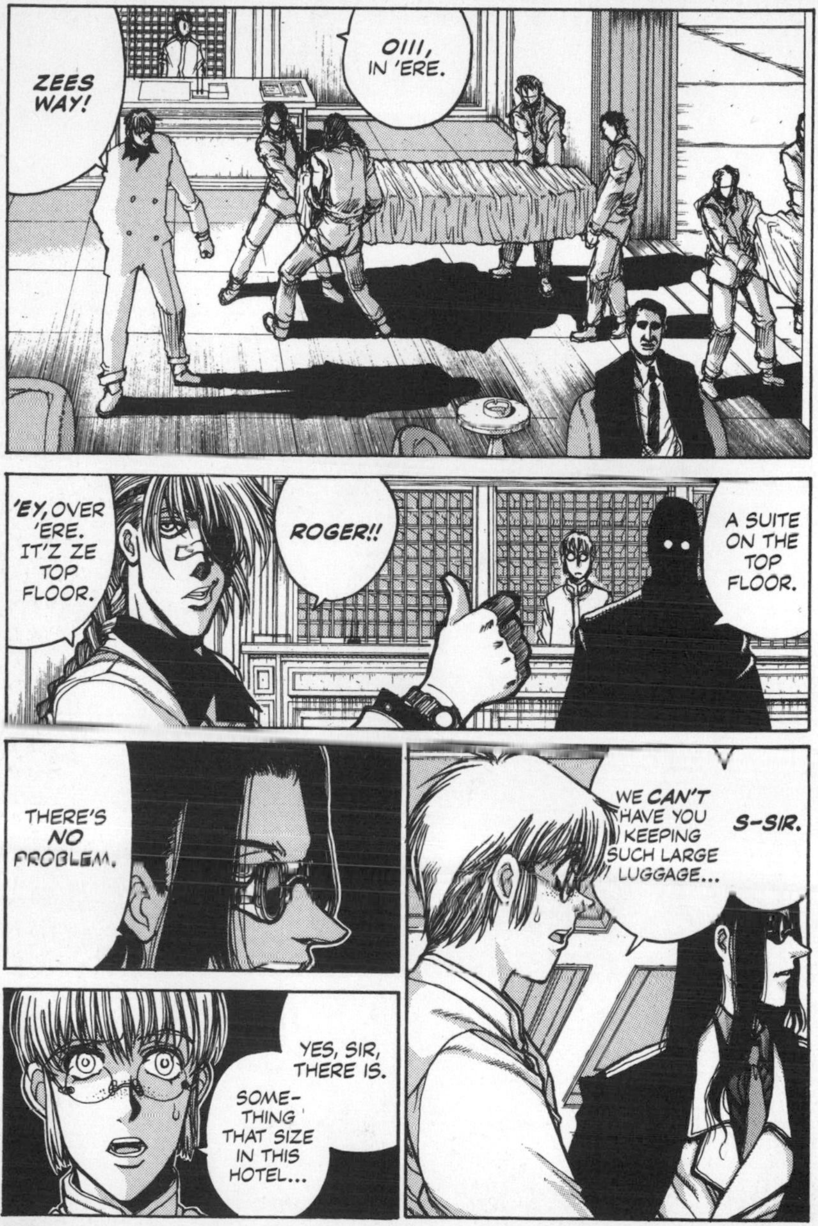
OIII, IN 'ERE.
ZEES WAY!
A SUITE ON THE TOP FLOOR.
ROGER!!
'EY, OVER 'ERE. IT'Z ZE TOP FLOOR.
S-SIR.
WE CAN'T HAVE YOU KEEPING SUCH LARGE LUGGAGE...
THERE'S NO PROBLEM.
YES, SIR, THERE IS.
SOME-THING THAT SIZE IN THIS HOTEL...

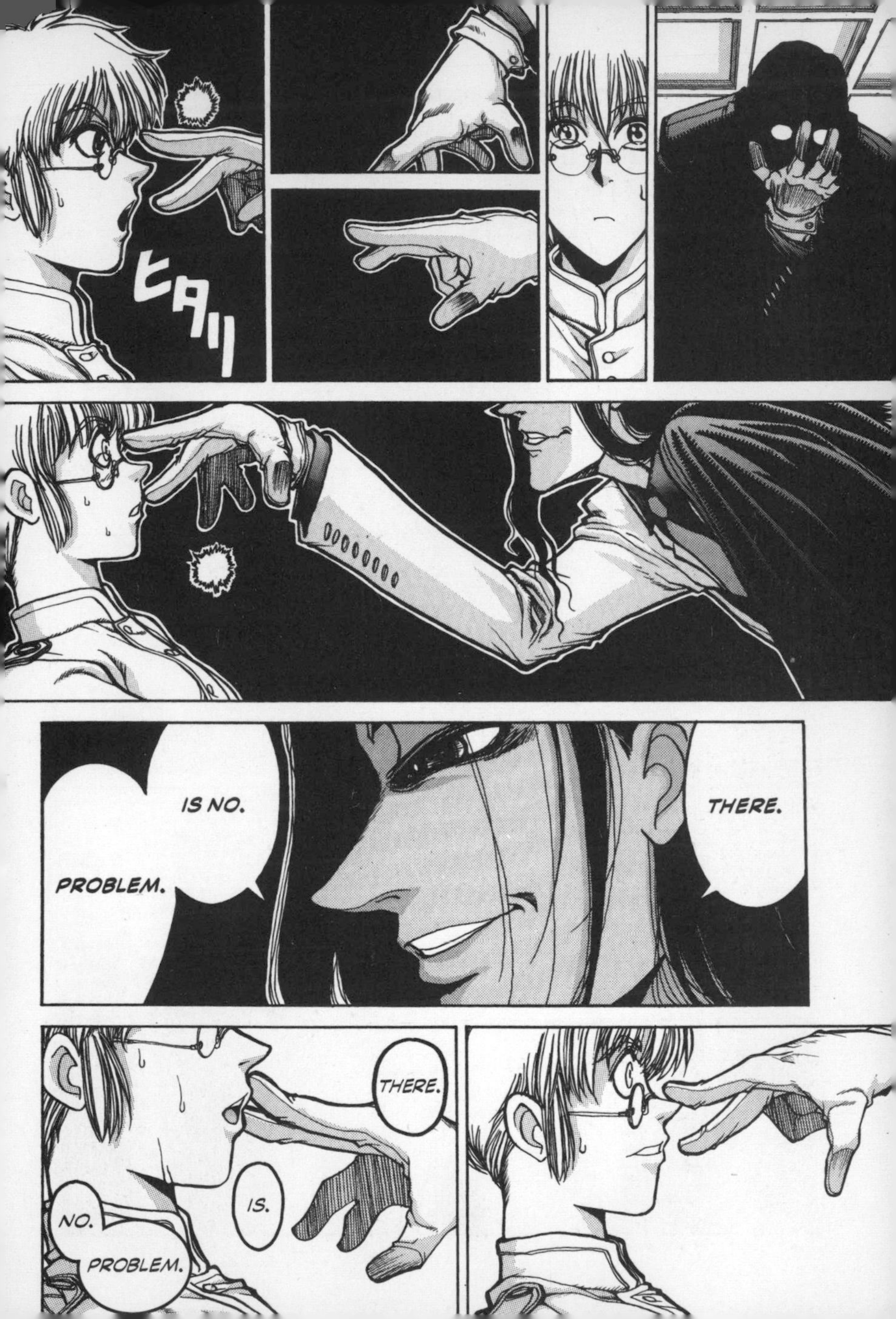
ヒタリ
THERE.
IS NO.
PROBLEM.
THERE.
IS.
NO.
PROBLEM.

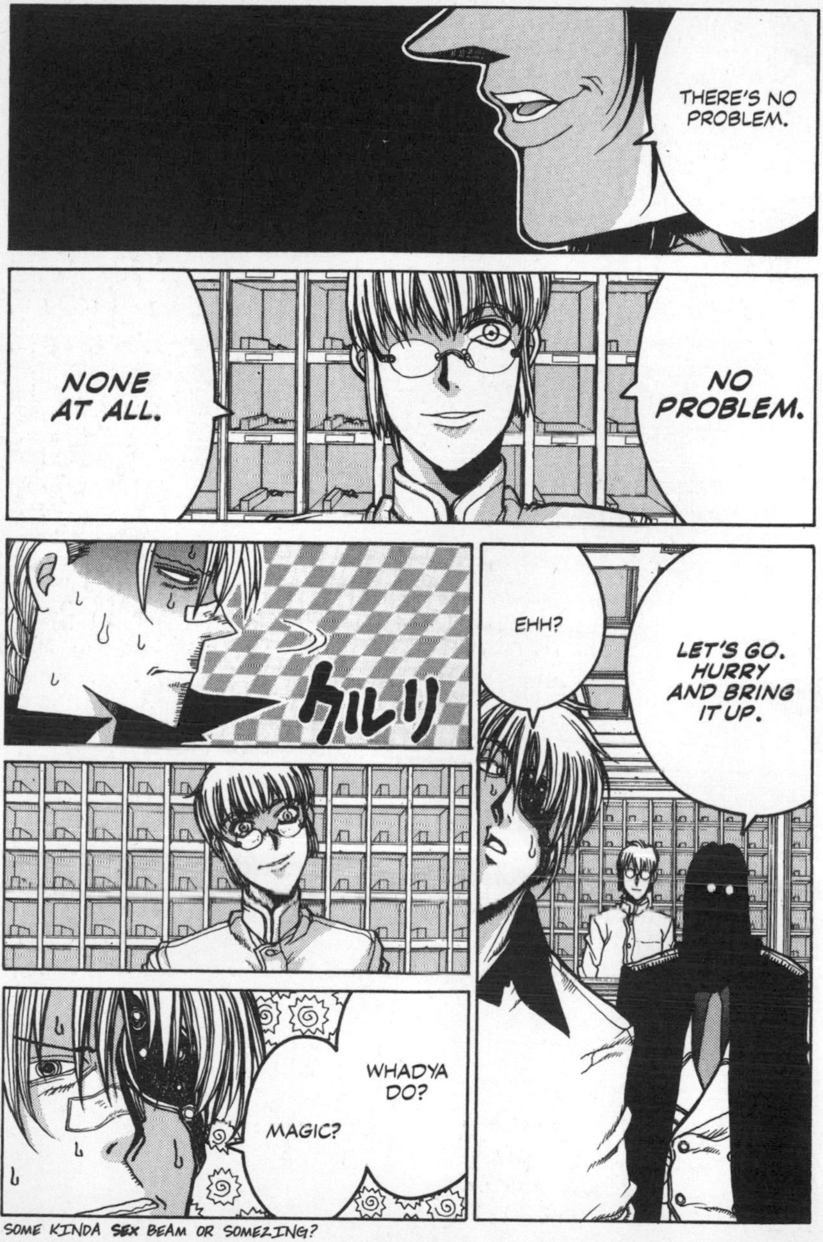
THERE'S NO PROBLEM.
NO PROBLEM.
NONE AT ALL.
LET'S GO. HURRY AND BRING IT UP.
EHH?
クルリ
WHADYA DO?
MAGIC?

SOME KINDA **SEX** BEAM OR SOMEZING?

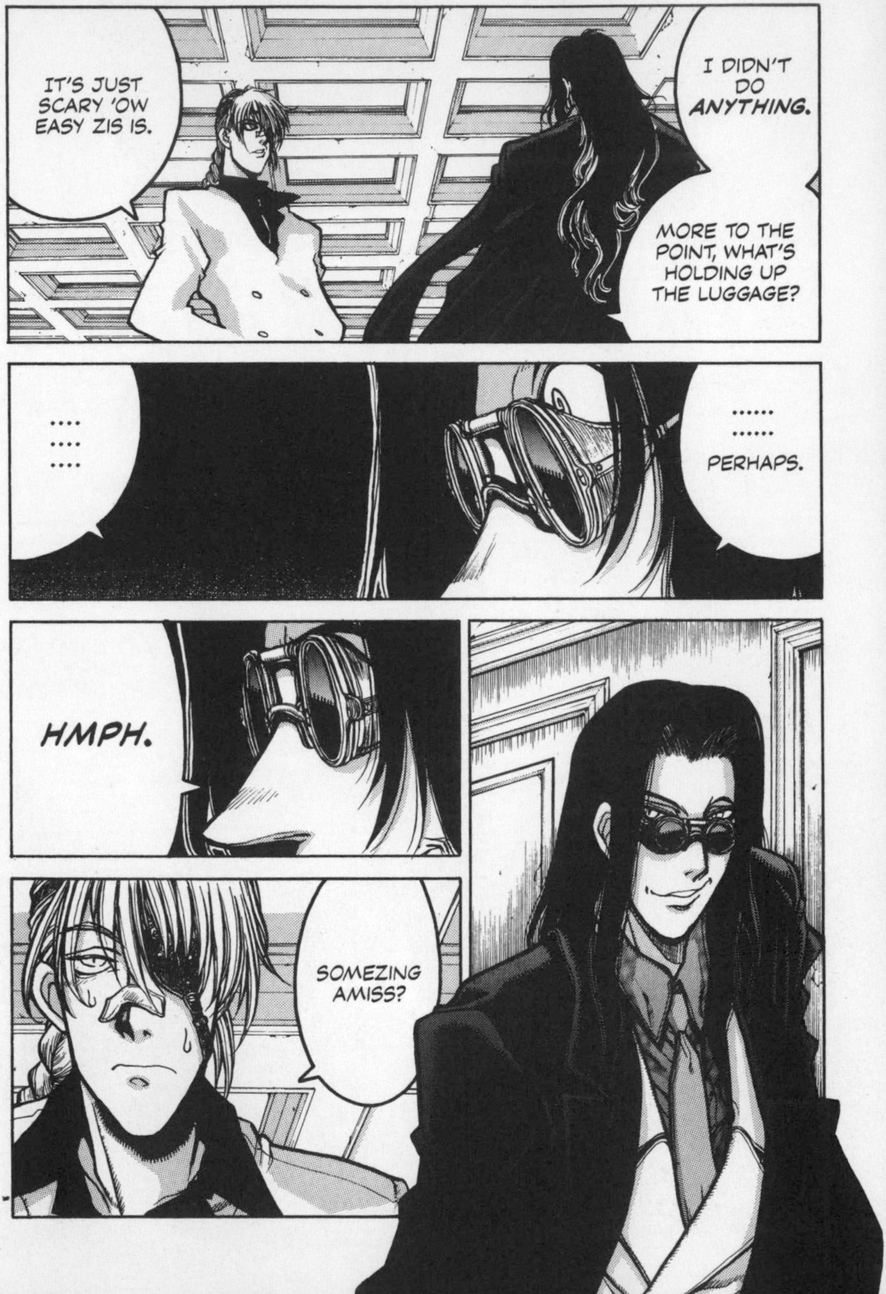
I DIDN'T DO ANYTHING.
IT'S JUST SCARY 'OW EASY ZIS IS.
MORE TO THE POINT, WHAT'S HOLDING UP THE LUGGAGE?
......
......
PERHAPS.
....
....
....
HMPH.
SOMEZING AMISS?

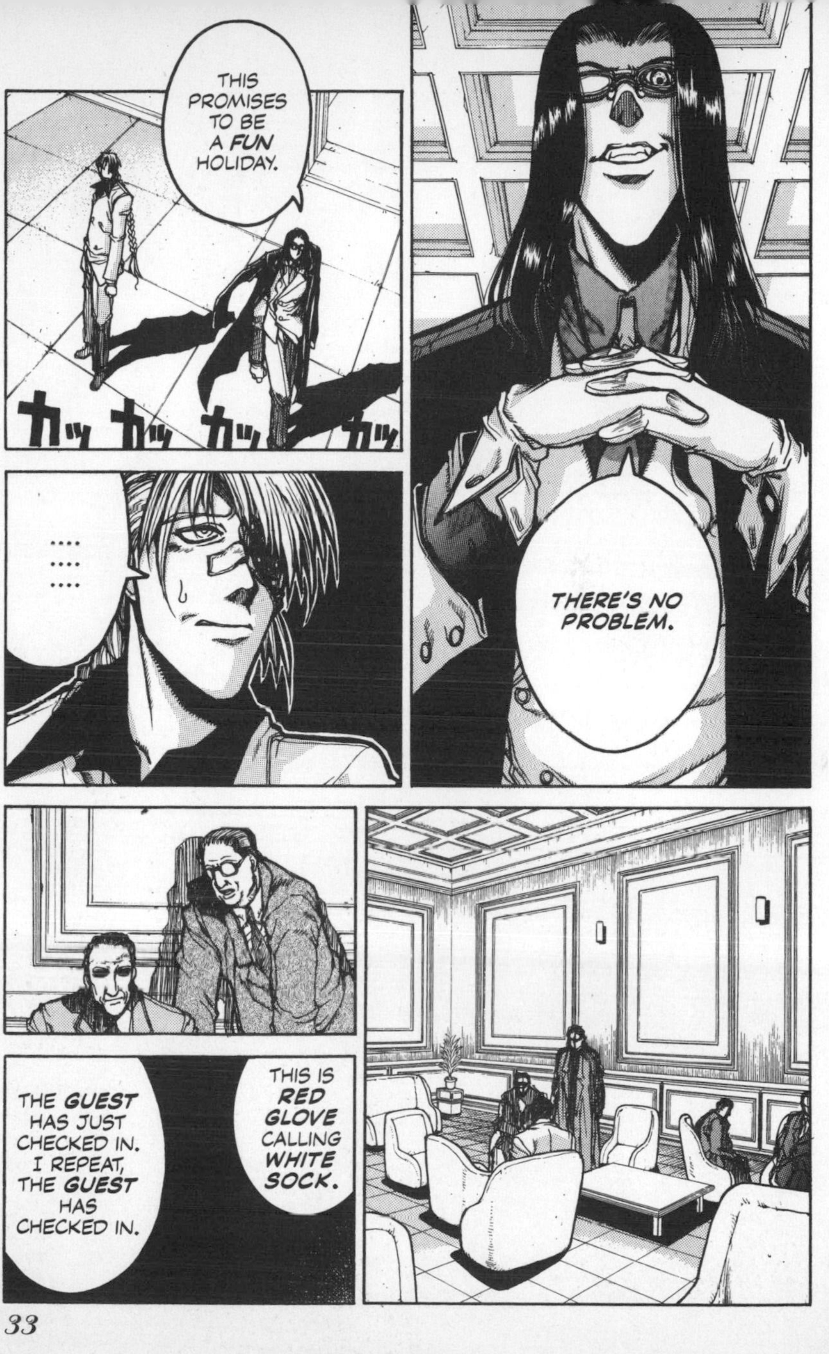
THERE'S NO PROBLEM.
THIS PROMISES TO BE A FUN HOLIDAY.
カッ カッ カッ カッ
....
....
....
THIS IS RED GLOVE CALLING WHITE SOCK.
THE GUEST HAS JUST CHECKED IN. I REPEAT, THE GUEST HAS CHECKED IN.

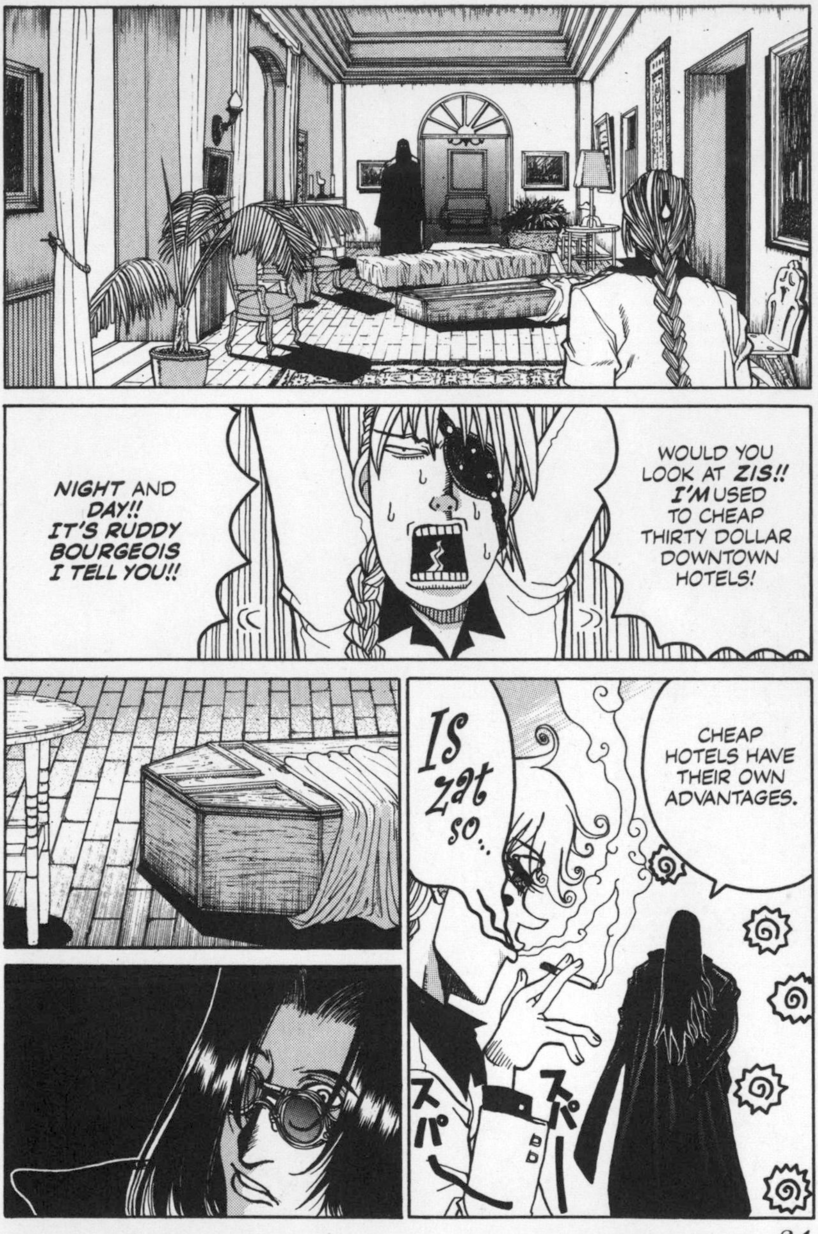
WOULD YOU LOOK AT ZIS!! I'M USED TO CHEAP THIRTY DOLLAR DOWNTOWN HOTELS!
NIGHT AND DAY!! IT'S RUDDY BOURGEOIS I TELL YOU!!
CHEAP HOTELS HAVE THEIR OWN ADVANTAGES.
Is zat so...
スパー
スパー

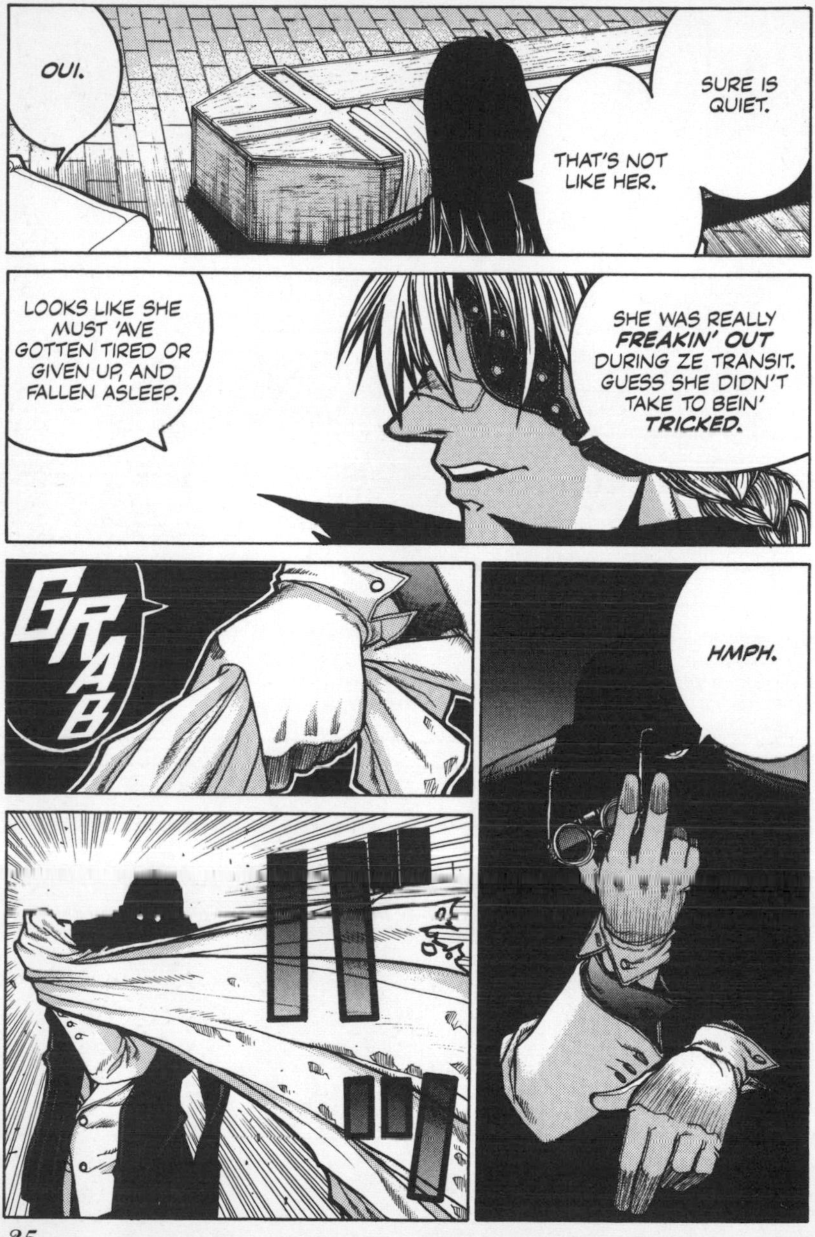
SURE IS QUIET.
THAT'S NOT LIKE HER.
OUI.
SHE WAS REALLY FREAKIN' OUT DURING ZE TRANSIT. GUESS SHE DIDN'T TAKE TO BEIN' TRICKED.
LOOKS LIKE SHE MUST 'AVE GOTTEN TIRED OR GIVEN UP, AND FALLEN ASLEEP.
HMPH.
GRAB

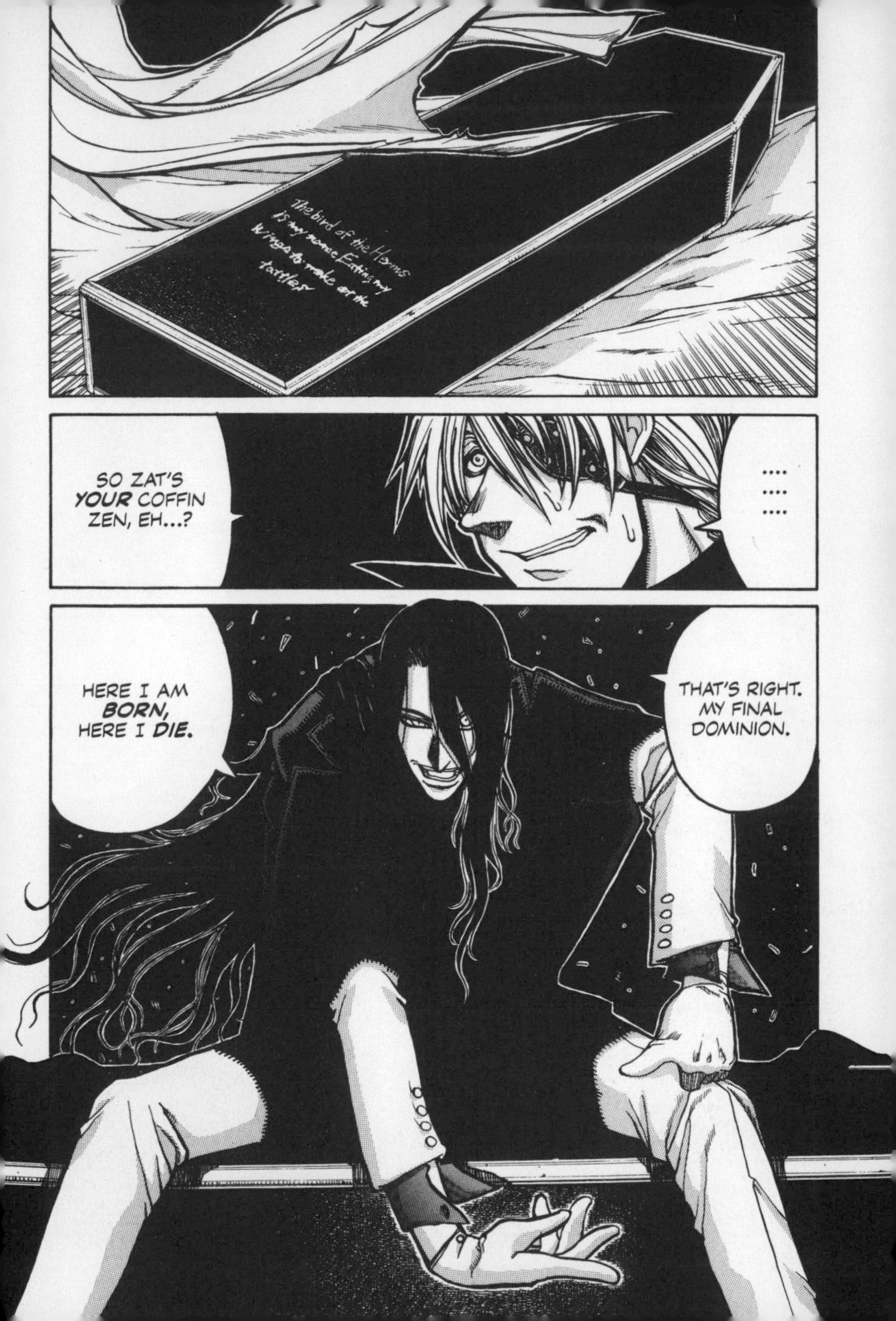
The bird of the Herms
is my name Eating my
wings to make at the
tattles
....
....
....
SO ZAT'S **YOUR** COFFIN ZEN, EH...?
THAT'S RIGHT. MY FINAL DOMINION.
HERE I AM **BORN**, HERE I **DIE**.

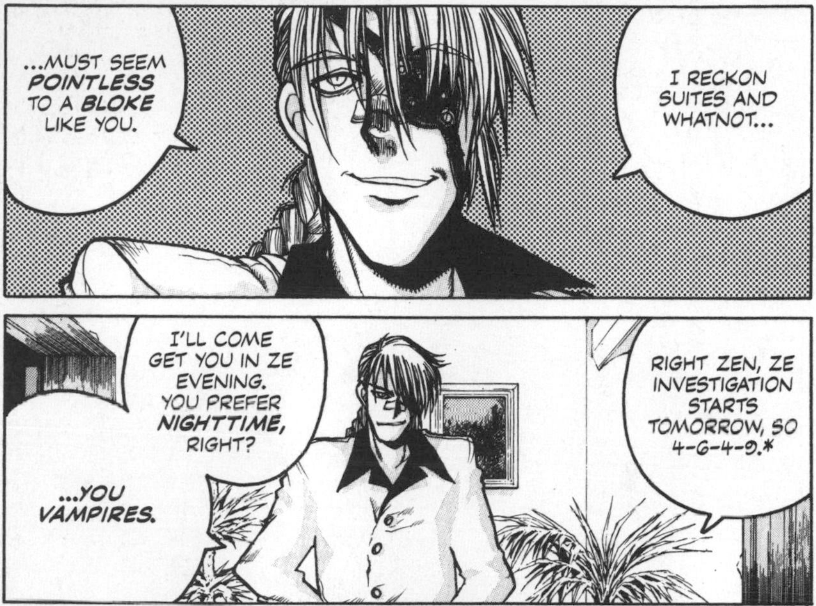
I RECKON SUITES AND WHATNOT...
...MUST SEEM POINTLESS TO A BLOKE LIKE YOU.
RIGHT ZEN, ZE INVESTIGATION STARTS TOMORROW, SO 4-6-4-9.*
I'LL COME GET YOU IN ZE EVENING. YOU PREFER NIGHTTIME, RIGHT?
...YOU VAMPIRES.

*Japanese numerical pun 4=YO, 6=RO, 4=SHI, 9=KU + YOROSHIKU=UNTIL LATER.

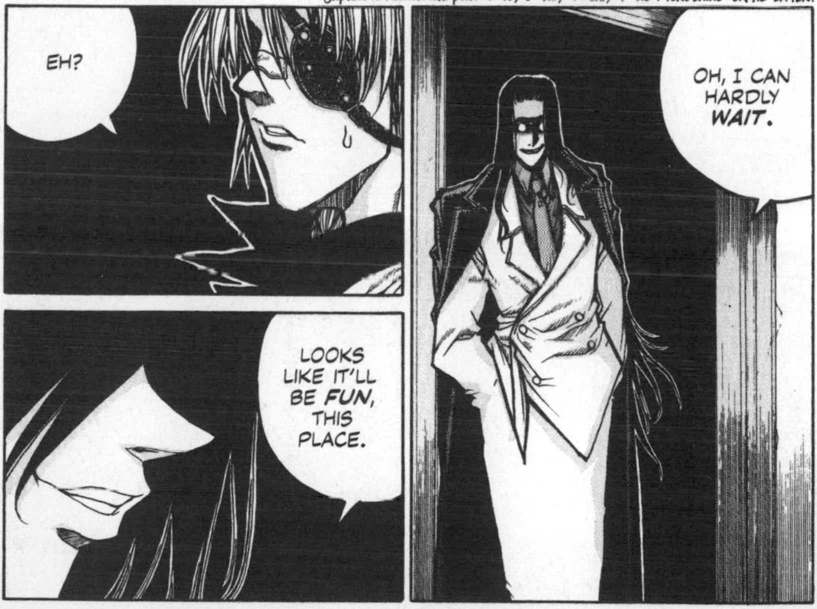
OH, I CAN HARDLY WAIT.
EH?
LOOKS LIKE IT'LL BE FUN, THIS PLACE.

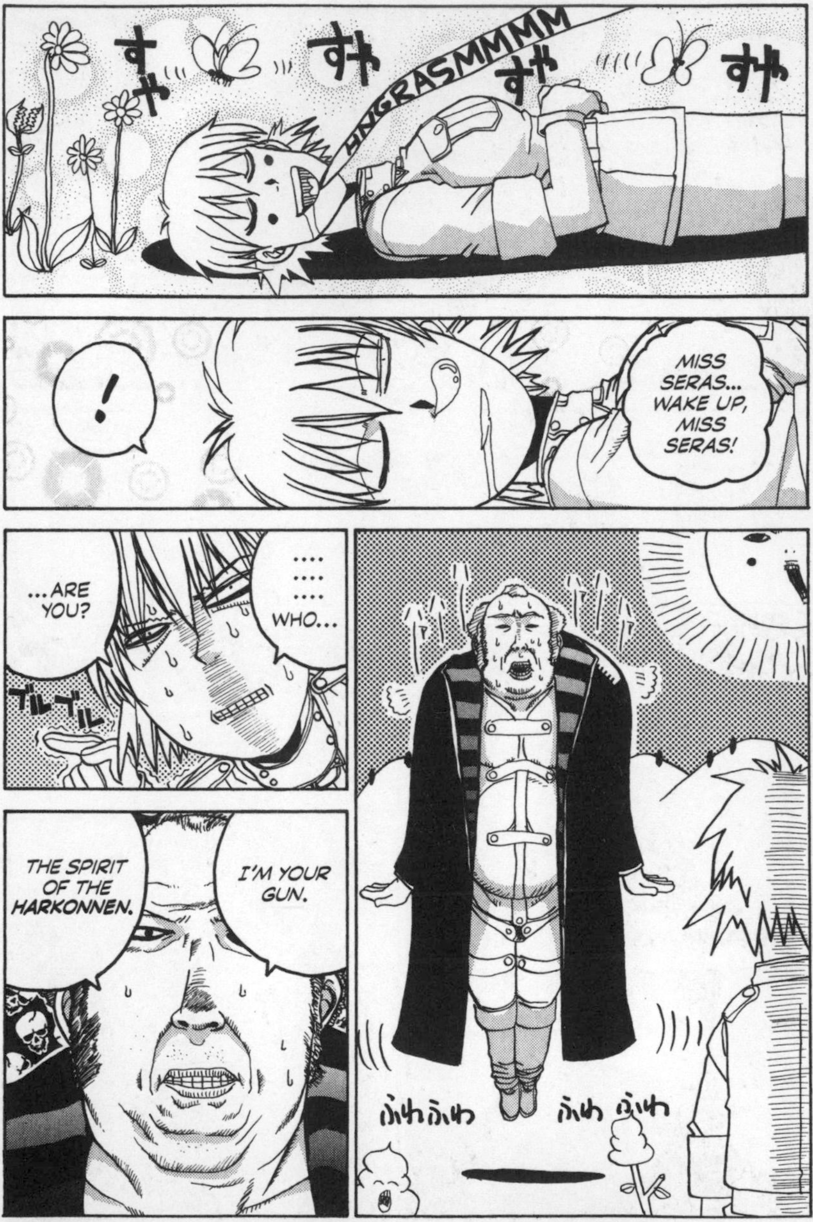
すや
すや
HNGRASMMMM
すや
すや
MISS SERAS... WAKE UP, MISS SERAS!
!
ふわ ふわ
ふわふわ
....
WHO...
...ARE YOU?
ブルブル
I'M YOUR GUN.
THE SPIRIT OF THE HARKONNEN.

SEEKING AN ASSISTANT? HELP MEEEE! I'M SEEKING HELP FROM ANY DEDICATED PERSON IN THE TOKYO SUBURBS WHO CAN COME IN ABOUT 7-10 DAYS A MONTH. PLEASE SEND YOUR PORTFOLIO AND RESUME TO THE EDITORIAL DEPARTMENT. I WILL TEACH YOU THE SKILLS YOU NEED FOR THE JOB, SO I WELCOME ANYONE WHO IS DEDICATED! -KOHTA HIRANO

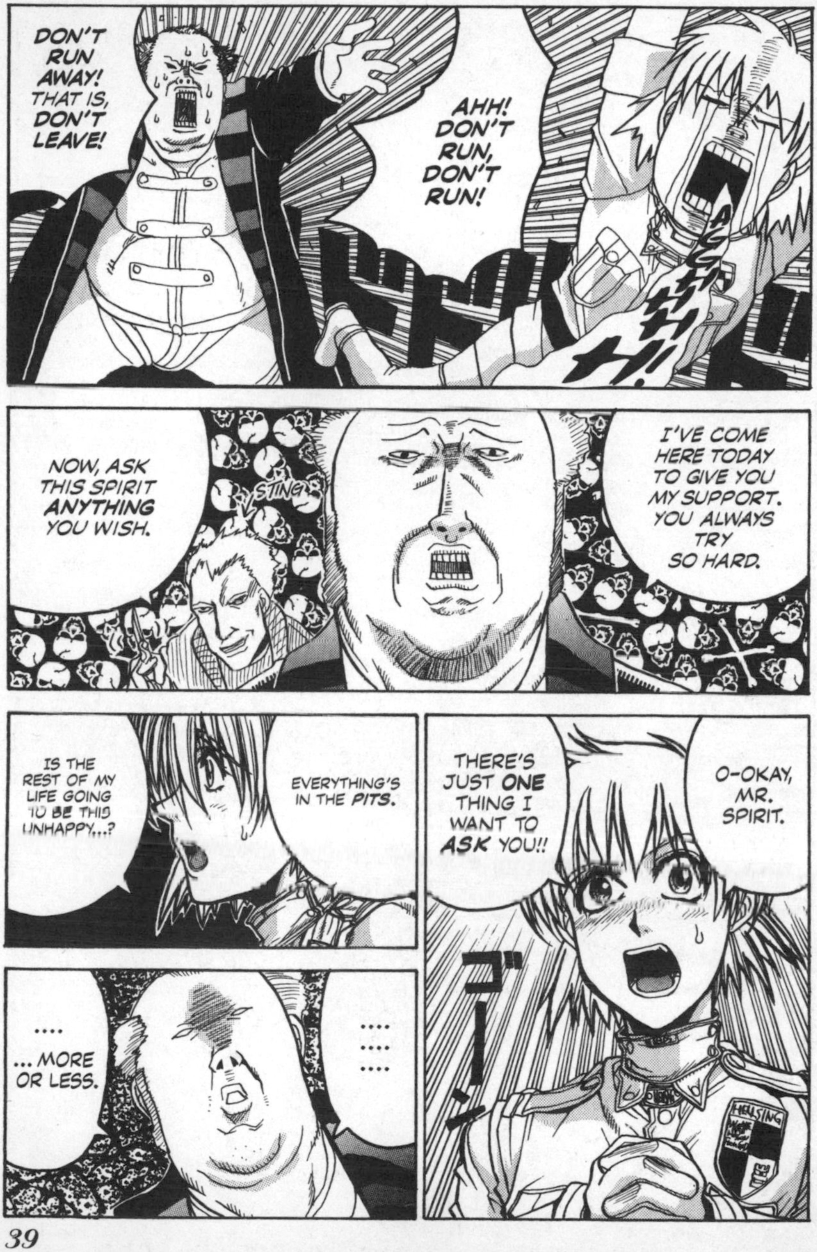
AHH! DON'T RUN, DON'T RUN!
DON'T RUN AWAY! THAT IS, DON'T LEAVE!
I'VE COME HERE TODAY TO GIVE YOU MY SUPPORT. YOU ALWAYS TRY SO HARD.
STING
NOW, ASK THIS SPIRIT **ANYTHING** YOU WISH.
O-OKAY, MR. SPIRIT.
THERE'S JUST **ONE** THING I WANT TO **ASK** YOU!!
EVERYTHING'S IN THE *PITS*.
IS THE REST OF MY LIFE GOING TO BE THIS UNHAPPY...?
....
....
....
....
... MORE OR LESS.

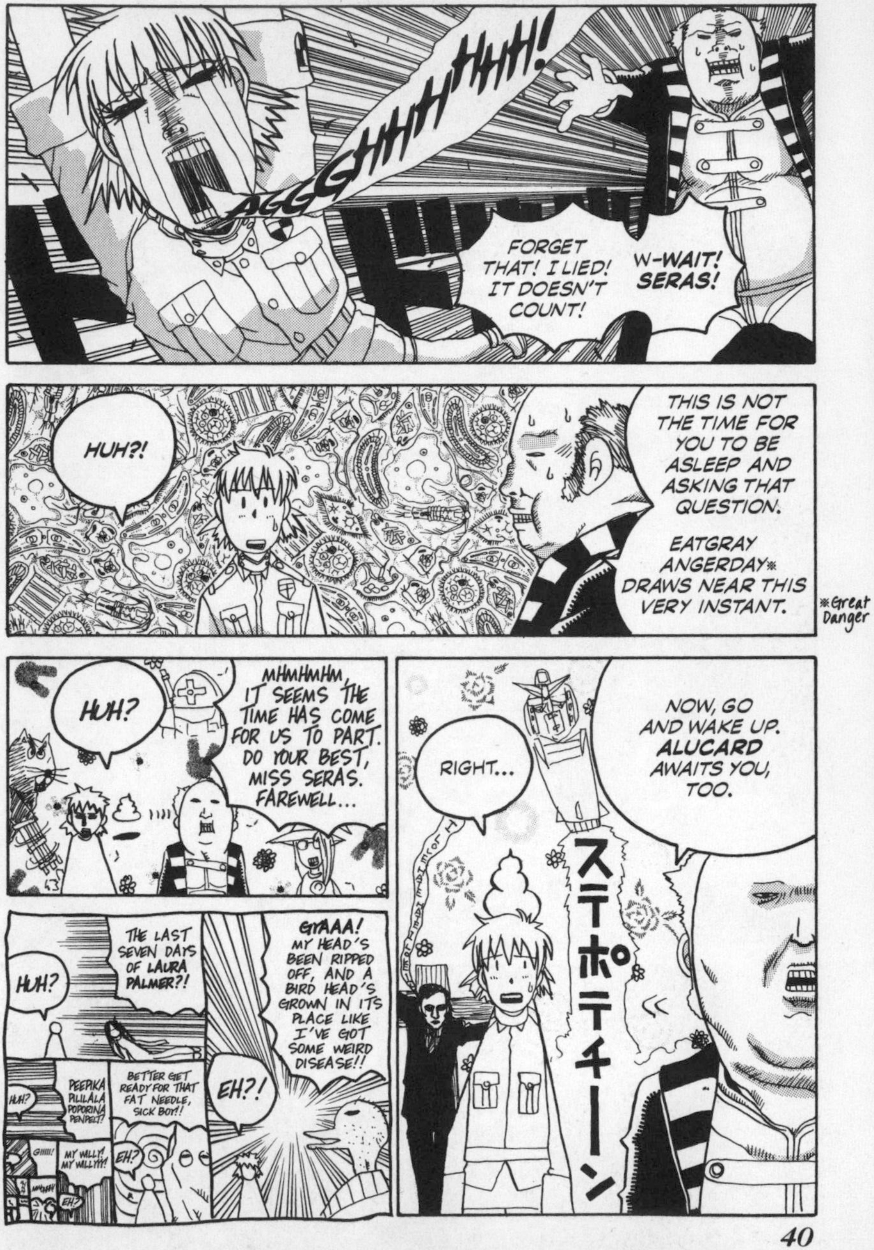
AGGGHHHHHHHHH!
W-WAIT! SERAS!
FORGET THAT! I LIED! IT DOESN'T COUNT!
THIS IS NOT THE TIME FOR YOU TO BE ASLEEP AND ASKING THAT QUESTION.
EATGRAY ANGERDAY※ DRAWS NEAR THIS VERY INSTANT.
※Great Danger
HUH?!
NOW, GO AND WAKE UP. ALUCARD AWAITS YOU, TOO.
RIGHT...
ステポテチーン
MHMHMHM, IT SEEMS THE TIME HAS COME FOR US TO PART. DO YOUR BEST, MISS SERAS. FAREWELL...
HUH?
GYAAA! MY HEAD'S BEEN RIPPED OFF, AND A BIRD HEAD'S GROWN IN ITS PLACE LIKE I'VE GOT SOME WEIRD DISEASE!!
THE LAST SEVEN DAYS OF LAURA PALMER?!
HUH?
EH?!
BETTER GET READY FOR THAT FAT NEEDLE, SICK BOY!!
EH?
PEEPIKA PILILALA POPORINA PENPELT?
HUH?
MY WILLY! MY WILLYYY!
GIIIII!
EH?

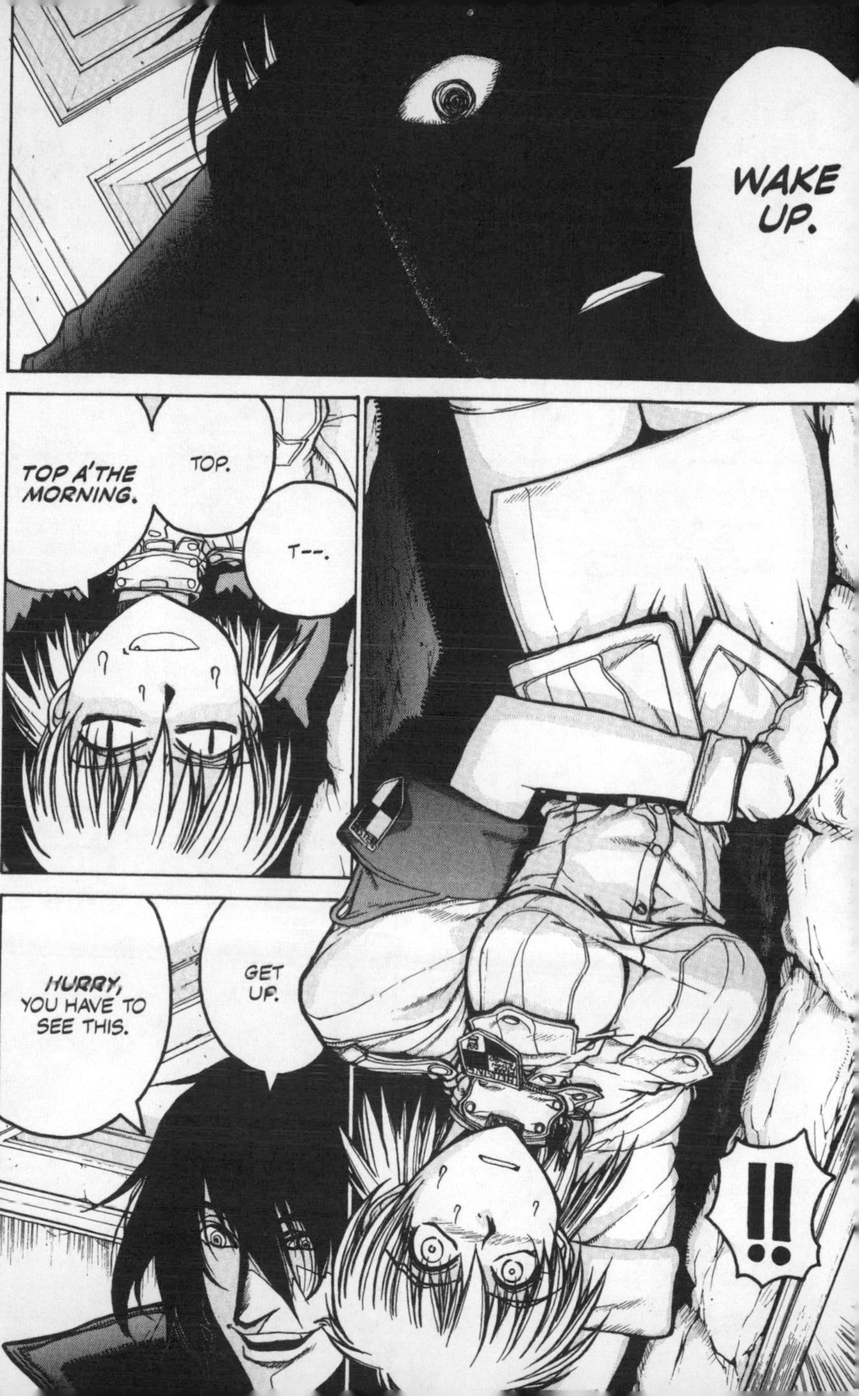
WAKE UP.
!!
T--.
TOP.
TOP A'THE MORNING.
GET UP.
HURRY, YOU HAVE TO SEE THIS.

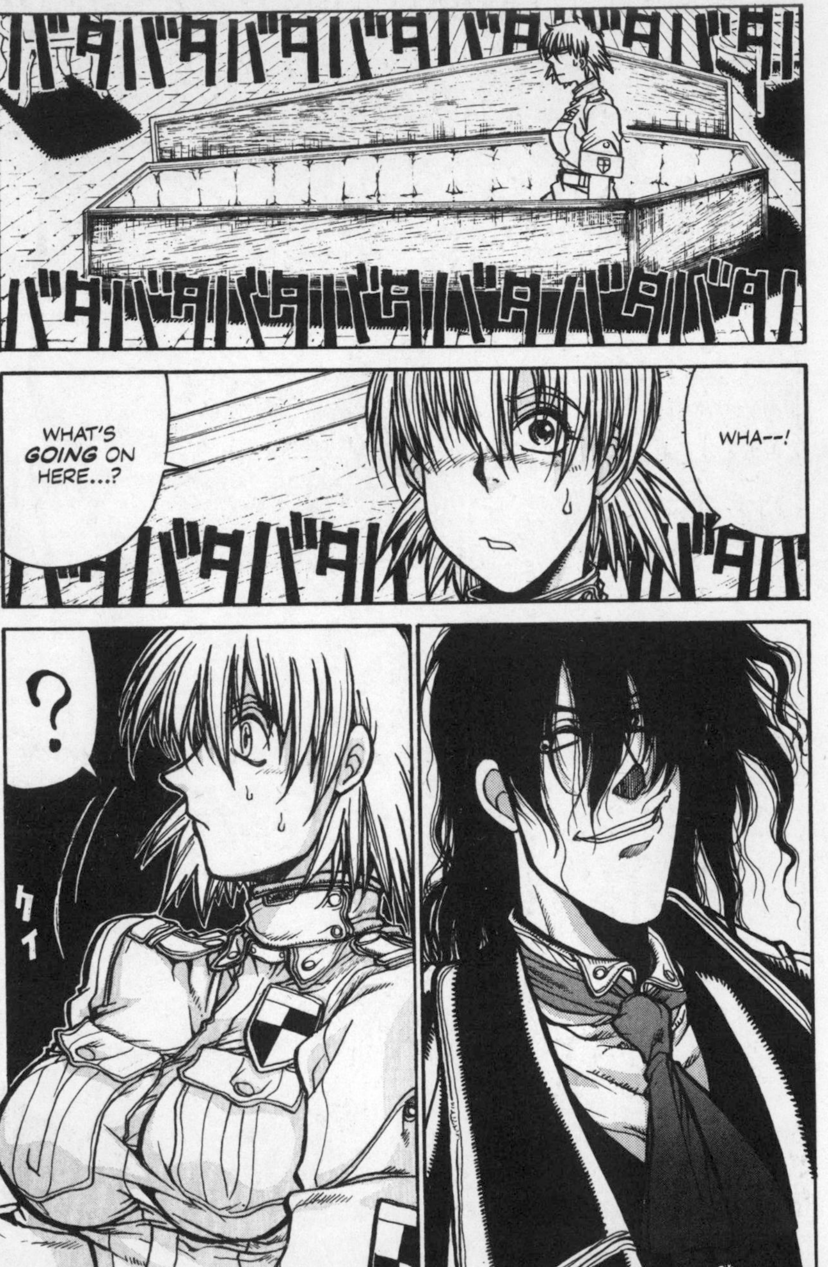
バタバタバタバタバタバタ!
バタバタバタバタバタバタ!
WHA--!
WHAT'S GOING ON HERE...?
バタバタバタ
?
クイ

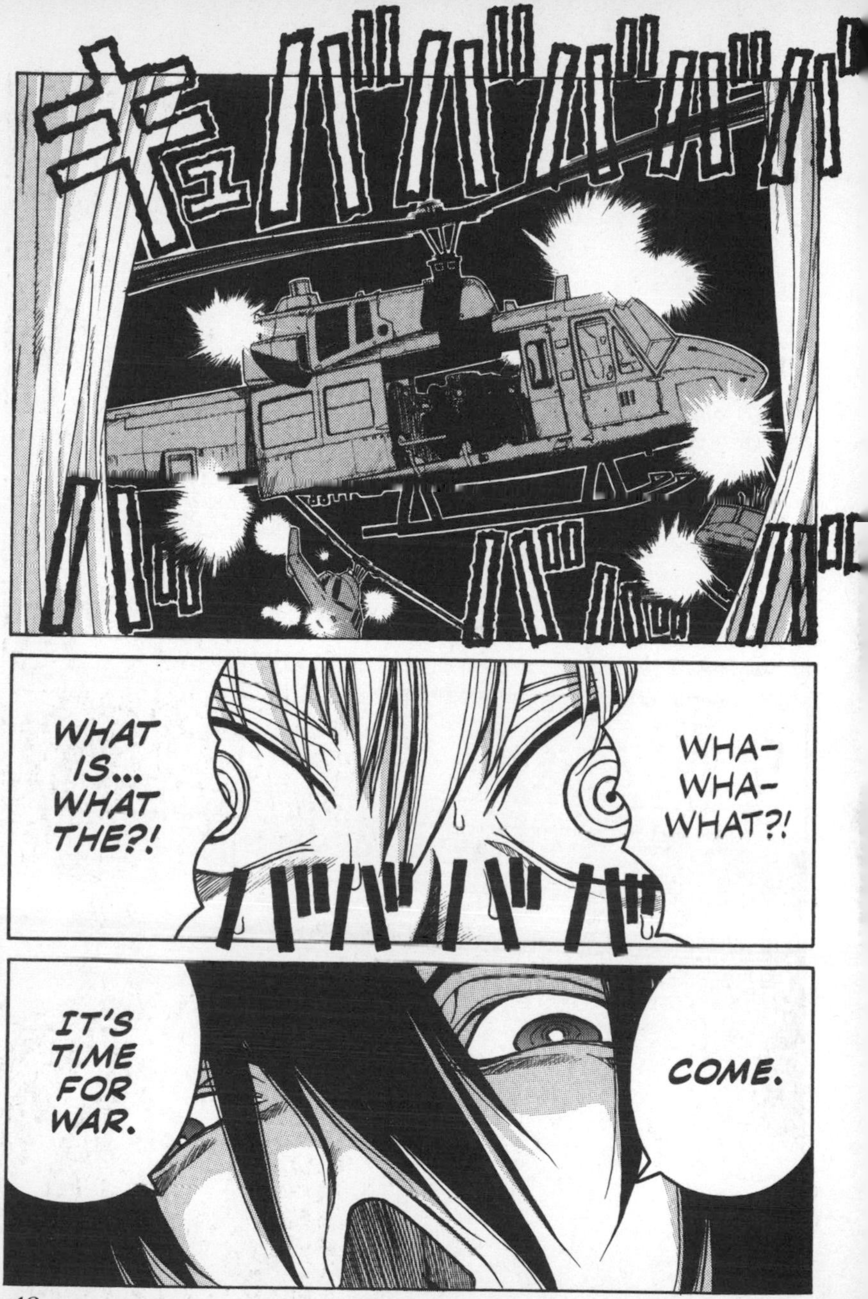
WHA- WHA- WHAT?!
WHAT IS... WHAT THE?!
COME.
IT'S TIME FOR WAR.

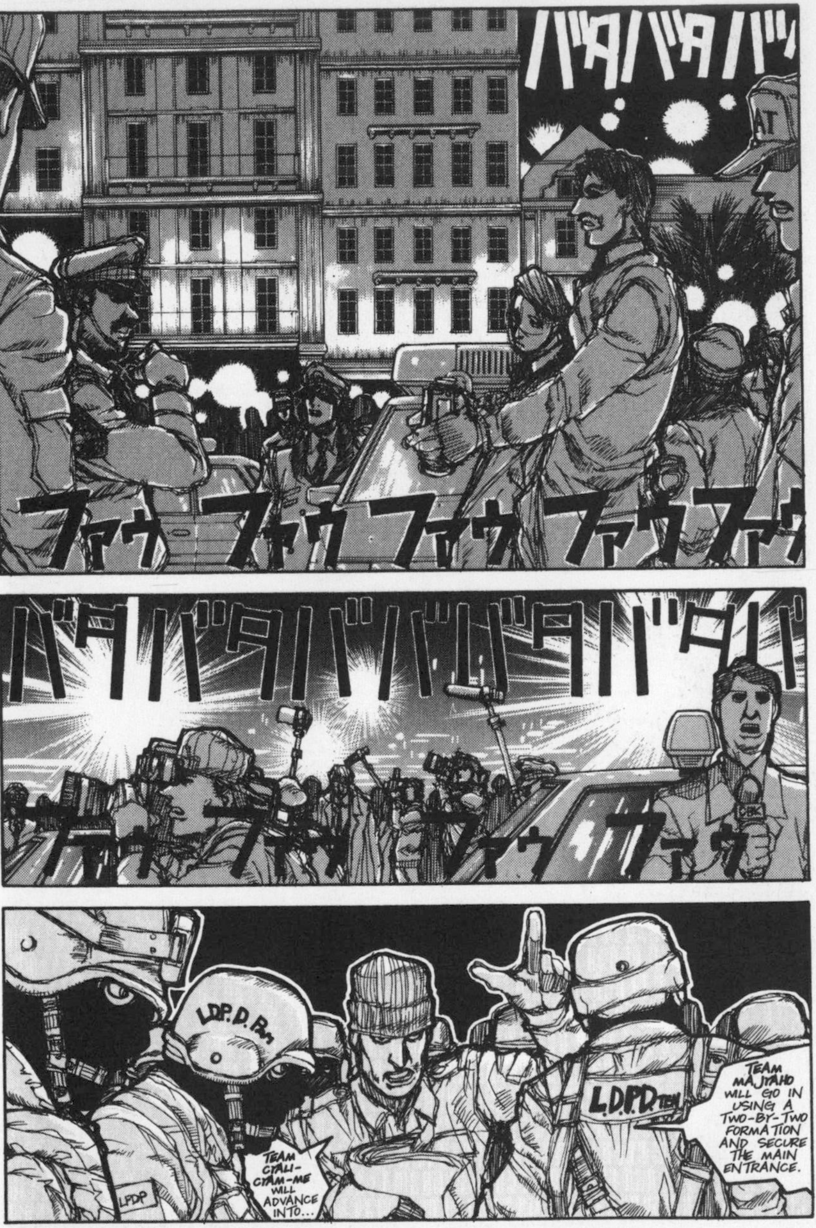
バタバタバッ
ファウ ファウ ファウ ファウ ファウ
L.D.P.D TEM
TEAM MAJYAHO WILL GO IN USING A TWO-BY-TWO FORMATION AND SECURE THE MAIN ENTRANCE.
TEAM CYALI-CYAM-ME WILL ADVANCE INTO...
LPDP

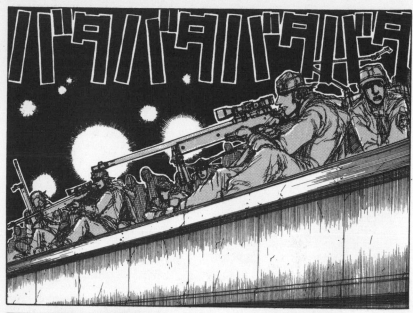

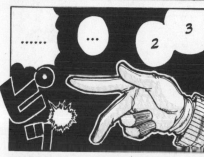

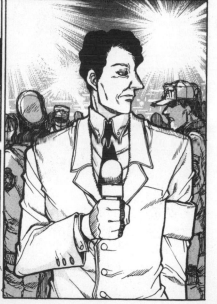

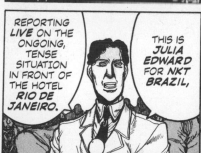

バタバタバタ!!バタ
3
2
...
......
ピッ
THIS IS JULIA EDWARD FOR NKT BRAZIL,
REPORTING LIVE ON THE ONGOING, TENSE SITUATION IN FRONT OF THE HOTEL RIO DE JANEIRO.

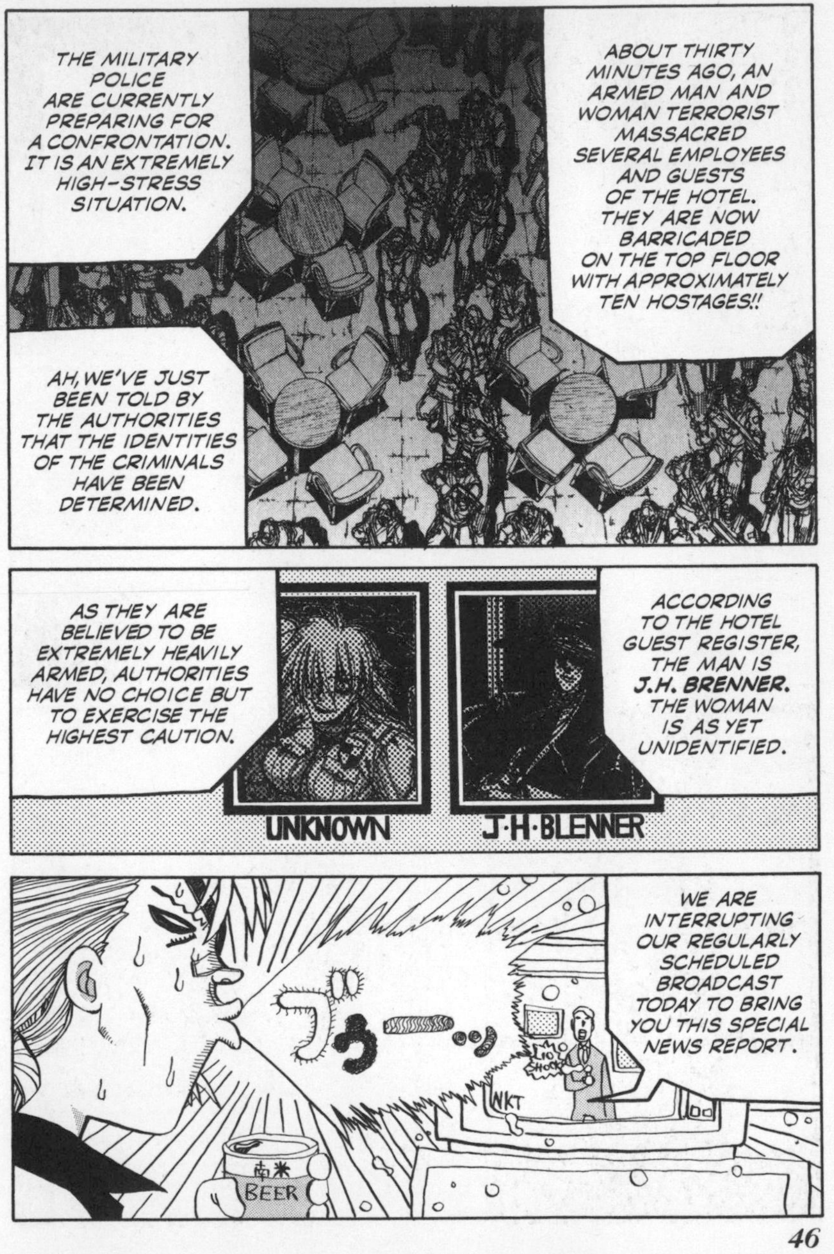
ABOUT THIRTY MINUTES AGO, AN ARMED MAN AND WOMAN TERRORIST MASSACRED SEVERAL EMPLOYEES AND GUESTS OF THE HOTEL. THEY ARE NOW BARRICADED ON THE TOP FLOOR WITH APPROXIMATELY TEN HOSTAGES!!
THE MILITARY POLICE ARE CURRENTLY PREPARING FOR A CONFRONTATION. IT IS AN EXTREMELY HIGH-STRESS SITUATION.
AH, WE'VE JUST BEEN TOLD BY THE AUTHORITIES THAT THE IDENTITIES OF THE CRIMINALS HAVE BEEN DETERMINED.
ACCORDING TO THE HOTEL GUEST REGISTER, THE MAN IS J.H. BRENNER. THE WOMAN IS AS YET UNIDENTIFIED.
J·H·BLENNER
UNKNOWN
AS THEY ARE BELIEVED TO BE EXTREMELY HEAVILY ARMED, AUTHORITIES HAVE NO CHOICE BUT TO EXERCISE THE HIGHEST CAUTION.
WE ARE INTERRUPTING OUR REGULARLY SCHEDULED BROADCAST TODAY TO BRING YOU THIS SPECIAL NEWS REPORT.
LIO SHOCK
NKT
BEER

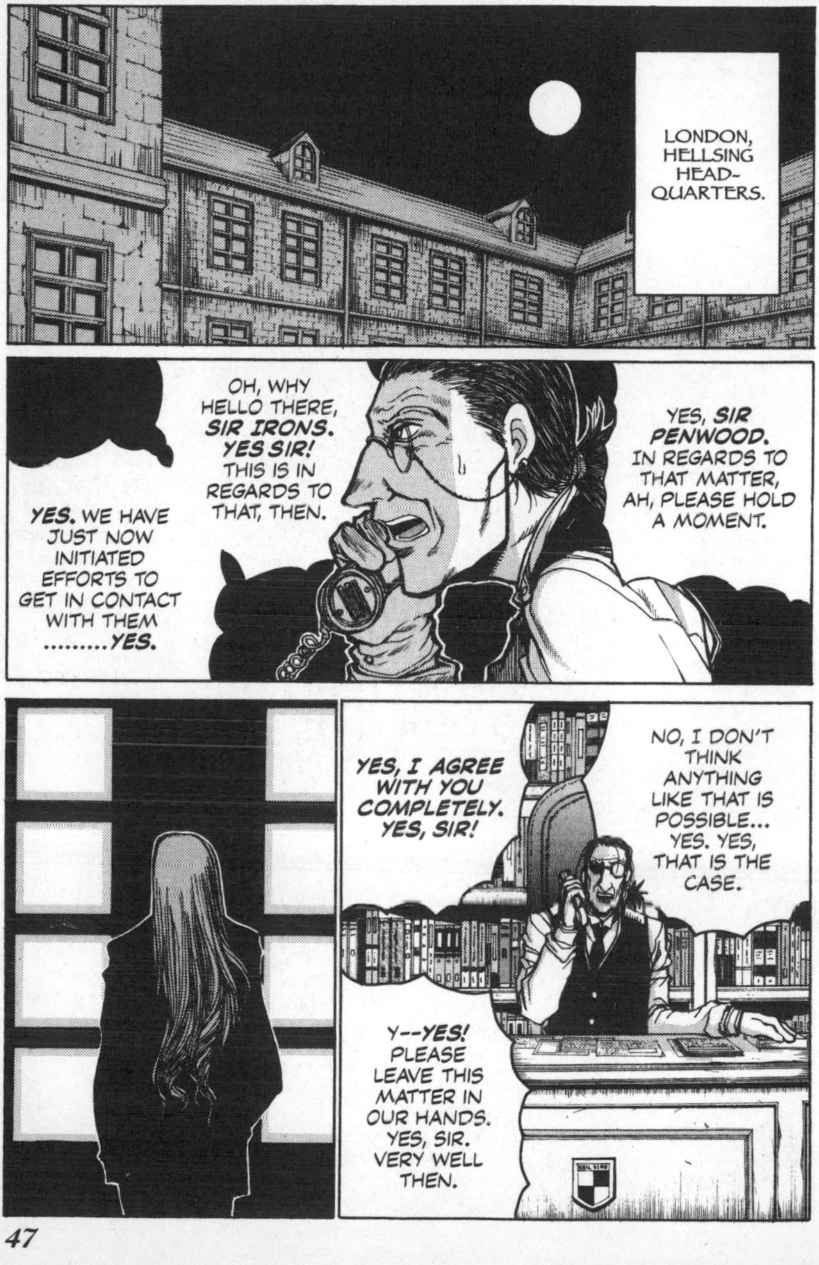
LONDON, HELLSING HEAD-QUARTERS.
YES, SIR PENWOOD. IN REGARDS TO THAT MATTER, AH, PLEASE HOLD A MOMENT.
OH, WHY HELLO THERE, SIR IRONS. YES SIR! THIS IS IN REGARDS TO THAT, THEN.
YES. WE HAVE JUST NOW INITIATED EFFORTS TO GET IN CONTACT WITH THEM ....YES.
NO, I DON'T THINK ANYTHING LIKE THAT IS POSSIBLE... YES. YES, THAT IS THE CASE.
YES, I AGREE WITH YOU COMPLETELY. YES, SIR!
Y--YES! PLEASE LEAVE THIS MATTER IN OUR HANDS. YES, SIR. VERY WELL THEN.

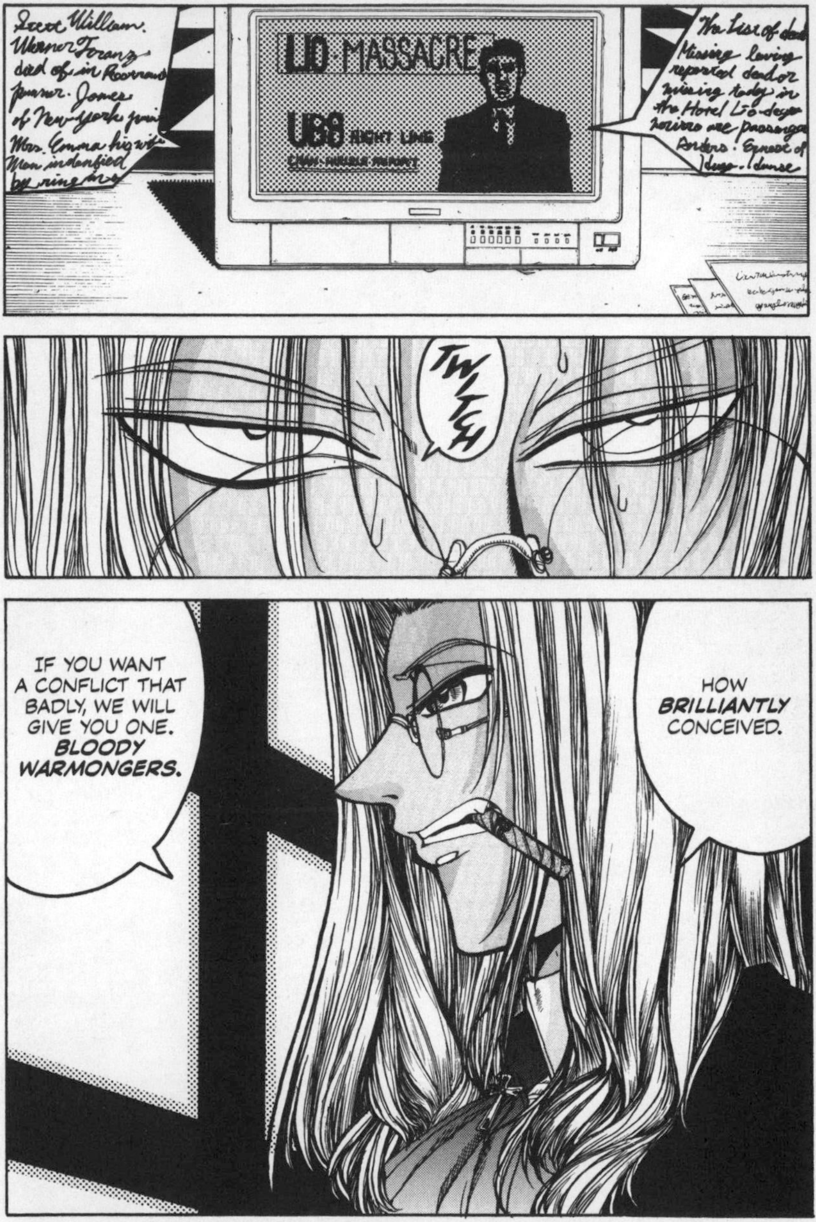
LIO MASSACRE
TWITCH
HOW BRILLIANTLY CONCEIVED.
IF YOU WANT A CONFLICT THAT BADLY, WE WILL GIVE YOU ONE. BLOODY WARMONGERS.

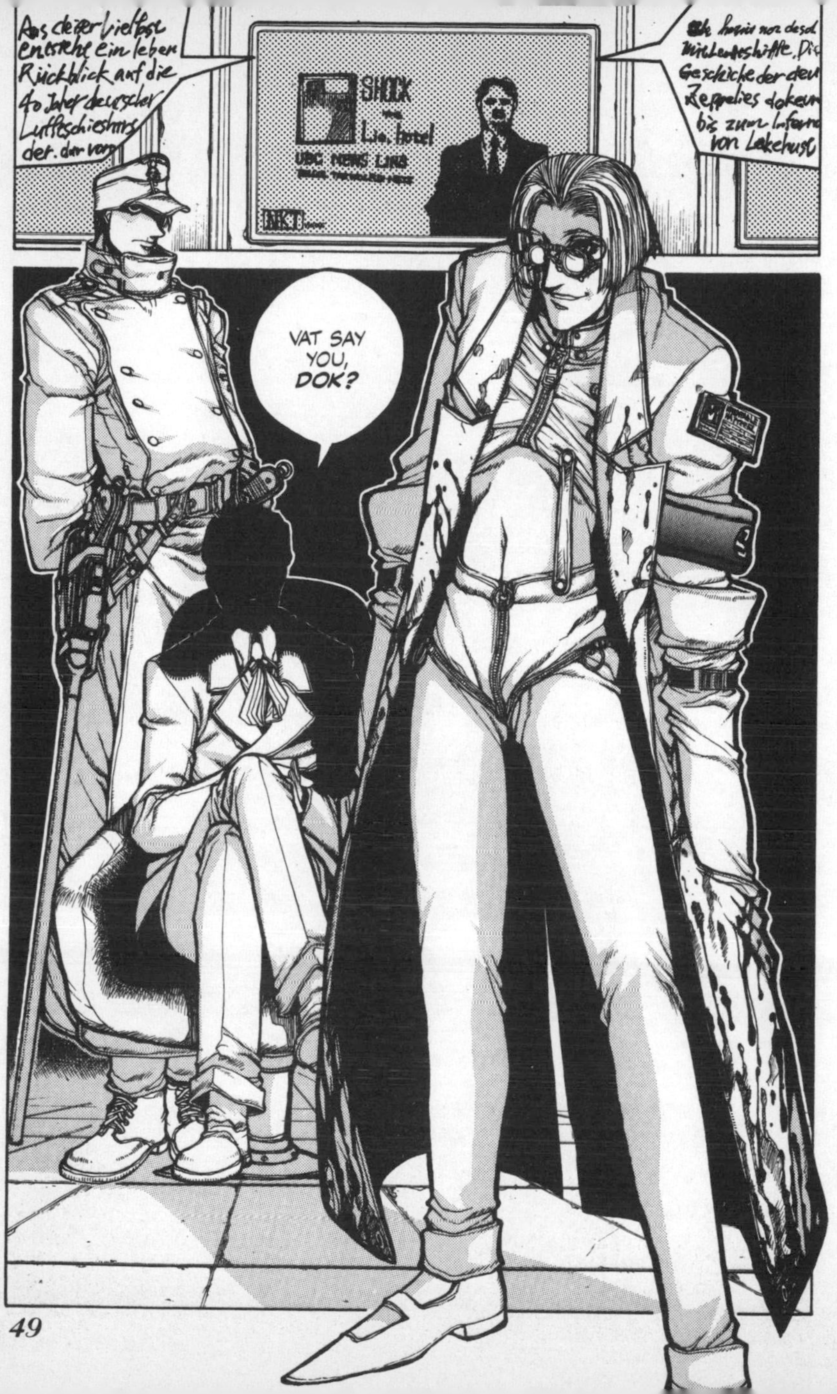
VAT SAY YOU, DOK?

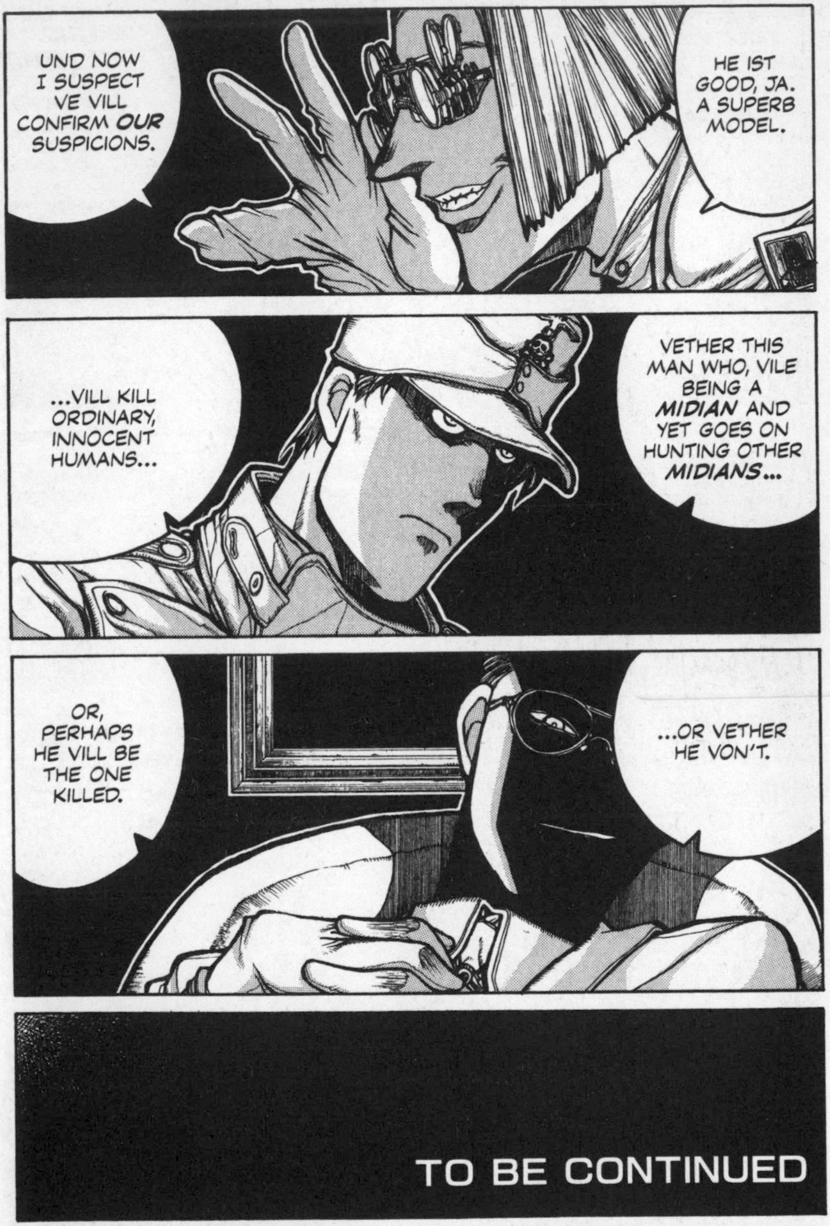
HE IST GOOD, JA. A SUPERB MODEL.
UND NOW I SUSPECT VE VILL CONFIRM OUR SUSPICIONS.
VETHER THIS MAN WHO, VILE BEING A MIDIAN AND YET GOES ON HUNTING OTHER MIDIANS...
...VILL KILL ORDINARY, INNOCENT HUMANS...
...OR VETHER HE VON'T.
OR, PERHAPS HE VILL BE THE ONE KILLED.
TO BE CONTINUED

ORDER 2 / END

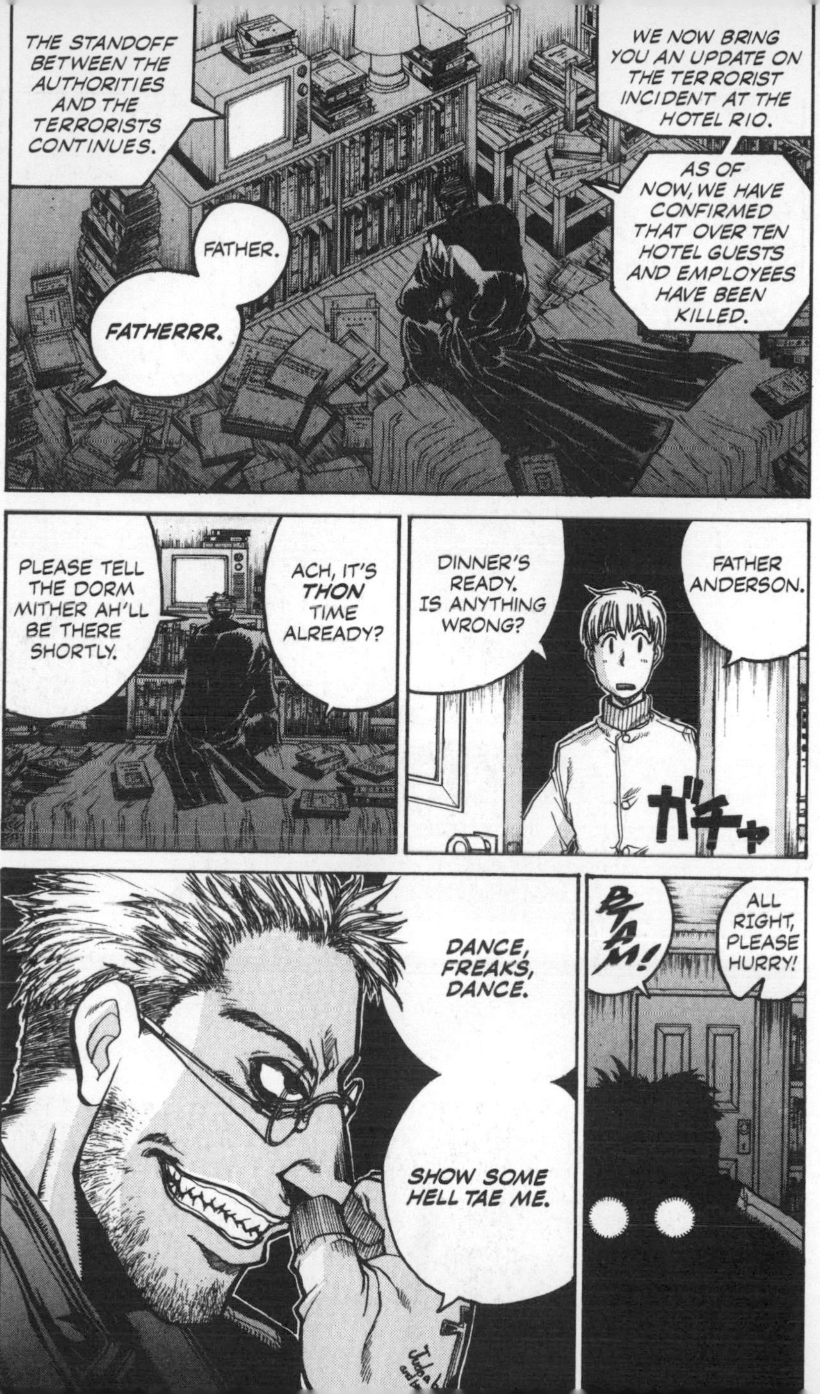
WE NOW BRING YOU AN UPDATE ON THE TERRORIST INCIDENT AT THE HOTEL RIO.
AS OF NOW, WE HAVE CONFIRMED THAT OVER TEN HOTEL GUESTS AND EMPLOYEES HAVE BEEN KILLED.
THE STANDOFF BETWEEN THE AUTHORITIES AND THE TERRORISTS CONTINUES.
FATHER.
FATHERRR.
FATHER ANDERSON.
DINNER'S READY. IS ANYTHING WRONG?
ガチャ
ACH, IT'S THON TIME ALREADY?
PLEASE TELL THE DORM MITHER AH'LL BE THERE SHORTLY.
ALL RIGHT, PLEASE HURRY!
BLAM!
DANCE, FREAKS, DANCE.
SHOW SOME HELL TAE ME.

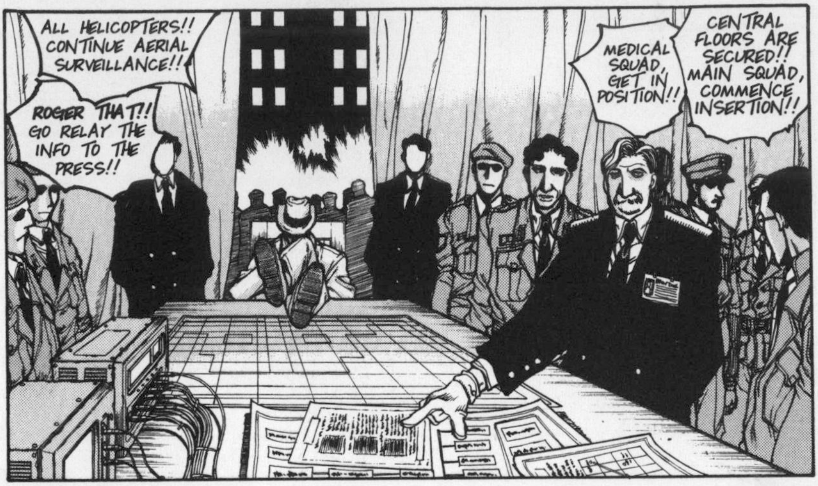
CENTRAL FLOORS ARE SECURED!! MAIN SQUAD, COMMENCE INSERTION!!
MEDICAL SQUAD, GET IN POSITION!!
ALL HELICOPTERS!! CONTINUE AERIAL SURVEILLANCE!!
ROGIER THAT!! GO RELAY THE INFO TO THE PRESS!!

ORDER 03

エレベーター　アクション

ELEVATOR ACTION②

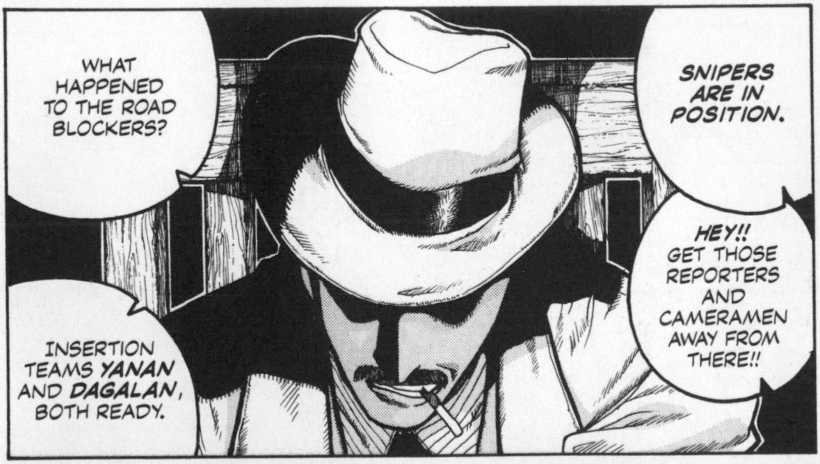
SNIPERS ARE IN POSITION.
WHAT HAPPENED TO THE ROAD BLOCKERS?
HEY!! GET THOSE REPORTERS AND CAMERAMEN AWAY FROM THERE!!
INSERTION TEAMS YANAN AND DAGALAN, BOTH READY.

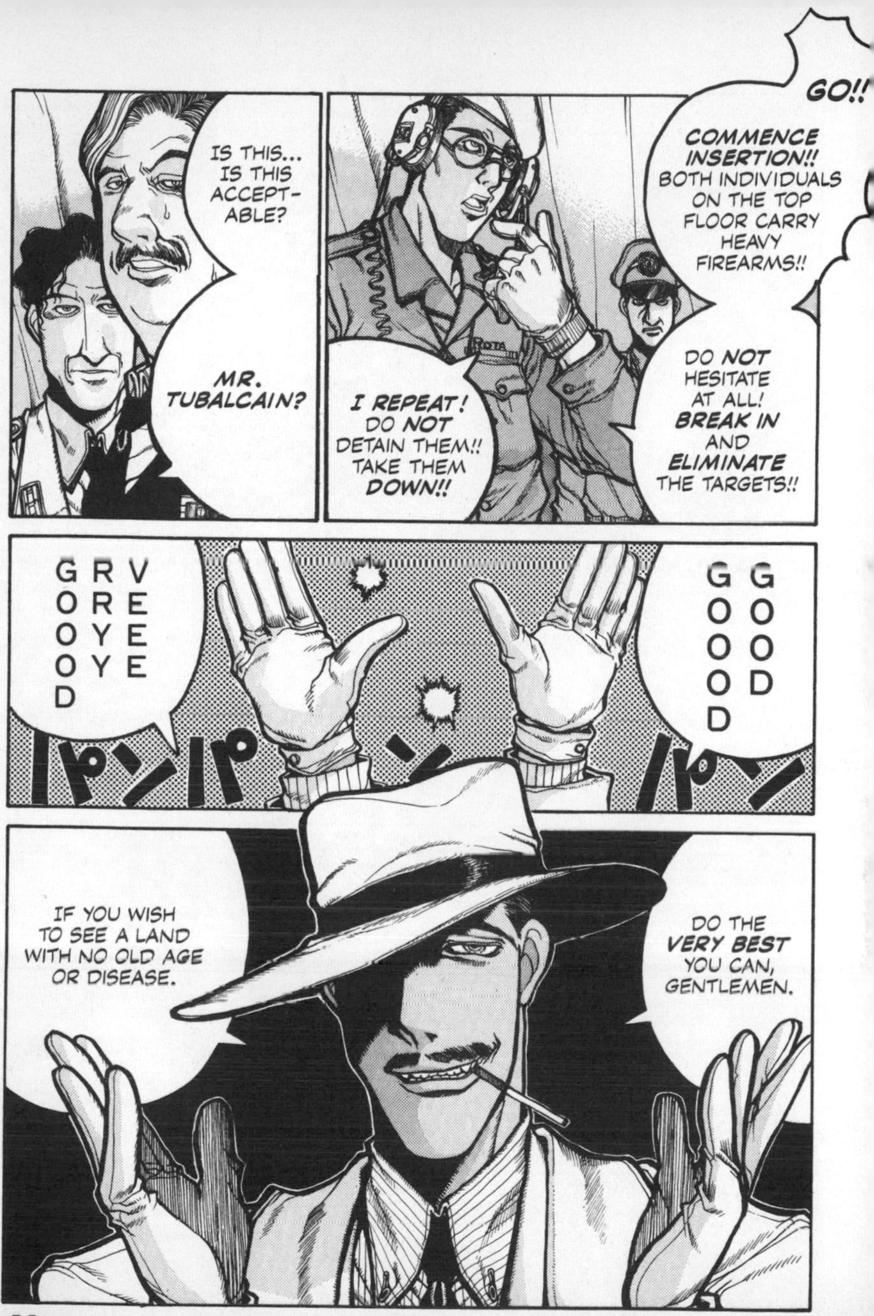
GO!!
COMMENCE INSERTION!! BOTH INDIVIDUALS ON THE TOP FLOOR CARRY HEAVY FIREARMS!!
DO NOT HESITATE AT ALL! BREAK IN AND ELIMINATE THE TARGETS!!
I REPEAT! DO NOT DETAIN THEM!! TAKE THEM DOWN!!
IS THIS... IS THIS ACCEPT-ABLE?
MR. TUBALCAIN?
GOOD GOOOOD
VEEE RRYY GOOOOD
DO THE VERY BEST YOU CAN, GENTLEMEN.
IF YOU WISH TO SEE A LAND WITH NO OLD AGE OR DISEASE.

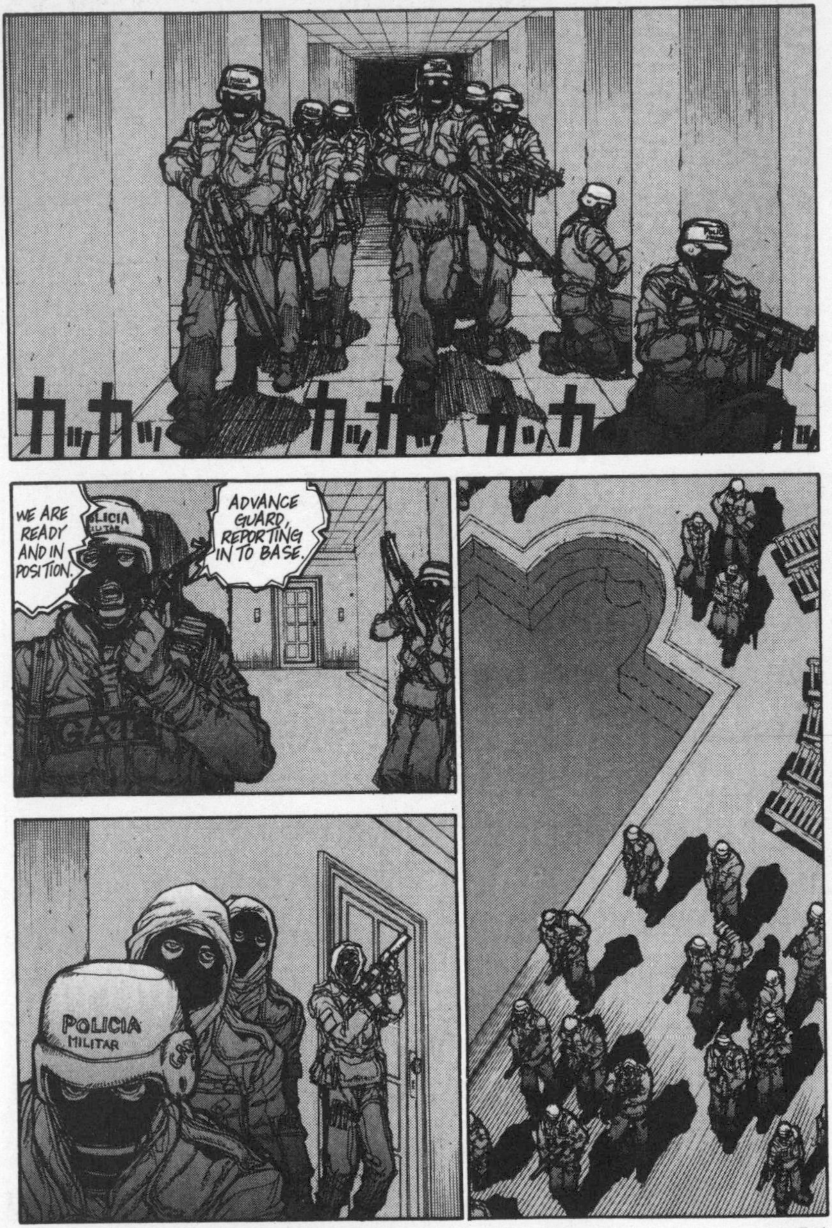
カッカッ カッカッ カッカッ
ADVANCE GUARD, REPORTING IN TO BASE.
WE ARE READY AND IN POSITION.
POLICIA MILITAR

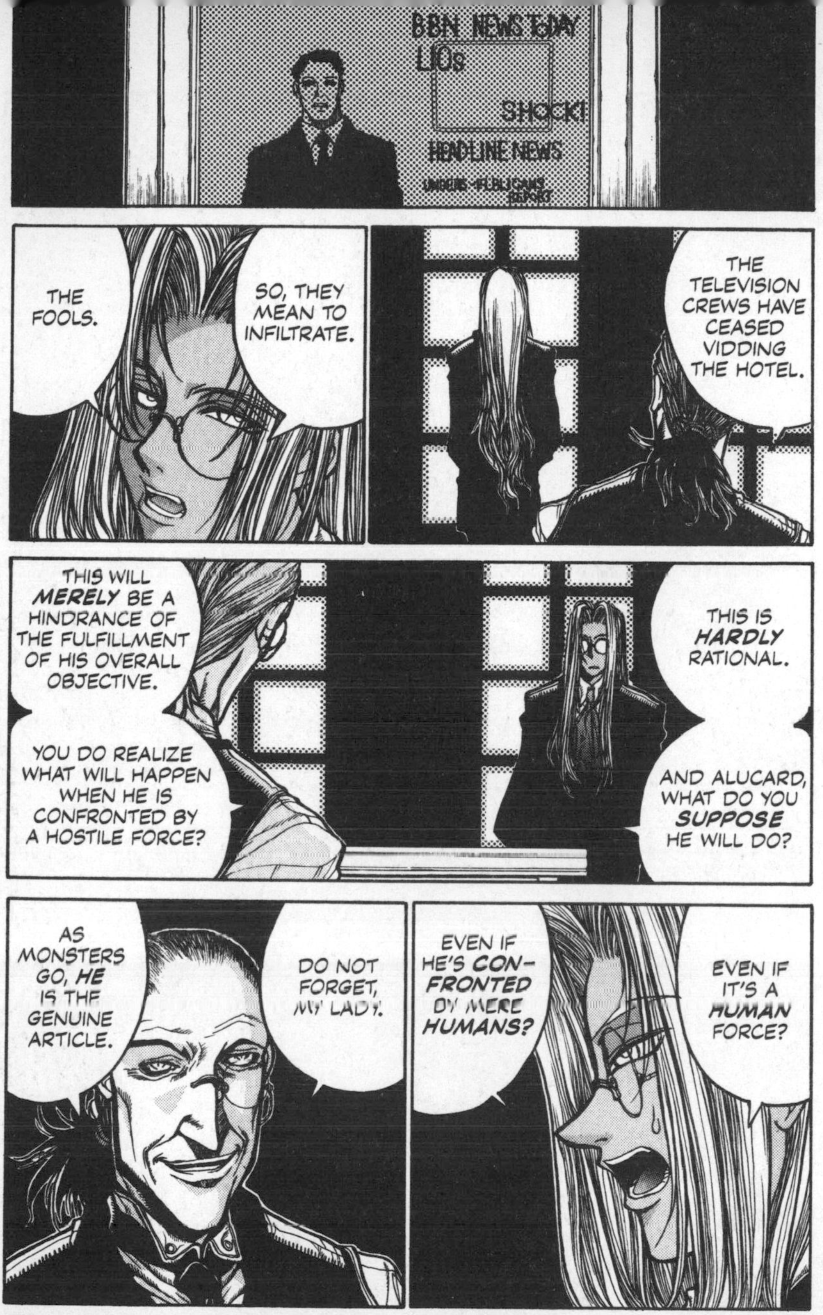
BBN NEWS TODAY
LIOs
SHOCK!
HEADLINE NEWS
THE TELEVISION CREWS HAVE CEASED VIDDING THE HOTEL.
SO, THEY MEAN TO INFILTRATE.
THE FOOLS.
THIS IS HARDLY RATIONAL.
AND ALUCARD, WHAT DO YOU SUPPOSE HE WILL DO?
THIS WILL MERELY BE A HINDRANCE OF THE FULFILLMENT OF HIS OVERALL OBJECTIVE.
YOU DO REALIZE WHAT WILL HAPPEN WHEN HE IS CONFRONTED BY A HOSTILE FORCE?
EVEN IF IT'S A HUMAN FORCE?
EVEN IF HE'S CONFRONTED BY MERE HUMANS?
DO NOT FORGET, MY LADY.
AS MONSTERS GO, HE IS THE GENUINE ARTICLE.

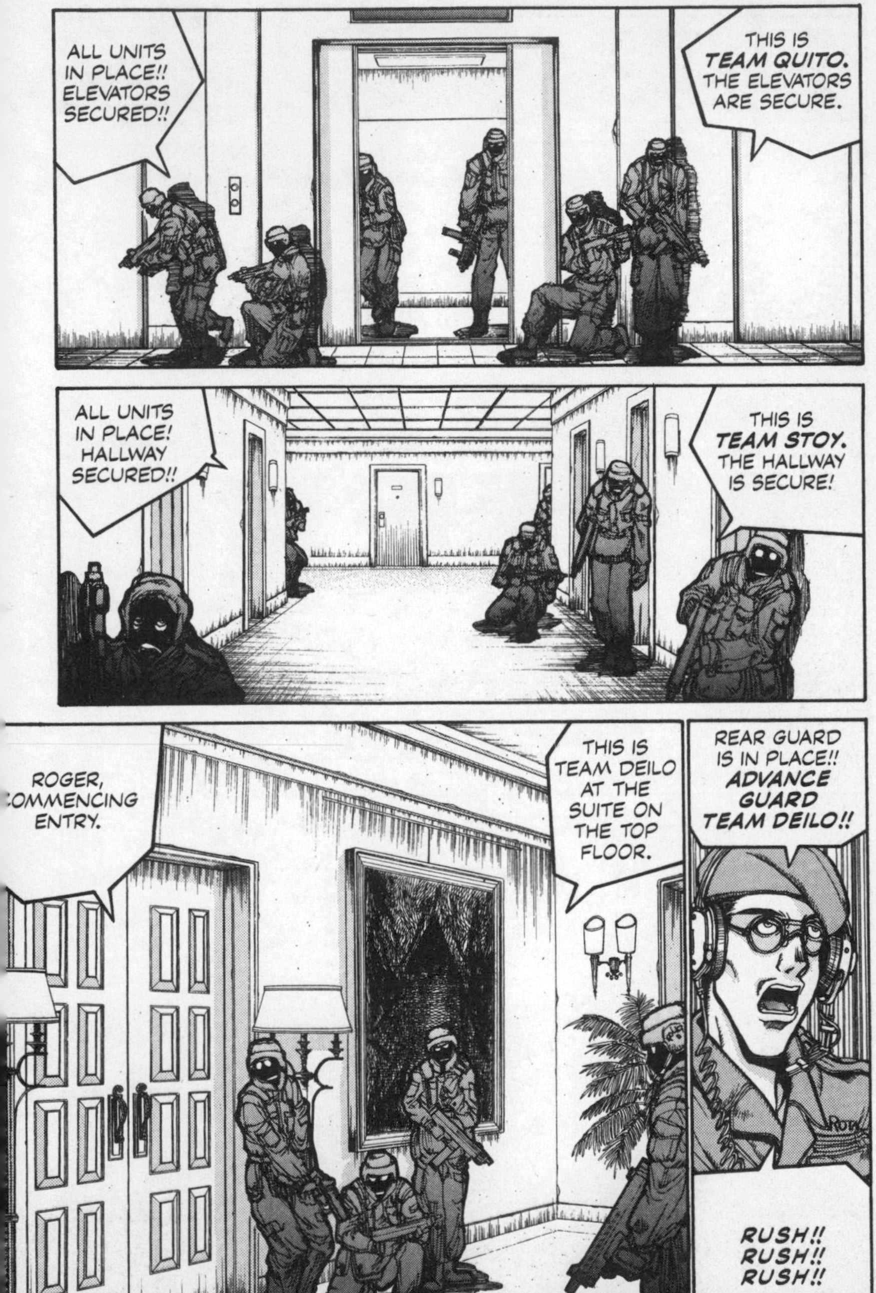
THIS IS TEAM QUITO. THE ELEVATORS ARE SECURE.
ALL UNITS IN PLACE!! ELEVATORS SECURED!!
THIS IS TEAM STOY. THE HALLWAY IS SECURE!
ALL UNITS IN PLACE! HALLWAY SECURED!!
REAR GUARD IS IN PLACE!! ADVANCE GUARD TEAM DEILO!!
RUSH!! RUSH!! RUSH!!
THIS IS TEAM DEILO AT THE SUITE ON THE TOP FLOOR.
ROGER, COMMENCING ENTRY.

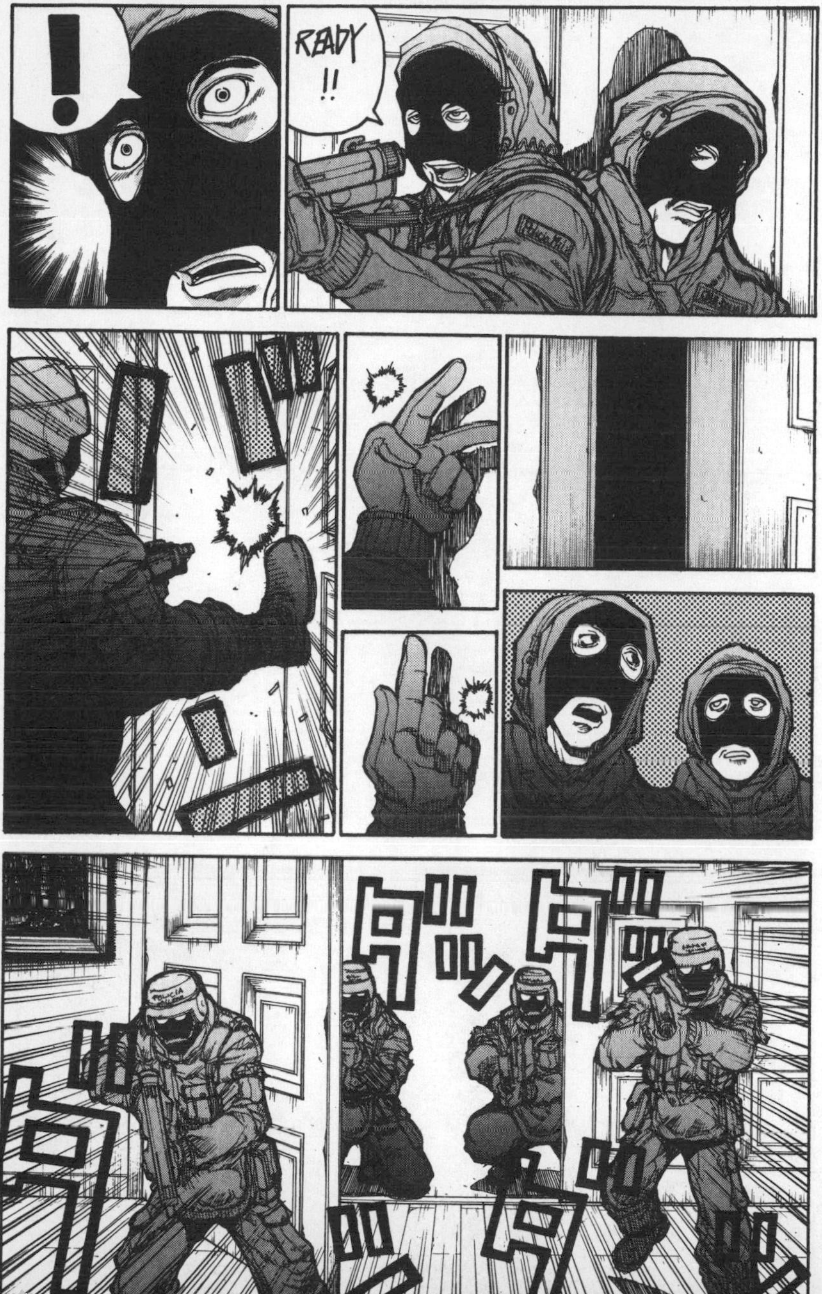
READY !!
!

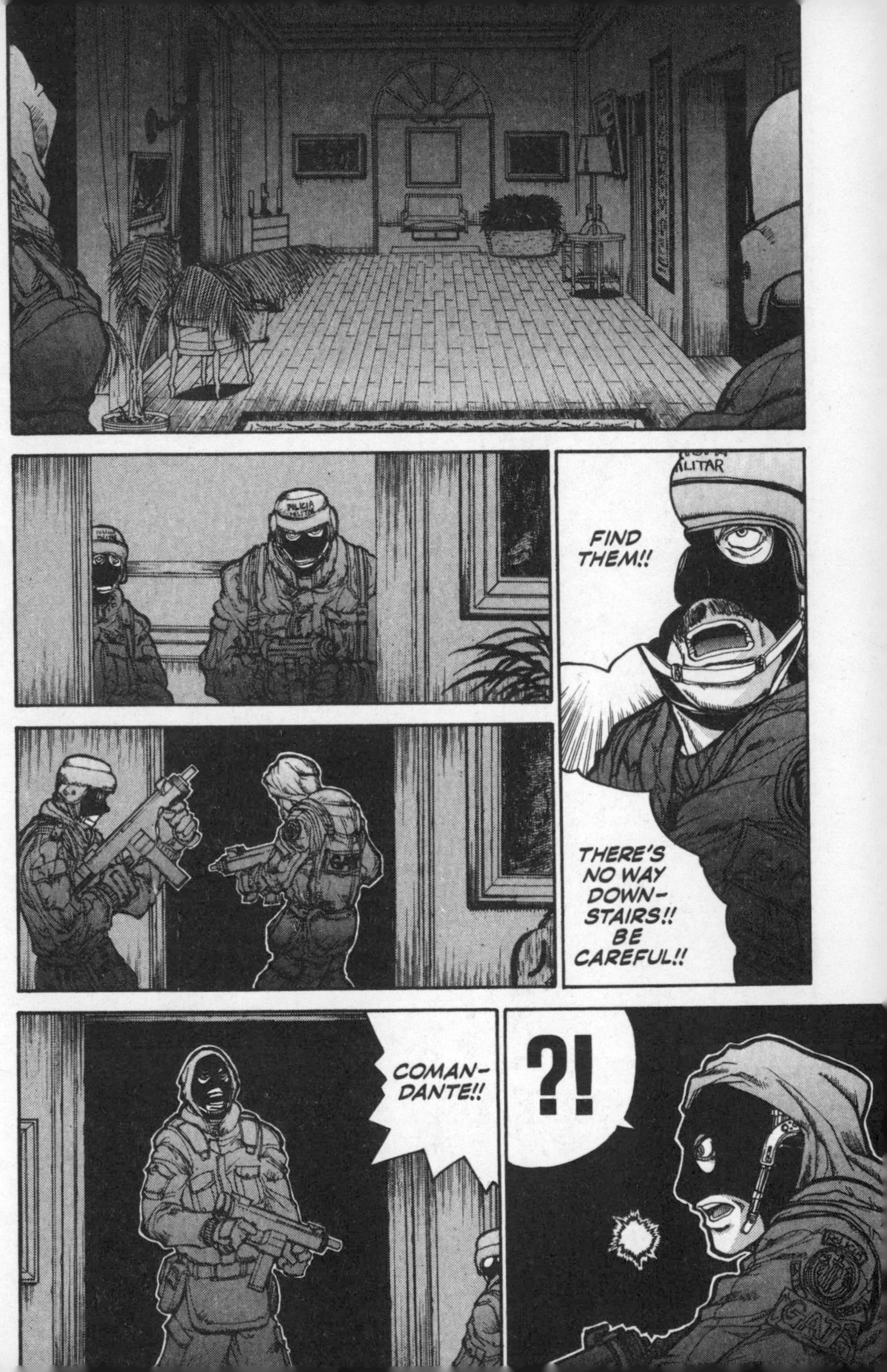
FIND THEM!!
THERE'S NO WAY DOWN-STAIRS!! BE CAREFUL!!
?!
COMAN-DANTE!!

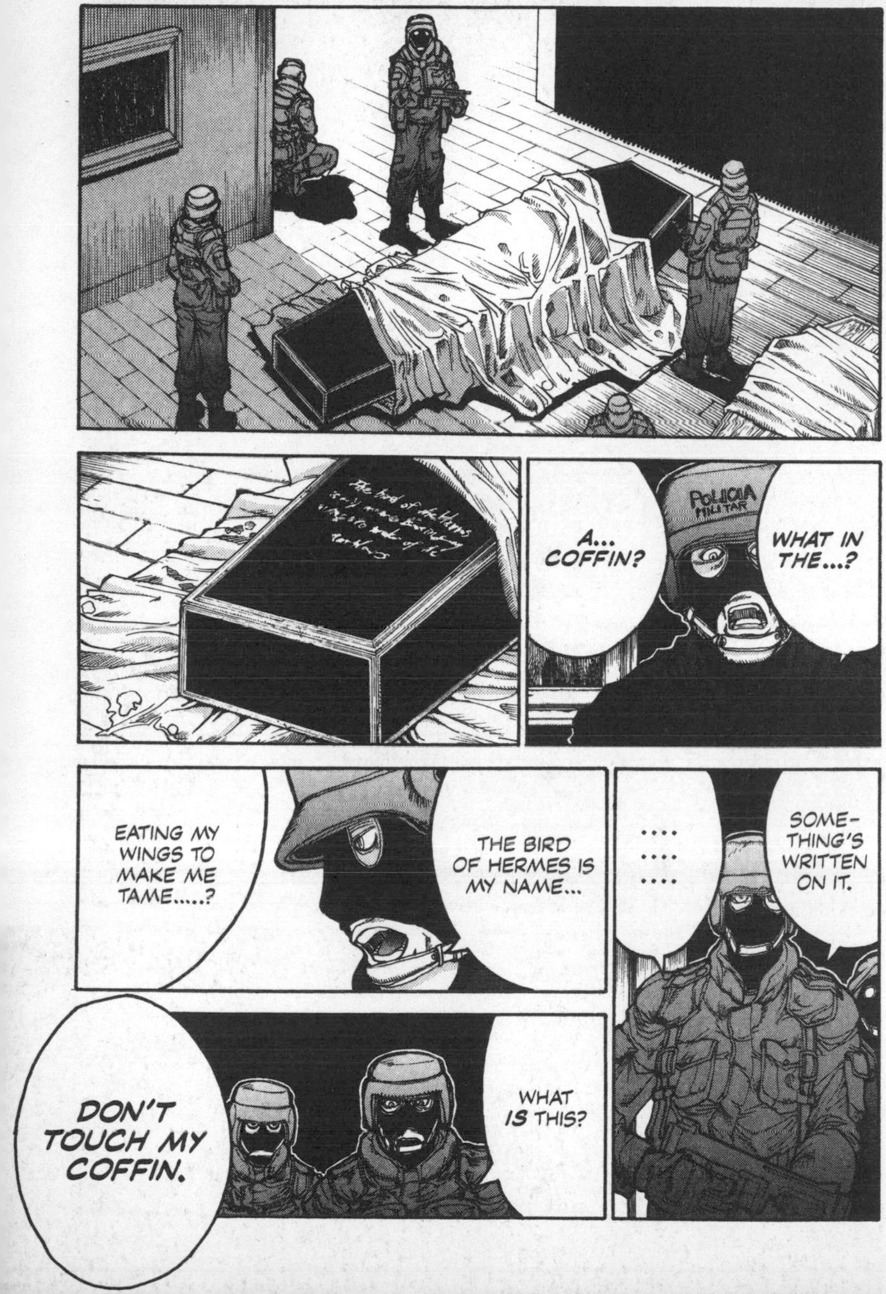
WHAT IN THE...?
A... COFFIN?
SOME-THING'S WRITTEN ON IT.
....
THE BIRD OF HERMES IS MY NAME...
EATING MY WINGS TO MAKE ME TAME.....?
WHAT *IS* THIS?
DON'T TOUCH MY COFFIN.

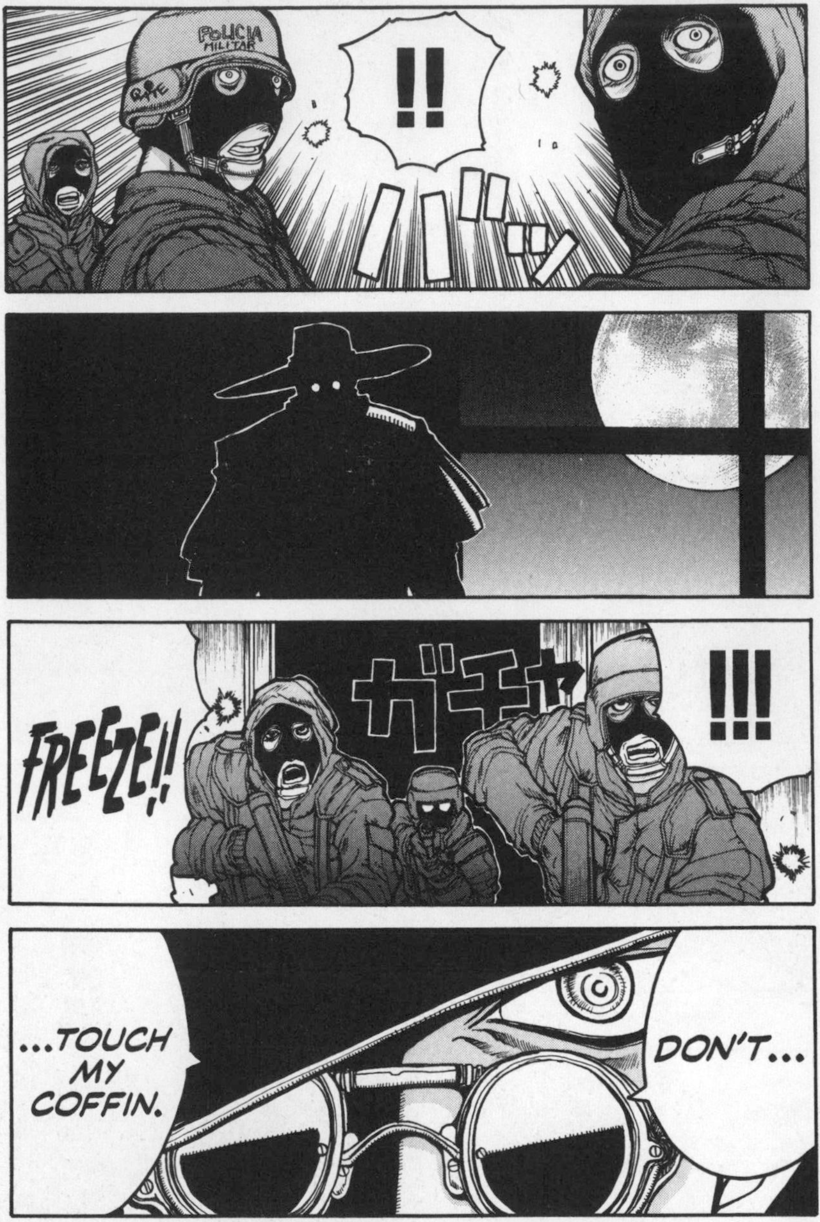
POLICIA
MILITAR
!!
!!!
ガチャ
FREEZE!!
DON'T...
...TOUCH MY COFFIN.

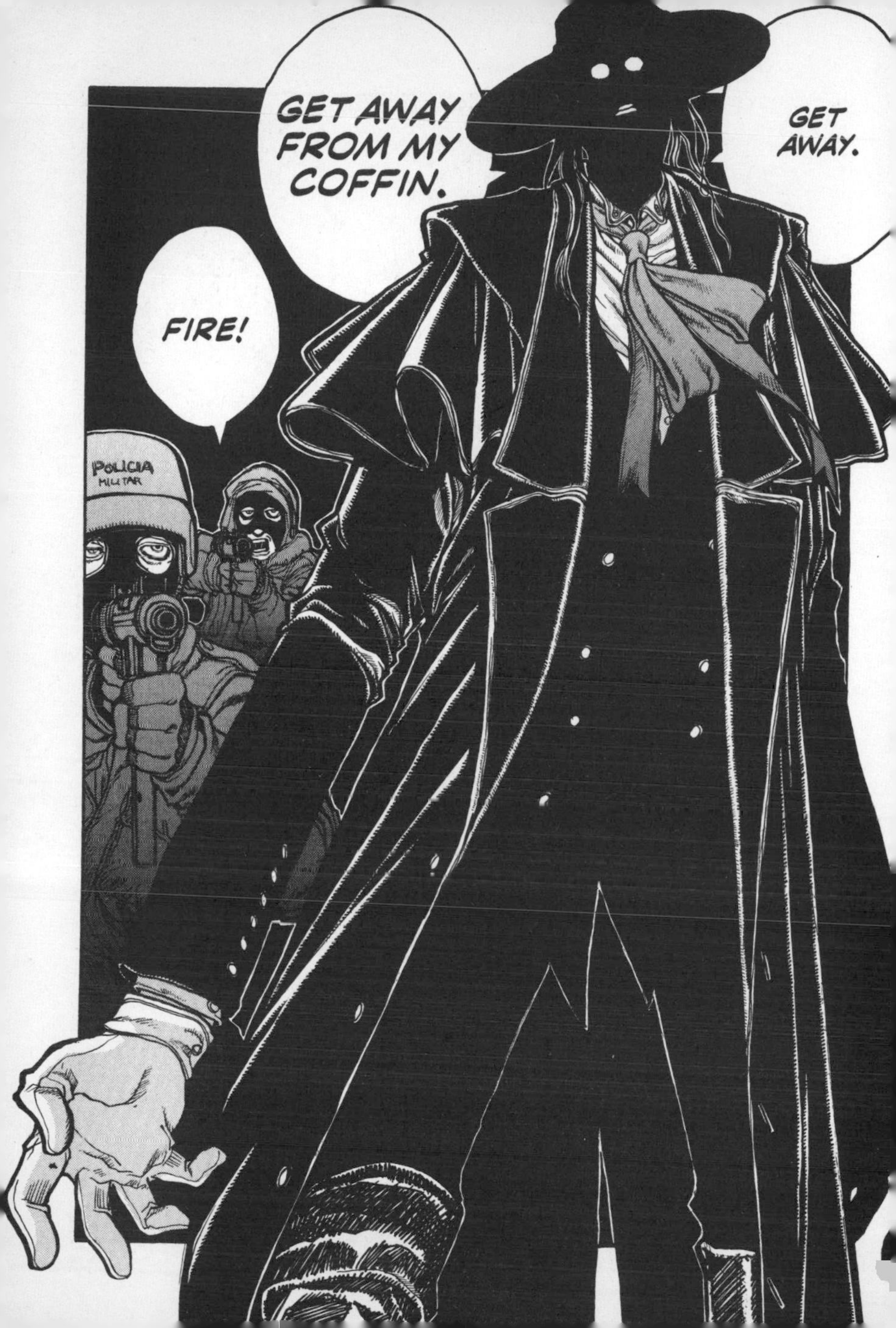
GET AWAY.
GET AWAY FROM MY COFFIN.
FIRE!
POLICIA MILITAR

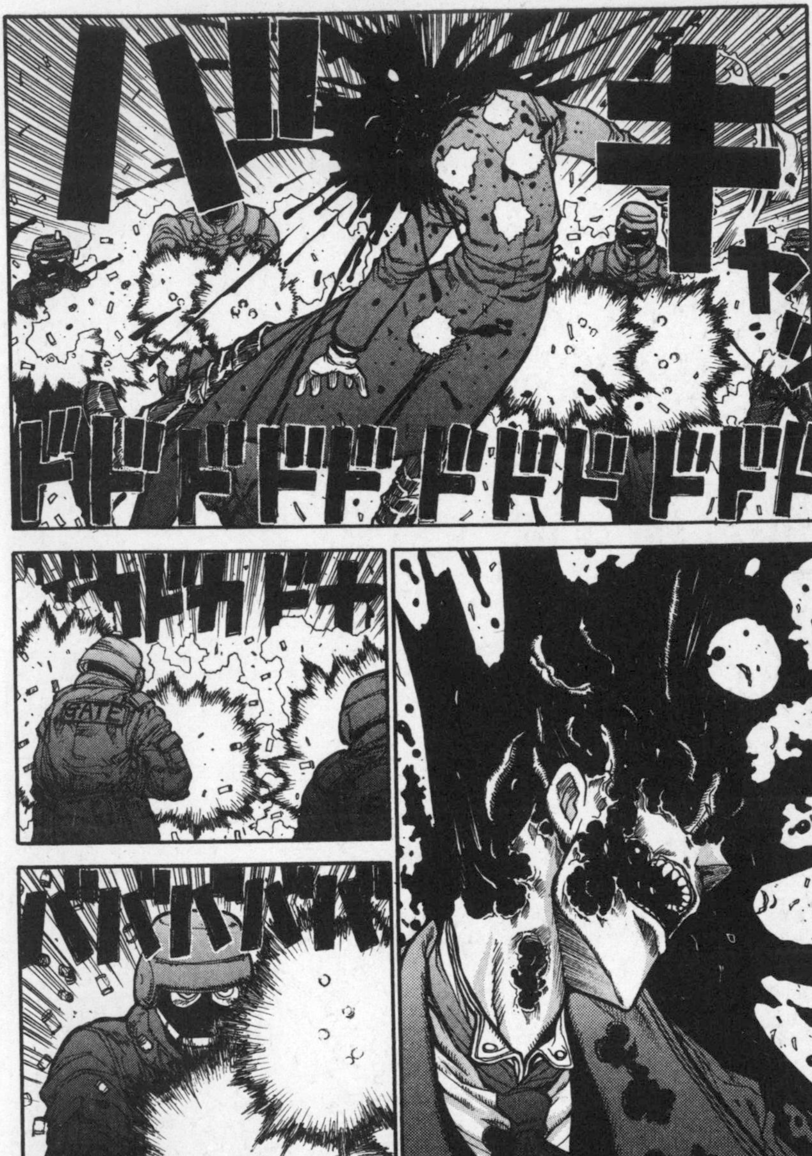
バキャッ
ドドドドドドドドドドド
GATE
ババババ

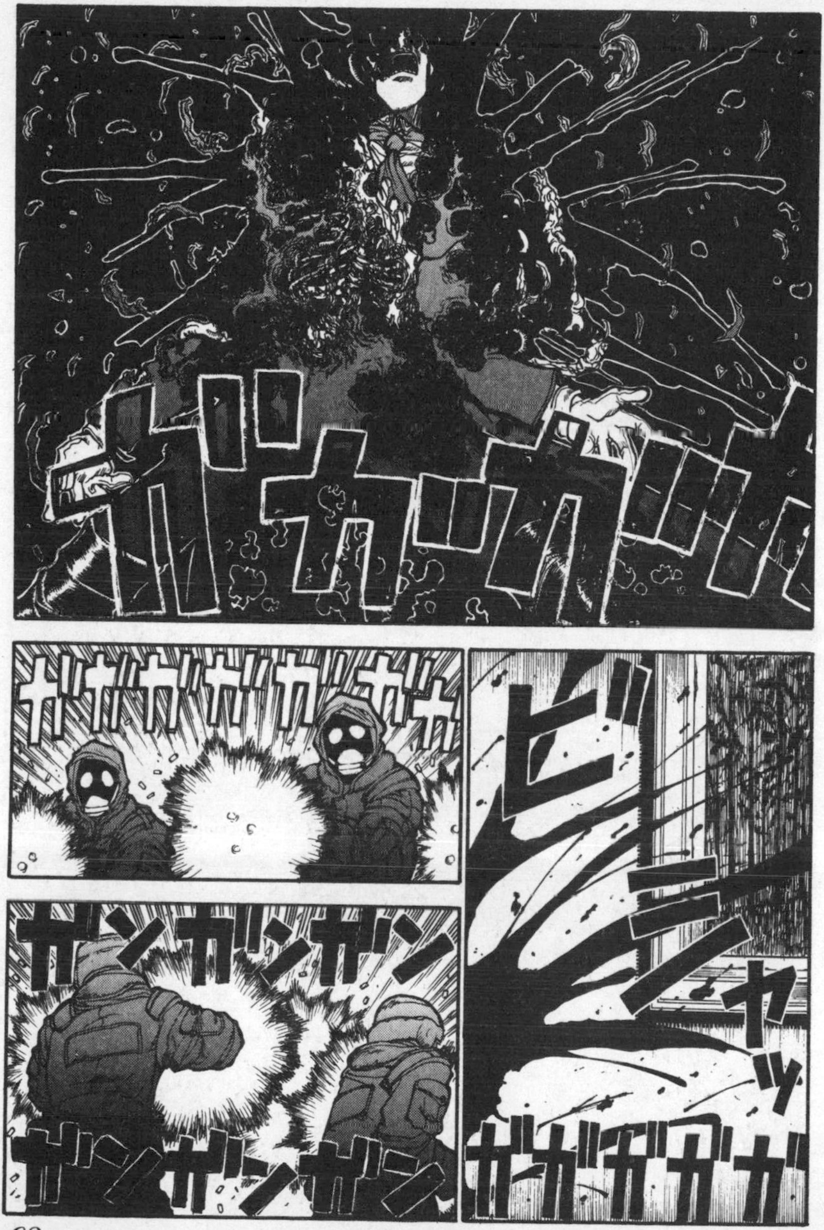
ガカッグーン
ビシャッ
ガガガガガ
ガガガガガガガ
ガンガンガン
ガンガンガン

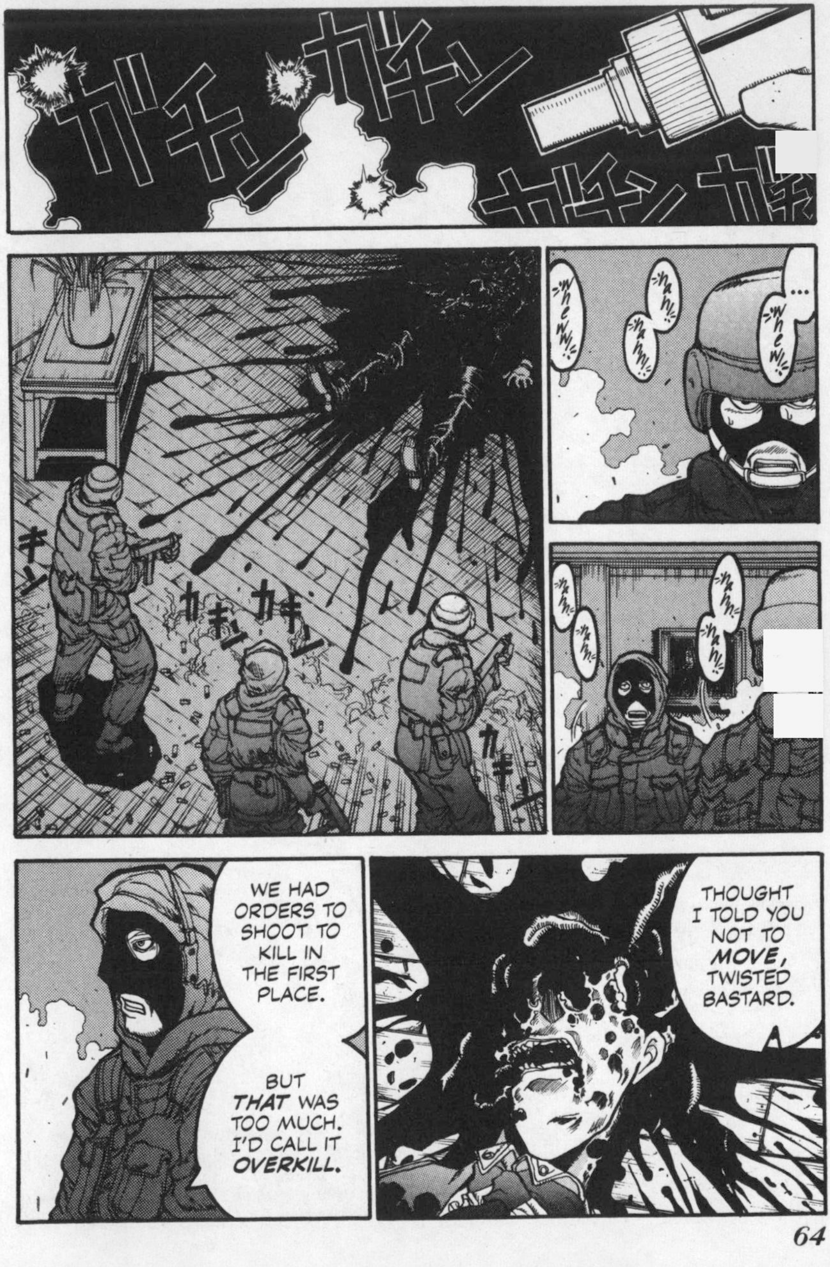
...
whew!
hah!
hah!
whew!
hah hah
THOUGHT I TOLD YOU NOT TO **MOVE**, TWISTED BASTARD.
WE HAD ORDERS TO SHOOT TO KILL IN THE FIRST PLACE.
BUT **THAT** WAS TOO MUCH. I'D CALL IT **OVERKILL.**

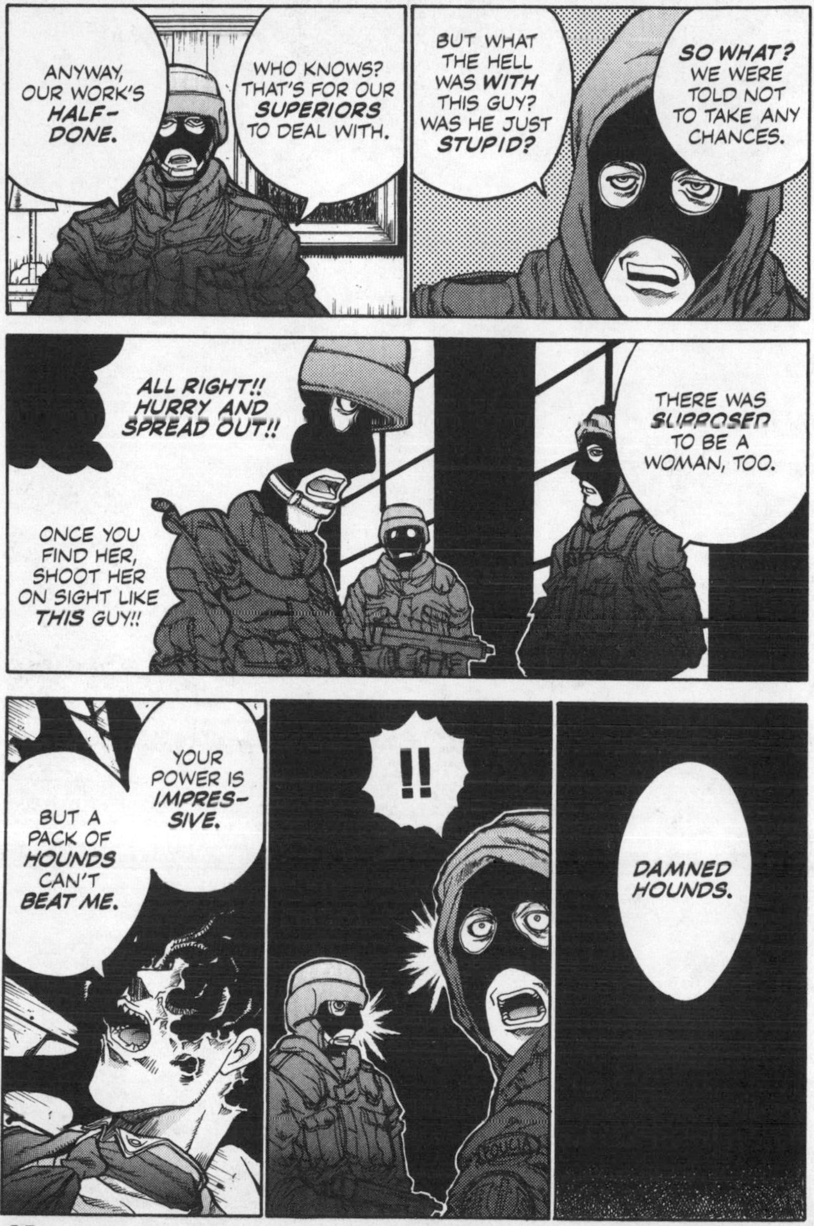
SO WHAT? WE WERE TOLD NOT TO TAKE ANY CHANCES.
BUT WHAT THE HELL WAS WITH THIS GUY? WAS HE JUST STUPID?
WHO KNOWS? THAT'S FOR OUR SUPERIORS TO DEAL WITH.
ANYWAY, OUR WORK'S HALF-DONE.
THERE WAS SUPPOSED TO BE A WOMAN, TOO.
ALL RIGHT!! HURRY AND SPREAD OUT!!
ONCE YOU FIND HER, SHOOT HER ON SIGHT LIKE THIS GUY!!
DAMNED HOUNDS.
!!
YOUR POWER IS IMPRES-SIVE.
BUT A PACK OF HOUNDS CAN'T BEAT ME.

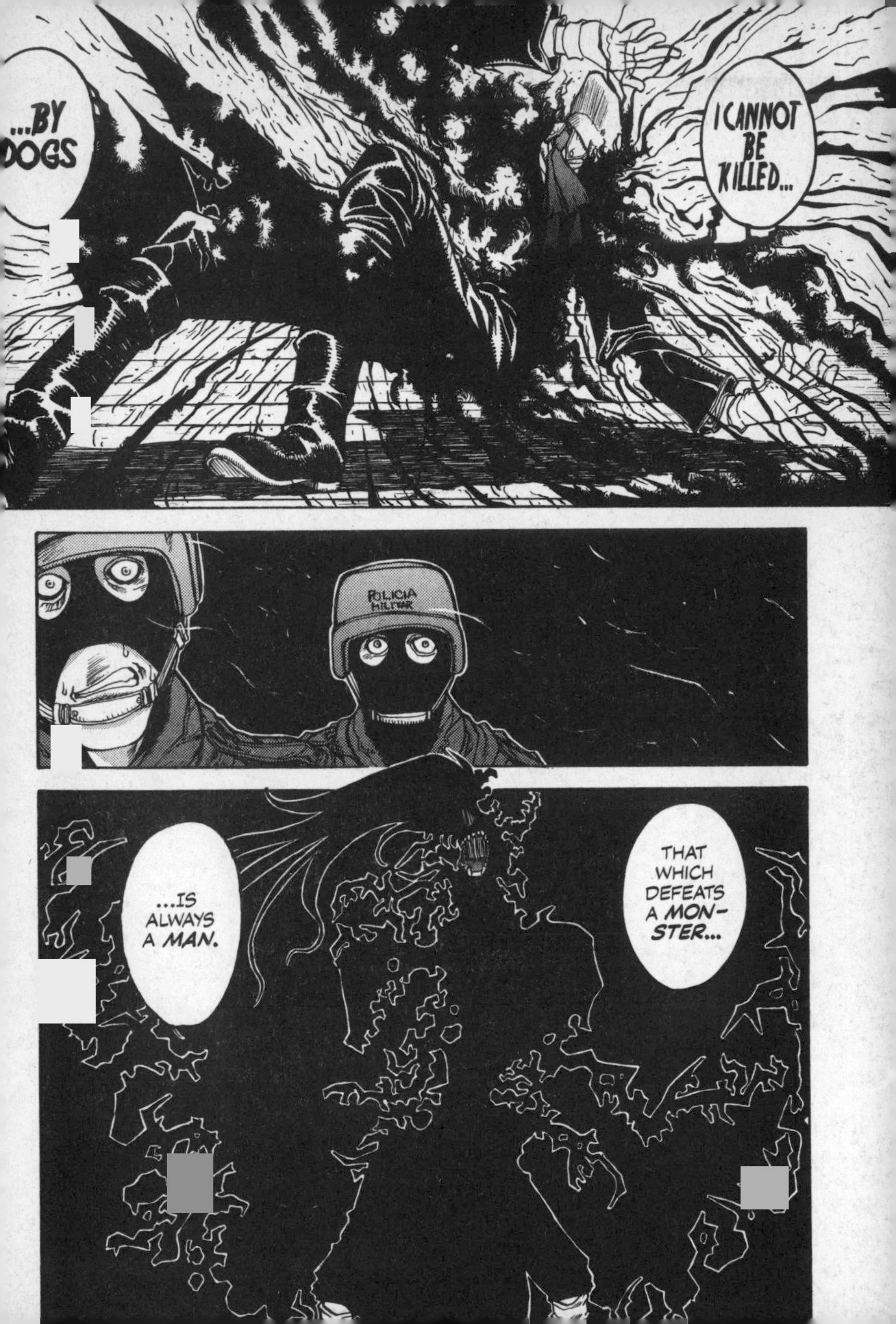
I CANNOT BE KILLED...
...BY DOGS
POLICIA MILITAR
THAT WHICH DEFEATS A MONSTER...
...IS ALWAYS A MAN.

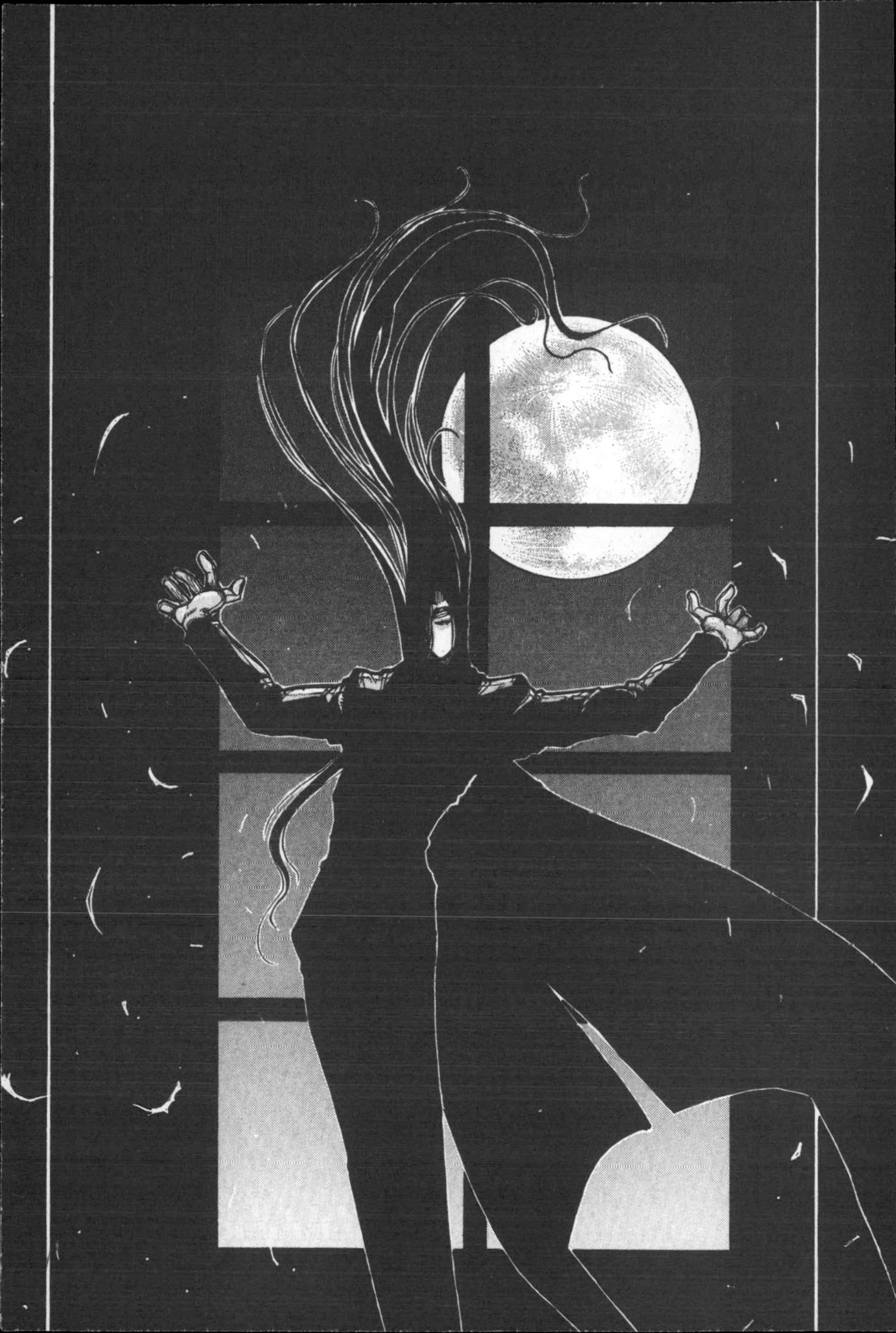

AHHHH

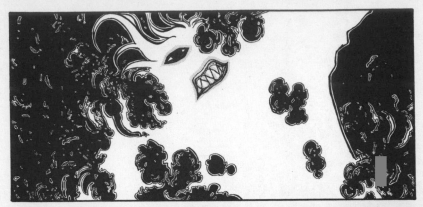

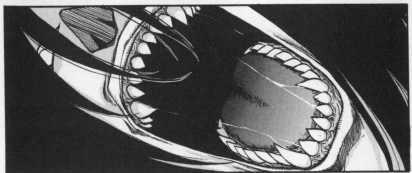

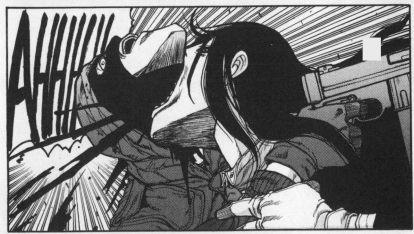

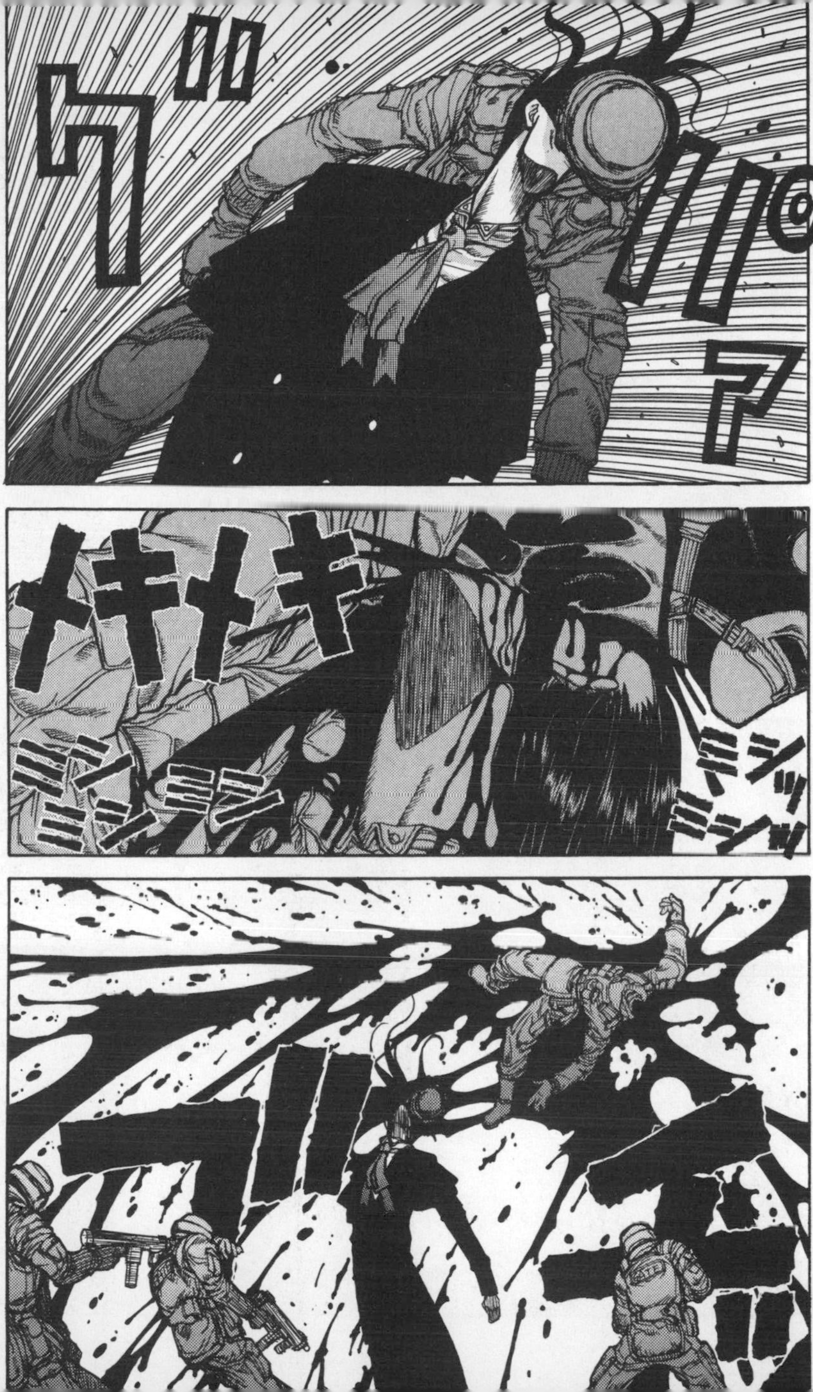
パア
ヴ
メキメキ
ミシッ
ミシッ
ミシ
ミシ
ミシ
ミシ
ブチ!!

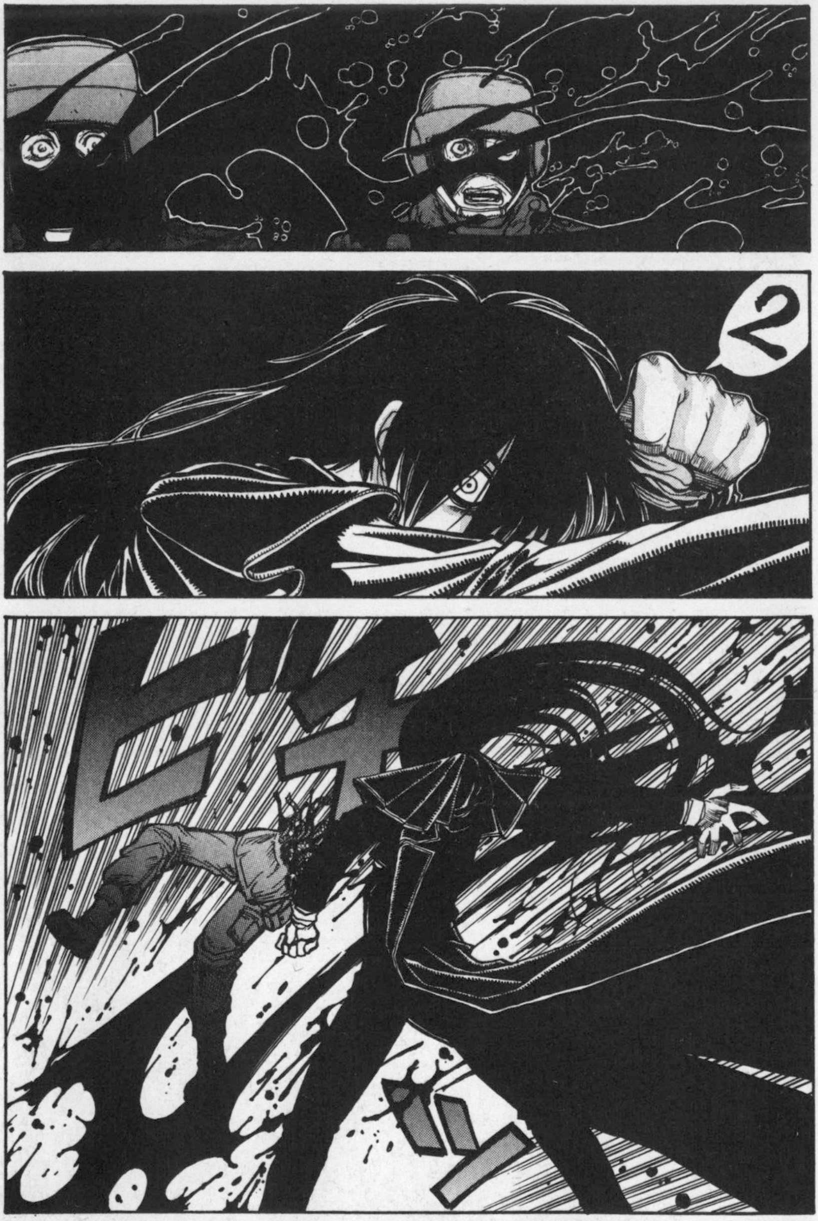
2

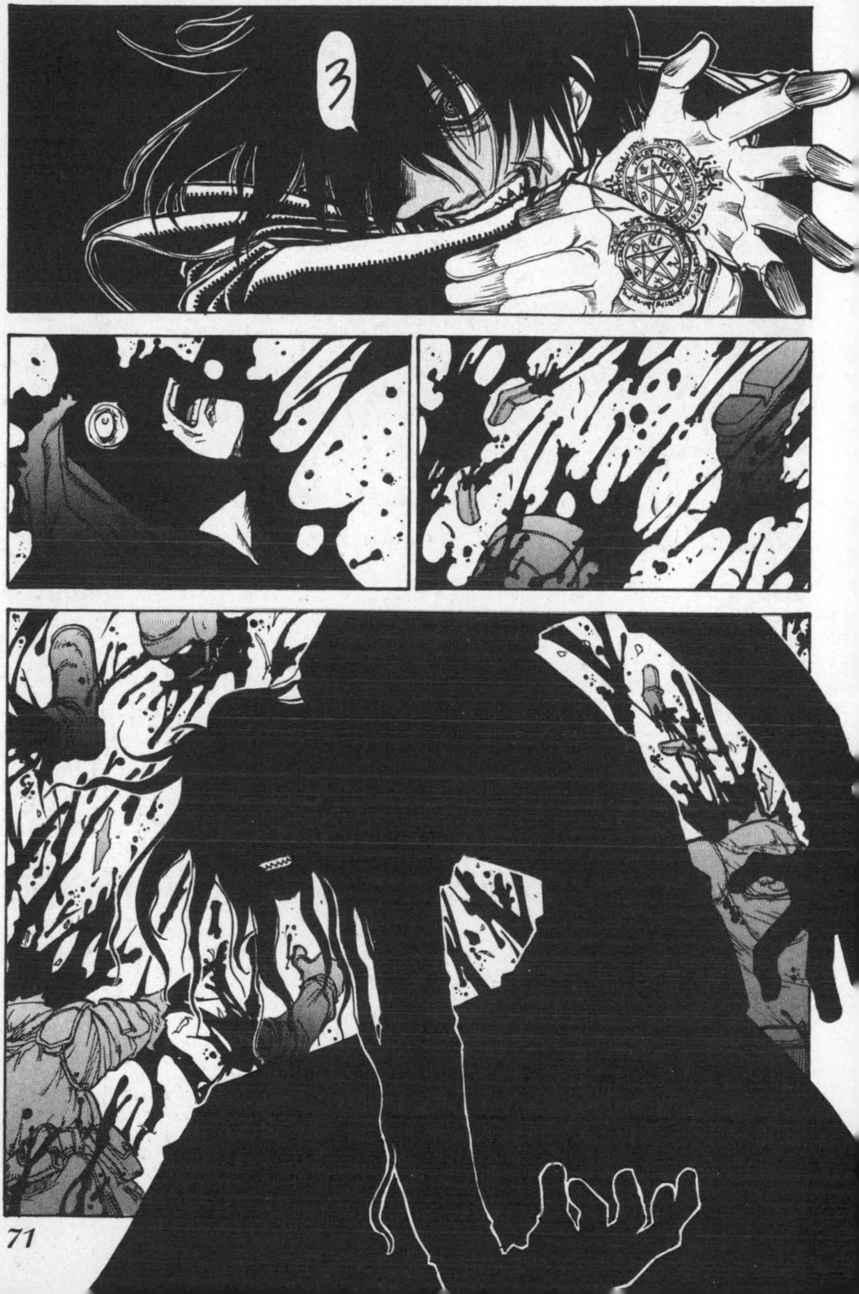
3

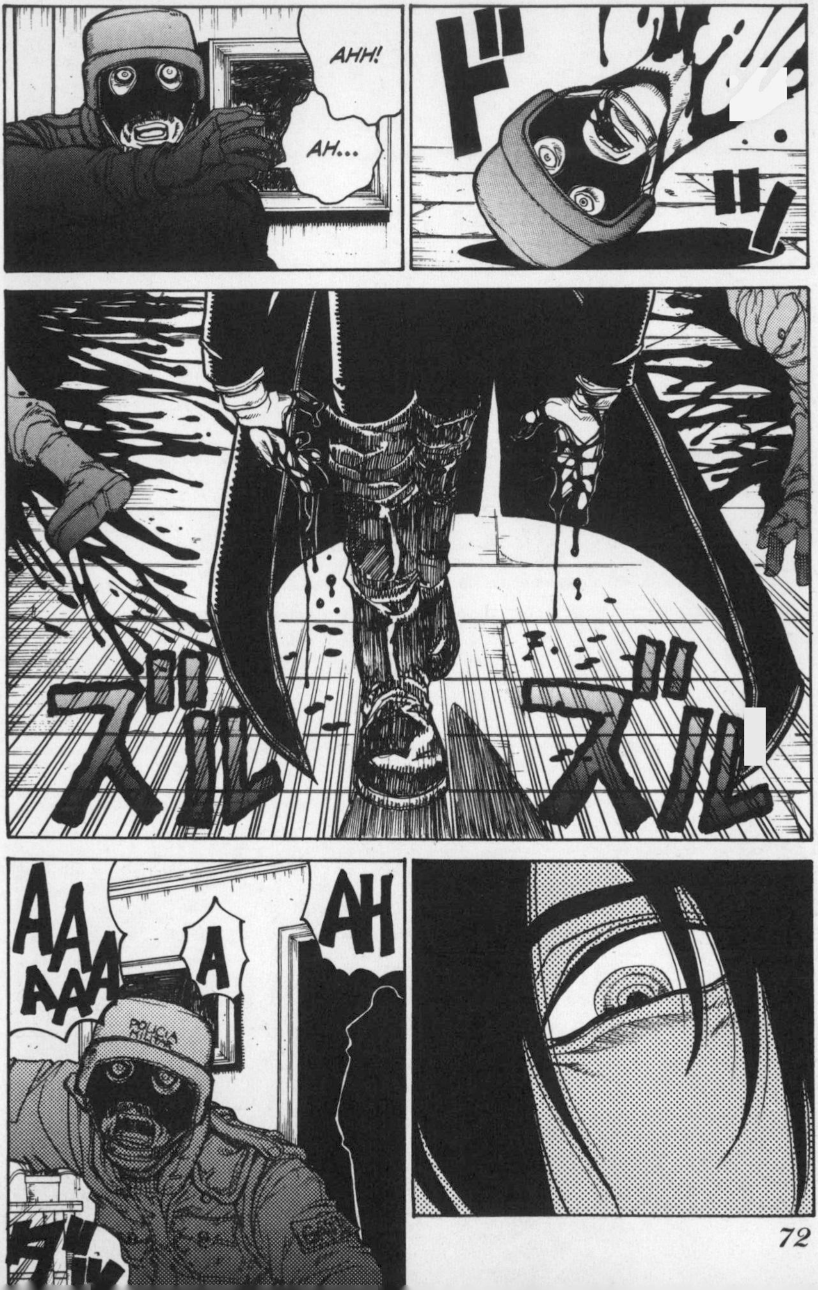
ドッ
AHH!
AH...
ズル
ズル
AH
A
AAAA AAAA

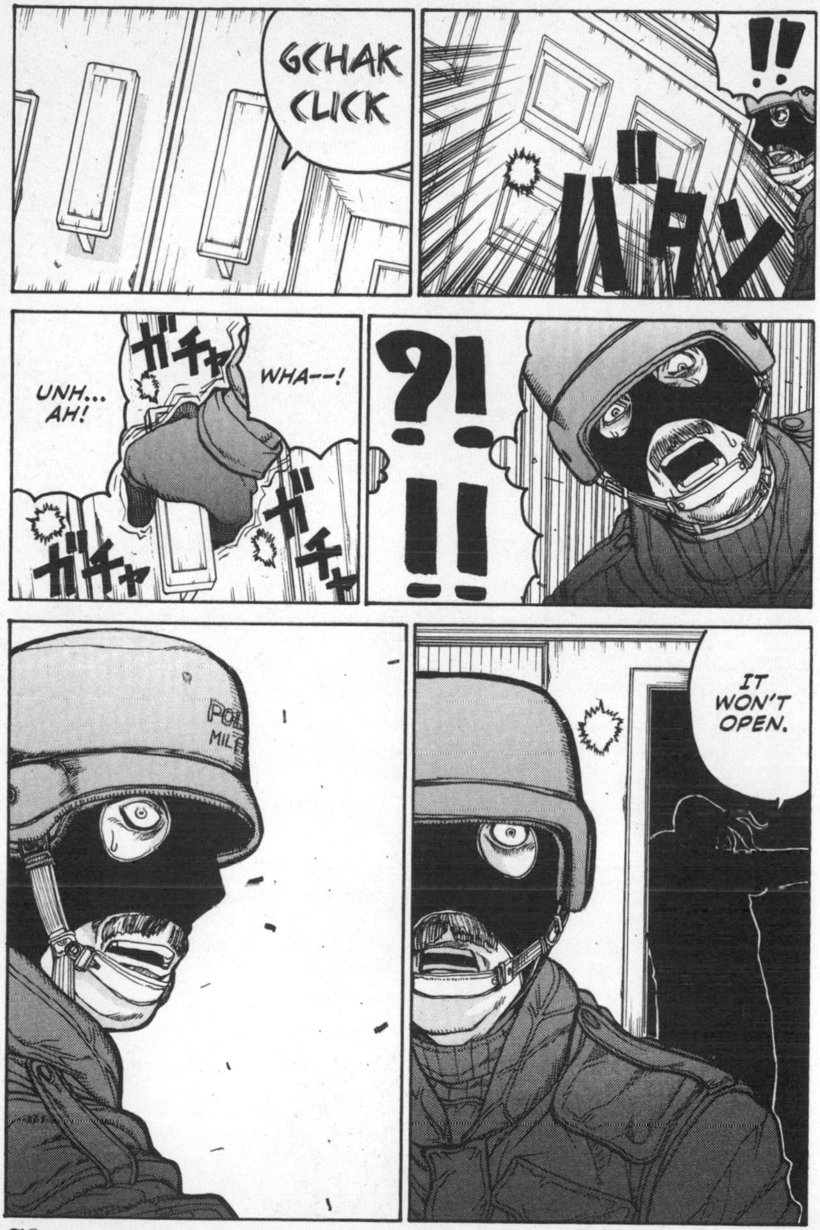
!!
バタン
GCHAK CLICK
?!!!
WHA--!
ガチャ
ガチャ
ガチャ
UNH... AH!
IT WON'T OPEN.

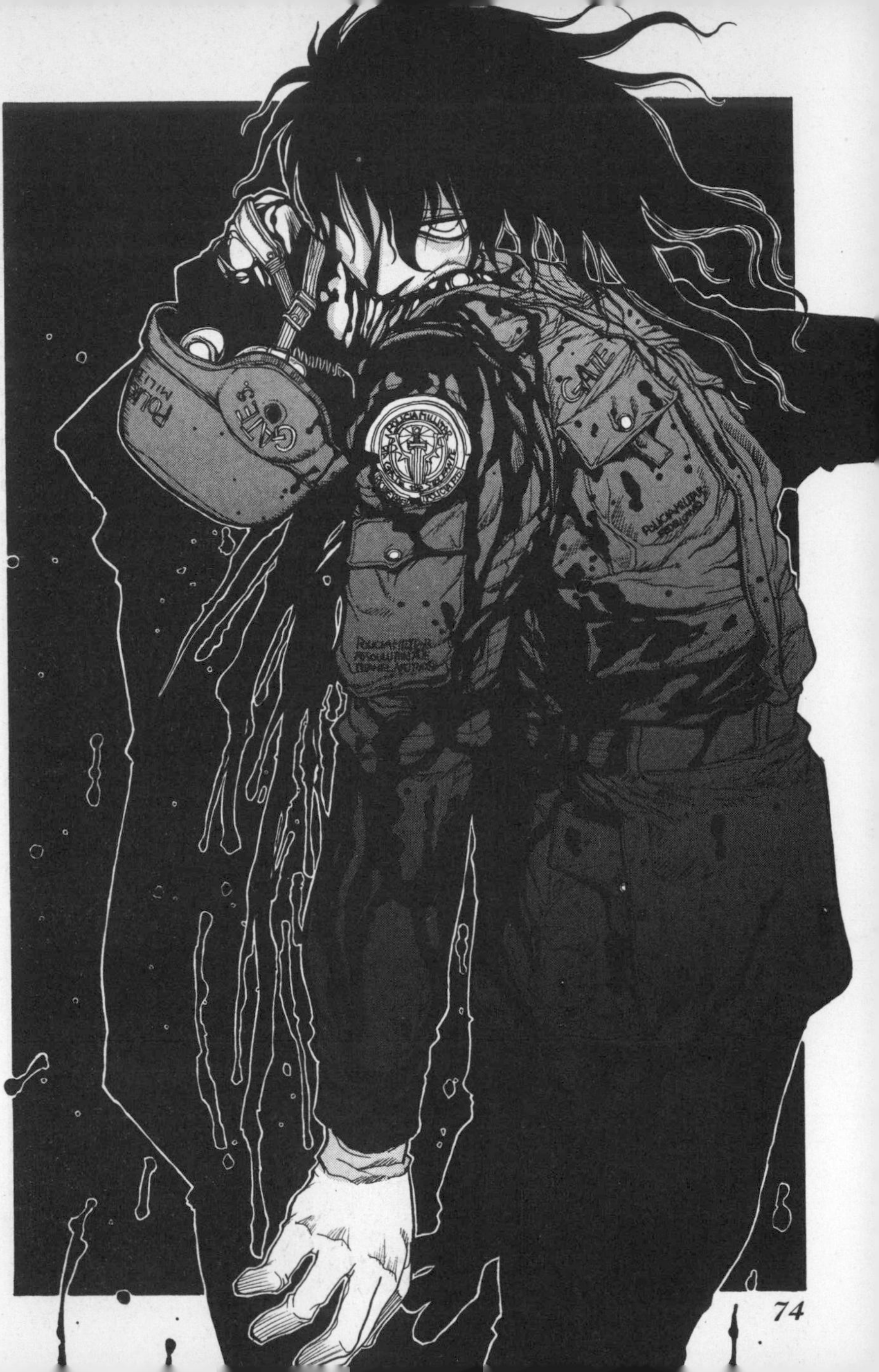
GATE'S
GATE

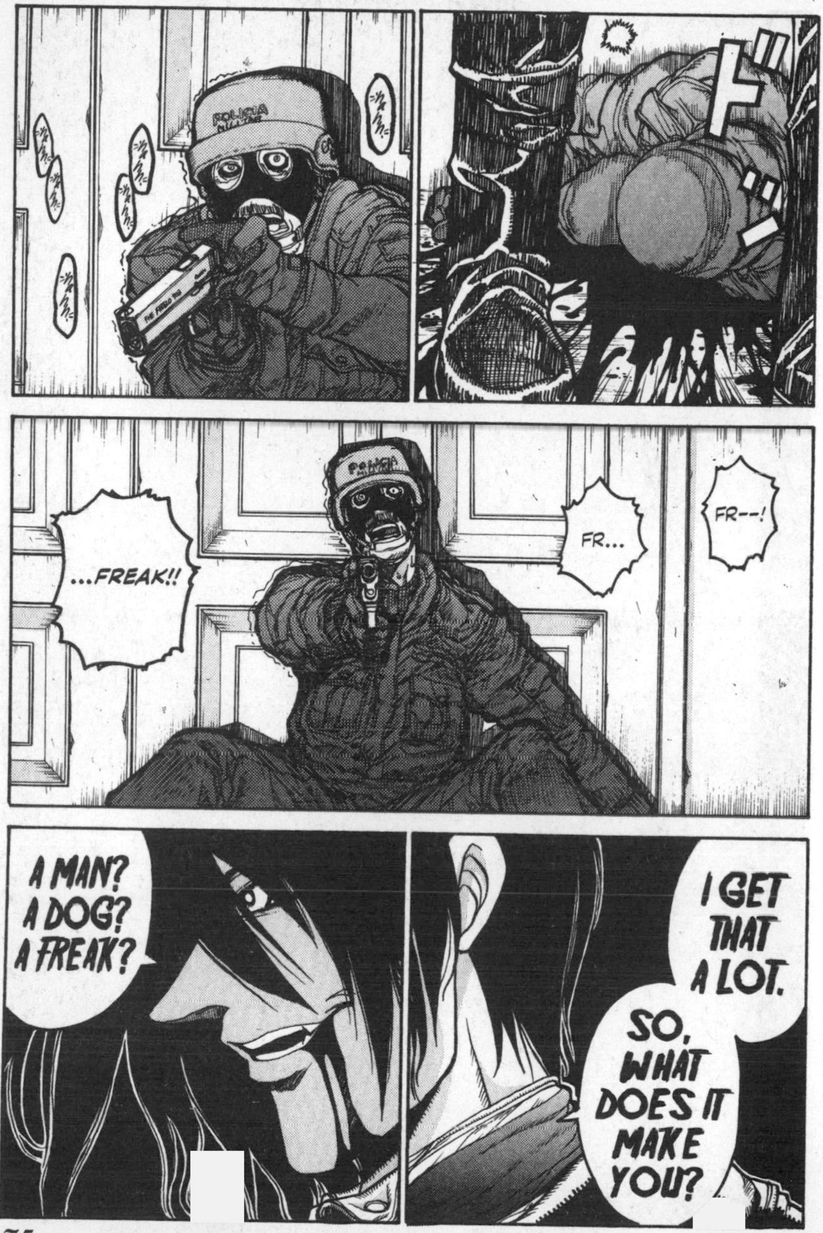
FR--!
FR...
...FREAK!!
I GET THAT A LOT.
SO, WHAT DOES IT MAKE YOU?
A MAN? A DOG? A FREAK?

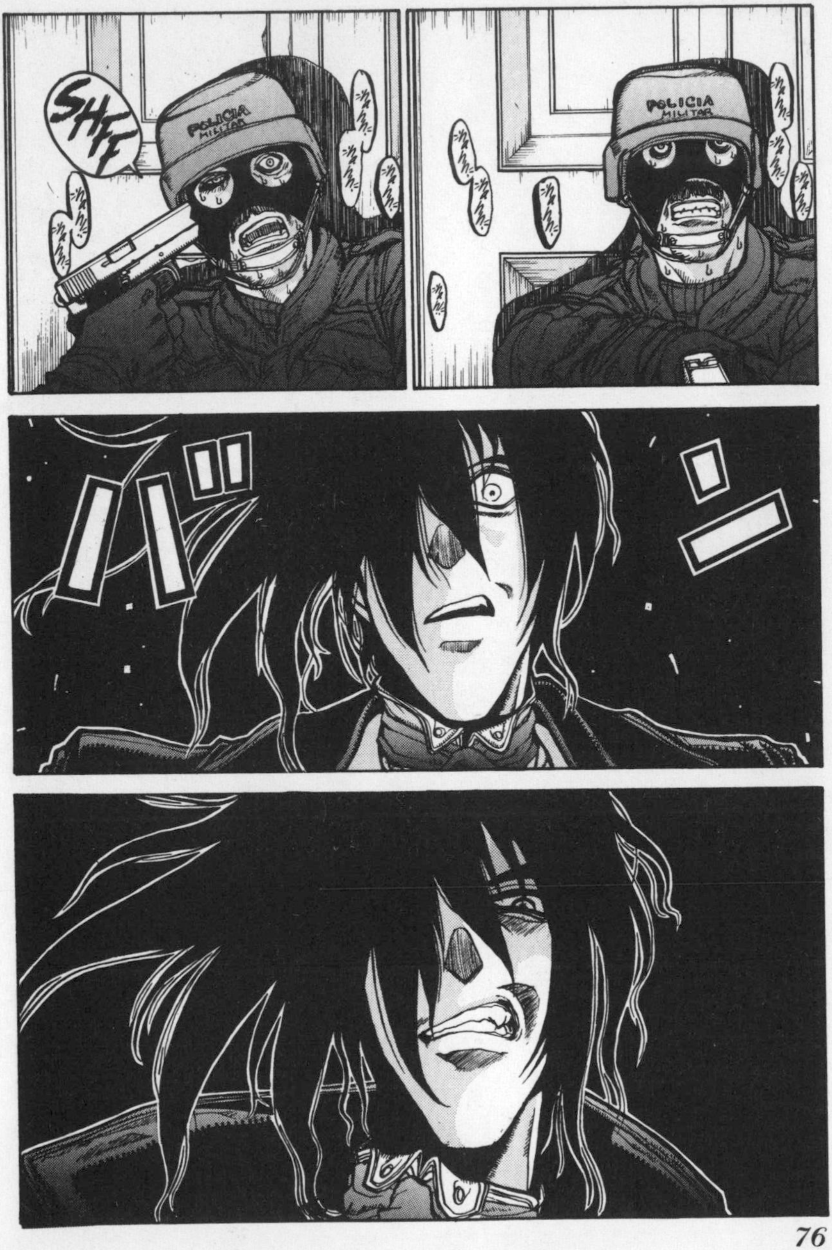
POLICIA MILITAR
SHFF
POLICIA MILITAR

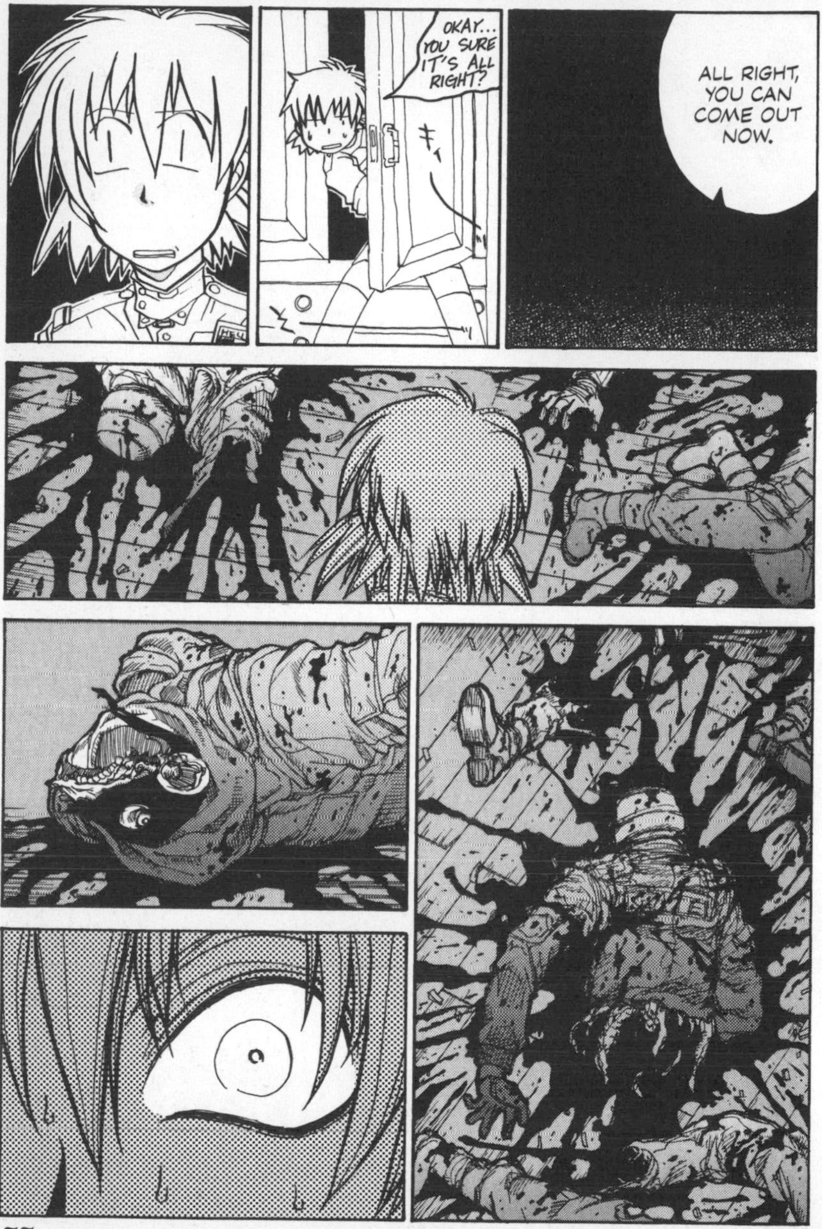
ALL RIGHT, YOU CAN COME OUT NOW.
OKAY... YOU SURE IT'S ALL RIGHT?

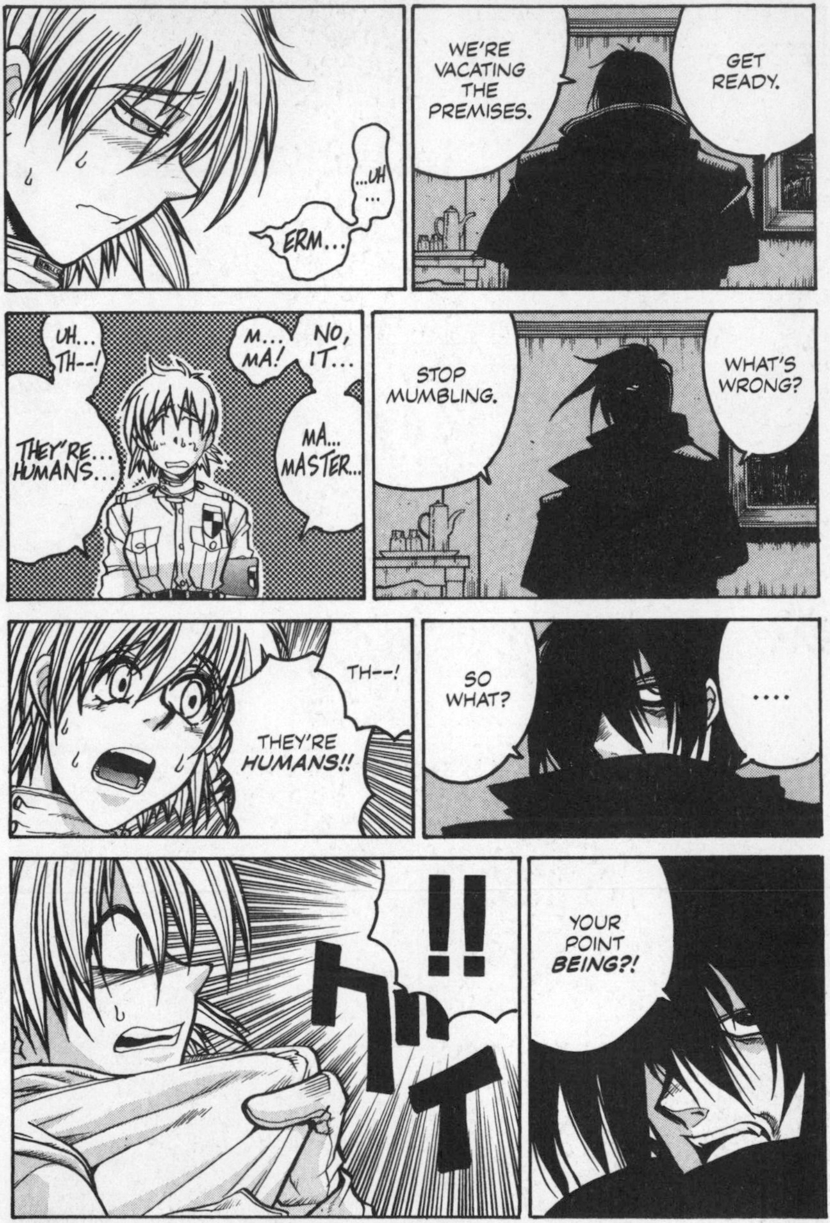
GET READY.
WE'RE VACATING THE PREMISES.
...UH ...
ERM...
WHAT'S WRONG?
STOP MUMBLING.
NO, IT...
M... MA!
UH... TH--!
MA... MASTER...
THEY'RE... HUMANS...
....
SO WHAT?
TH--!
THEY'RE **HUMANS!!**
YOUR POINT **BEING?!**
!!

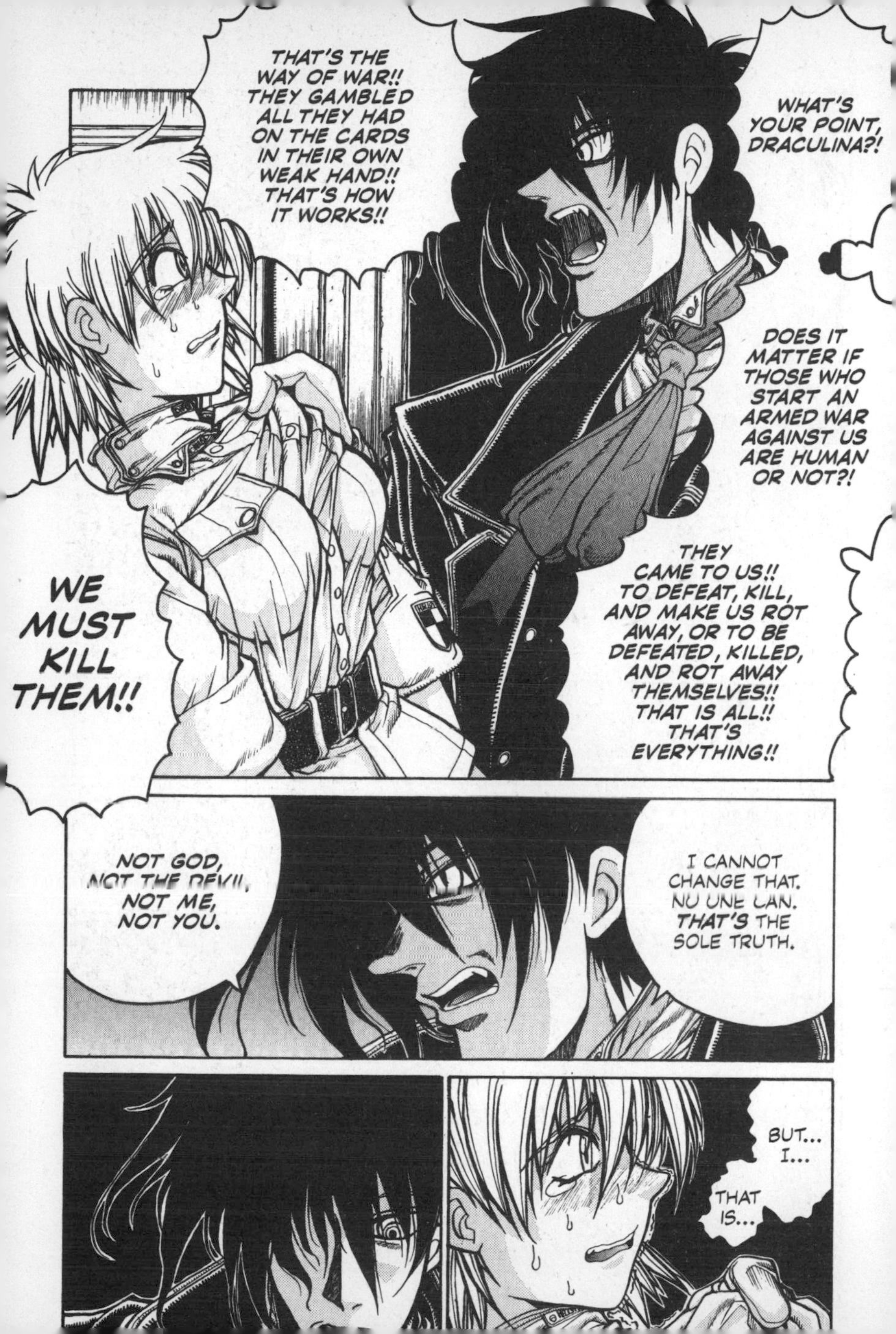
WHAT'S YOUR POINT, DRACULINA?!
DOES IT MATTER IF THOSE WHO START AN ARMED WAR AGAINST US ARE HUMAN OR NOT?!
THAT'S THE WAY OF WAR!! THEY GAMBLED ALL THEY HAD ON THE CARDS IN THEIR OWN WEAK HAND!! THAT'S HOW IT WORKS!!
THEY CAME TO US!! TO DEFEAT, KILL, AND MAKE US ROT AWAY, OR TO BE DEFEATED, KILLED, AND ROT AWAY THEMSELVES!! THAT IS ALL!! THAT'S EVERYTHING!!
WE MUST KILL THEM!!
I CANNOT CHANGE THAT. NO ONE CAN. THAT'S THE SOLE TRUTH.
NOT GOD, NOT THE DEVIL, NOT ME, NOT YOU.
BUT... I...
THAT IS...

THERE IT IS. *THAT'S IT EXACTLY.*

NO.

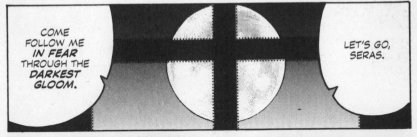

COME FOLLOW ME *IN FEAR* THROUGH THE *DARKEST GLOOM.*

LET'S GO, SERAS.

TO BE CONTINUED

Y-Y--!!

YES, SIR!!

ORDER 3 / END

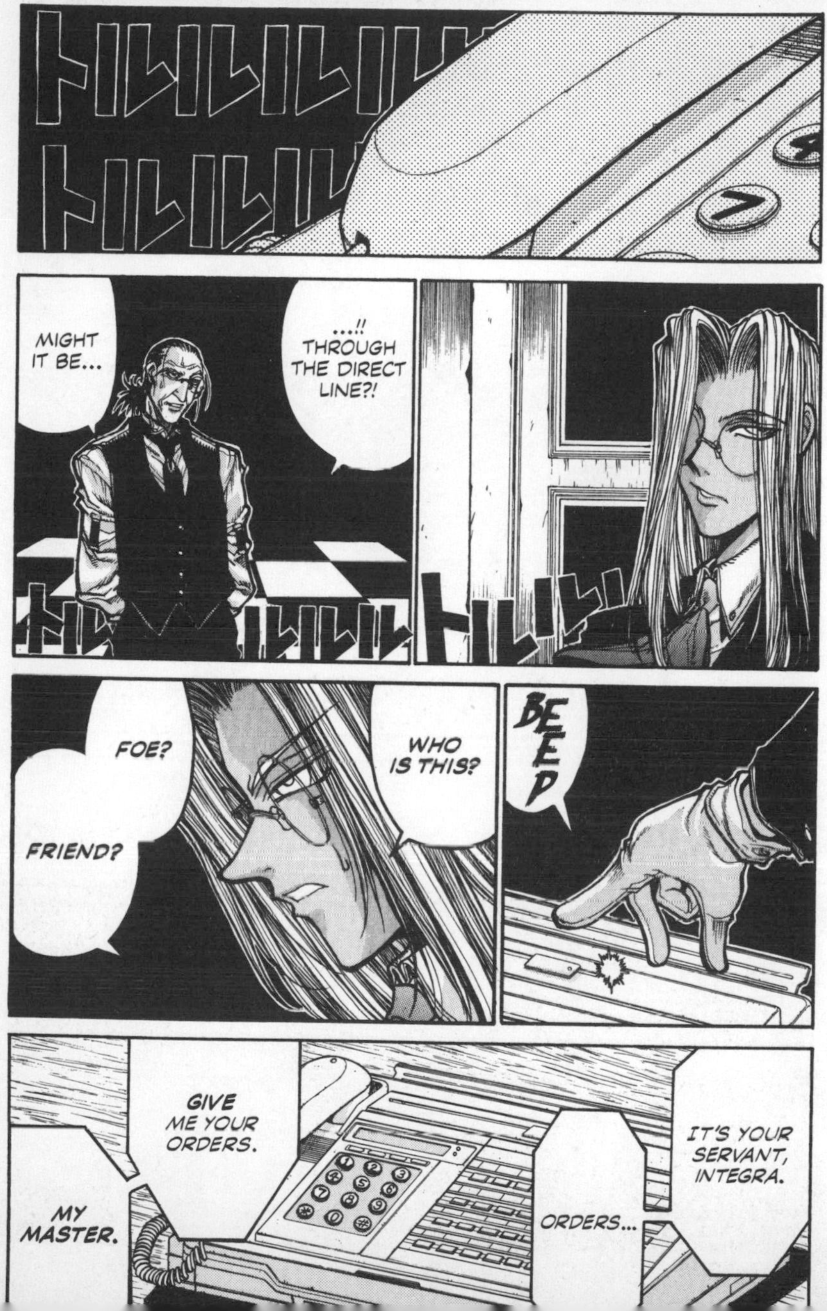
...!!
THROUGH THE DIRECT LINE?!
MIGHT IT BE...
BEEP
WHO IS THIS?
FOE?
FRIEND?
IT'S YOUR SERVANT, INTEGRA.
ORDERS...
GIVE ME YOUR ORDERS.
MY MASTER.

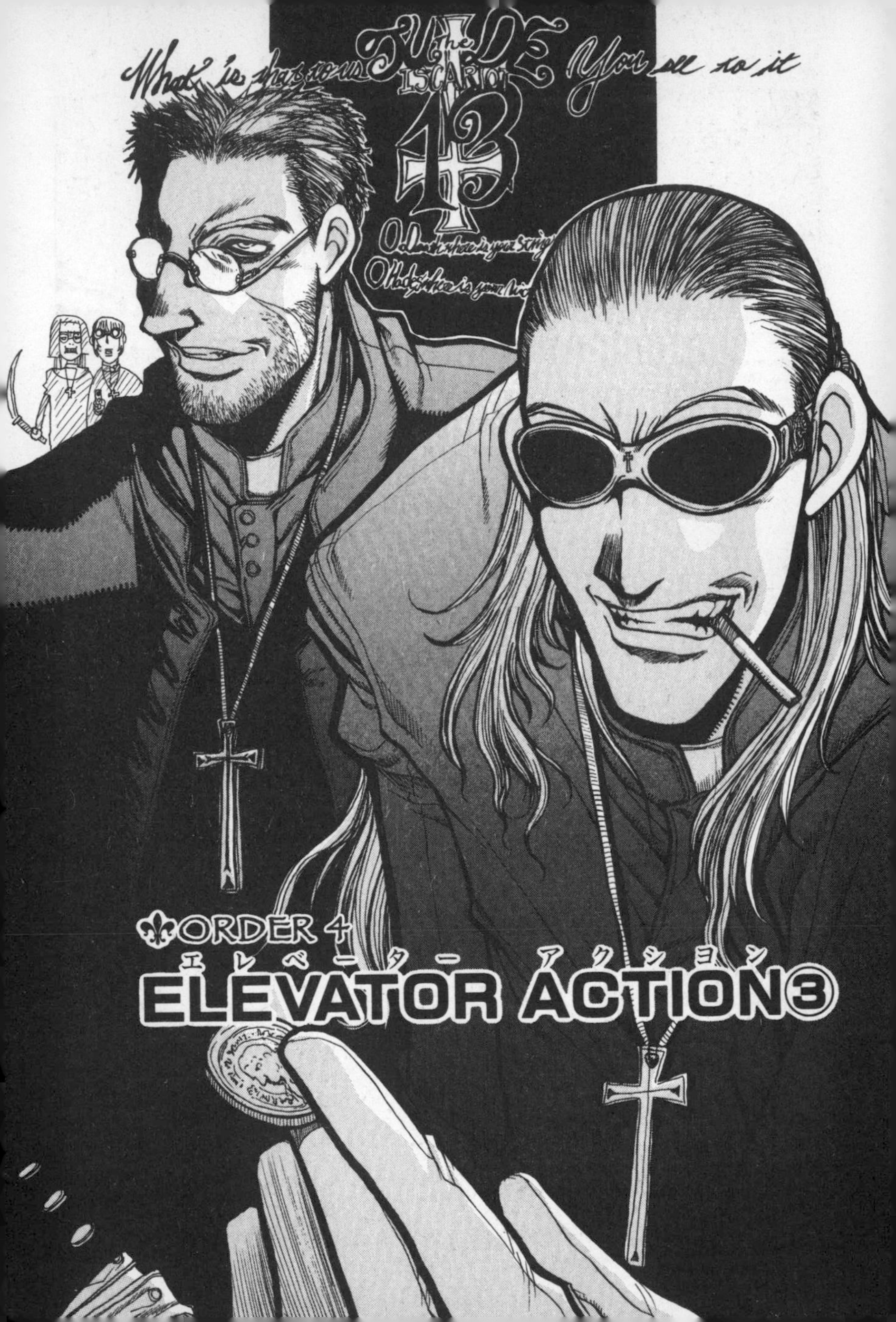
ISCARIOT
13
ORDER 4
エレベーター アクション
ELEVATOR ACTION③

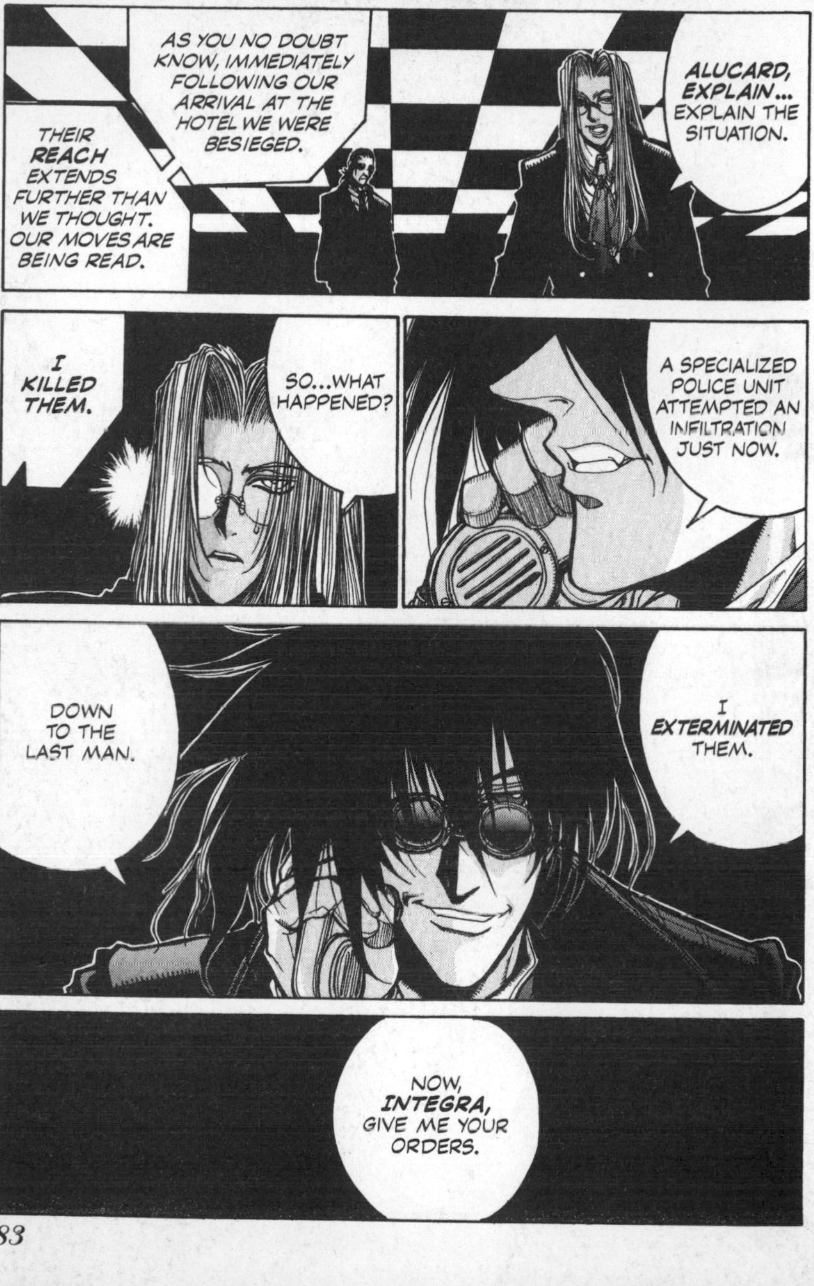
ALUCARD, EXPLAIN... EXPLAIN THE SITUATION.
AS YOU NO DOUBT KNOW, IMMEDIATELY FOLLOWING OUR ARRIVAL AT THE HOTEL WE WERE BESIEGED.
THEIR REACH EXTENDS FURTHER THAN WE THOUGHT. OUR MOVES ARE BEING READ.
A SPECIALIZED POLICE UNIT ATTEMPTED AN INFILTRATION JUST NOW.
SO...WHAT HAPPENED?
I KILLED THEM.
I EXTERMINATED THEM.
DOWN TO THE LAST MAN.
NOW, INTEGRA, GIVE ME YOUR ORDERS.

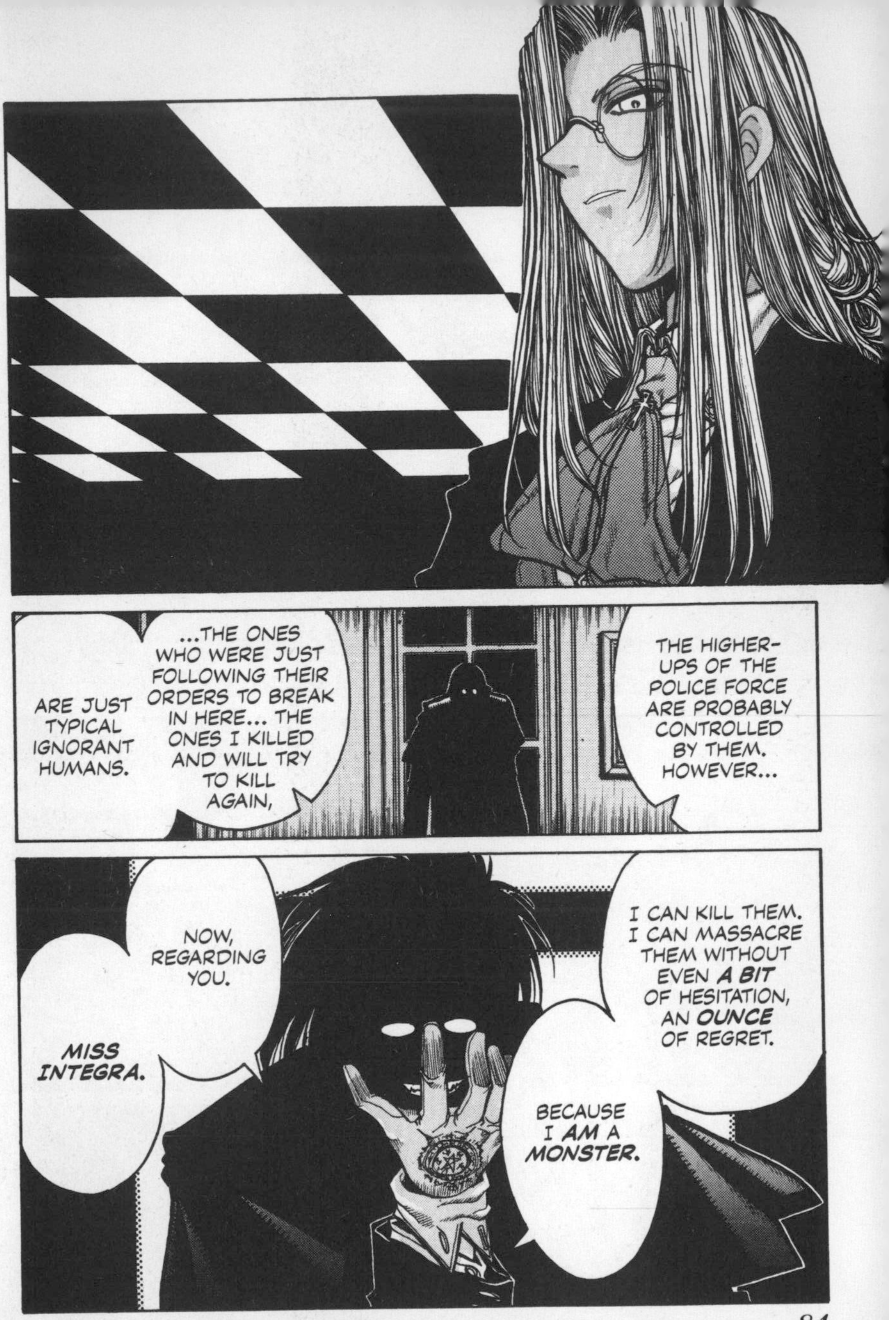
THE HIGHER-UPS OF THE POLICE FORCE ARE PROBABLY CONTROLLED BY THEM. HOWEVER...
...THE ONES WHO WERE JUST FOLLOWING THEIR ORDERS TO BREAK IN HERE... THE ONES I KILLED AND WILL TRY TO KILL AGAIN,
ARE JUST TYPICAL IGNORANT HUMANS.
I CAN KILL THEM. I CAN MASSACRE THEM WITHOUT EVEN *A BIT* OF HESITATION, AN *OUNCE* OF REGRET.
BECAUSE I *AM* A *MONSTER*.
NOW, REGARDING YOU.
MISS INTEGRA.

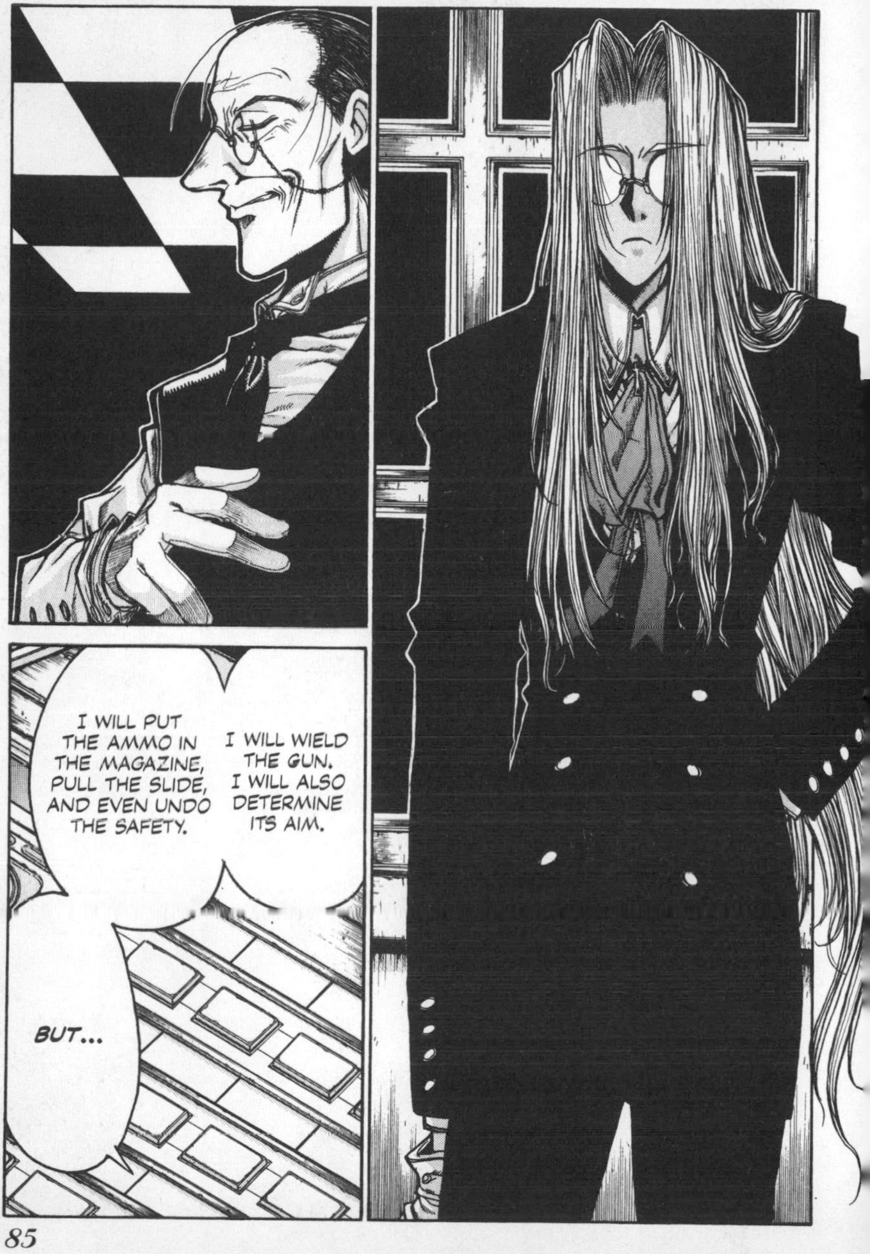
I WILL WIELD THE GUN. I WILL ALSO DETERMINE ITS AIM.
I WILL PUT THE AMMO IN THE MAGAZINE, PULL THE SLIDE, AND EVEN UNDO THE SAFETY.
BUT...

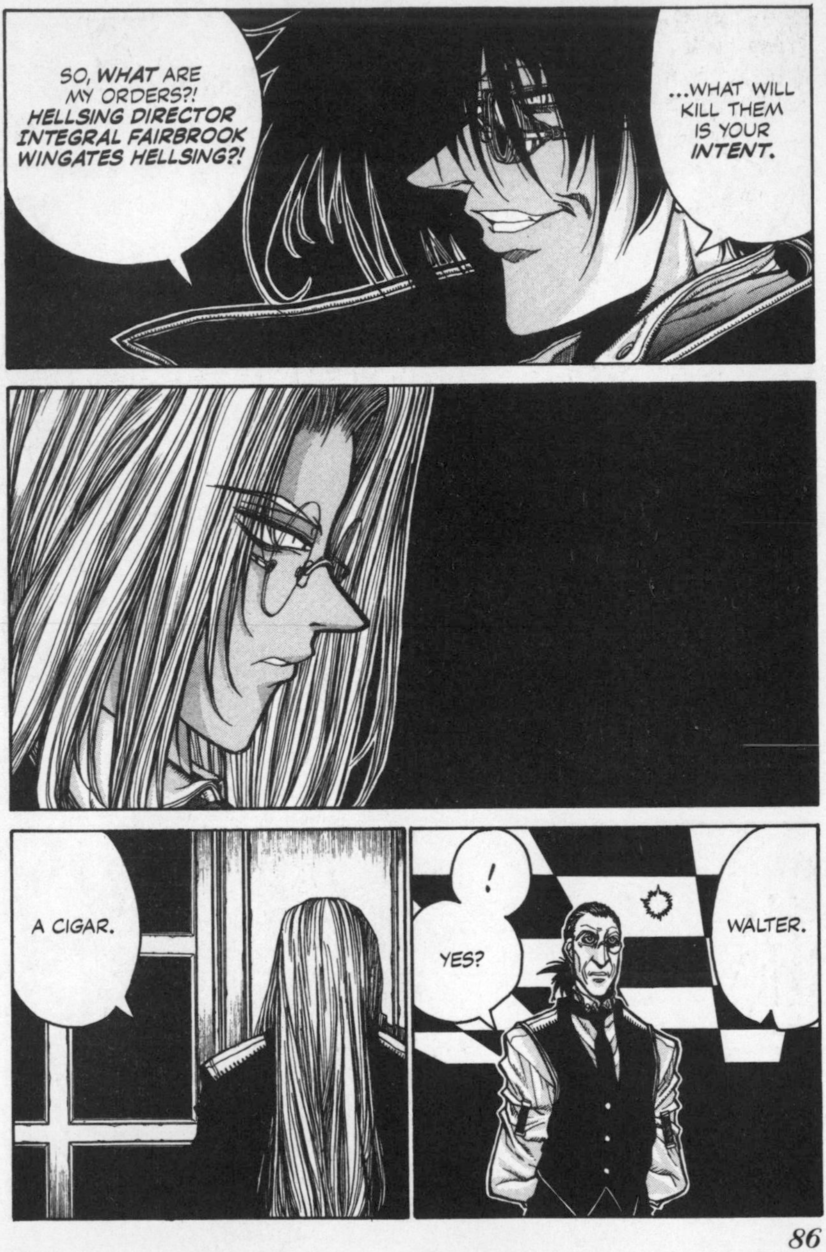
...WHAT WILL KILL THEM IS YOUR INTENT.
SO, WHAT ARE MY ORDERS?! HELLSING DIRECTOR INTEGRAL FAIRBROOK WINGATES HELLSING?!
WALTER.
!
YES?
A CIGAR.

NOTT NOTT NOTT

YES.

RIGHT AWAY.

HERE YOU ARE.

SLPP

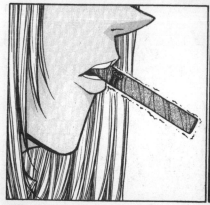

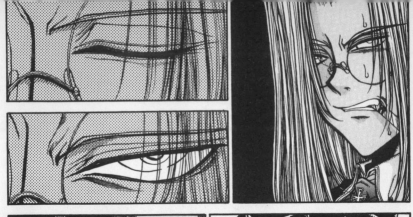

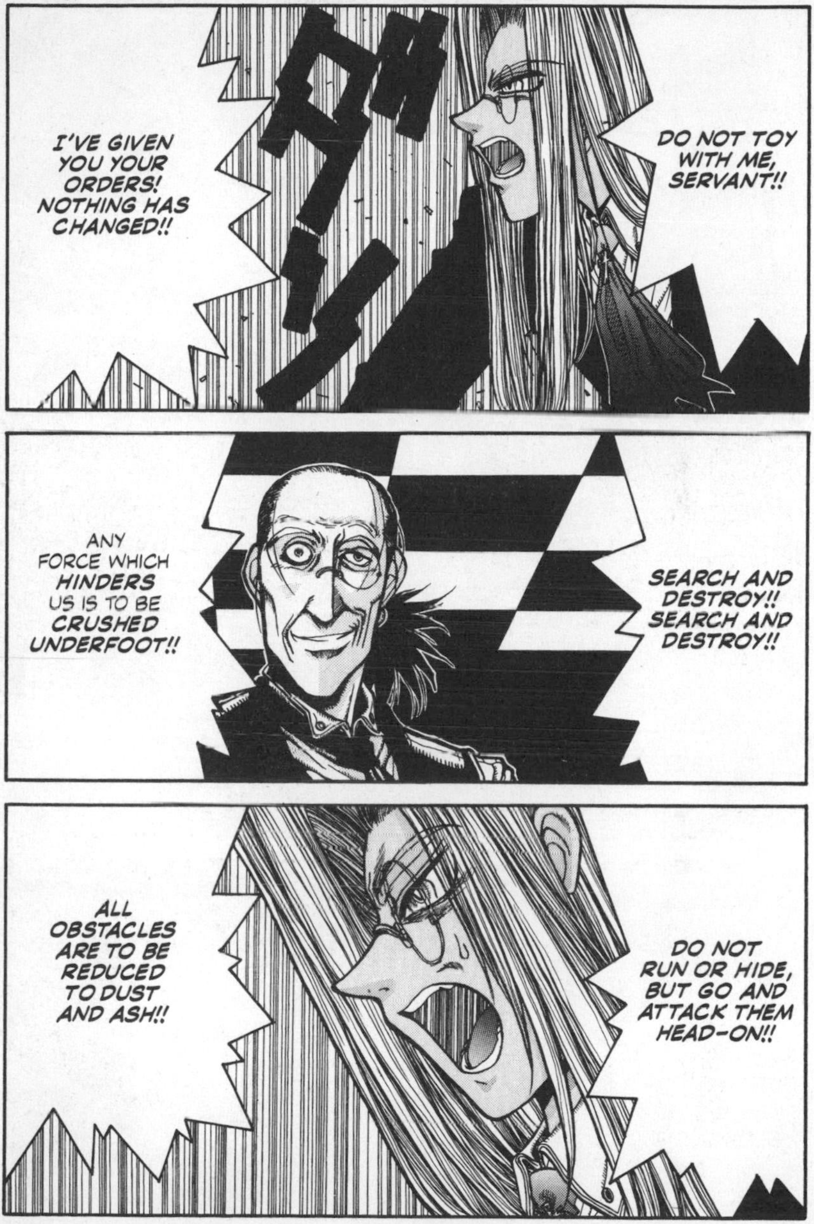
DO NOT TOY WITH ME, SERVANT!!
I'VE GIVEN YOU YOUR ORDERS! NOTHING HAS CHANGED!!
SEARCH AND DESTROY!! SEARCH AND DESTROY!!
ANY FORCE WHICH HINDERS US IS TO BE CRUSHED UNDERFOOT!!
DO NOT RUN OR HIDE, BUT GO AND ATTACK THEM HEAD-ON!!
ALL OBSTACLES ARE TO BE REDUCED TO DUST AND ASH!!

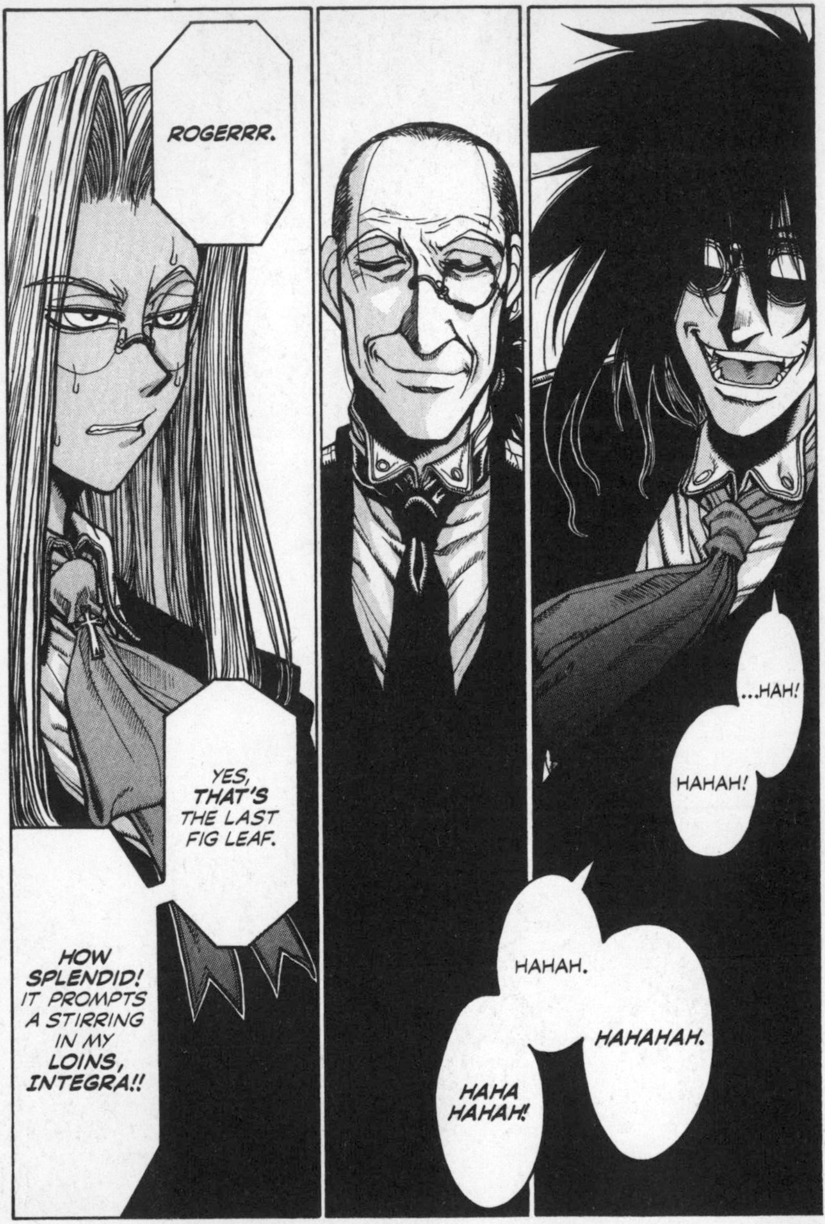
...HAH!
HAHAH!
HAHAH.
HAHAHAH.
HAHA HAHAH!
ROGERRR.
YES, THAT'S THE LAST FIG LEAF.
HOW SPLENDID! IT PROMPTS A STIRRING IN MY LOINS, INTEGRA!!

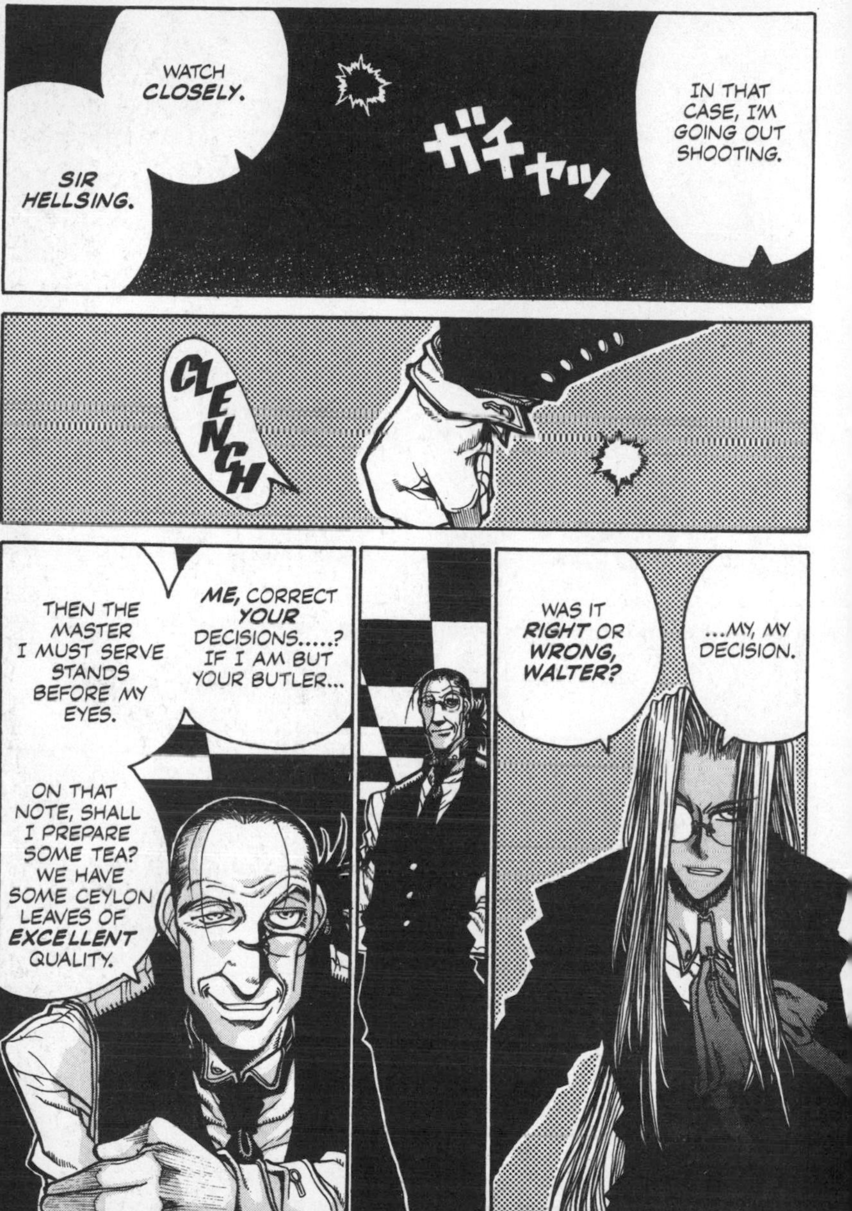
IN THAT CASE, I'M GOING OUT SHOOTING.
ガチャッ
WATCH CLOSELY.
SIR HELLSING.
.....
CLENCH
...MY, MY DECISION.
WAS IT RIGHT OR WRONG, WALTER?
ME, CORRECT YOUR DECISIONS.....? IF I AM BUT YOUR BUTLER...
THEN THE MASTER I MUST SERVE STANDS BEFORE MY EYES.
ON THAT NOTE, SHALL I PREPARE SOME TEA? WE HAVE SOME CEYLON LEAVES OF EXCELLENT QUALITY.

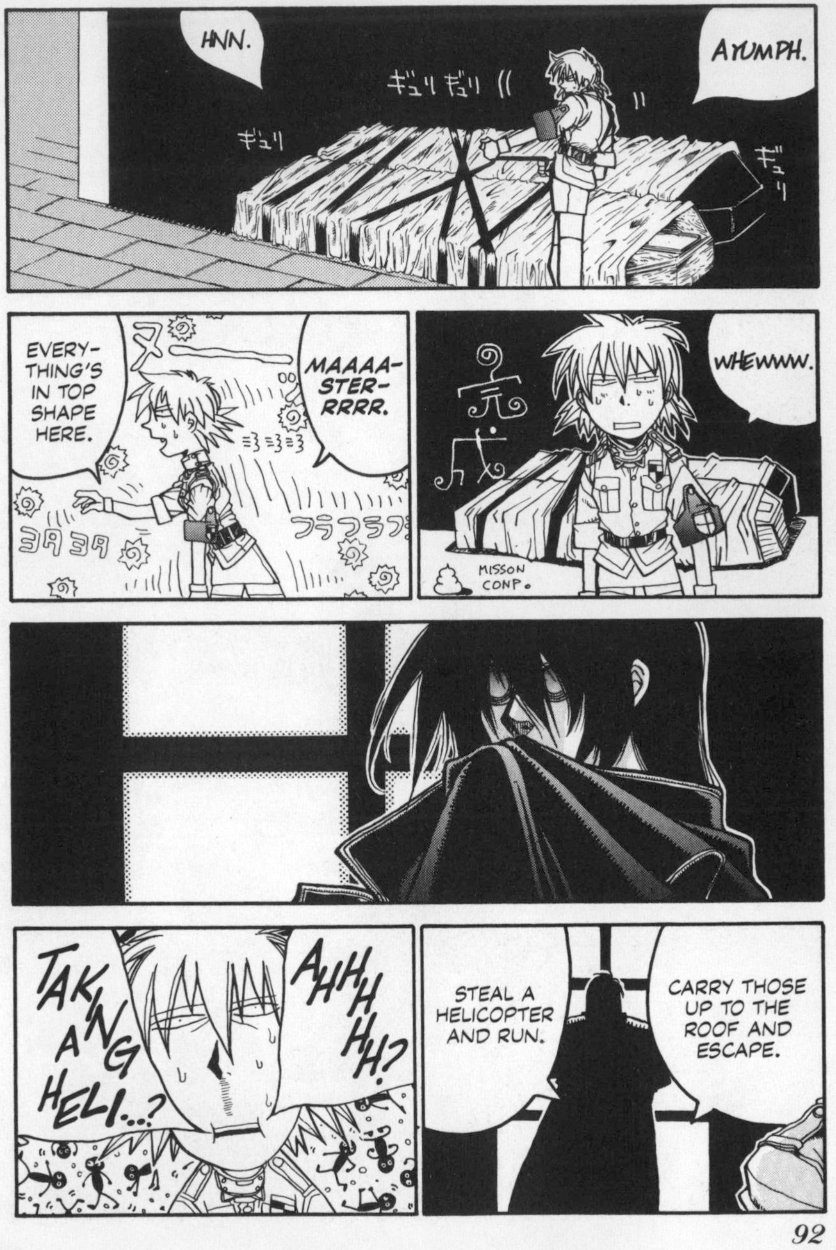
AYUMPH.
HNN.
WHEWWW.
MISSON CONP.
MAAAAA-STER-RRRR.
EVERY-THING'S IN TOP SHAPE HERE.
CARRY THOSE UP TO THE ROOF AND ESCAPE.
STEAL A HELICOPTER AND RUN.
AHHHHH?
TAKING A HELI...?

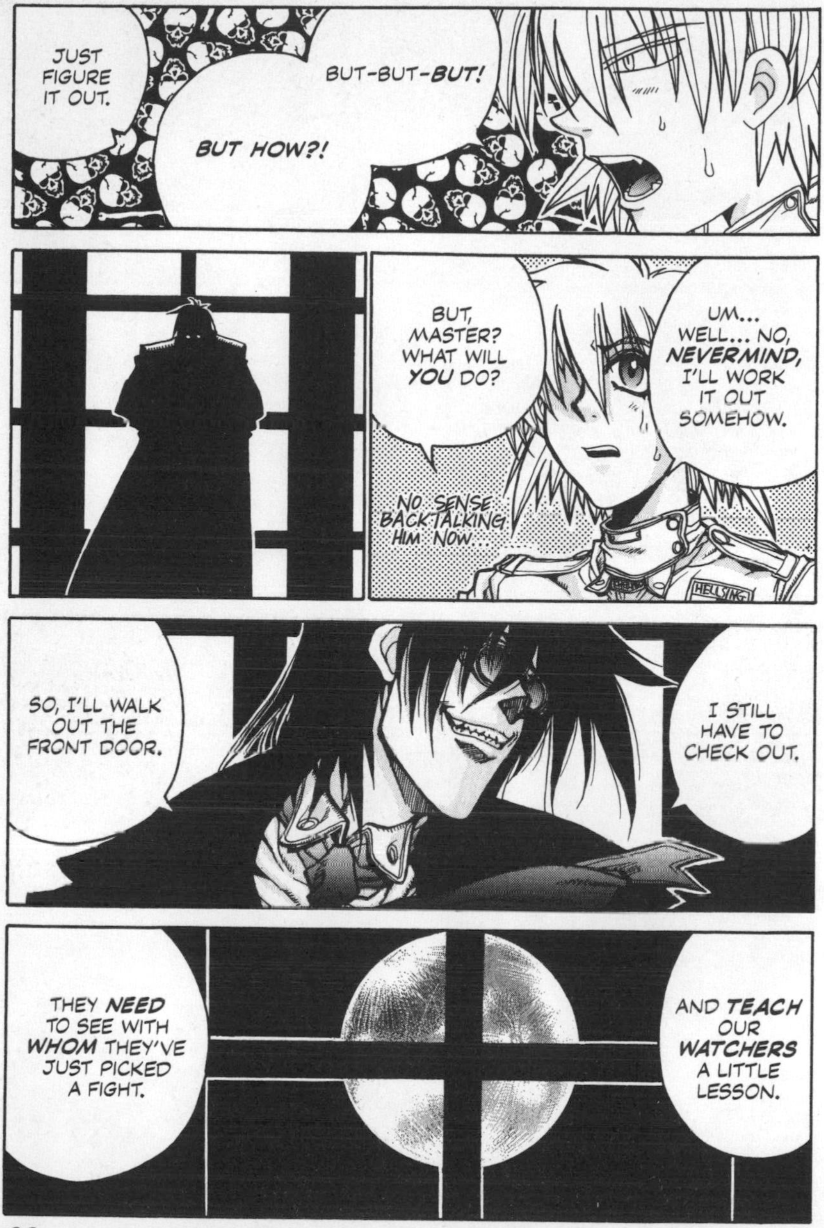
BUT-BUT-BUT!
BUT HOW?!
JUST FIGURE IT OUT.
UM... WELL... NO, NEVERMIND, I'LL WORK IT OUT SOMEHOW.
BUT, MASTER? WHAT WILL YOU DO?
NO SENSE BACKTALKING HIM NOW.
I STILL HAVE TO CHECK OUT.
SO, I'LL WALK OUT THE FRONT DOOR.
AND TEACH OUR WATCHERS A LITTLE LESSON.
THEY NEED TO SEE WITH WHOM THEY'VE JUST PICKED A FIGHT.

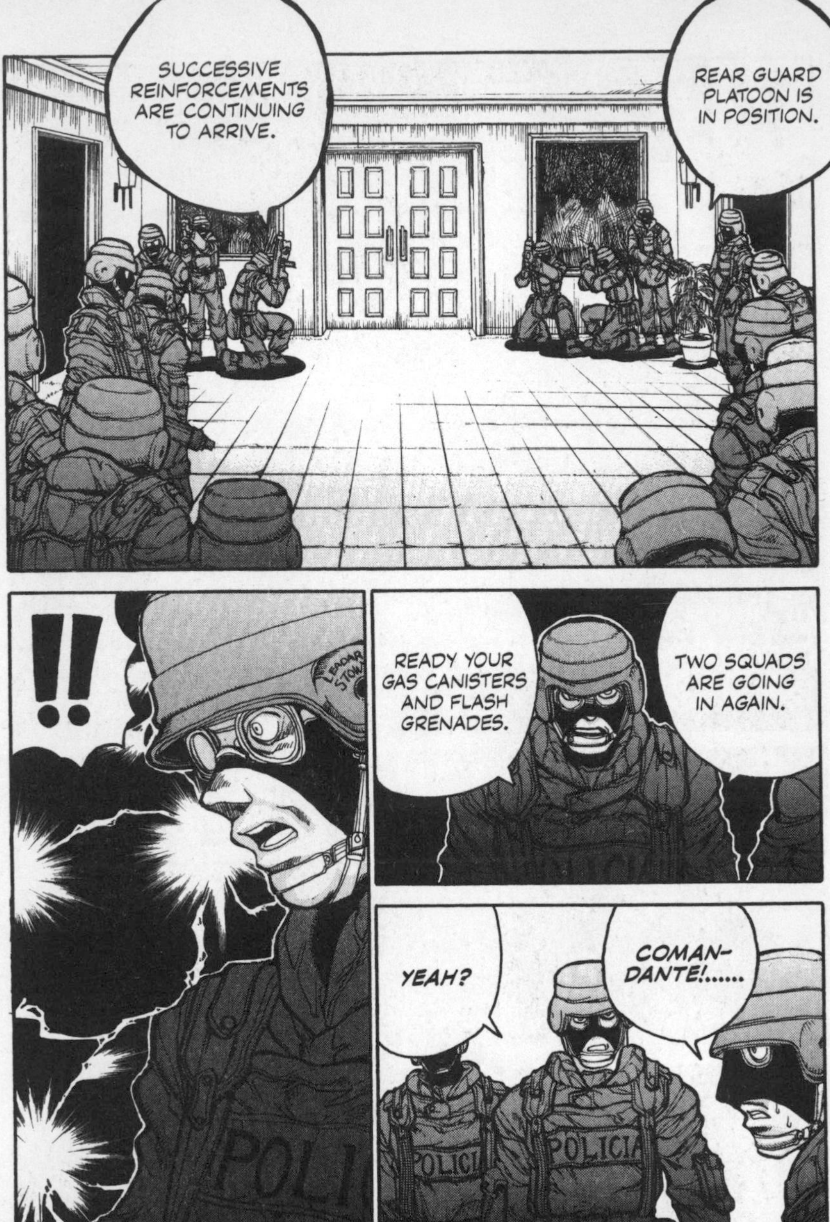
REAR GUARD PLATOON IS IN POSITION.
SUCCESSIVE REINFORCEMENTS ARE CONTINUING TO ARRIVE.
TWO SQUADS ARE GOING IN AGAIN.
READY YOUR GAS CANISTERS AND FLASH GRENADES.
COMAN-DANTE!......
YEAH?
!!
POLICIA
POLICIA

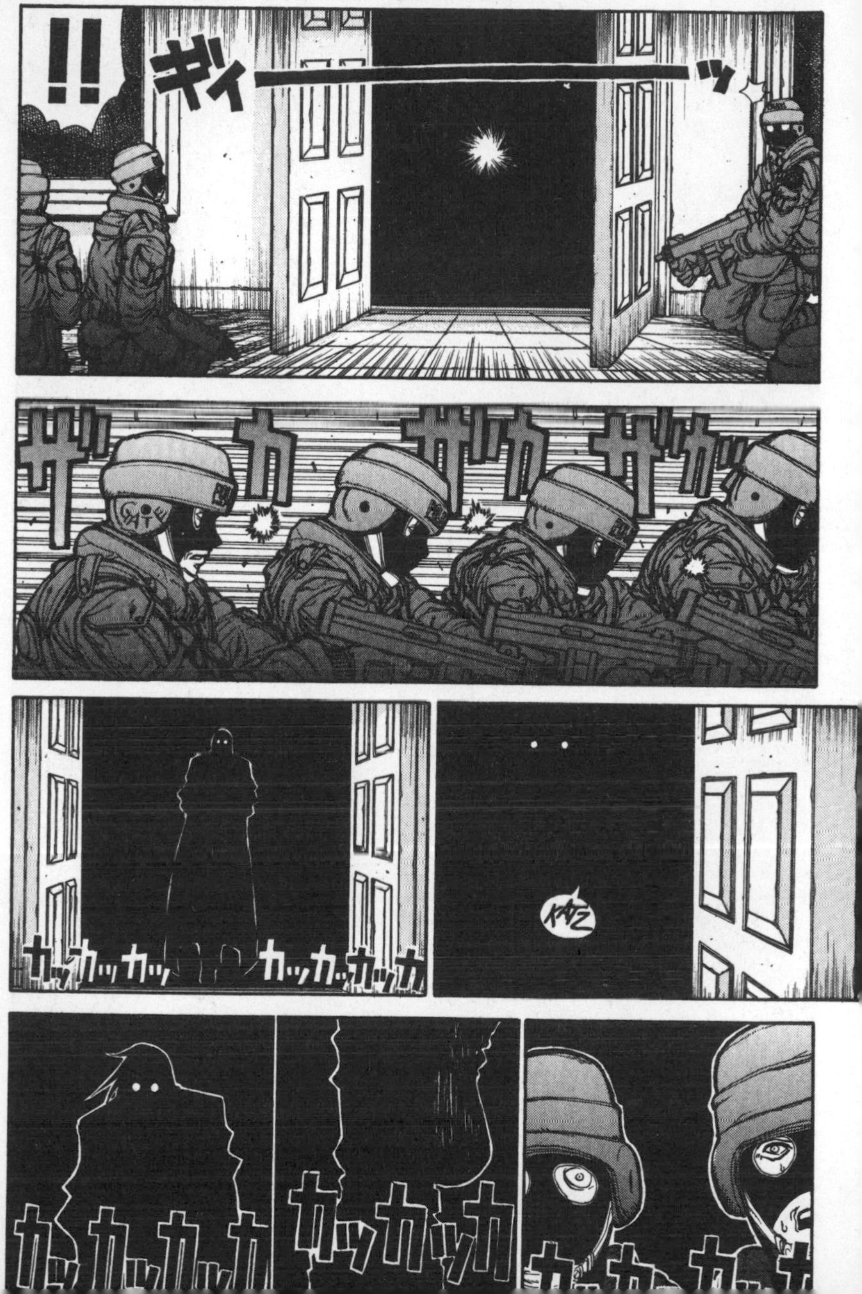

ギィーーーーッ
!!
ザッ カ ザッカ ザッカッ
カッカッカッ カッカッカッカ
カッカッカッカッ
カッカッカッカ

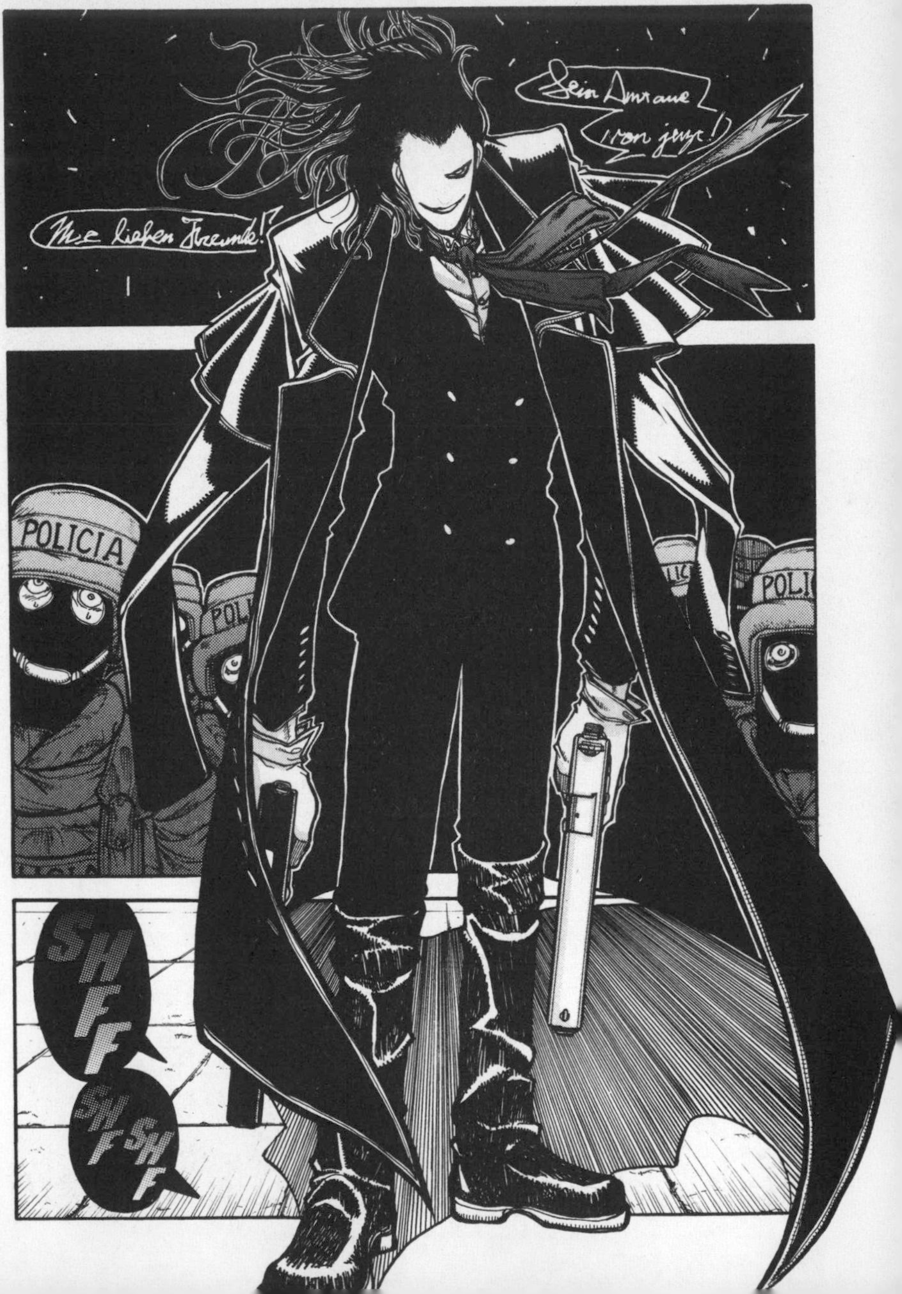

POLICIA
SHF
SHFSHF

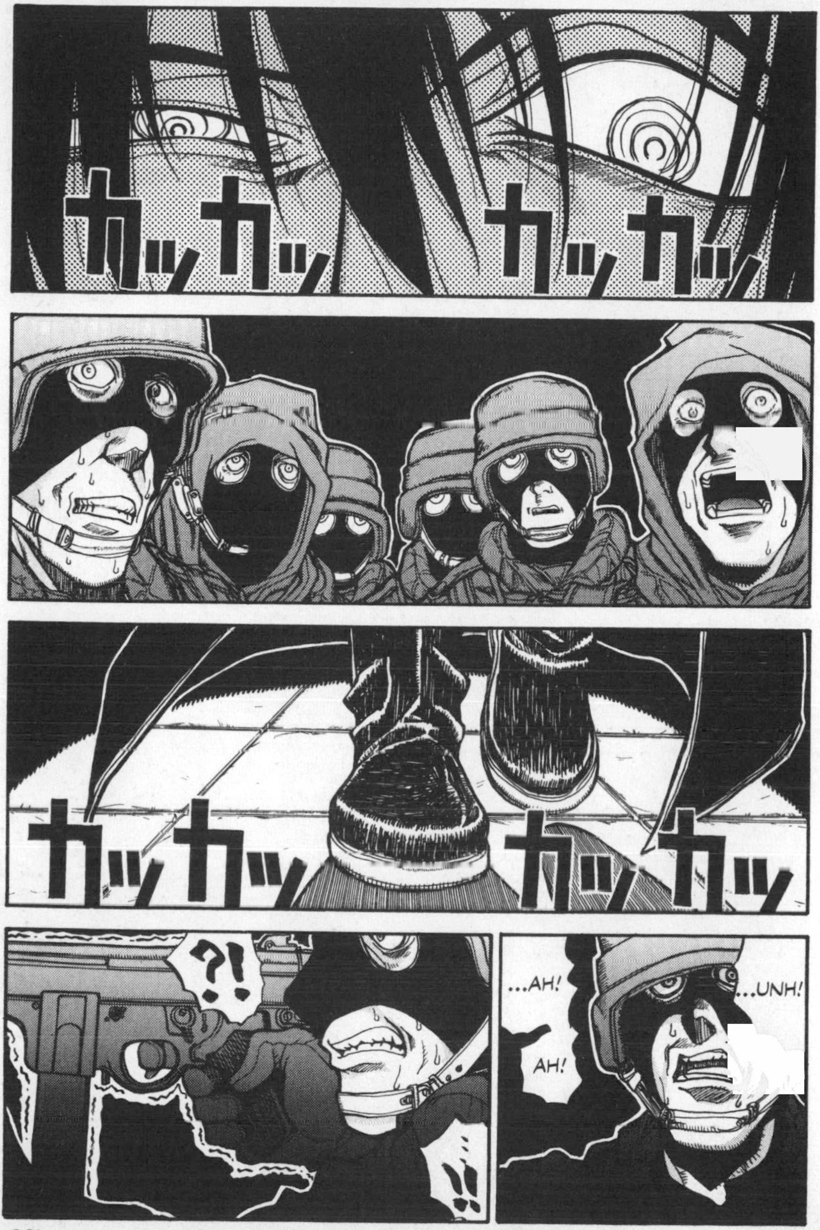
カッカッ
カッカッ
カッカッ
カッカッ
...UNH!
...AH!
AH!
?!
!!

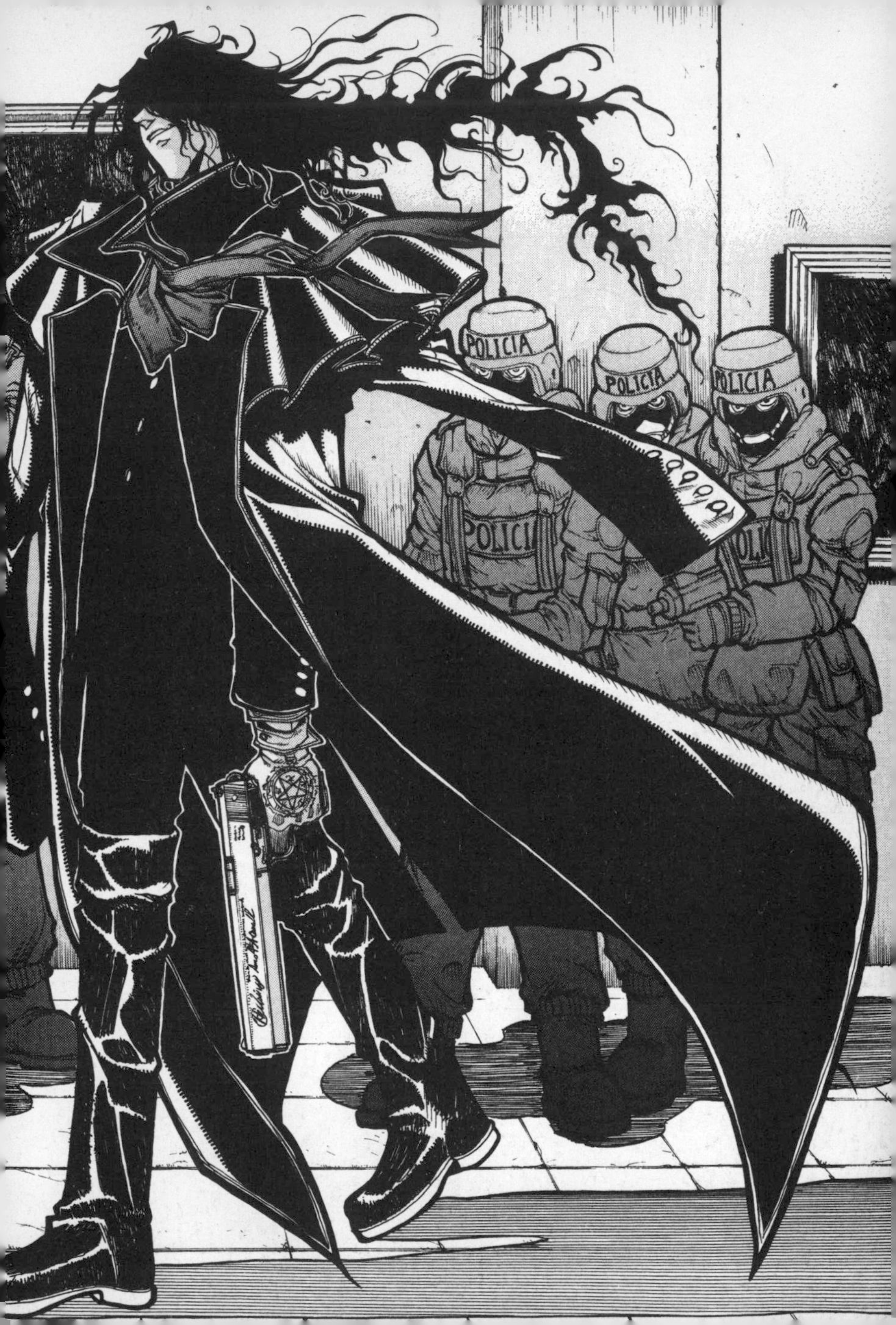
POLICIA
POLICIA
POLICIA
POLICIA
POLICIA

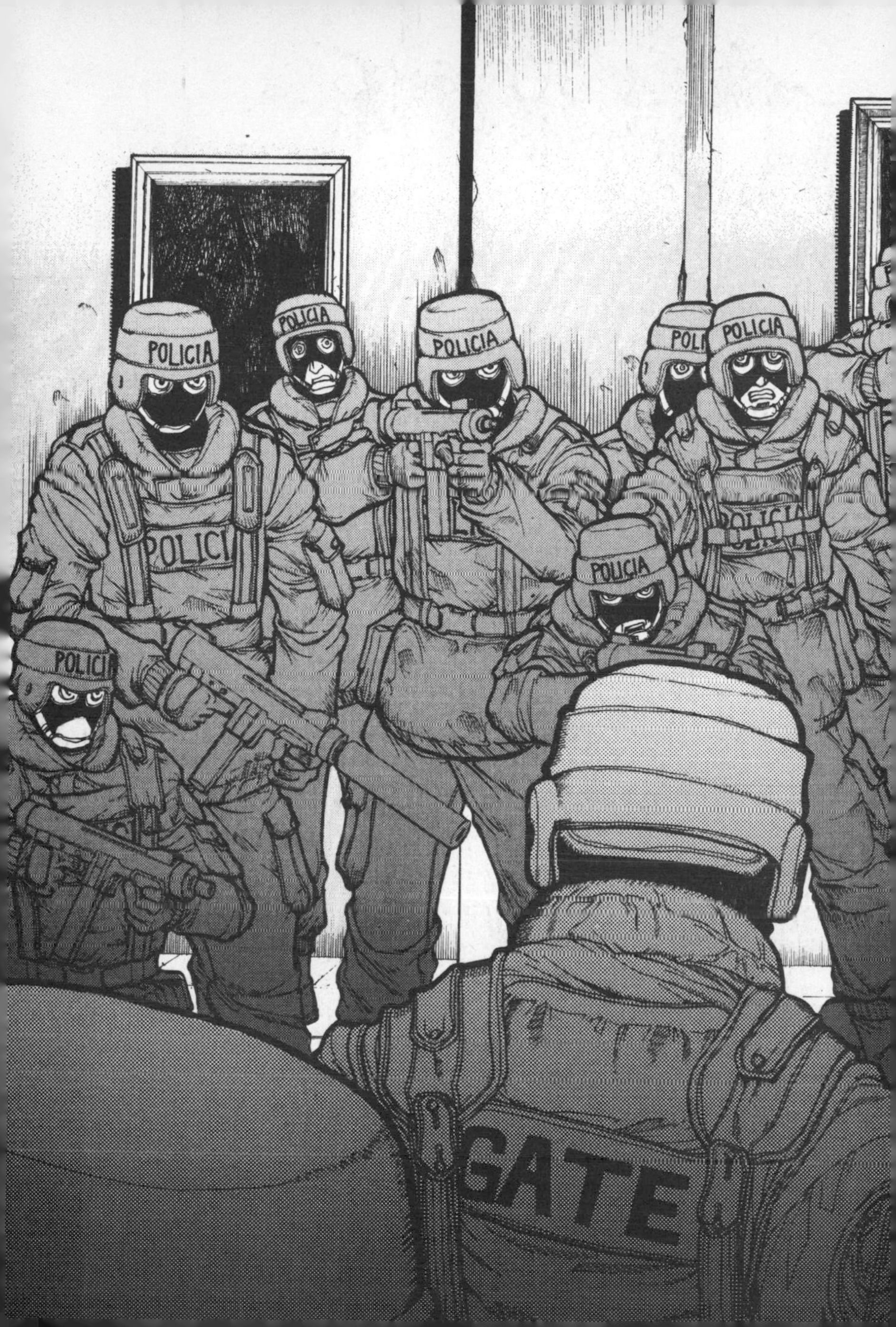
POLICIA
POLICIA
POLICIA
POLICIA
POLICIA
POLICI
POLICIA
POLICIA
GATE

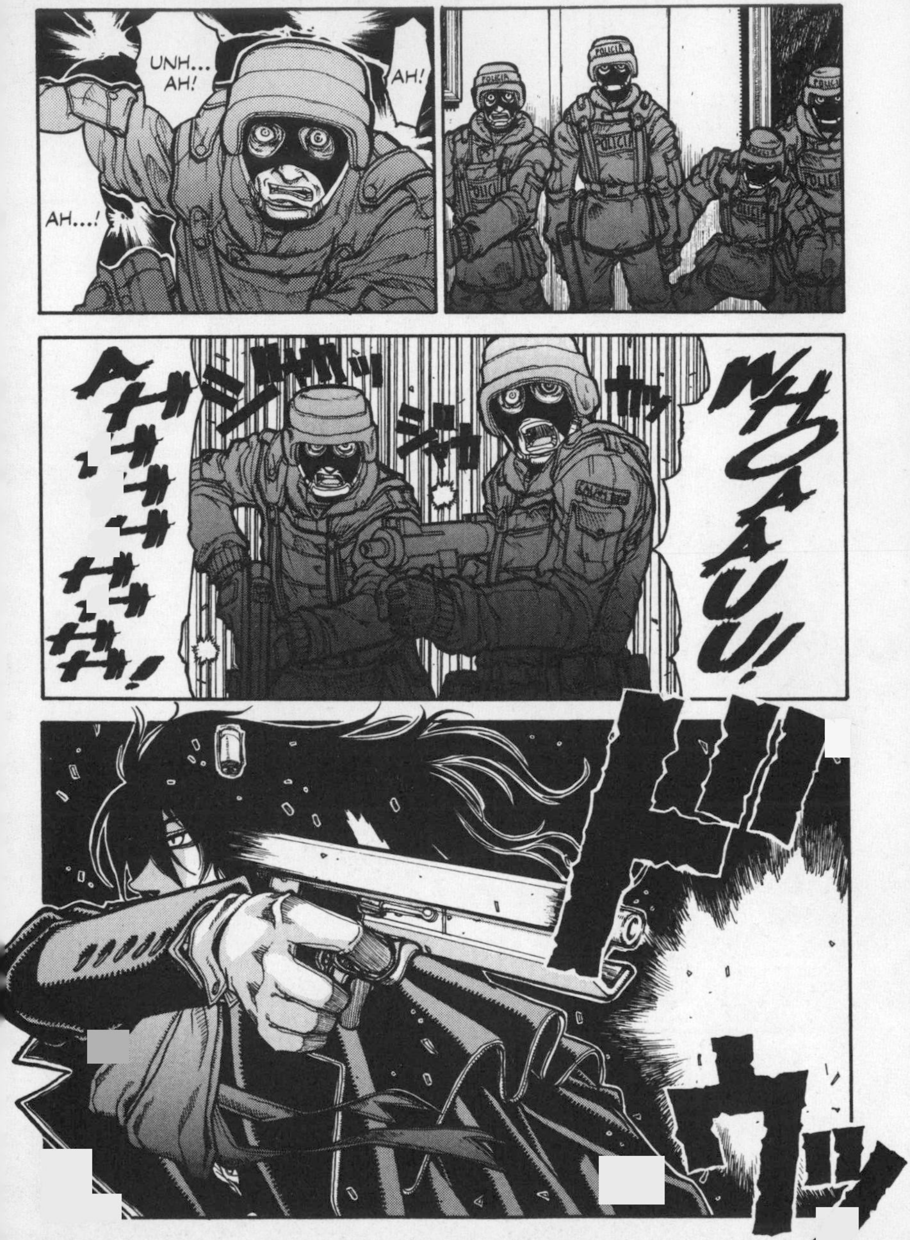
AH!
UNH... AH!
AH...!
WHOAAUU!

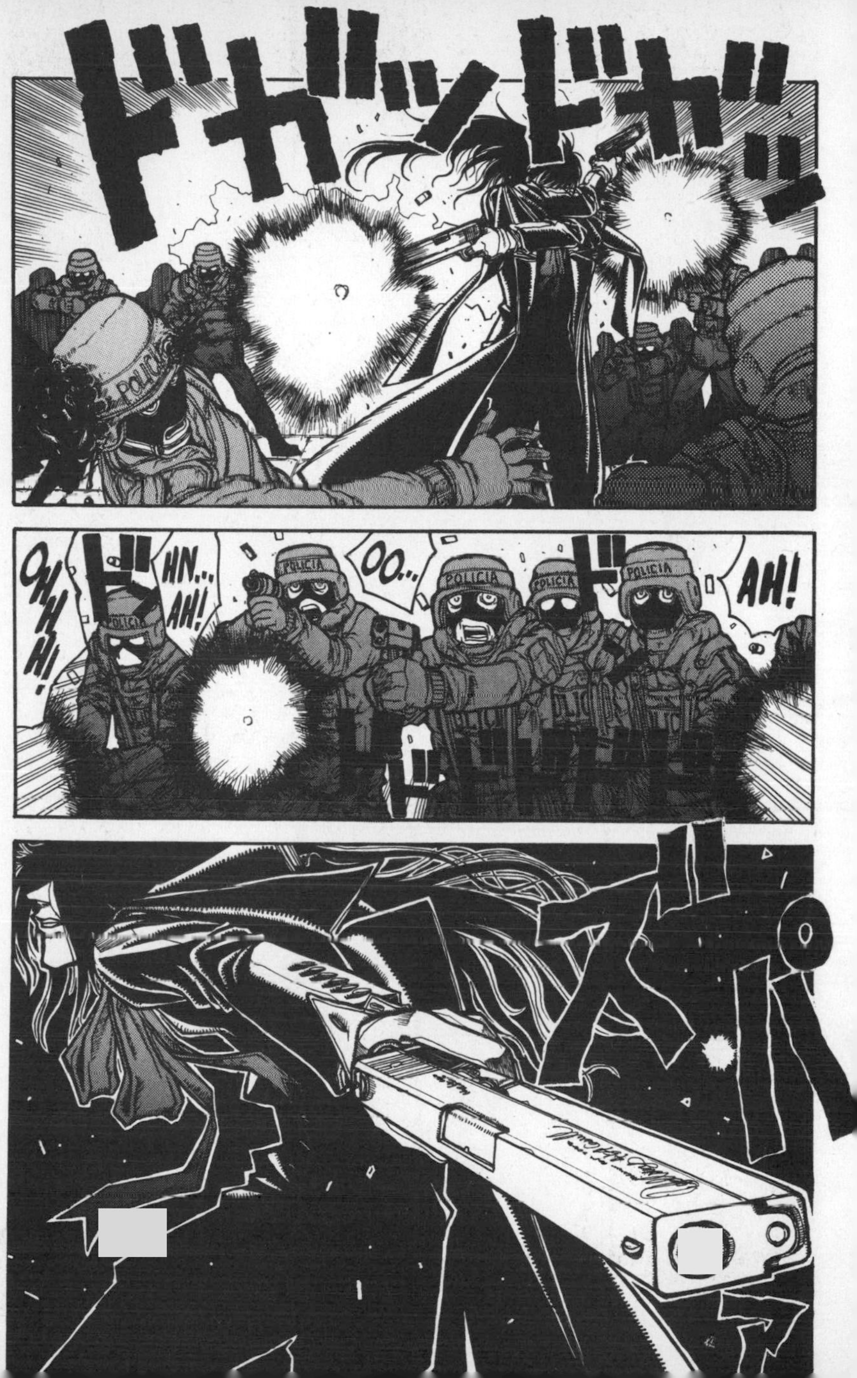
ドガッドガッ
POLICIA
AH!
OO...
HN... AH!
OHHHH!
ズオ

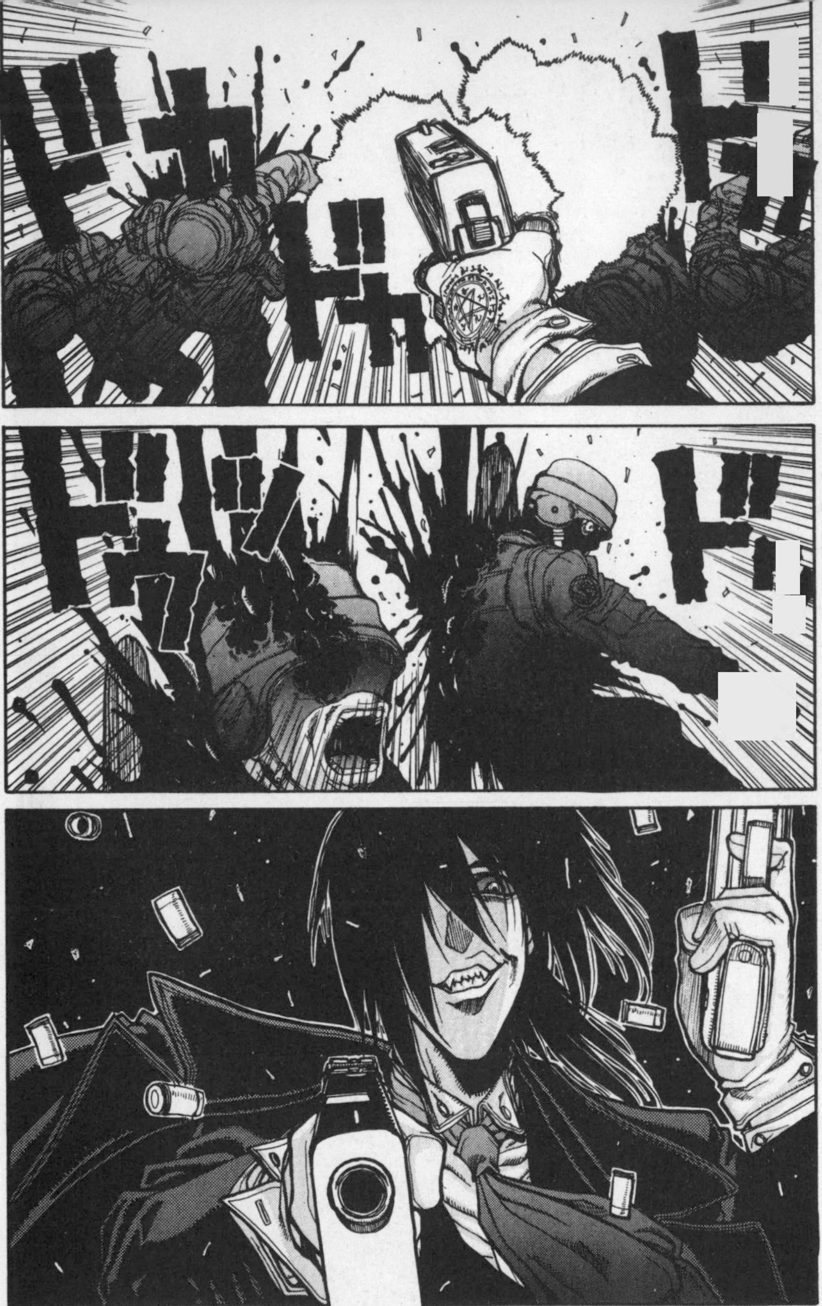
ドカ
ドカ
ドカ
ド
ドゥ

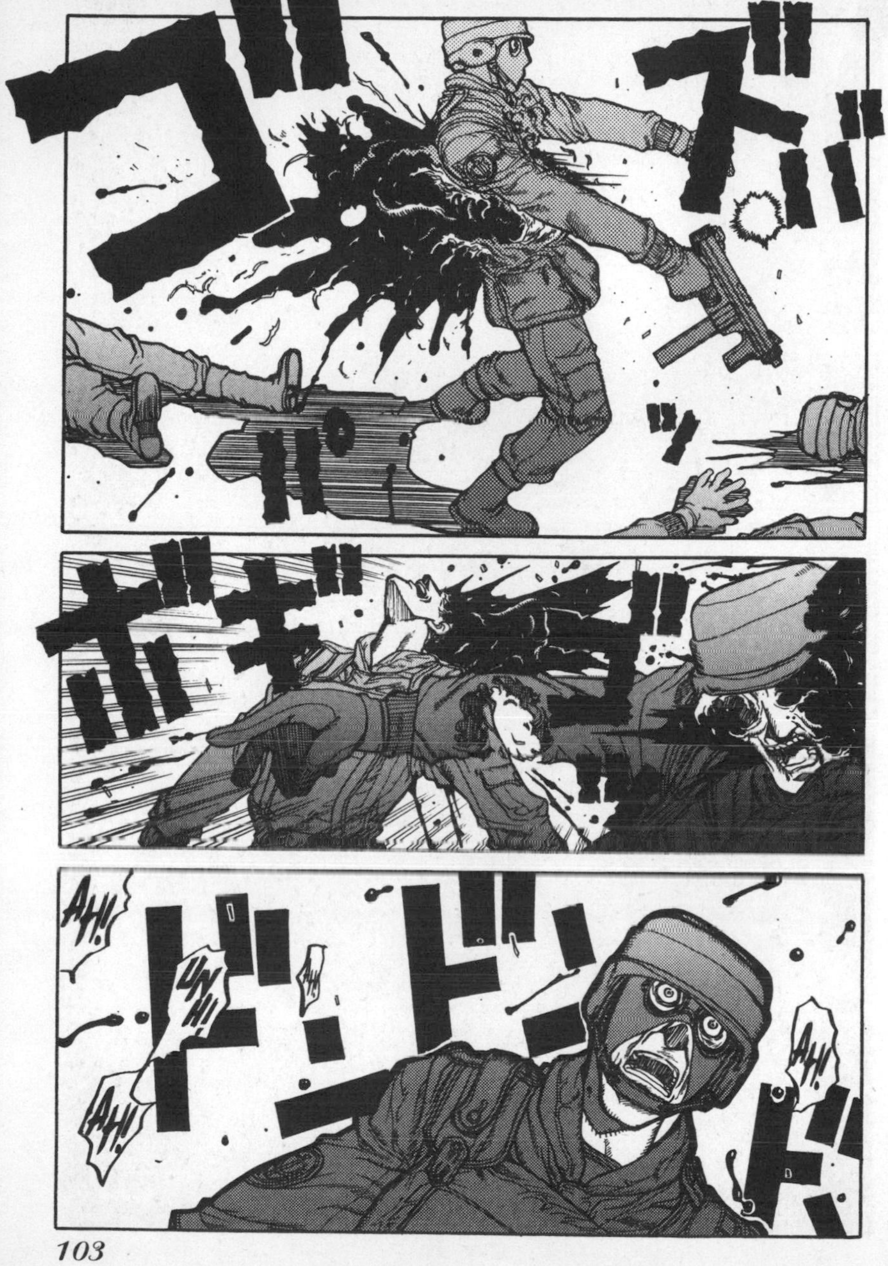
AH!
AH!
UNH!
AH!
AH!

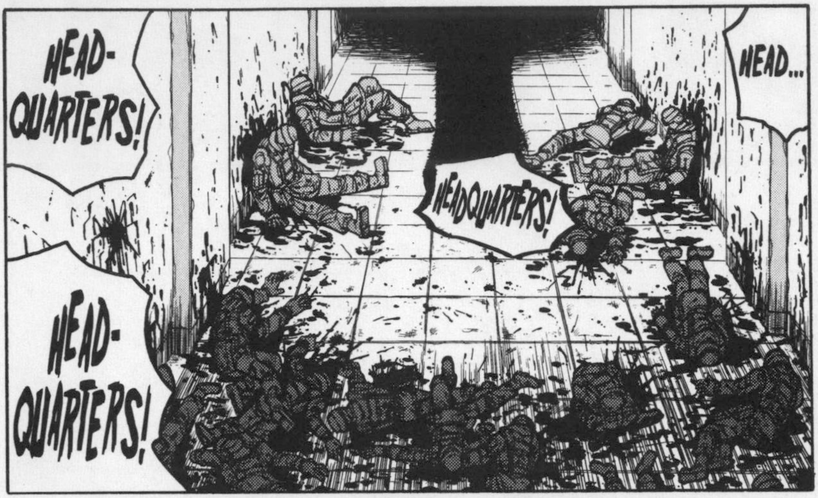
HEAD...
HEADQUARTERS!
HEAD-QUARTERS!
HEAD-QUARTERS!

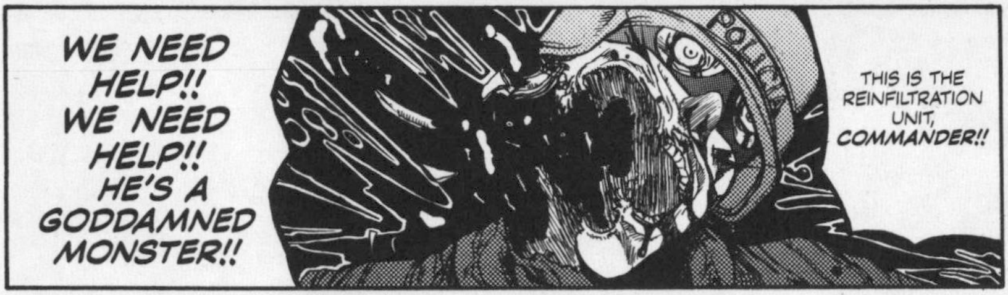
THIS IS THE REINFILTRATION UNIT, COMMANDER!!
WE NEED HELP!! WE NEED HELP!! HE'S A GODDAMNED MONSTER!!

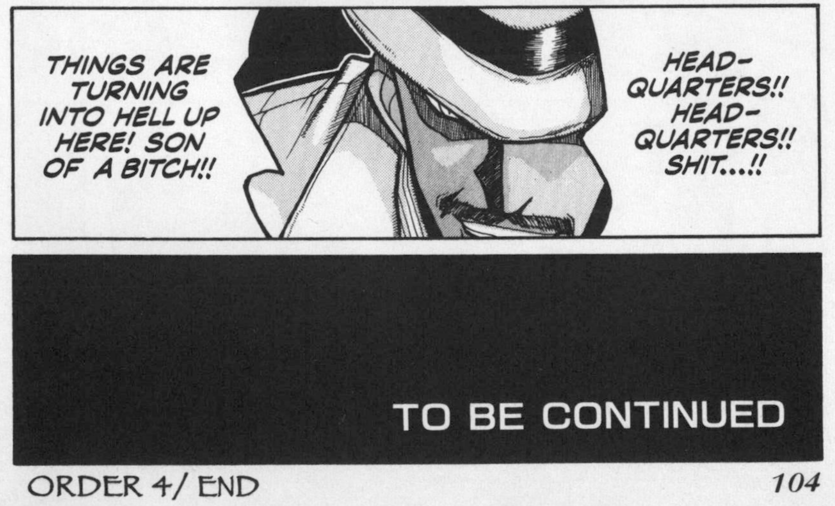
HEAD-QUARTERS!! HEAD-QUARTERS!! SHIT...!!
THINGS ARE TURNING INTO HELL UP HERE! SON OF A BITCH!!

TO BE CONTINUED

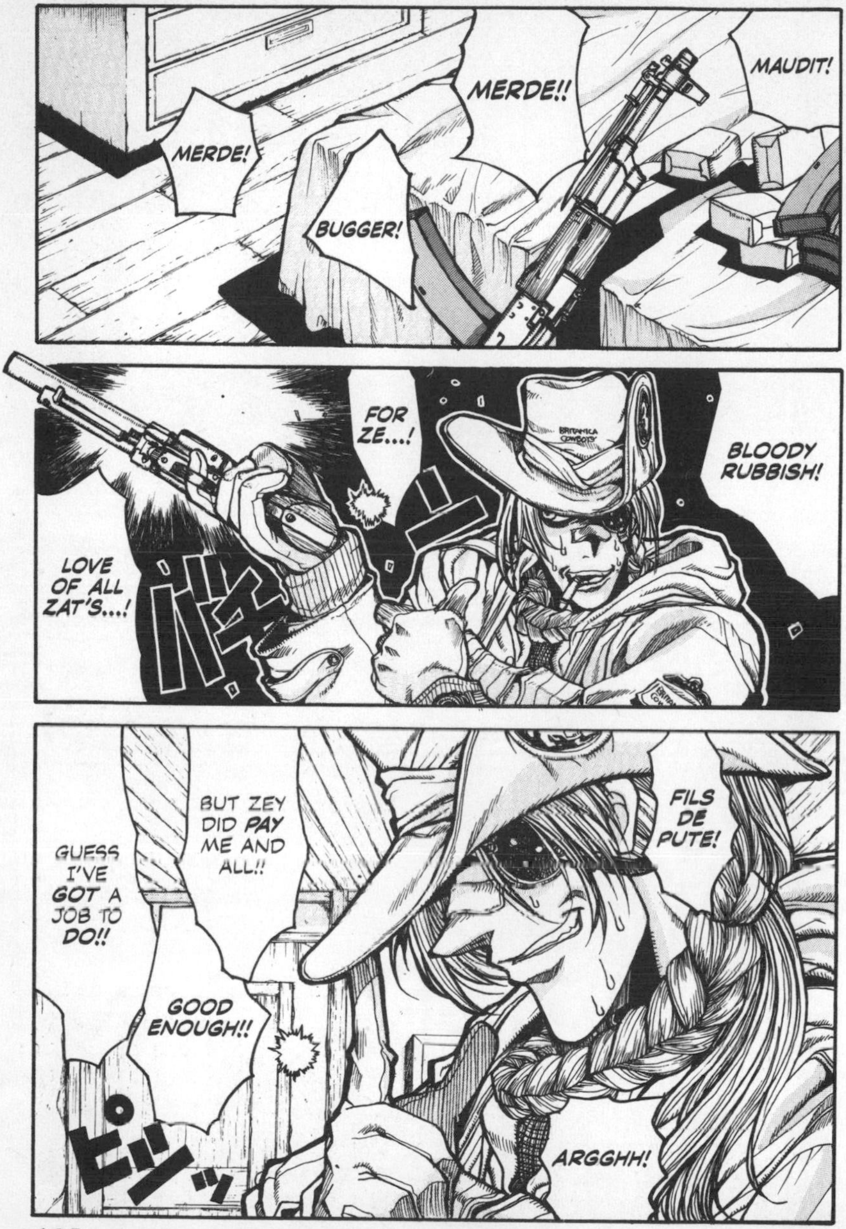
MAUDIT!
MERDE!!
MERDE!
BUGGER!
BLOODY RUBBISH!
FOR ZE...!
LOVE OF ALL ZAT'S...!
FILS DE PUTE!
BUT ZEY DID PAY ME AND ALL!!
GUESS I'VE GOT A JOB TO DO!!
GOOD ENOUGH!!
ARGGHH!

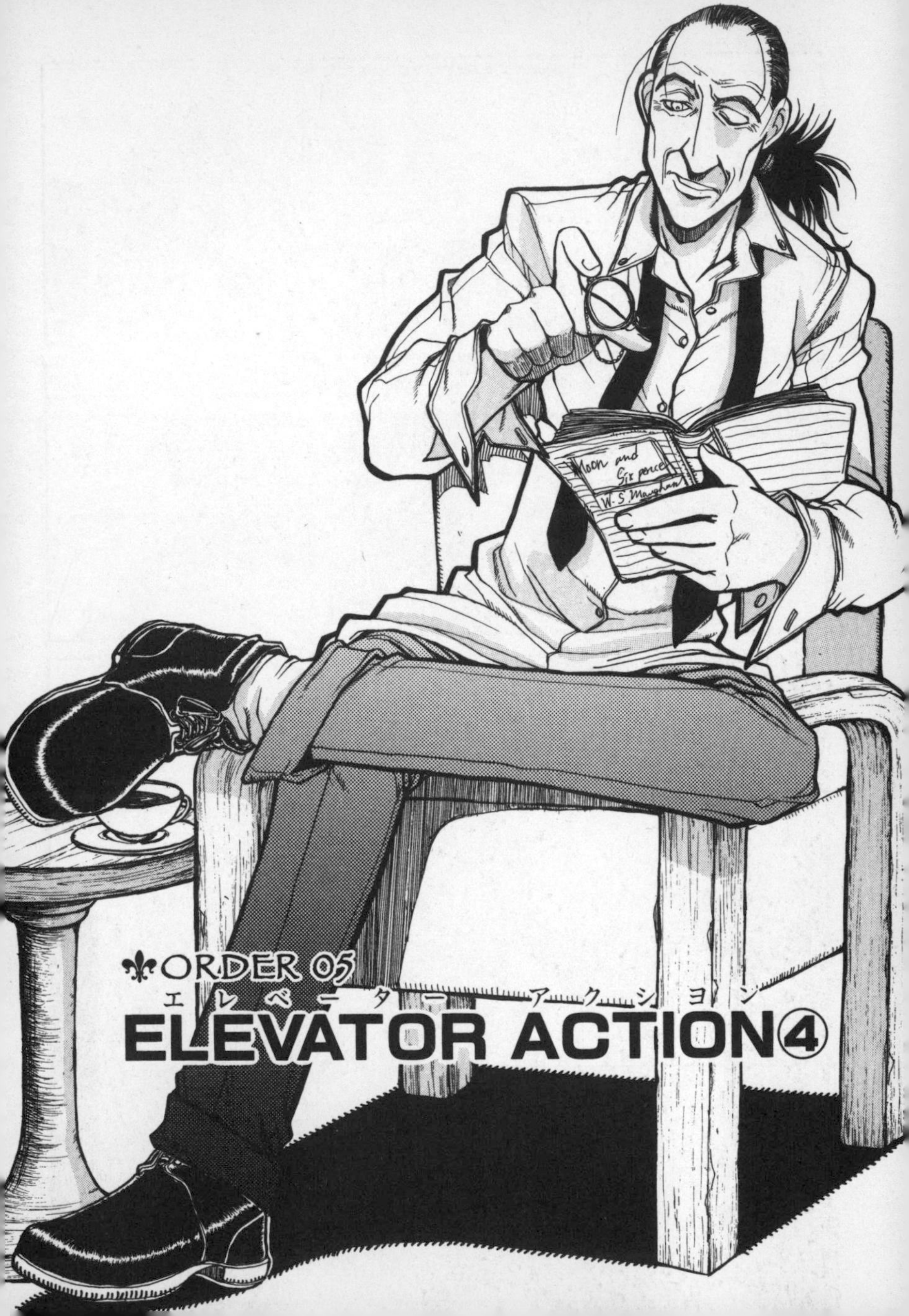
Moon and Six pence
W.S. Maugham

ORDER 05

エレベーターアクション
ELEVATOR ACTION④

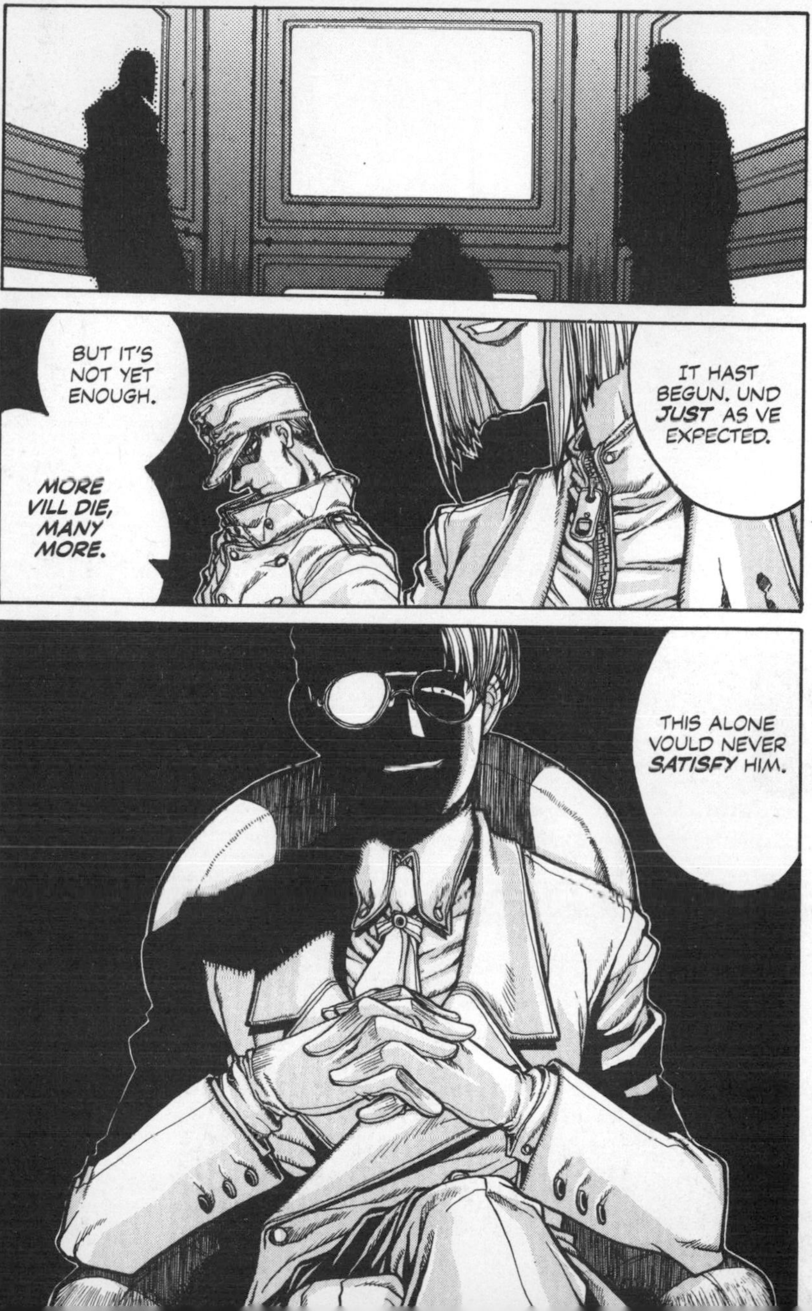
IT HAST BEGUN. UND *JUST* AS VE EXPECTED.
BUT IT'S NOT YET ENOUGH.
MORE VILL DIE, MANY MORE.
THIS ALONE VOULD NEVER *SATISFY* HIM.

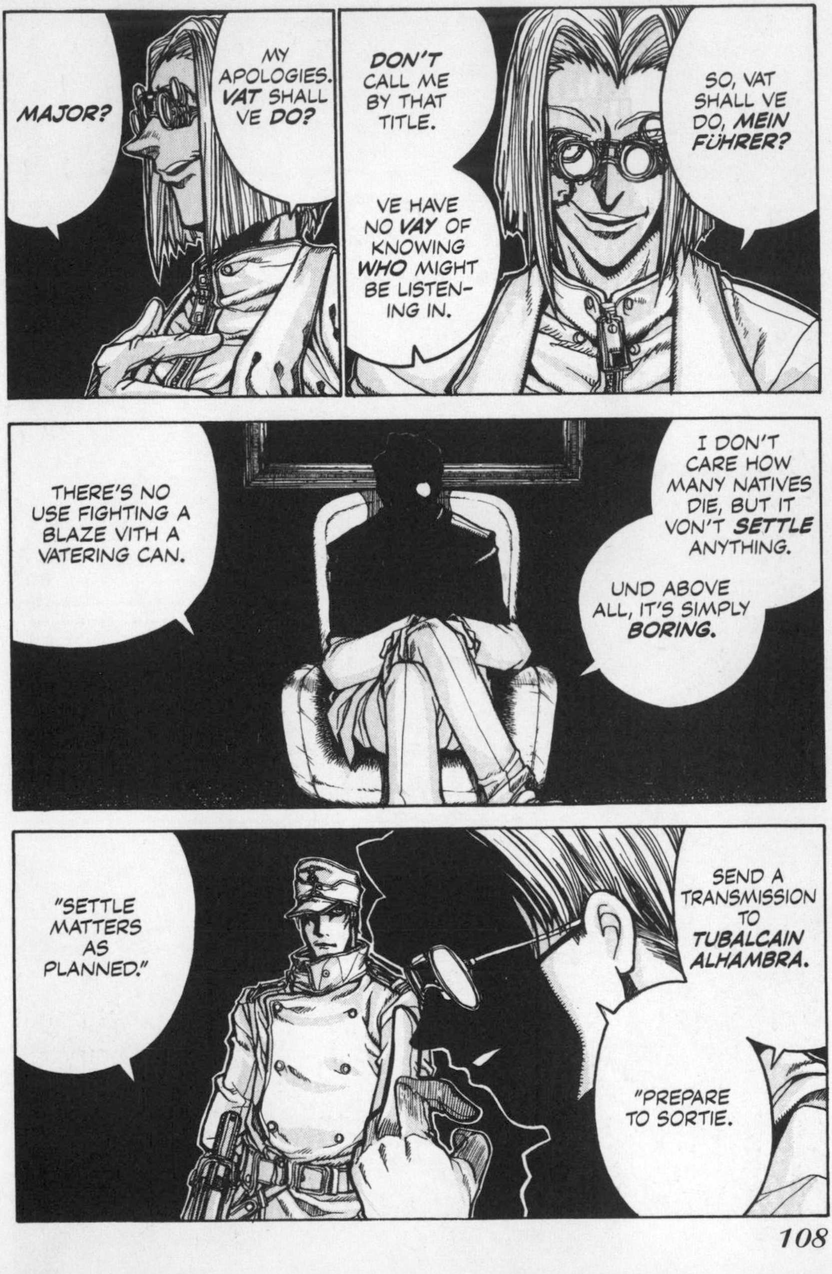
SO, VAT SHALL VE DO, MEIN FÜHRER?
DON'T CALL ME BY THAT TITLE.
VE HAVE NO VAY OF KNOWING WHO MIGHT BE LISTENING IN.
MY APOLOGIES. VAT SHALL VE DO?
MAJOR?
I DON'T CARE HOW MANY NATIVES DIE, BUT IT VON'T SETTLE ANYTHING.
UND ABOVE ALL, IT'S SIMPLY BORING.
THERE'S NO USE FIGHTING A BLAZE VITH A VATERING CAN.
SEND A TRANSMISSION TO TUBALCAIN ALHAMBRA.
"PREPARE TO SORTIE.
"SETTLE MATTERS AS PLANNED."

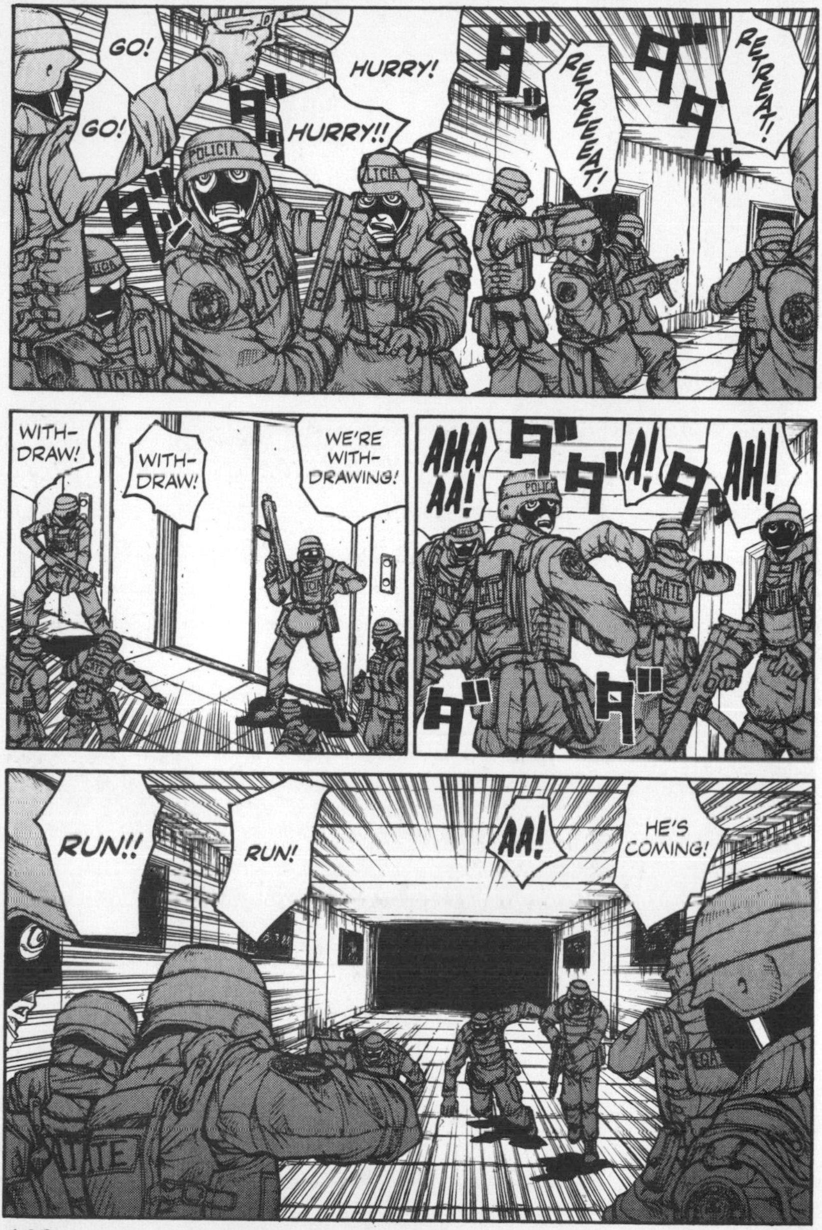
RETREAT!
RETREEEAT!
HURRY!
HURRY!!
GO!
GO!
AH!
A!
AHAAA!
WE'RE WITH-DRAWING!
WITH-DRAW!
WITH-DRAW!
HE'S COMING!
AA!
RUN!
RUN!!

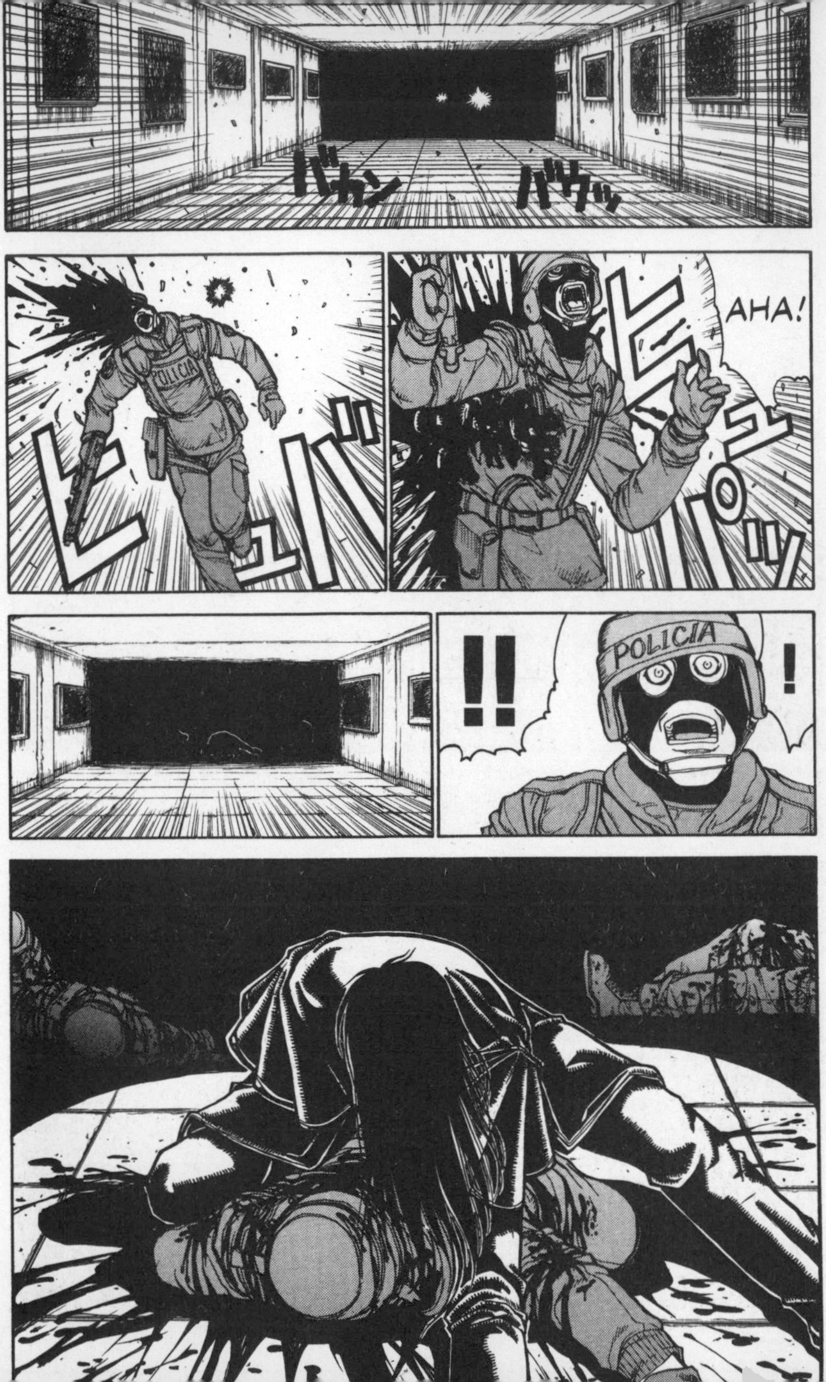
バカン
AHA!
ビュパッ
POLICIA
ビュバ
!!
!
POLICIA

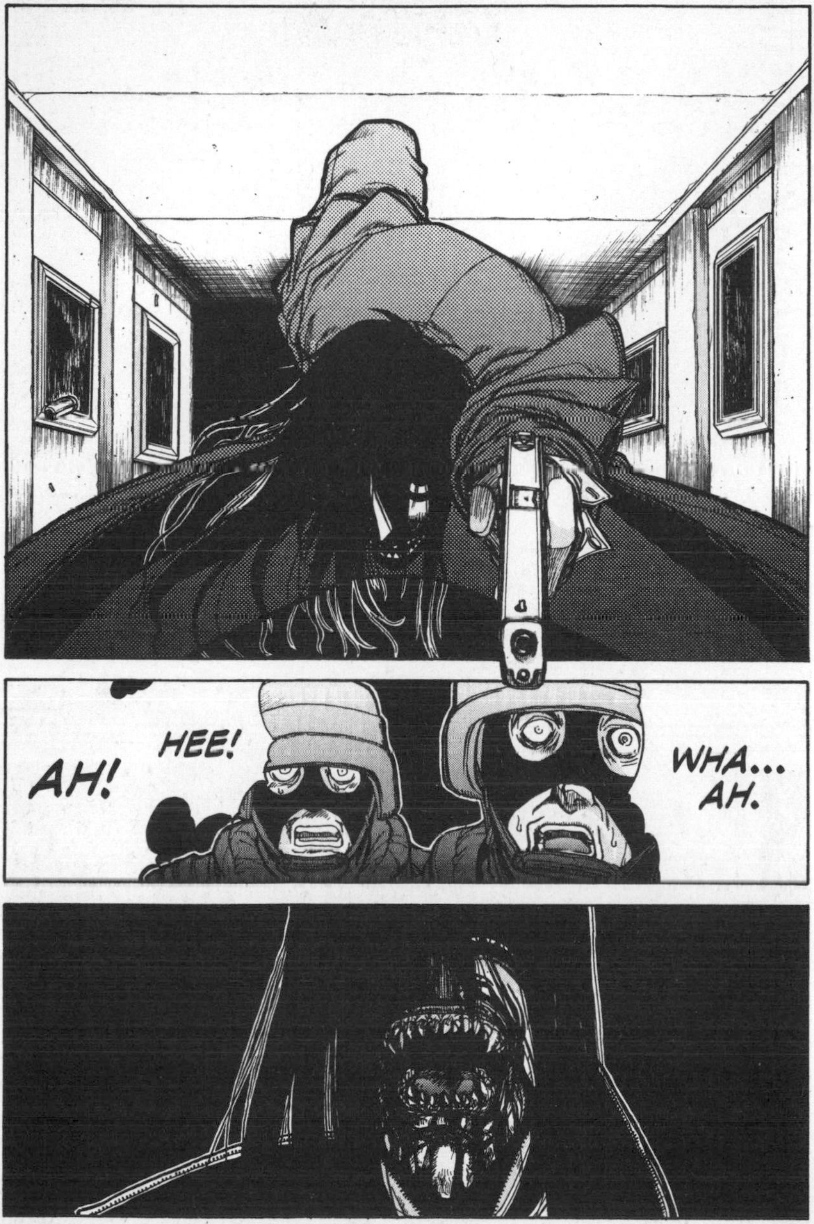
WHA... AH.
HEE!
AH!

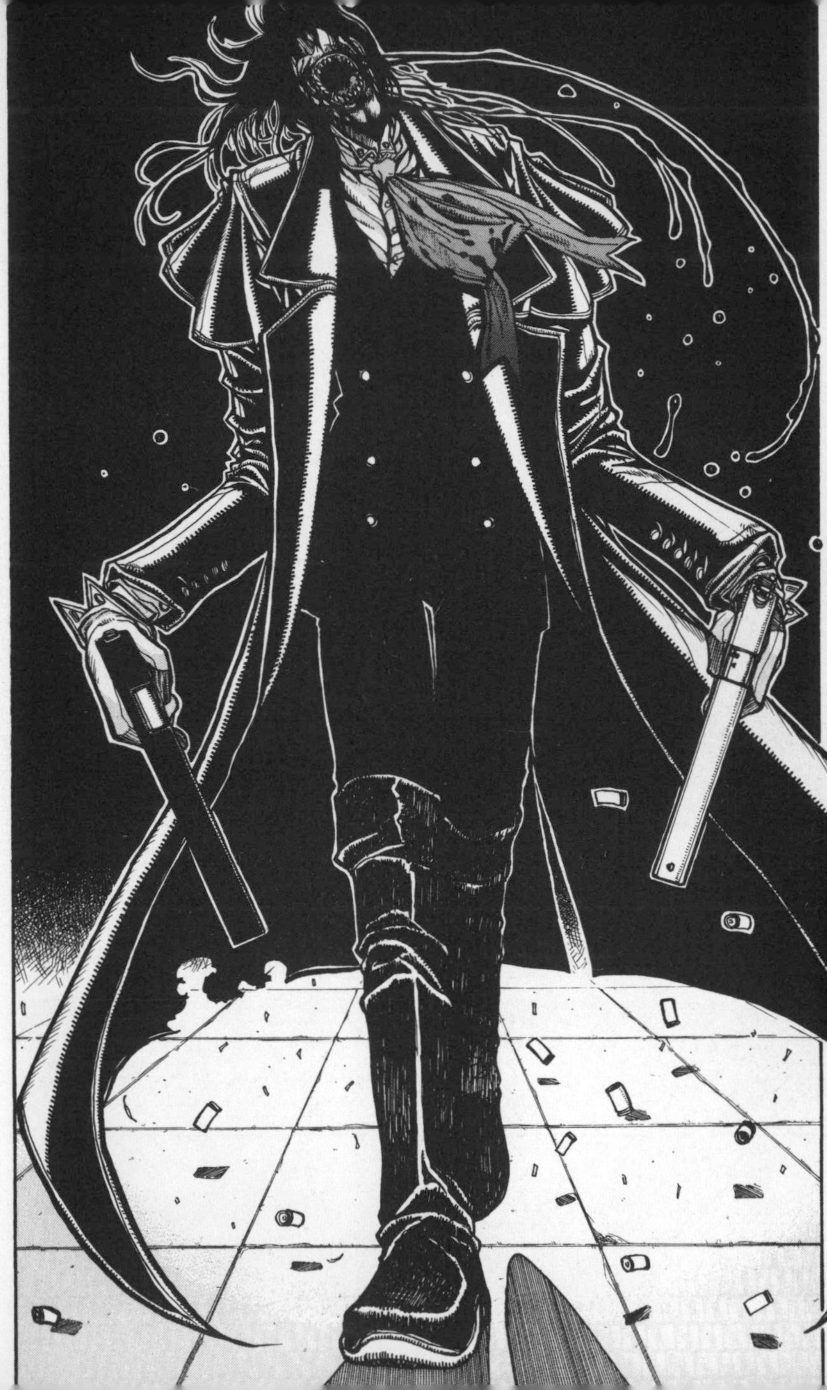

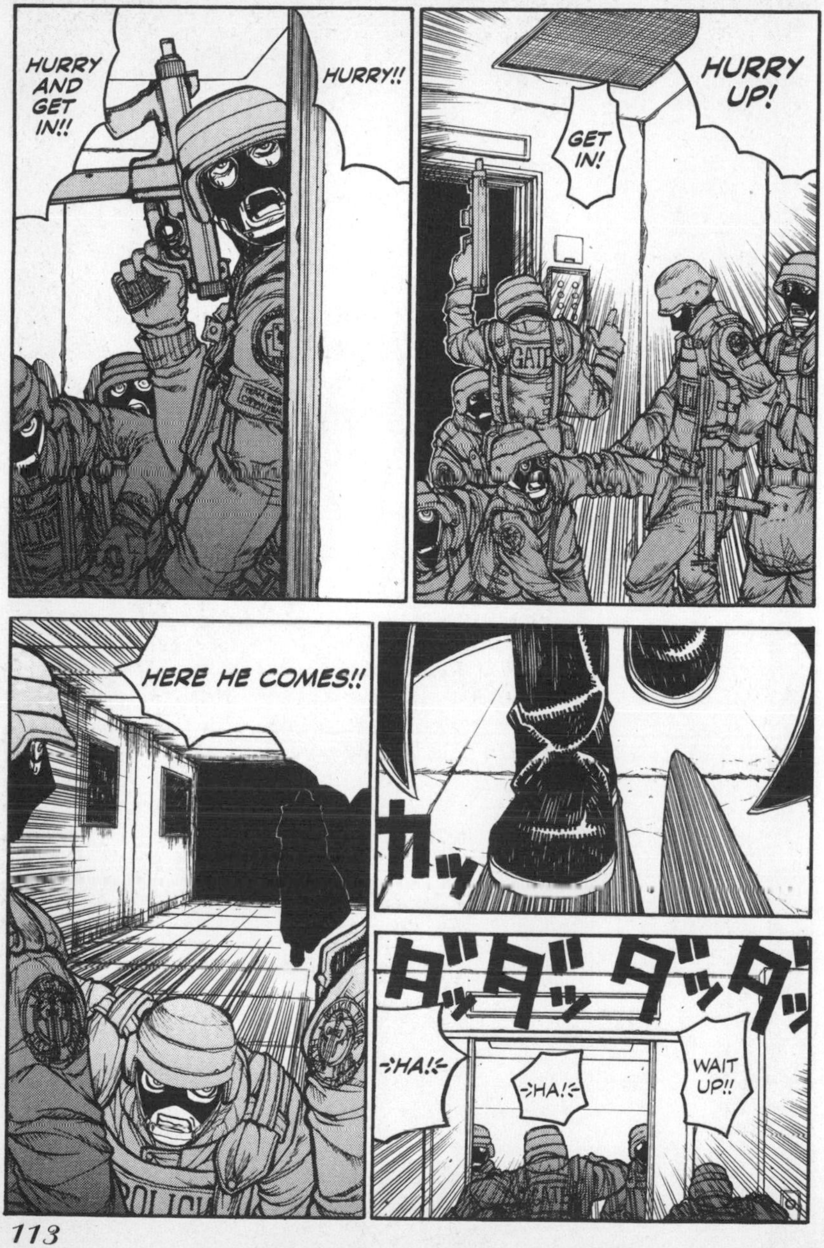
HURRY UP!
GET IN!
HURRY!!
HURRY AND GET IN!!
カッ
タッ ダッ タッ ダッ
WAIT UP!!
-HA!-
-HA!-
HERE HE COMES!!

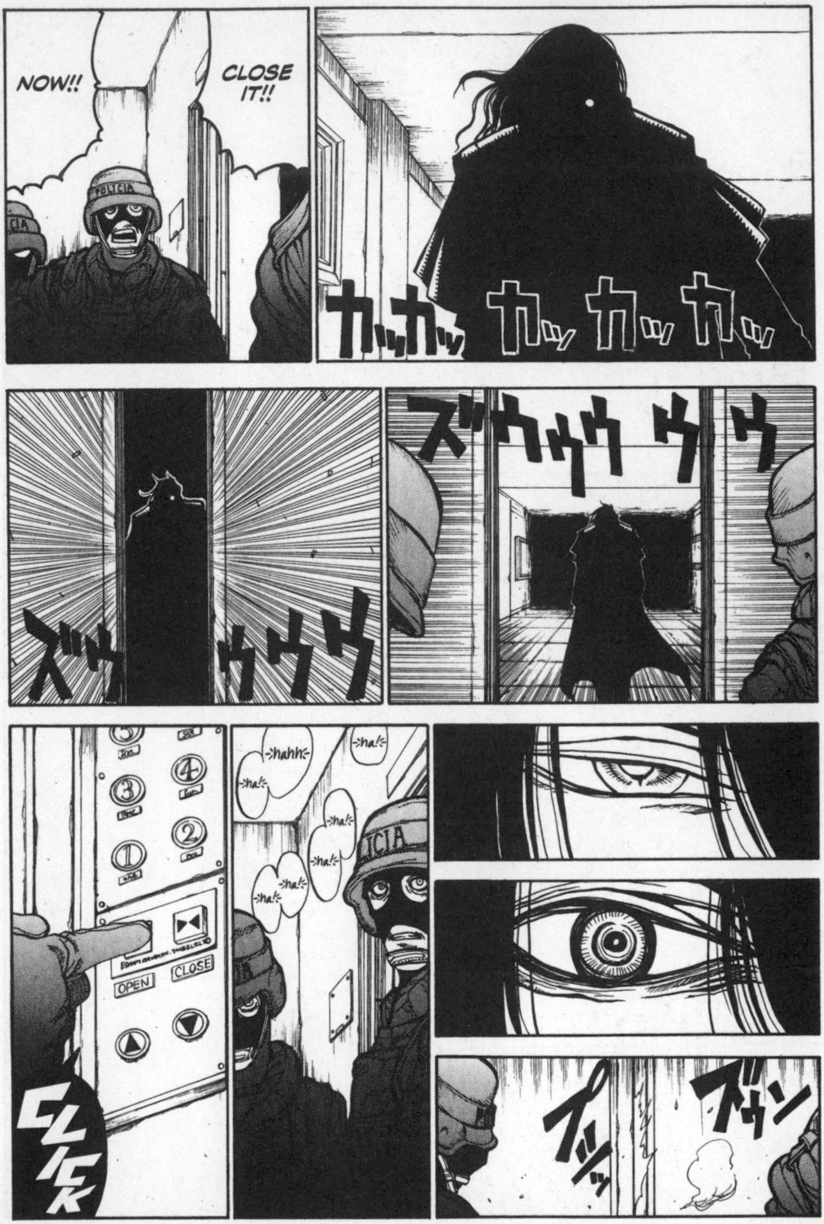
カッカッ
カッカッカッ
CLOSE IT!!
NOW!!
ズウウウ ウウ
ズウウウ
ズウン
ブツッ
-ha!-
-hahh-
-ha!-
-ha!-
-ha!-
-ha!-
-ha!-
CLOSE
OPEN
CLICK

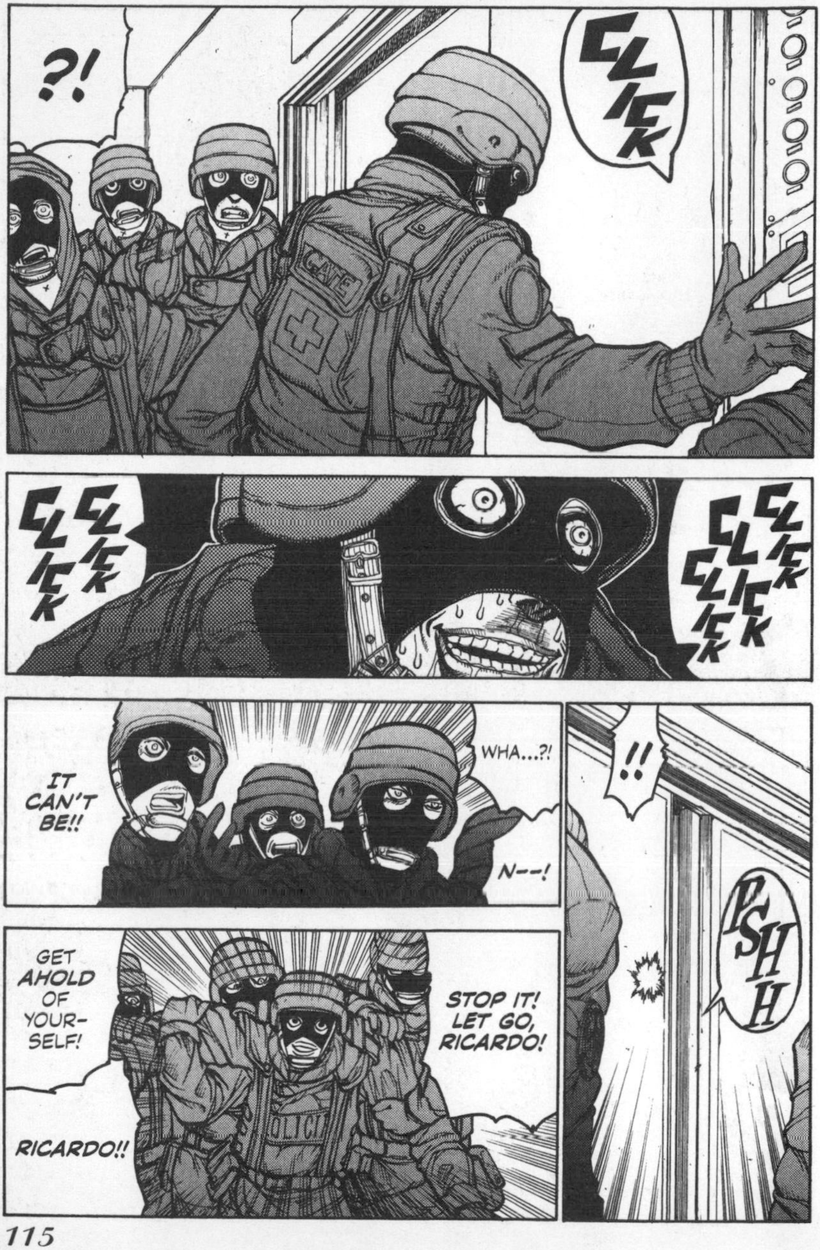
CLICK
?!
CLICK CLICK CLICK
CLICK CLICK
!!
PSHH
WHA...?!
N--!
IT CAN'T BE!!
STOP IT! LET GO, RICARDO!
GET AHOLD OF YOURSELF!
RICARDO!!

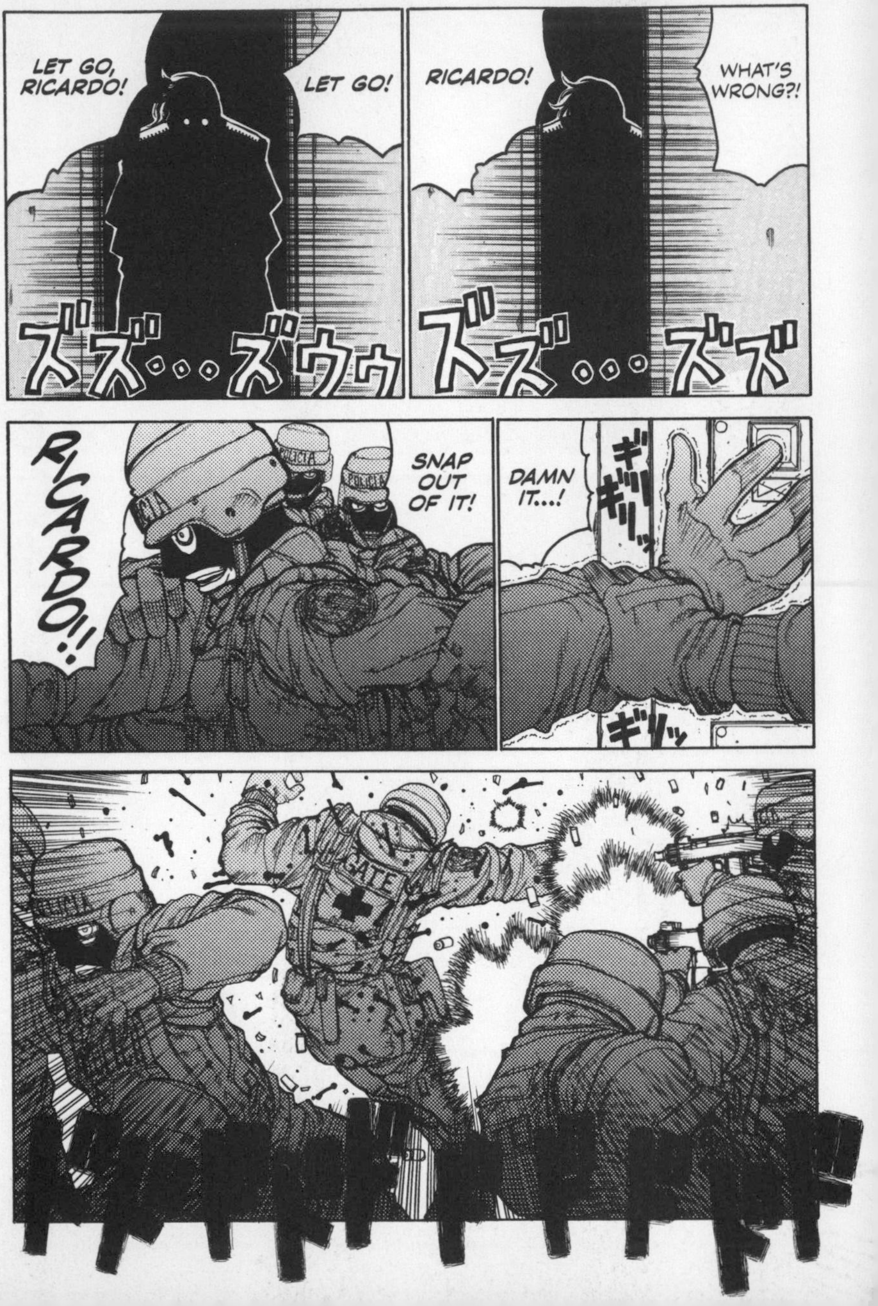
WHAT'S WRONG?!
RICARDO!
ドズ…ズズ
LET GO!
LET GO, RICARDO!
ズズ…ズウウ
DAMN IT...!
ギッ
ギリッ
ギリッ
SNAP OUT OF IT!
RICARDO!!!
GATE

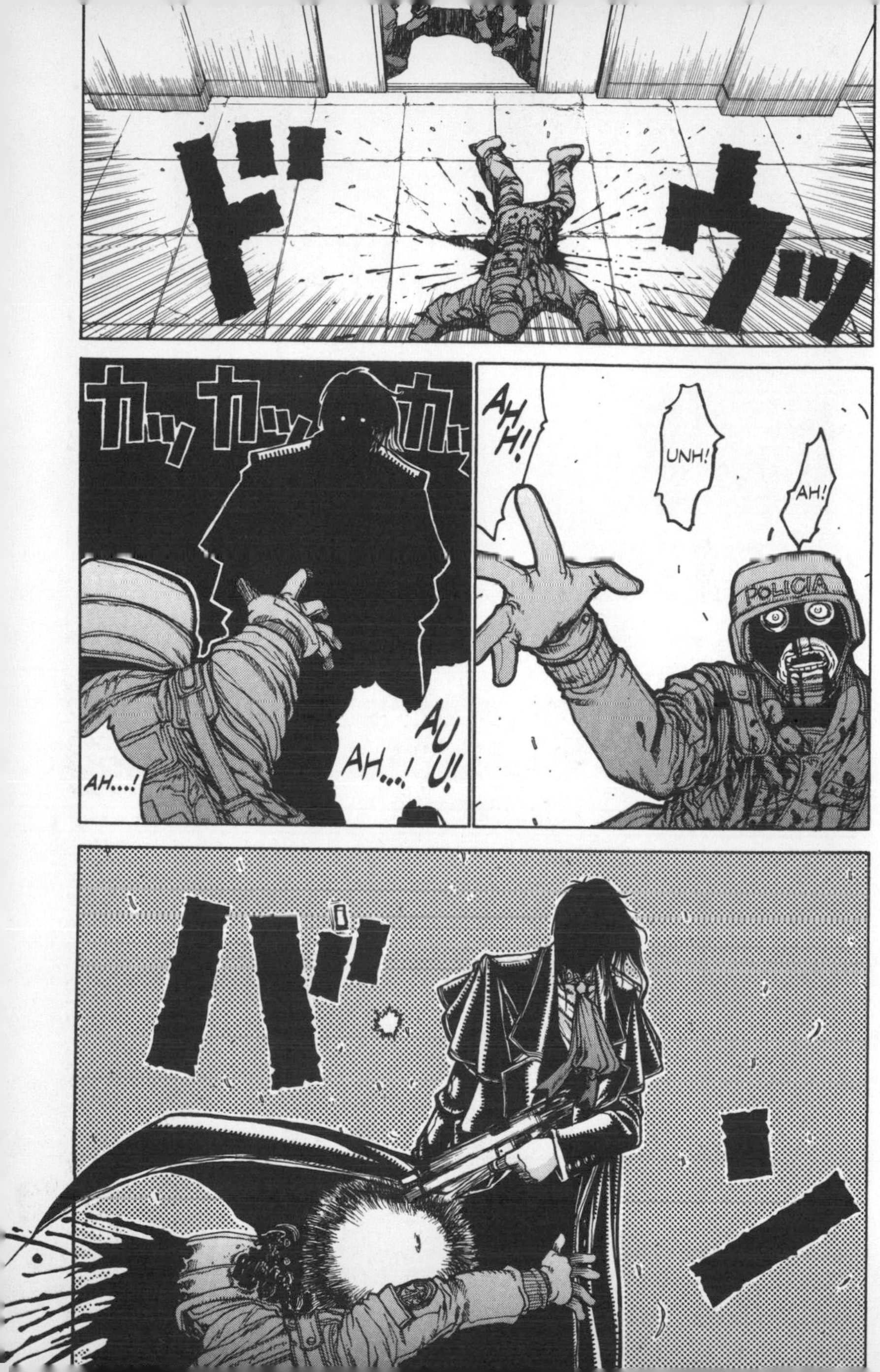
ドウッ
AHH!
UNH!
AH!
カッ カッ カッ
AUU!
AH...!
AH...!
バー

POLICIA
CLOSE IT!!
CLOSE IIIIT!!
ガチッ
open Sesami

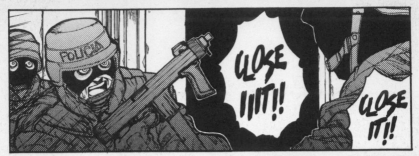

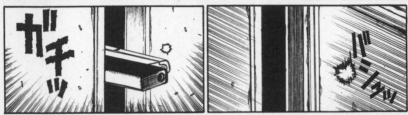

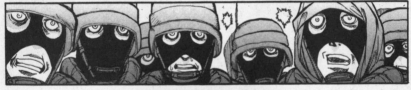

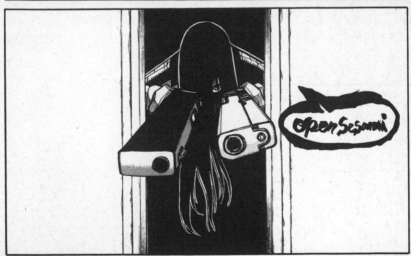

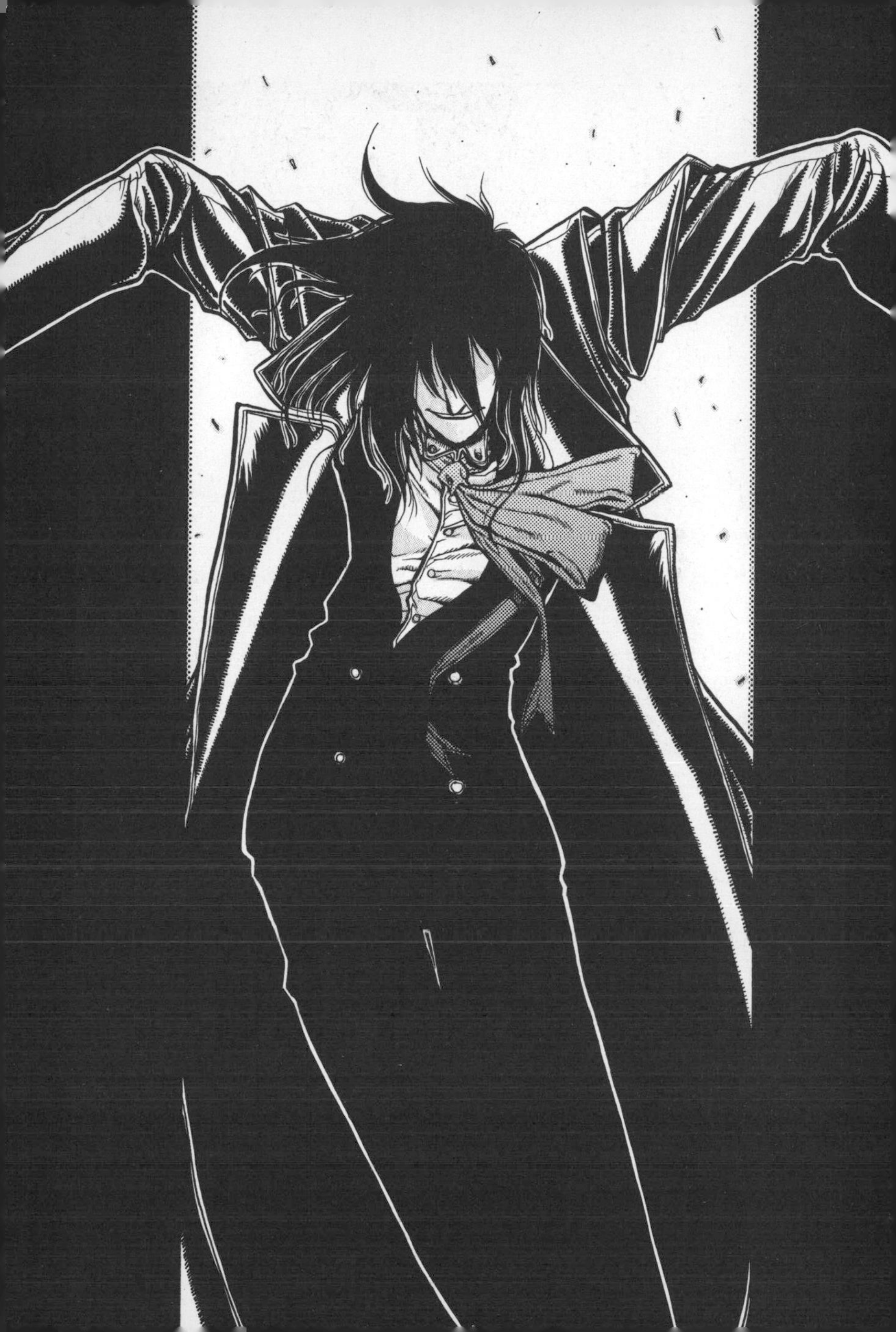

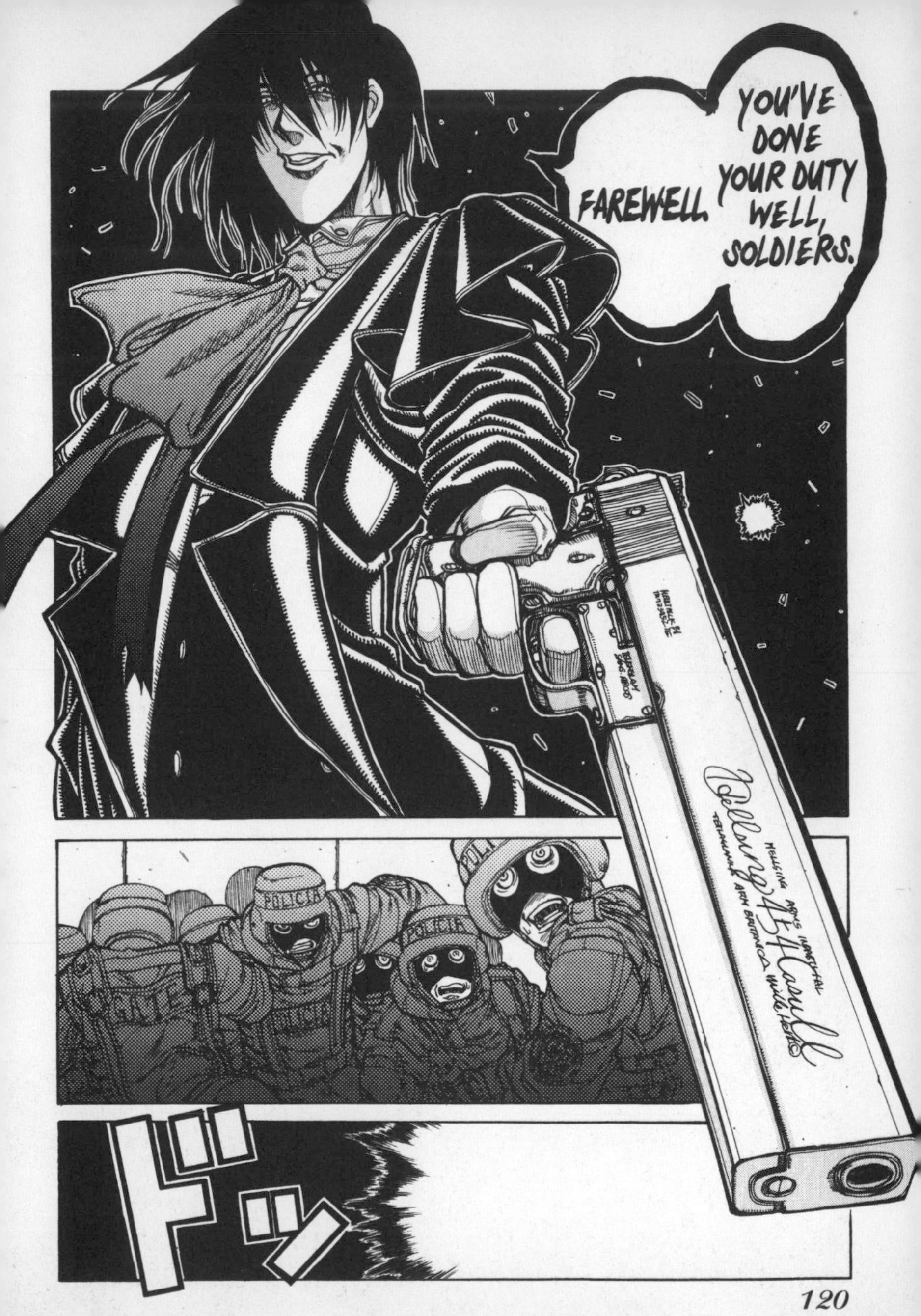
YOU'VE DONE YOUR DUTY WELL, SOLDIERS.
FAREWELL.
POLICIA
ドドッ

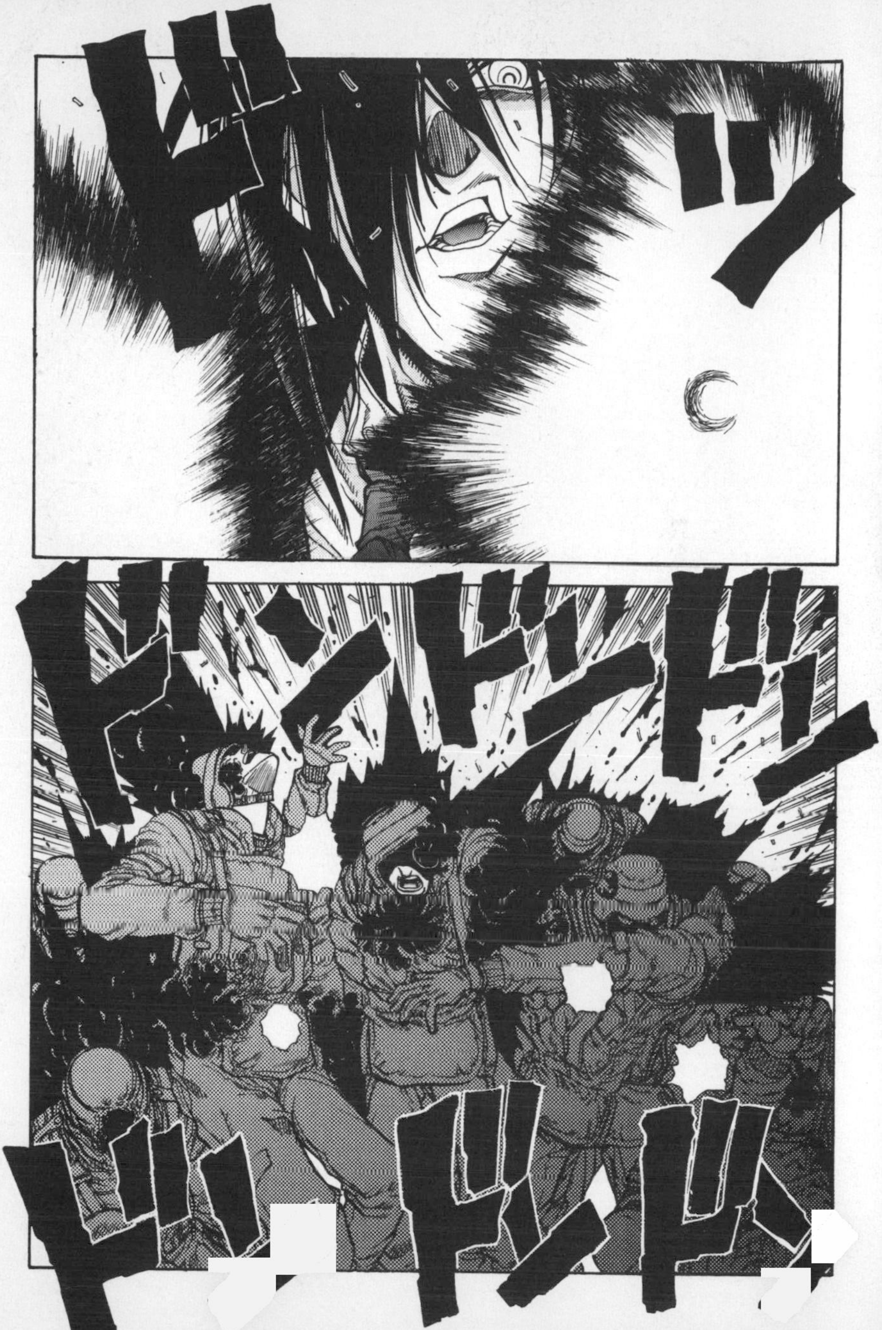

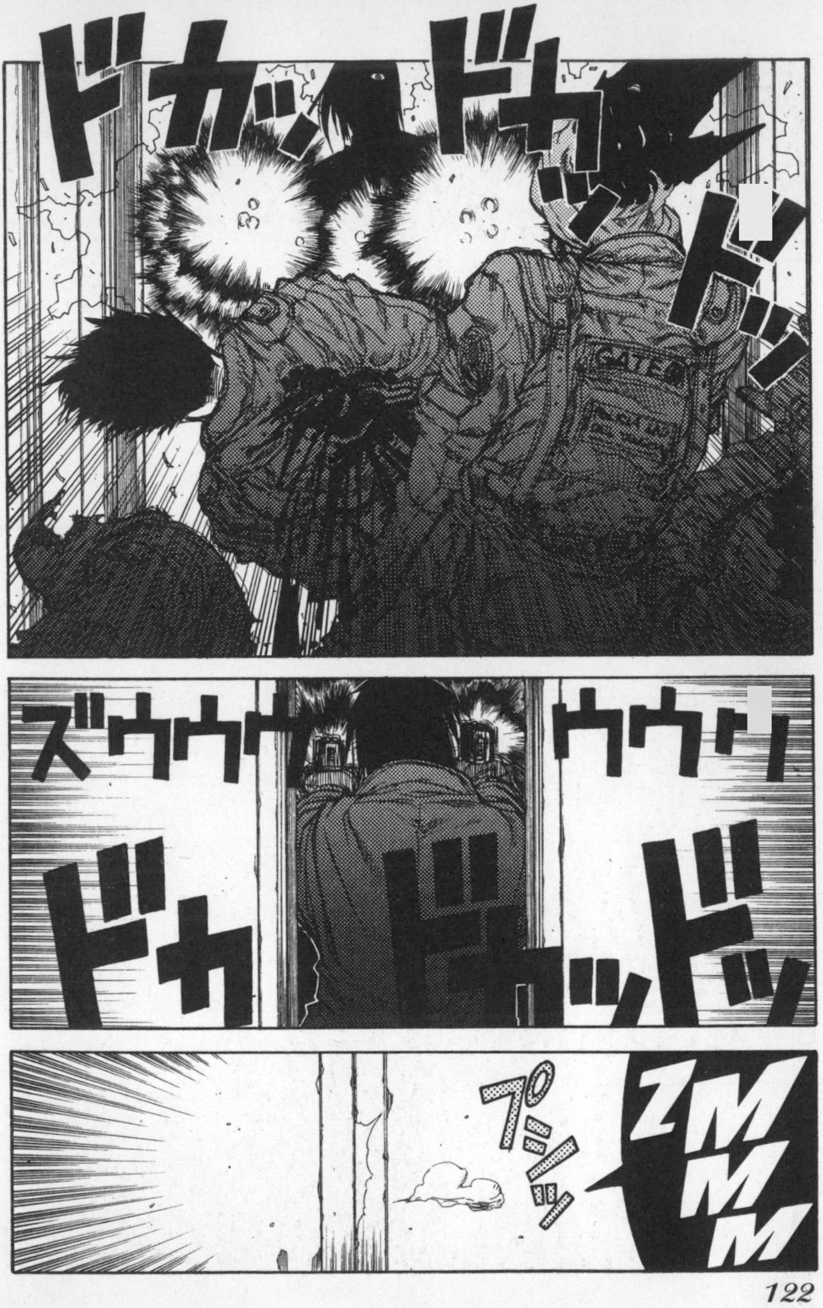
ドドッ
ドガッ ドガッ
GATE
ズウウウウウウ
ドドッ
ドガッ
ドカ
ZMMM
プシッ

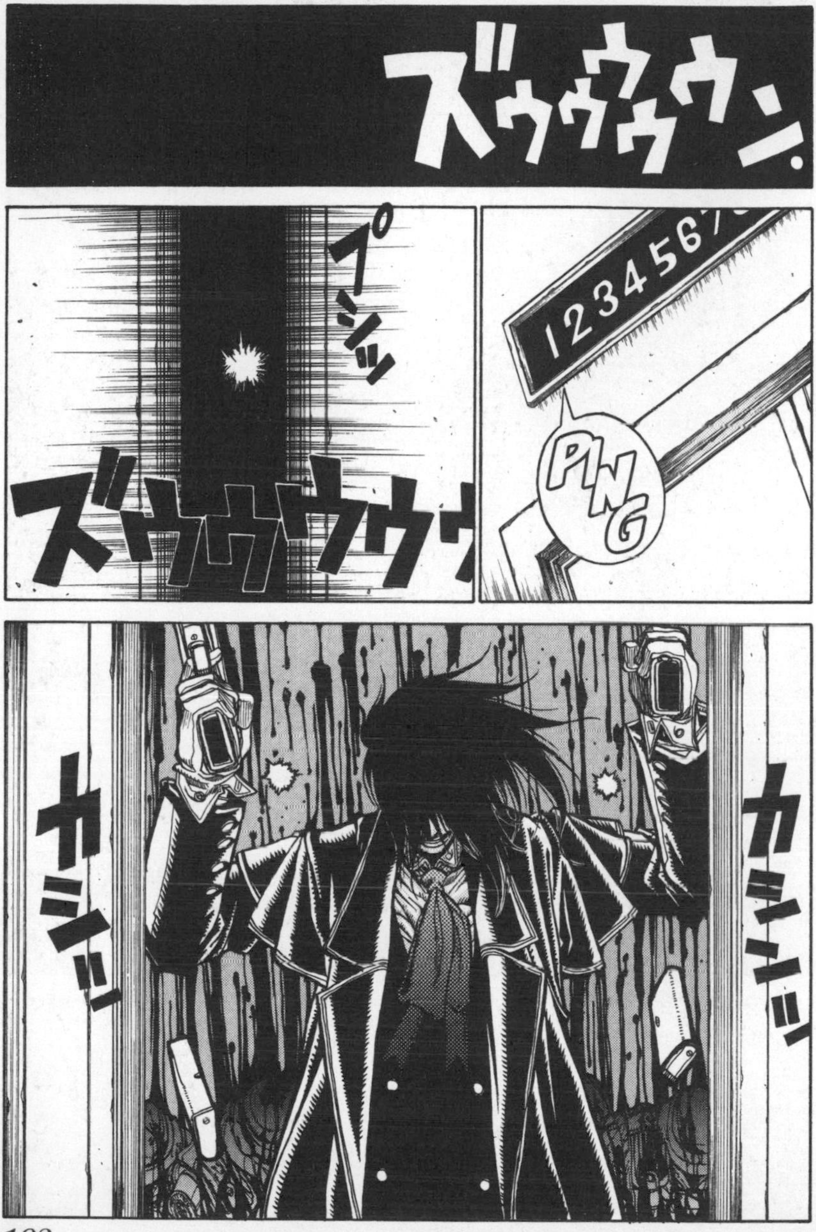
ズウウウウン.
1234567
PING
プシッ
ズウウウウウ

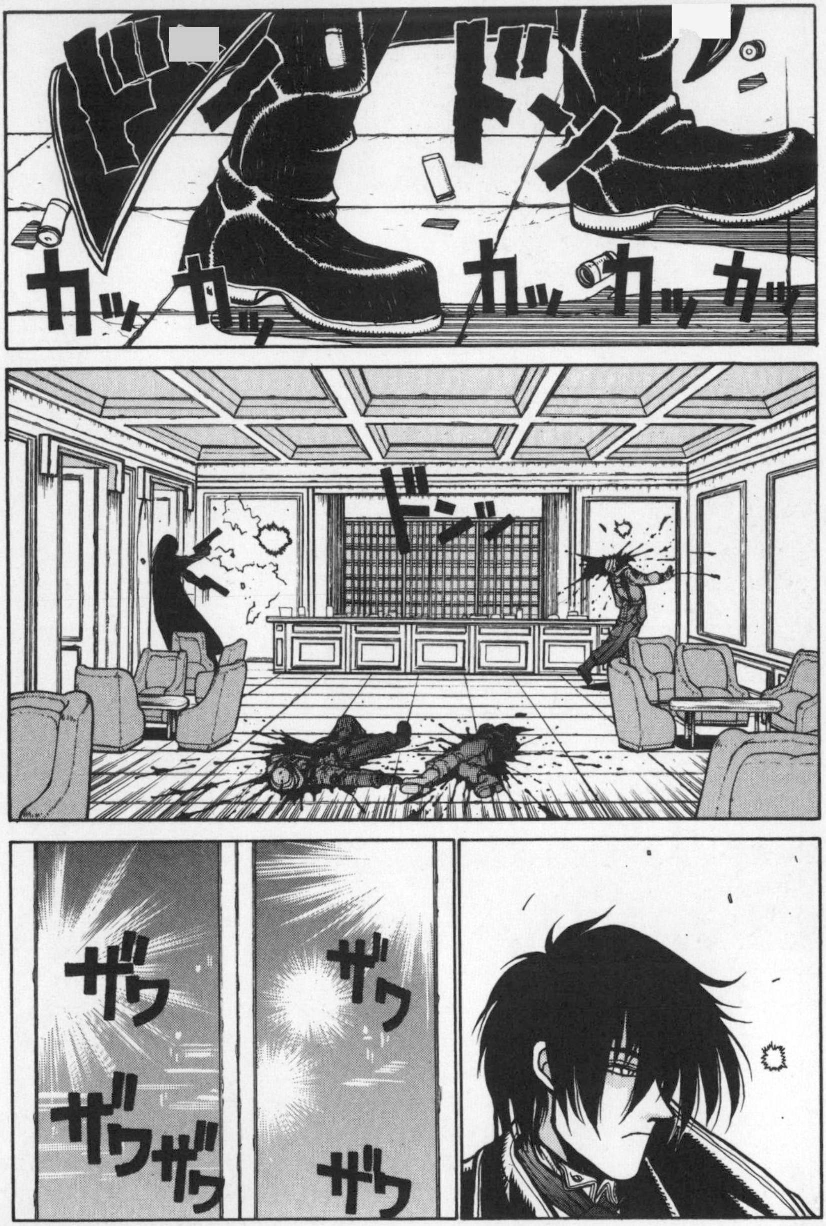
ドン
ドン
カッ カッ カッ
カッ カッ
ドンッ
ザワ
ザワ
ザワ
ザワザワ

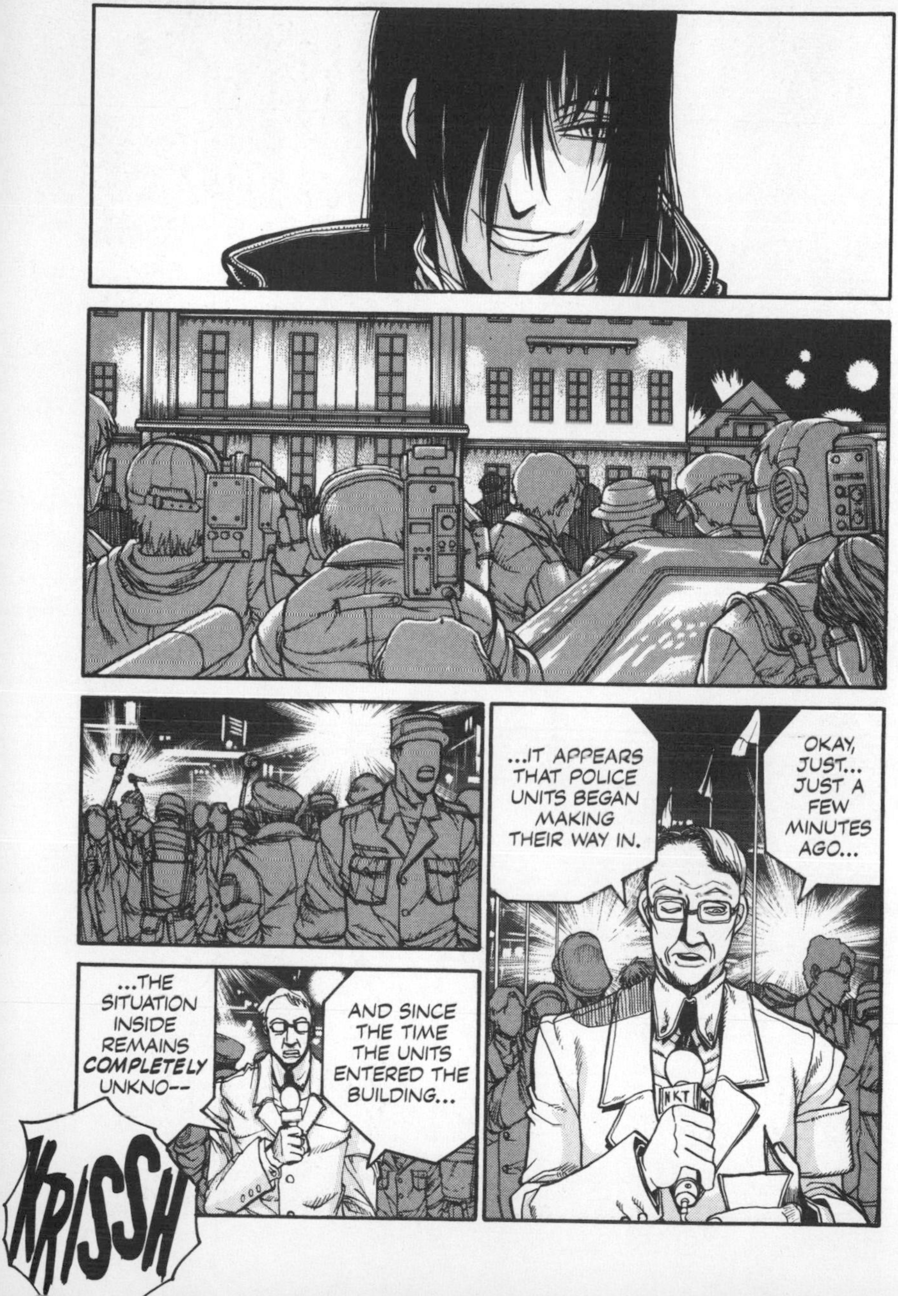
OKAY, JUST... JUST A FEW MINUTES AGO...
...IT APPEARS THAT POLICE UNITS BEGAN MAKING THEIR WAY IN.
AND SINCE THE TIME THE UNITS ENTERED THE BUILDING...
...THE SITUATION INSIDE REMAINS COMPLETELY UNKNO--
KRISSH

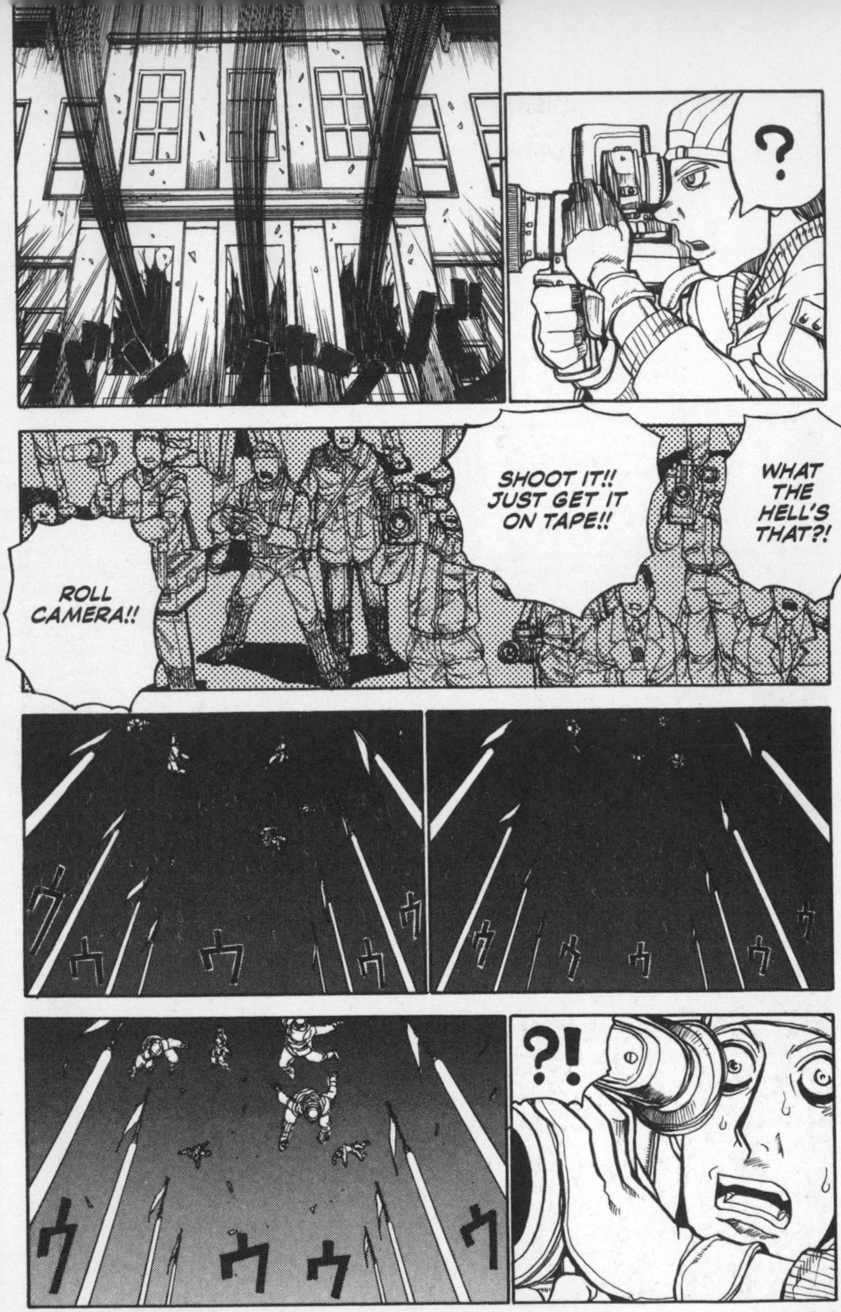
?
WHAT THE HELL'S THAT?!
SHOOT IT!! JUST GET IT ON TAPE!!
ROLL CAMERA!!
ウ ウ ウ ウ ウ
ウ ウ ウ ウ
?!
ウ ウ ウ ウ

AH...   WHA....!

UNH...
AH...

!!   AGH!   EE!

ZMFF   ZMFF

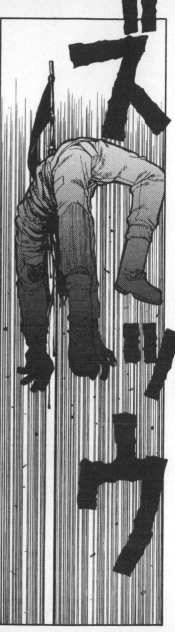

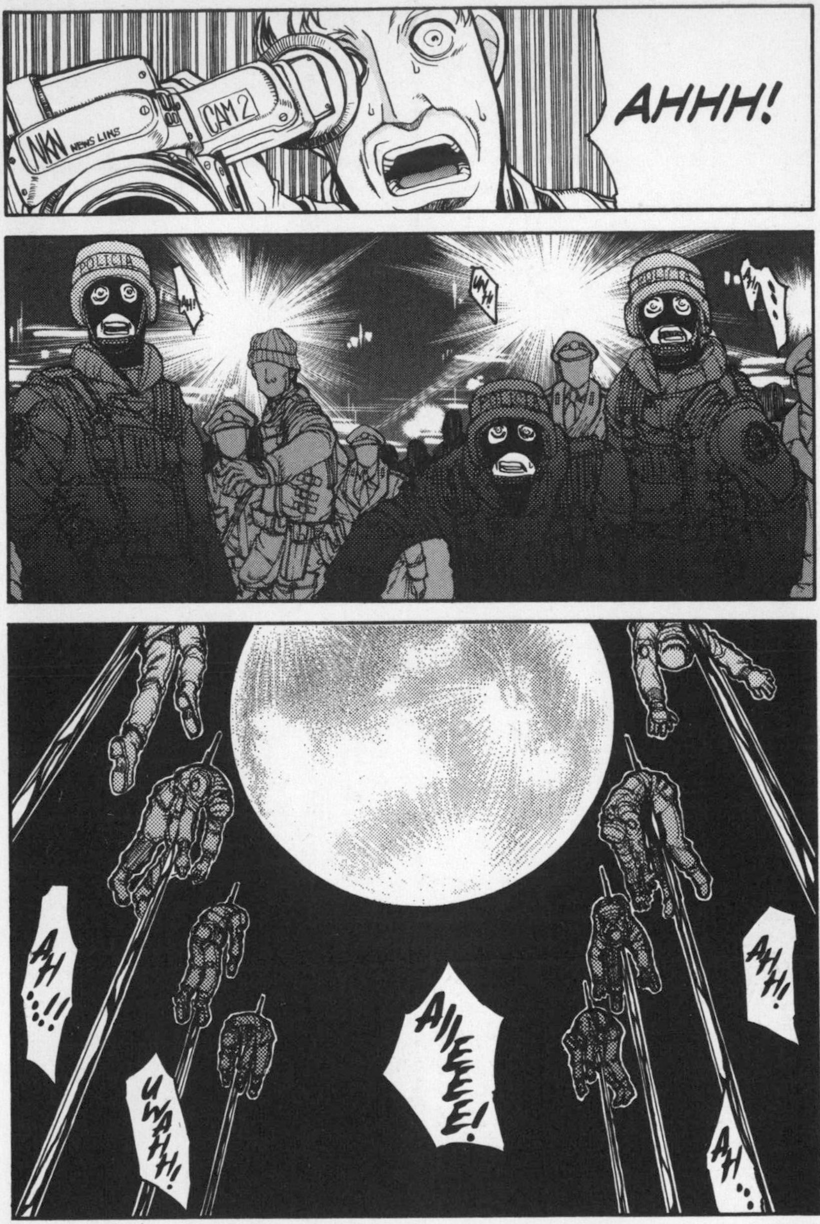
NKN NEWS LINS
CAM 2
AHHH!
AH!..
UNH!
AH!
AHH!
AIIEEEE!
AH...!!
AH...
UWAHH!

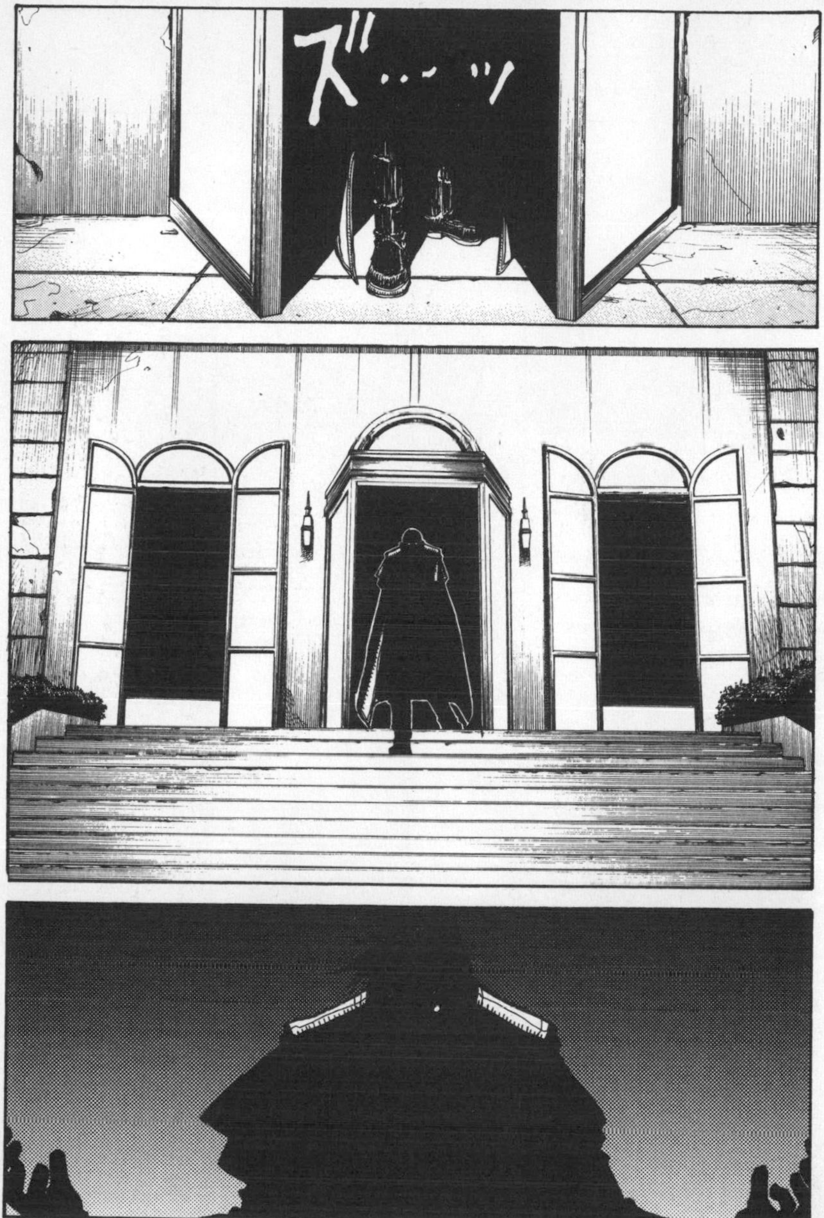
ズ‥ーッ

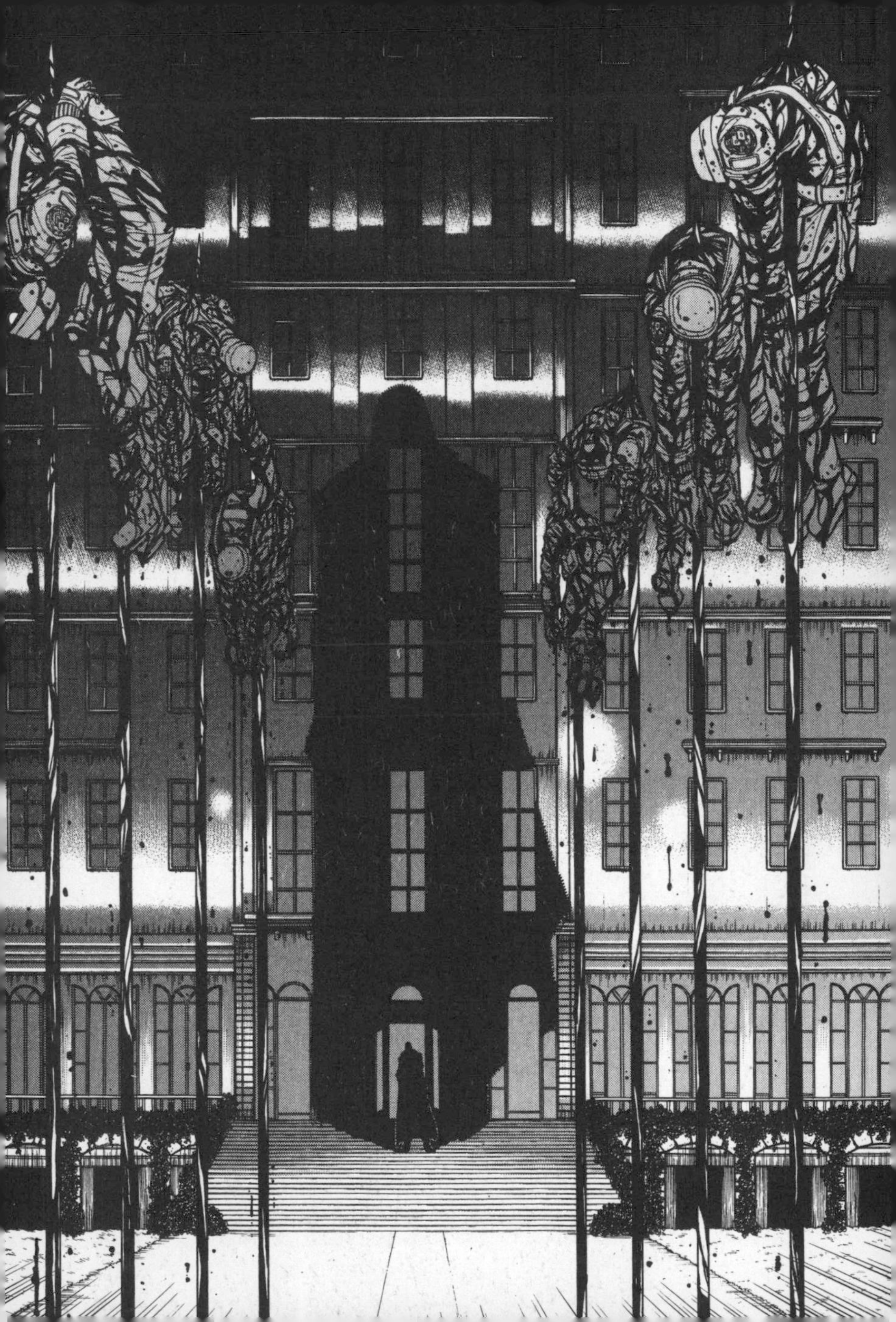

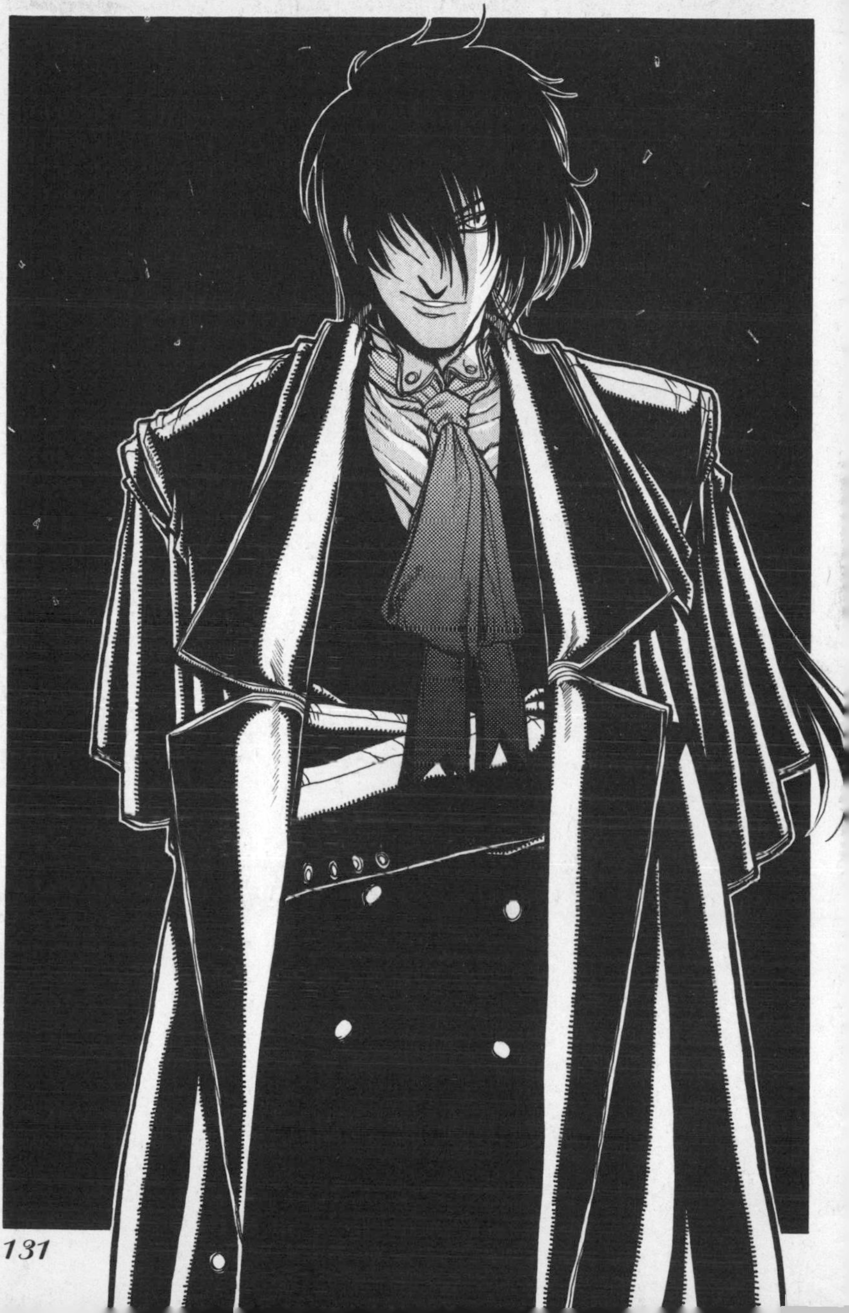

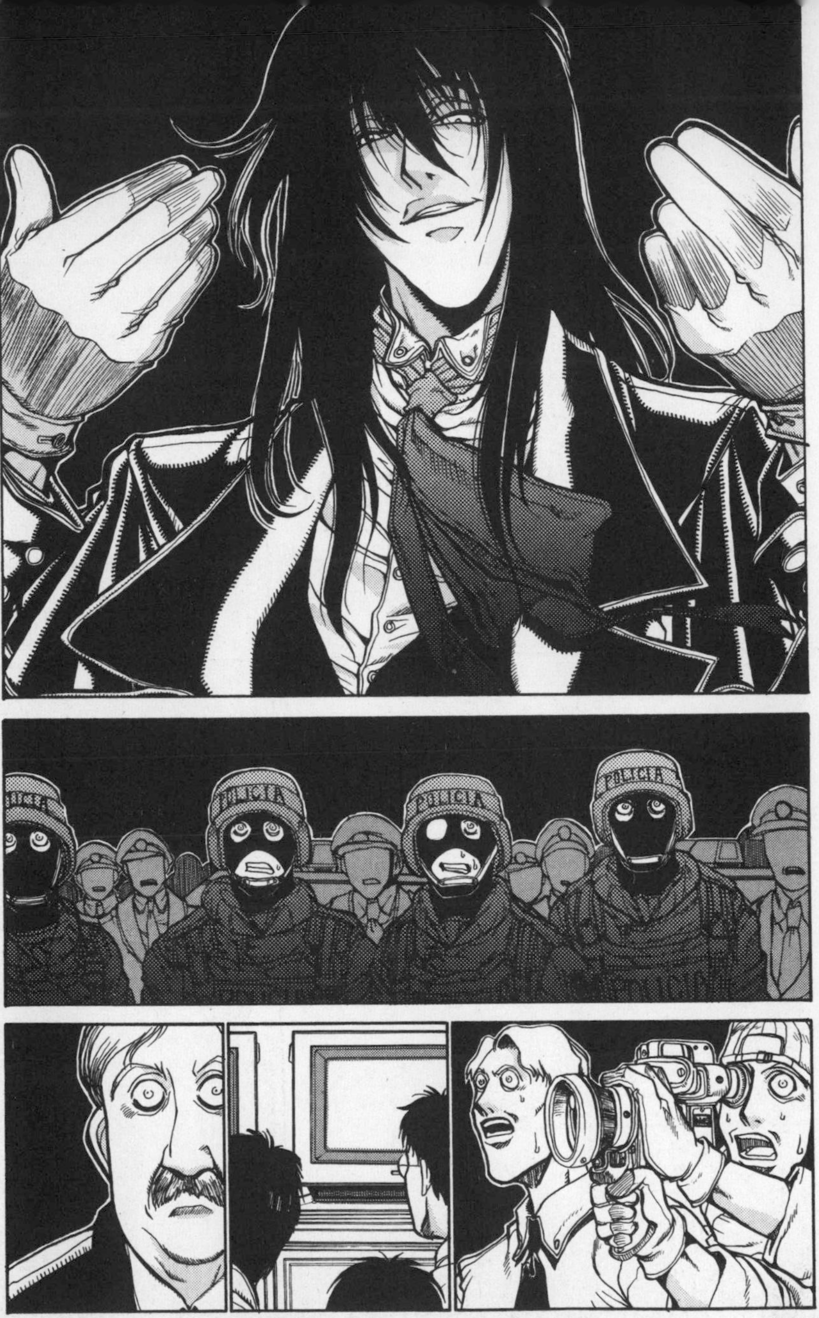
POLICIA
POLICIA
POLICIA

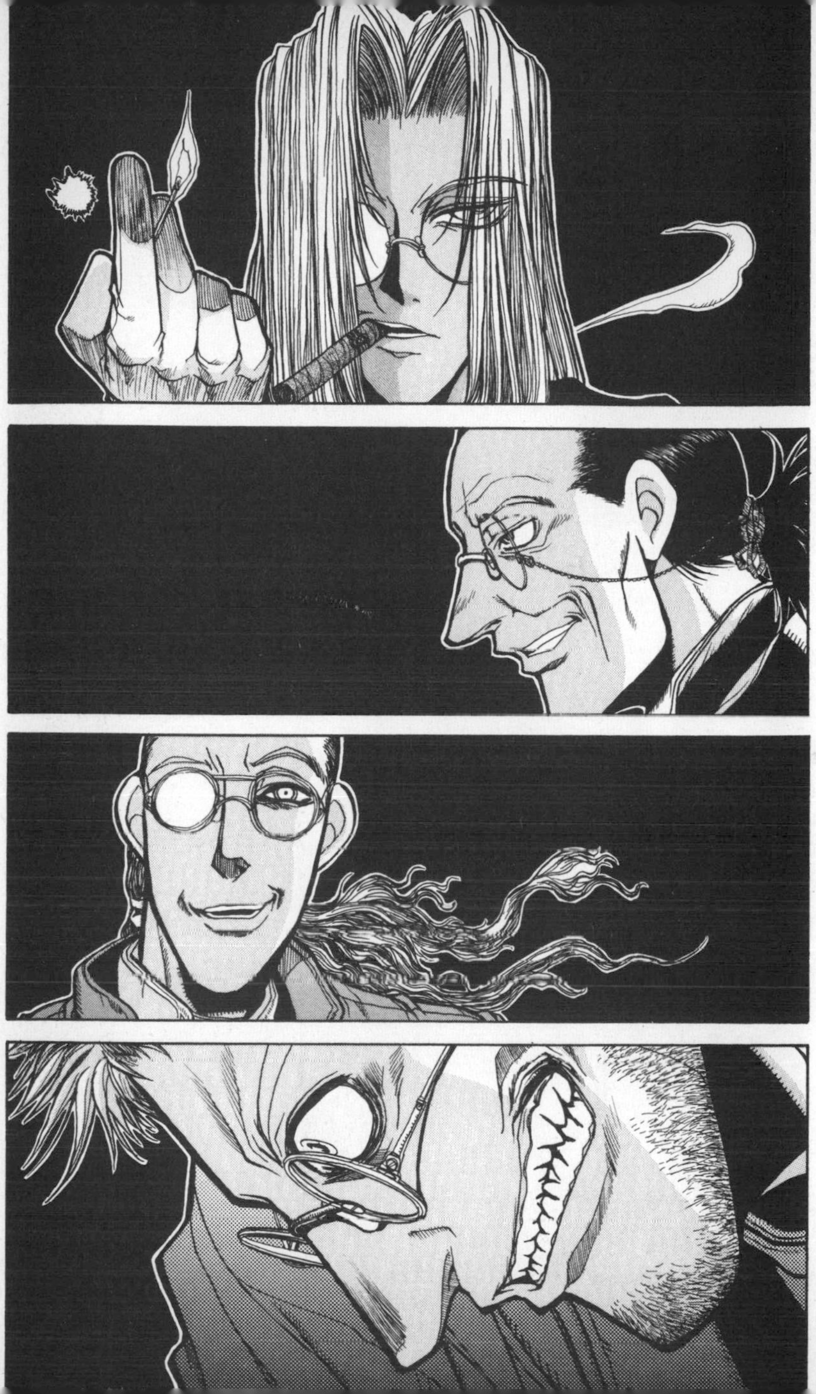

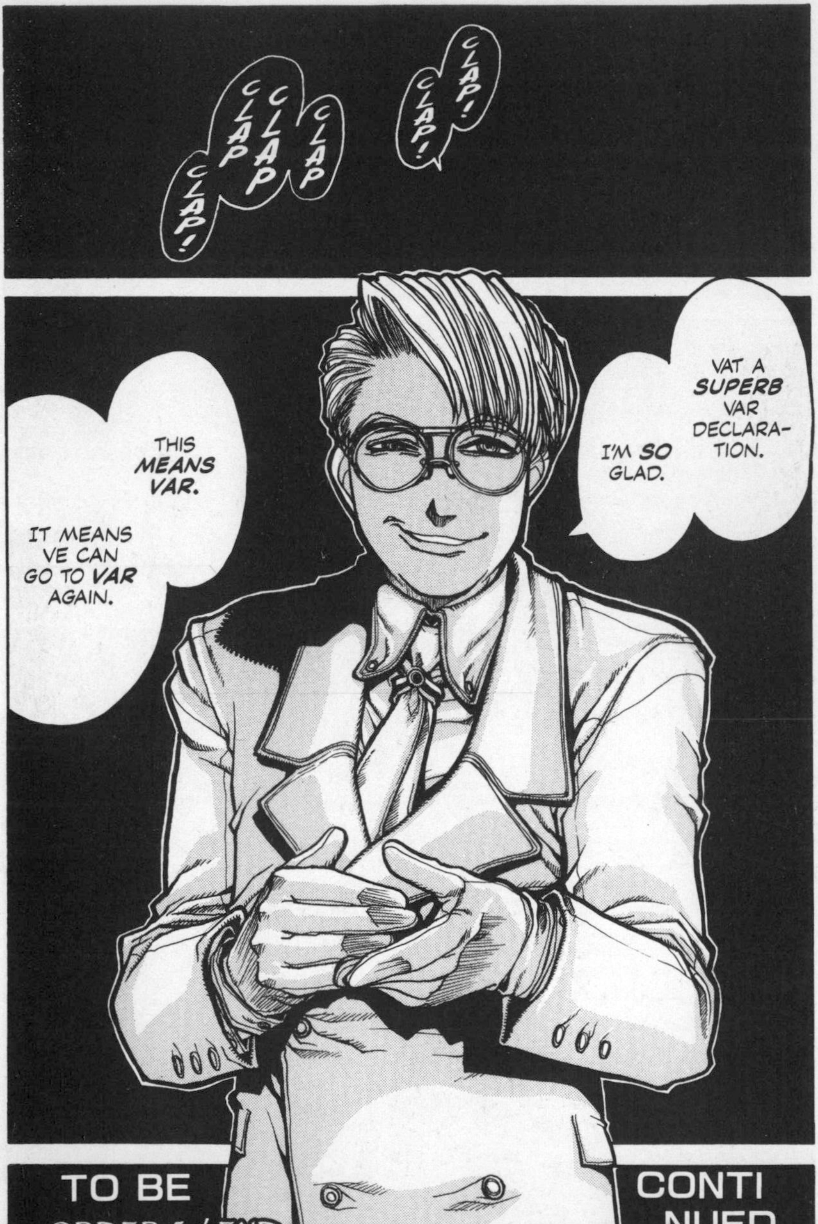
CLAP! CLAP!
CLAP
CLAP
CLAP
CLAP!
VAT A SUPERB VAR DECLARATION.
I'M SO GLAD.
THIS MEANS VAR.
IT MEANS VE CAN GO TO VAR AGAIN.
TO BE CONTI NUED
ORDER 5 / END

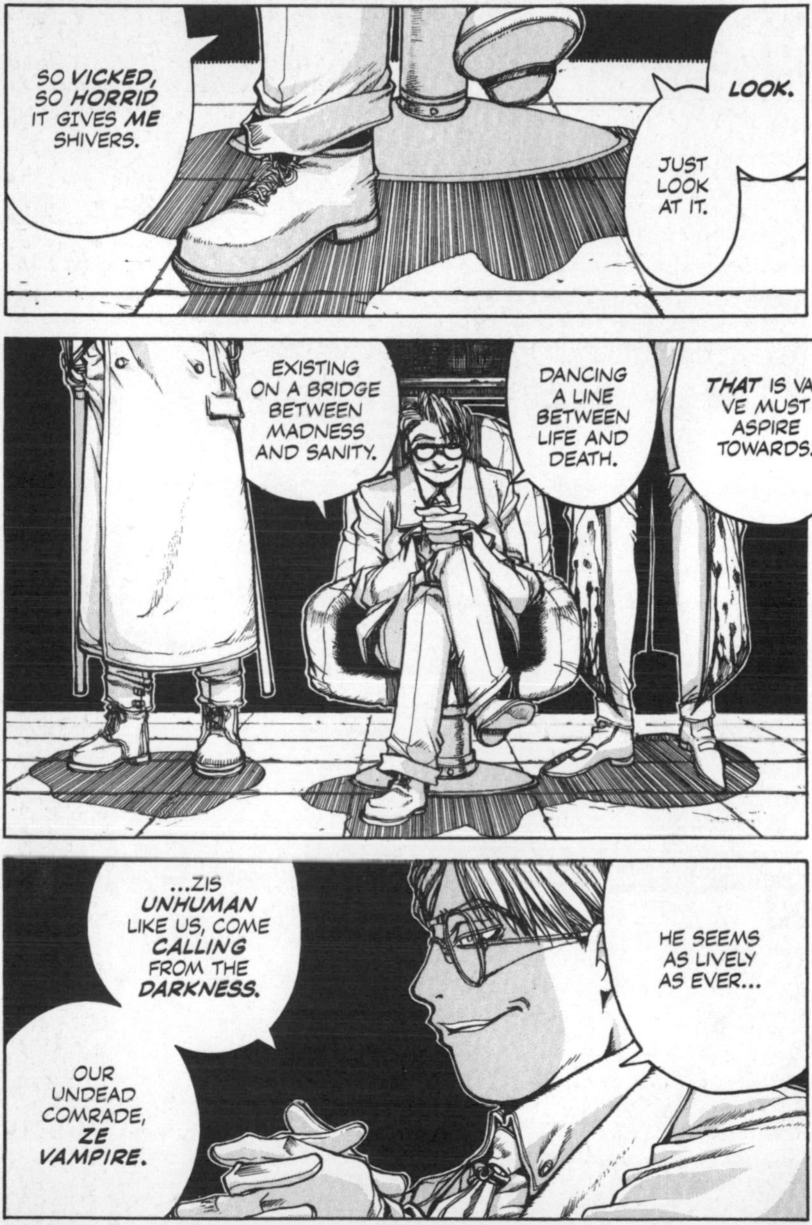
LOOK.
JUST LOOK AT IT.
SO VICKED, SO HORRID IT GIVES ME SHIVERS.
THAT IS VAT VE MUST ASPIRE TOWARDS.
DANCING A LINE BETWEEN LIFE AND DEATH.
EXISTING ON A BRIDGE BETWEEN MADNESS AND SANITY.
HE SEEMS AS LIVELY AS EVER...
...ZIS UNHUMAN LIKE US, COME CALLING FROM THE DARKNESS.
OUR UNDEAD COMRADE, ZE VAMPIRE.

ORDER 06

エレベーターアクション

ELEVATOR ACTION⑤

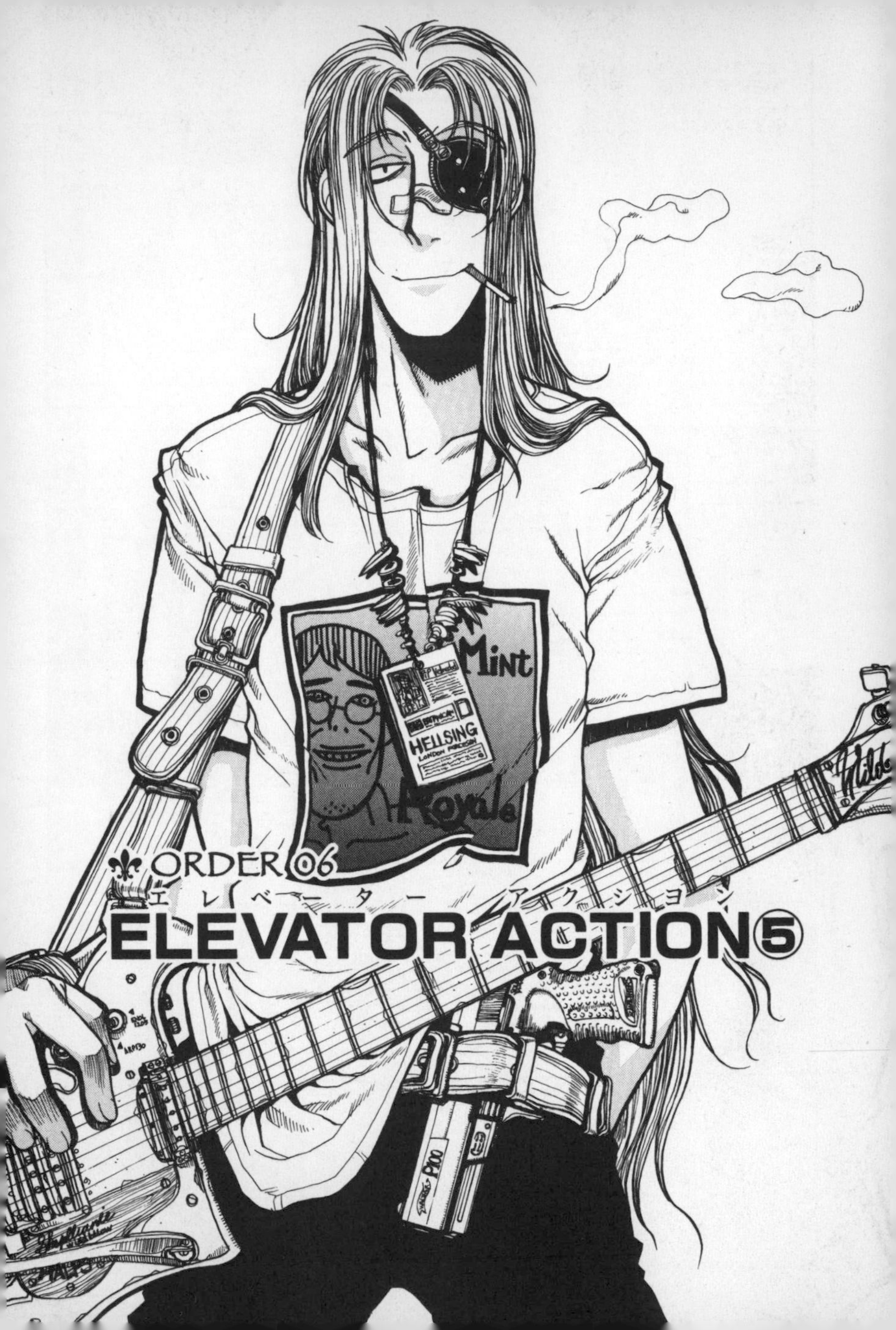
Mint
Royale
HELLSING
P100

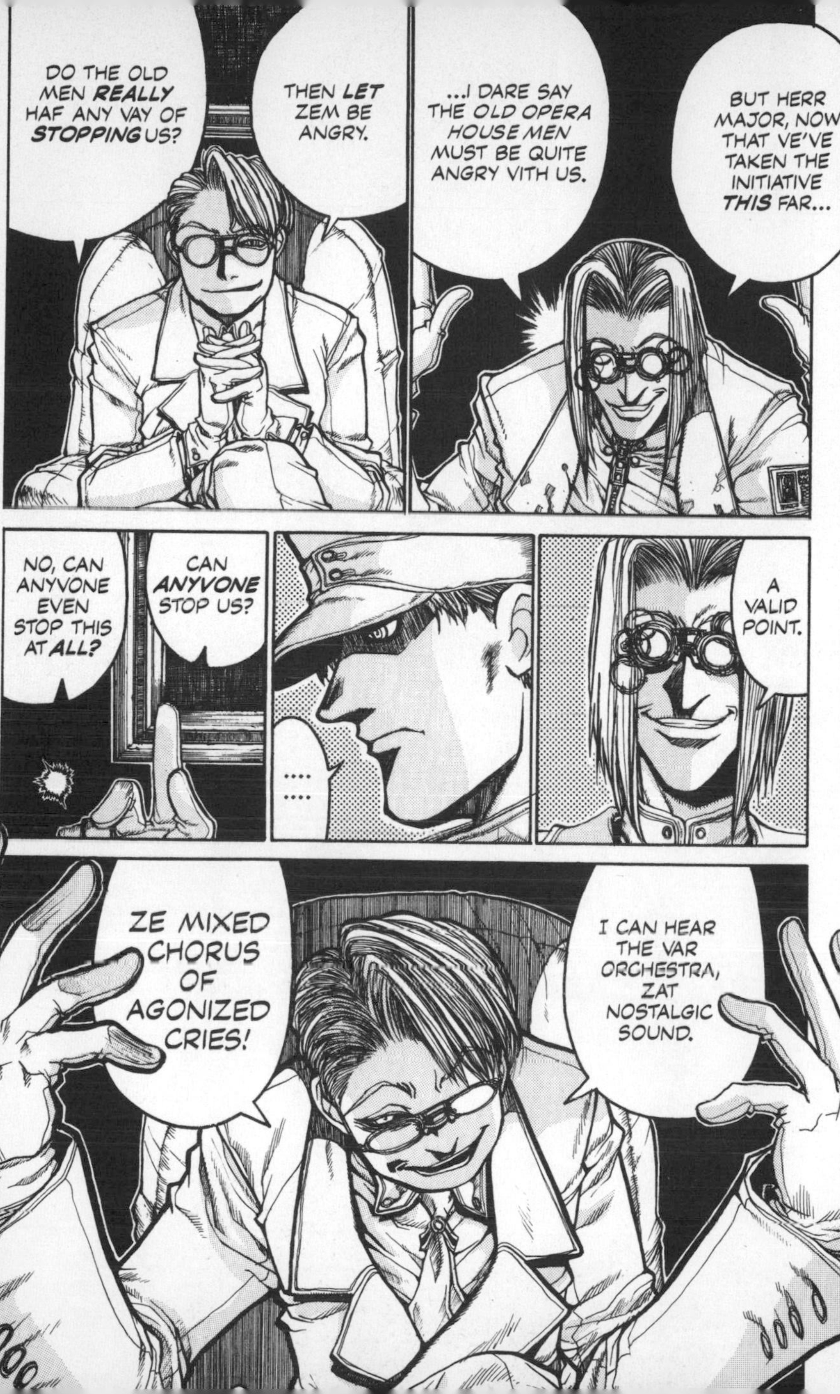
BUT HERR MAJOR, NOW THAT VE'VE TAKEN THE INITIATIVE THIS FAR...
...I DARE SAY THE OLD OPERA HOUSE MEN MUST BE QUITE ANGRY VITH US.
THEN LET ZEM BE ANGRY.
DO THE OLD MEN REALLY HAF ANY VAY OF STOPPING US?
A VALID POINT.
....
CAN ANYVONE STOP US?
NO, CAN ANYVONE EVEN STOP THIS AT ALL?
I CAN HEAR THE VAR ORCHESTRA, ZAT NOSTALGIC SOUND.
ZE MIXED CHORUS OF AGONIZED CRIES!

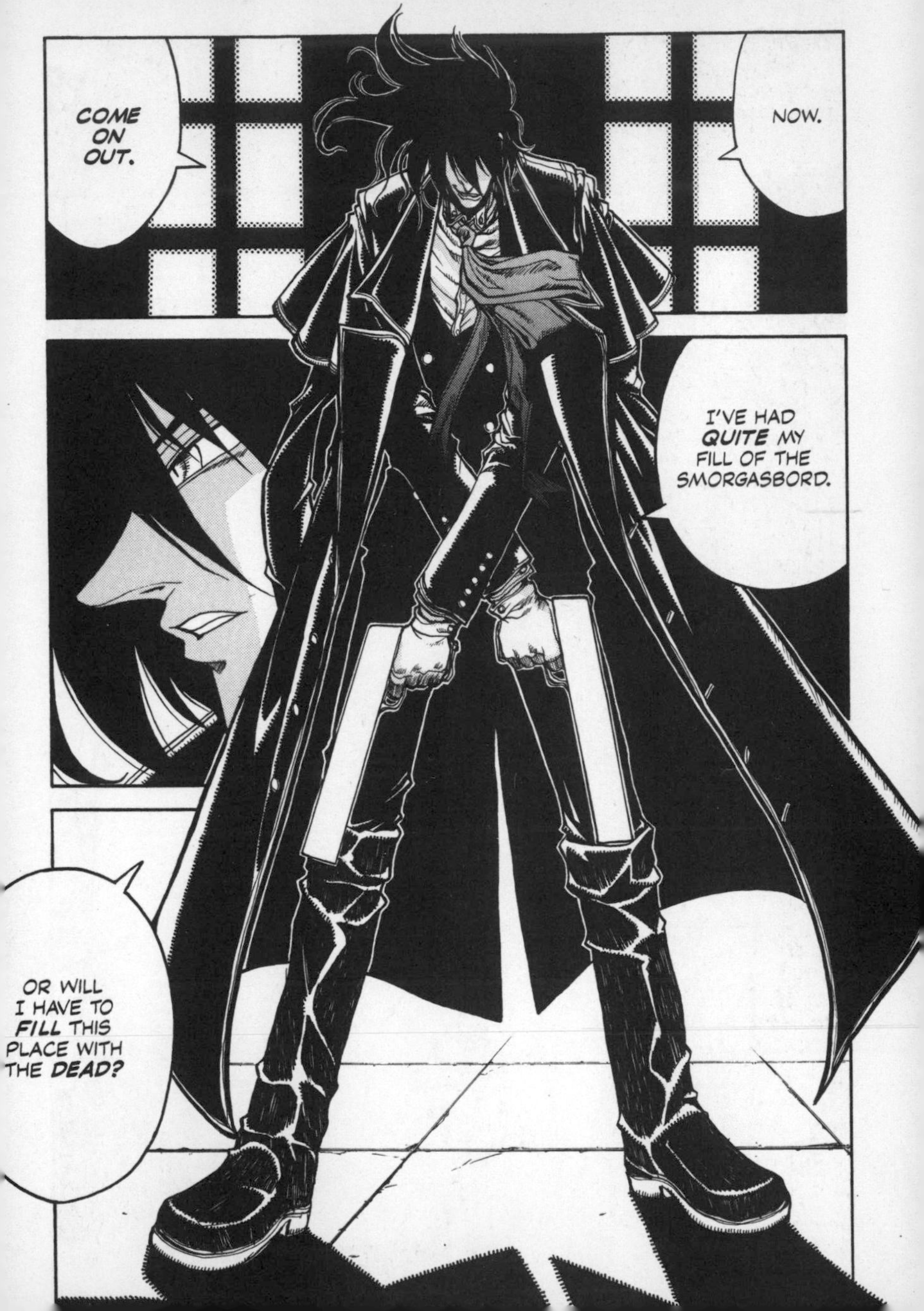
NOW.
COME ON OUT.
I'VE HAD QUITE MY FILL OF THE SMORGASBORD.
OR WILL I HAVE TO FILL THIS PLACE WITH THE DEAD?

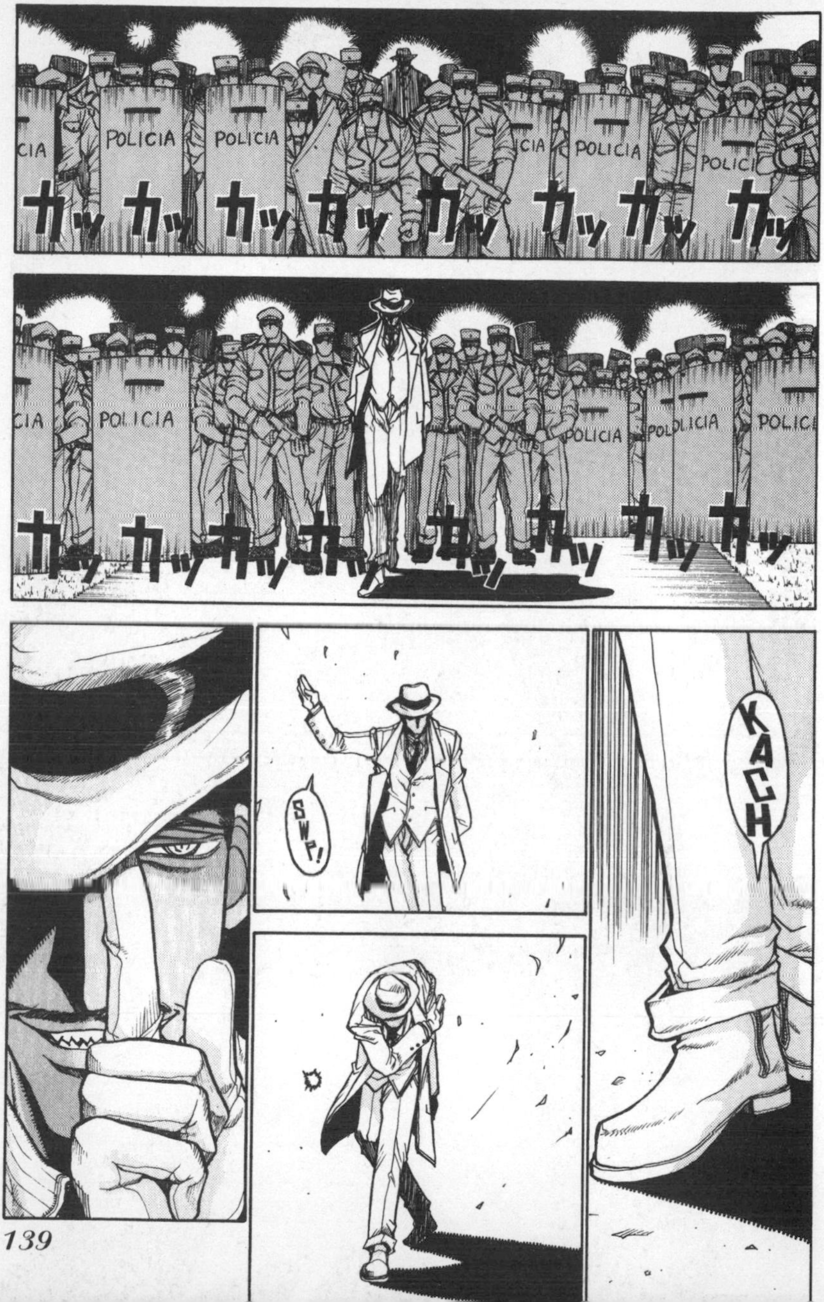
カッ
カッ
カッ
カッ
カッ
カッ
カッ
カッ
カッ
カッ
カッ
カッ
カッ
カッ
カッ
カッ
POLICIA
POLICIA
KACH
SWP!

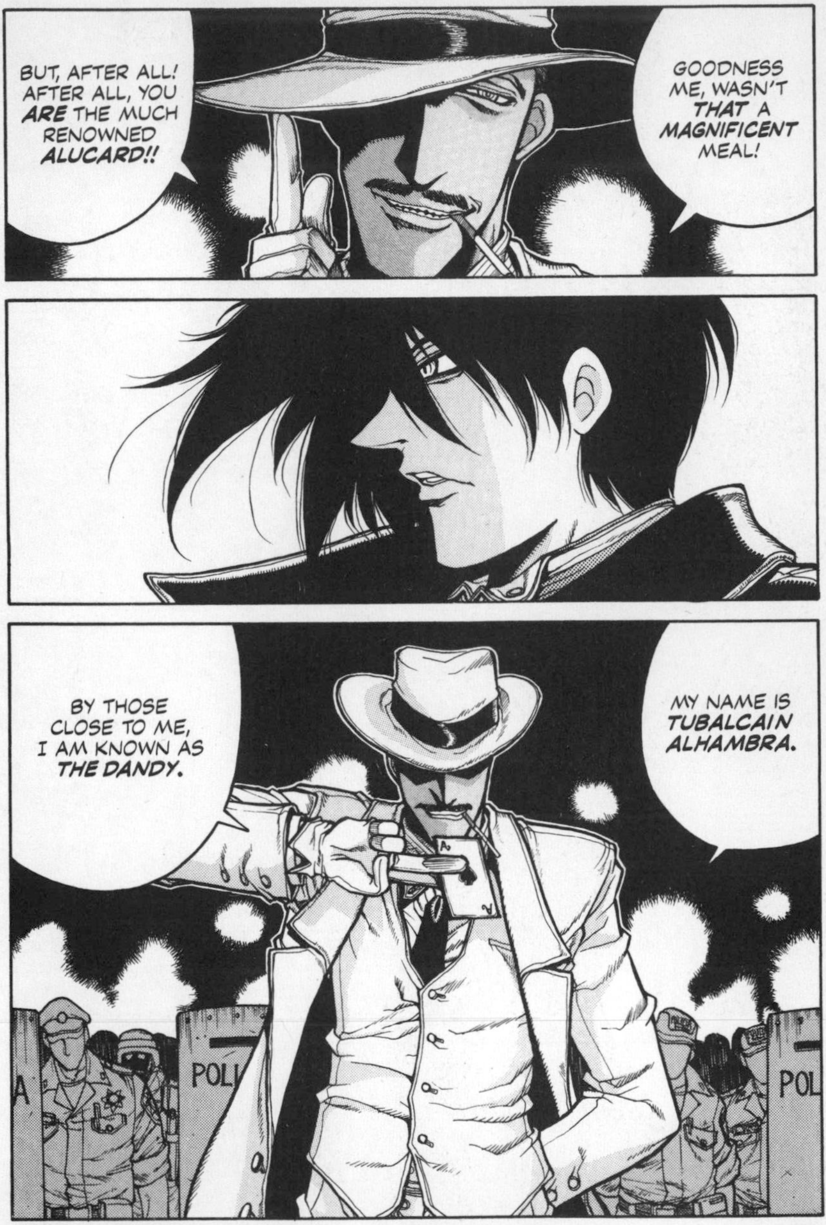
GOODNESS ME, WASN'T THAT A MAGNIFICENT MEAL!
BUT, AFTER ALL! AFTER ALL, YOU ARE THE MUCH RENOWNED ALUCARD!!
MY NAME IS TUBALCAIN ALHAMBRA.
BY THOSE CLOSE TO ME, I AM KNOWN AS THE DANDY.
POL
POLI

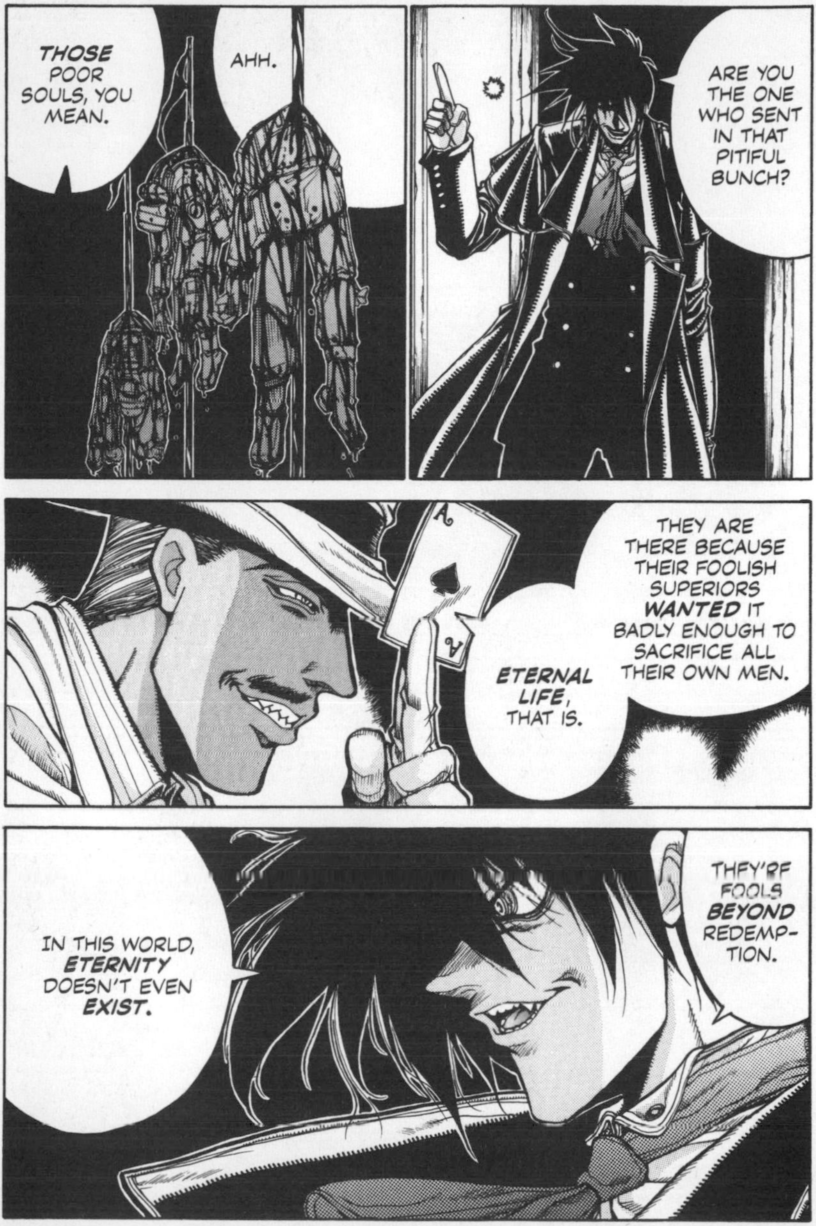
ARE YOU THE ONE WHO SENT IN THAT PITIFUL BUNCH?
AHH.
THOSE POOR SOULS, YOU MEAN.
THEY ARE THERE BECAUSE THEIR FOOLISH SUPERIORS *WANTED* IT BADLY ENOUGH TO SACRIFICE ALL THEIR OWN MEN.
ETERNAL LIFE, THAT IS.
THEY'RE FOOLS *BEYOND* REDEMPTION.
IN THIS WORLD, *ETERNITY* DOESN'T EVEN *EXIST*.

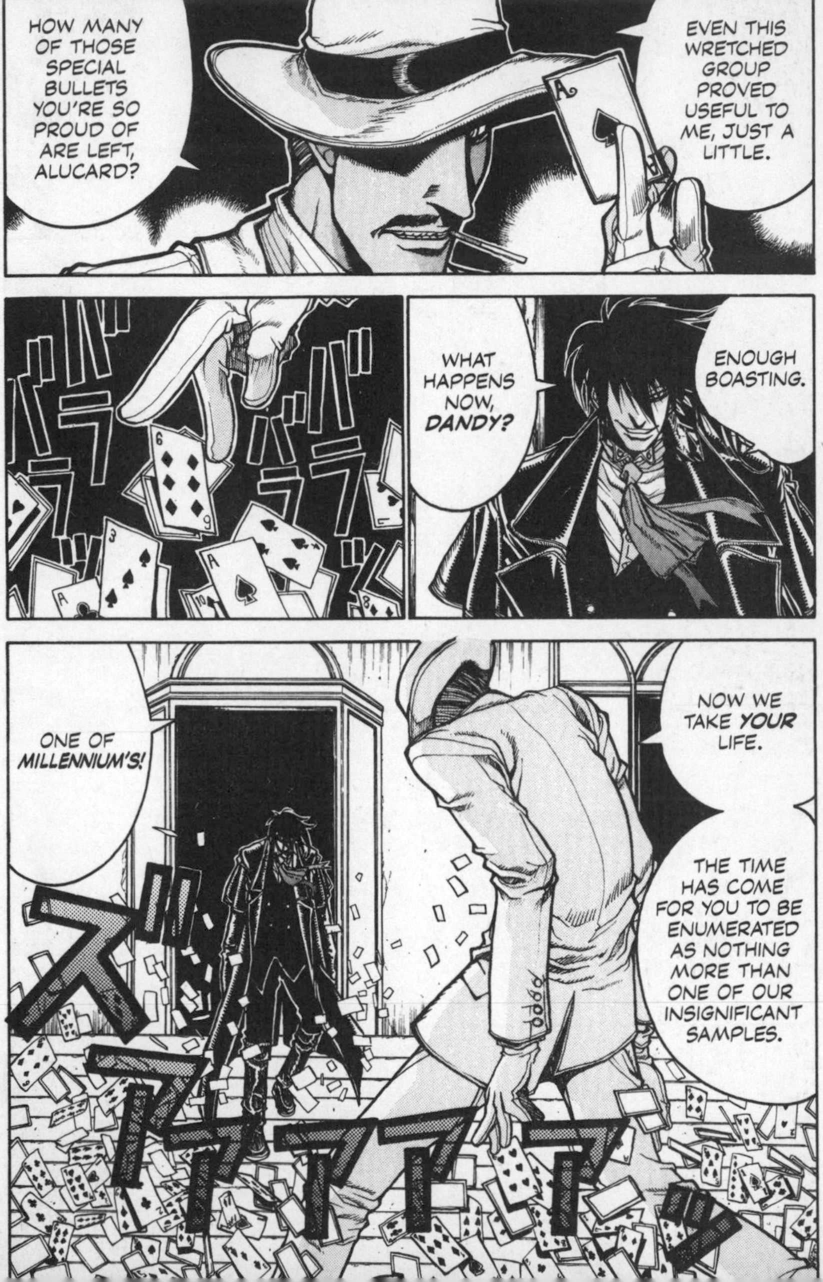
EVEN THIS WRETCHED GROUP PROVED USEFUL TO ME, JUST A LITTLE.
HOW MANY OF THOSE SPECIAL BULLETS YOU'RE SO PROUD OF ARE LEFT, ALUCARD?
ENOUGH BOASTING.
WHAT HAPPENS NOW, *DANDY?*
NOW WE TAKE *YOUR* LIFE.
THE TIME HAS COME FOR YOU TO BE ENUMERATED AS NOTHING MORE THAN ONE OF OUR INSIGNIFICANT SAMPLES.
ONE OF *MILLENNIUM'S!*

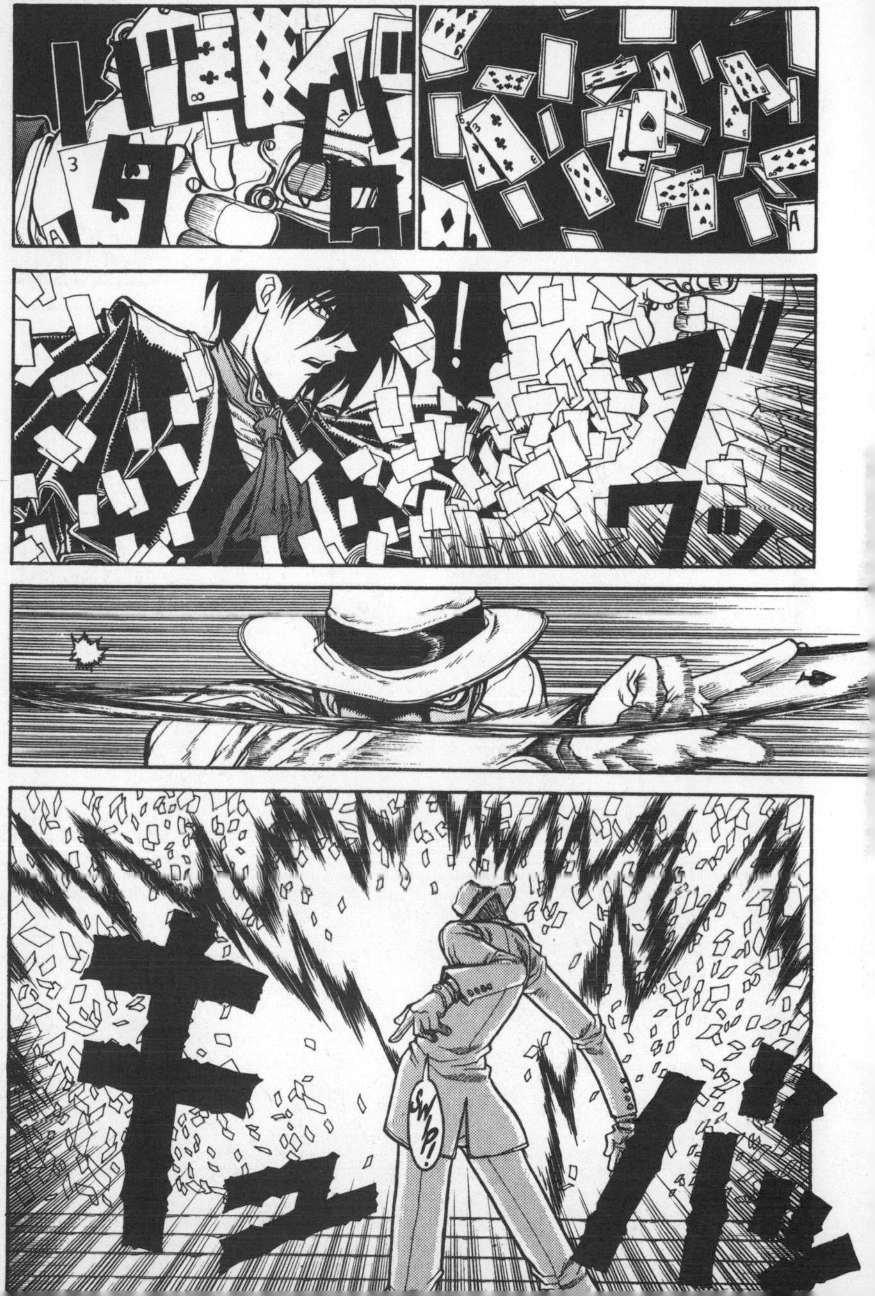
ブワッ
!
SWIP!

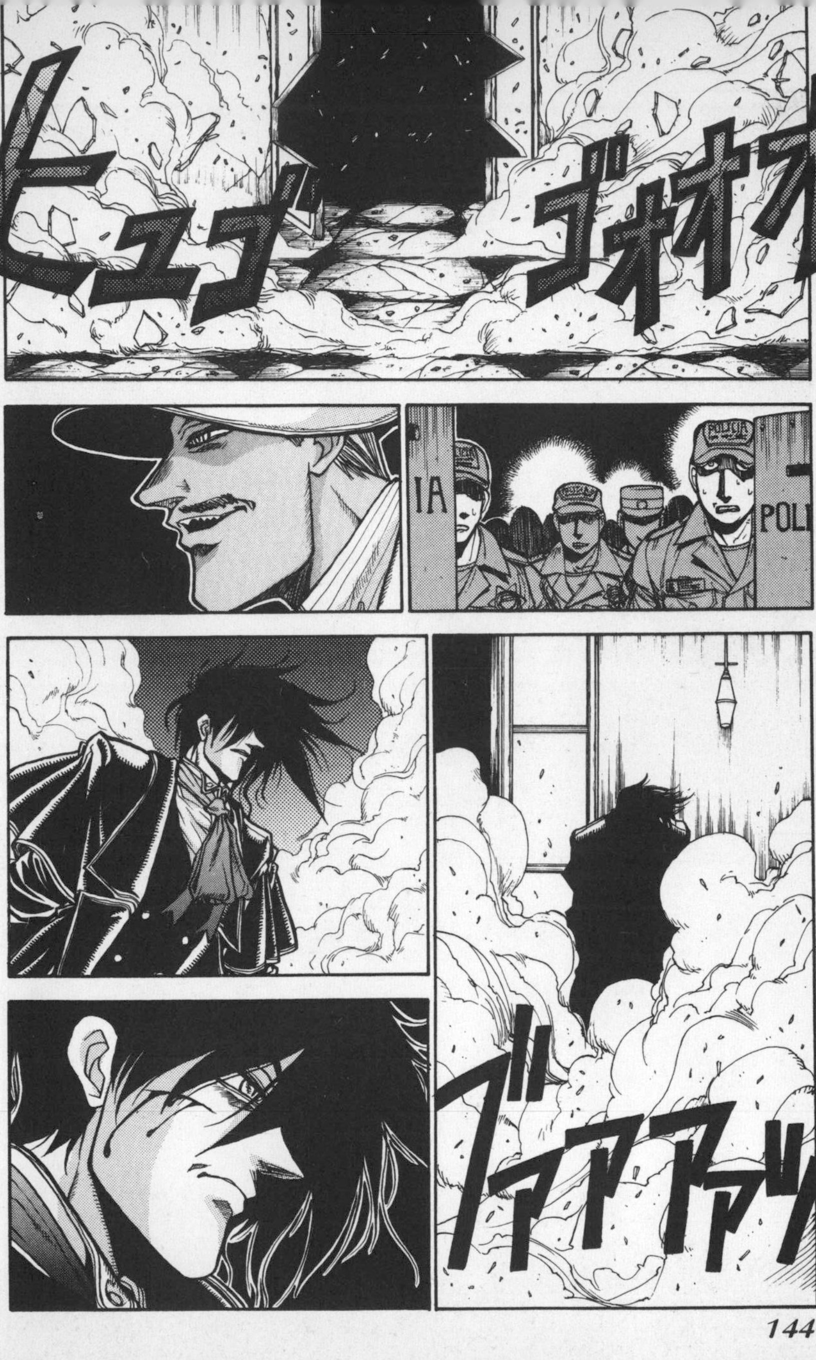
ヒュゴ
ゴオオオ
POLI
IA
ブァアアアッ

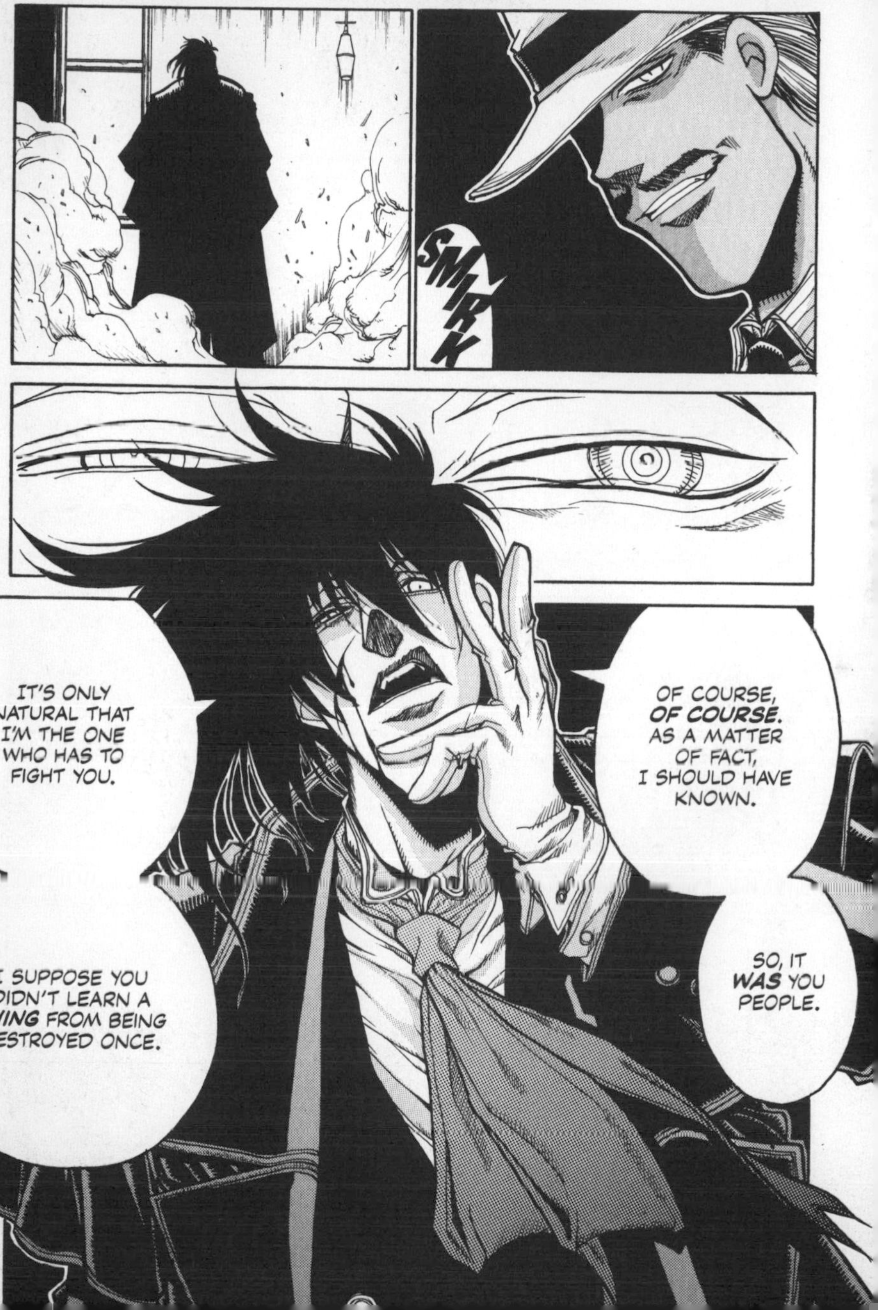
SMIRK
OF COURSE, *OF COURSE.* AS A MATTER OF FACT, I SHOULD HAVE KNOWN.
SO, IT **WAS** YOU PEOPLE.
IT'S ONLY NATURAL THAT I'M THE ONE WHO HAS TO FIGHT YOU.
I SUPPOSE YOU DIDN'T LEARN A ***THING*** FROM BEING DESTROYED ONCE.

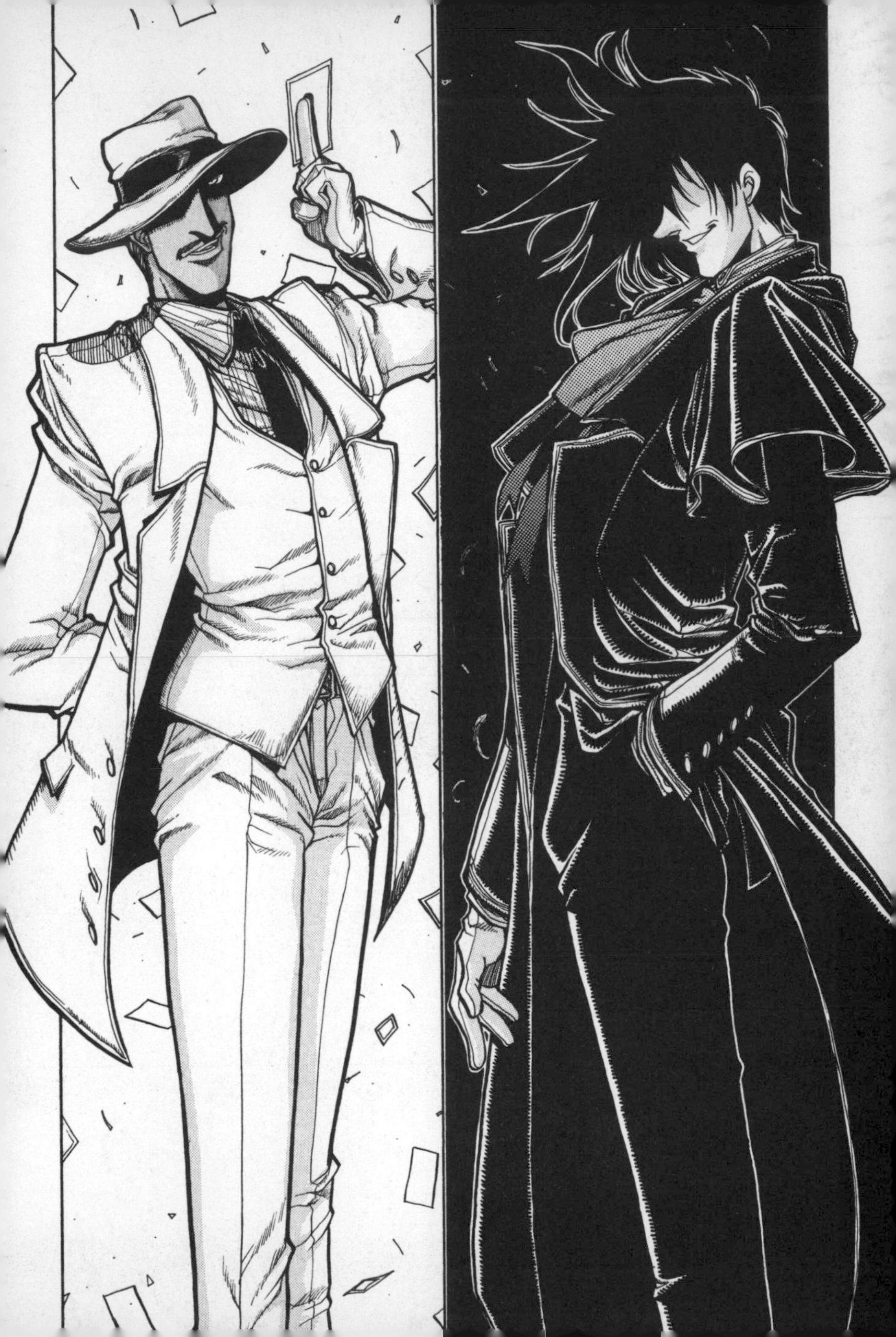

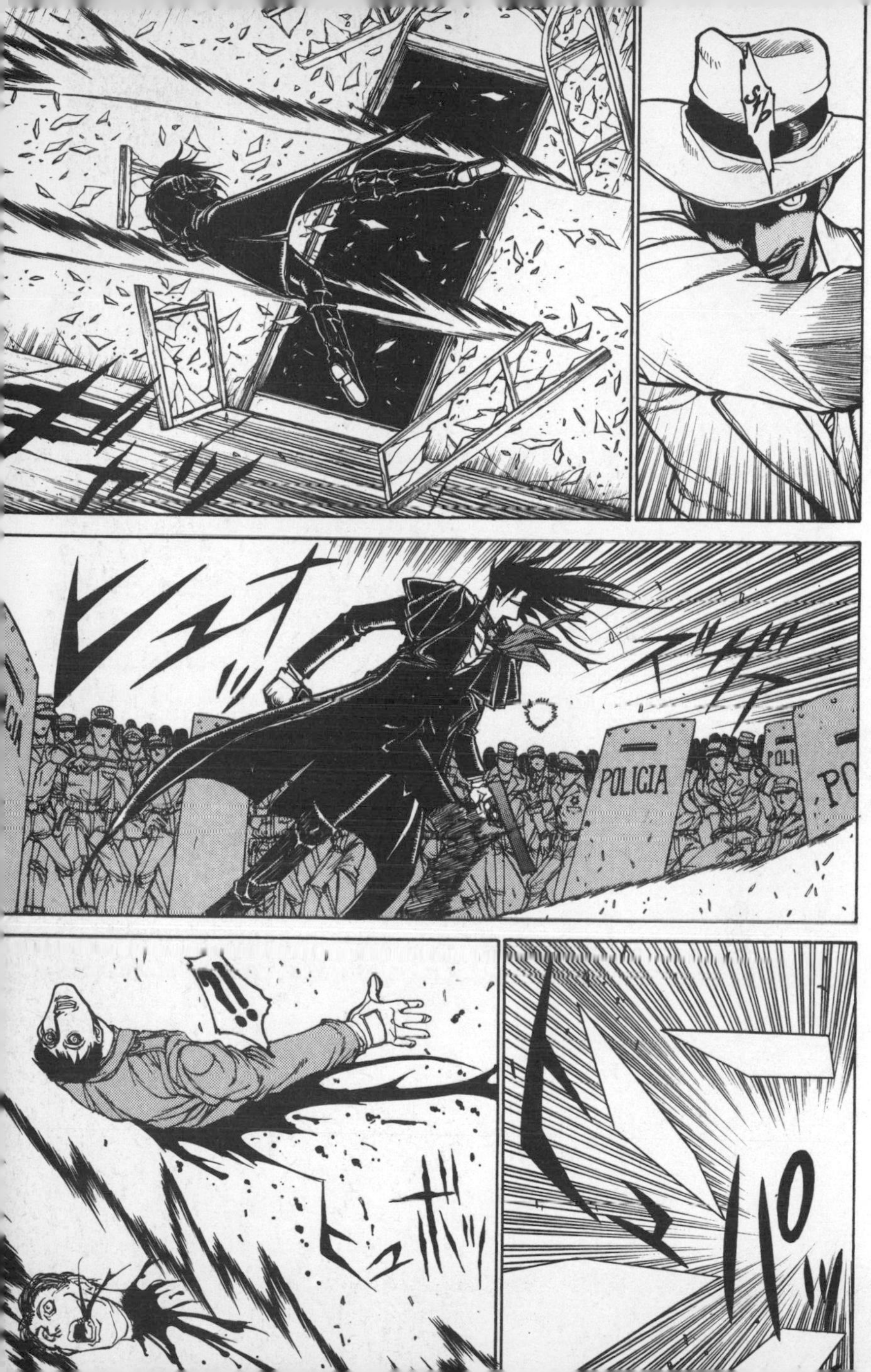
POLICIA

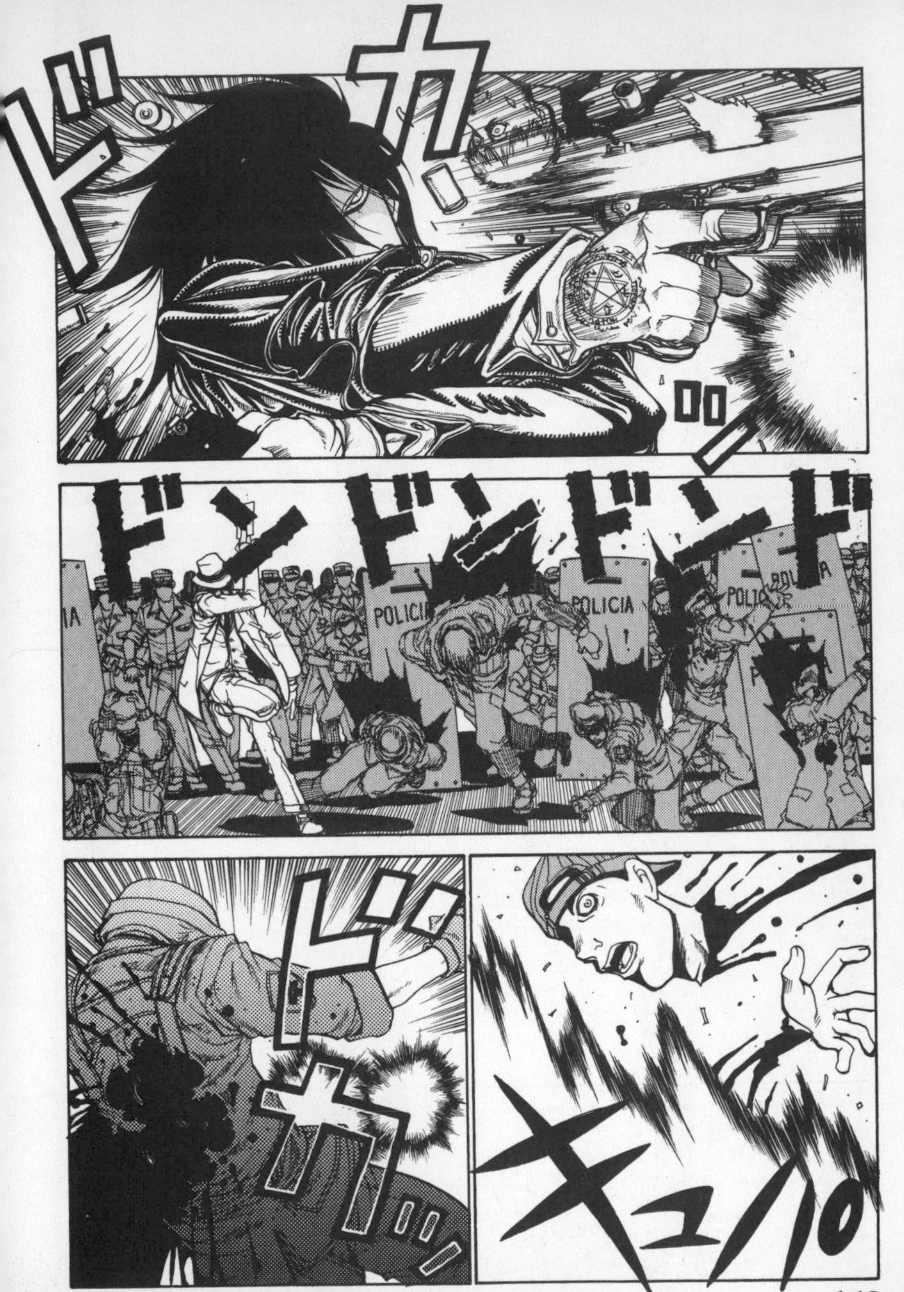
ドカ
ドンドンドンド
POLICIA
キュパ
ドガ

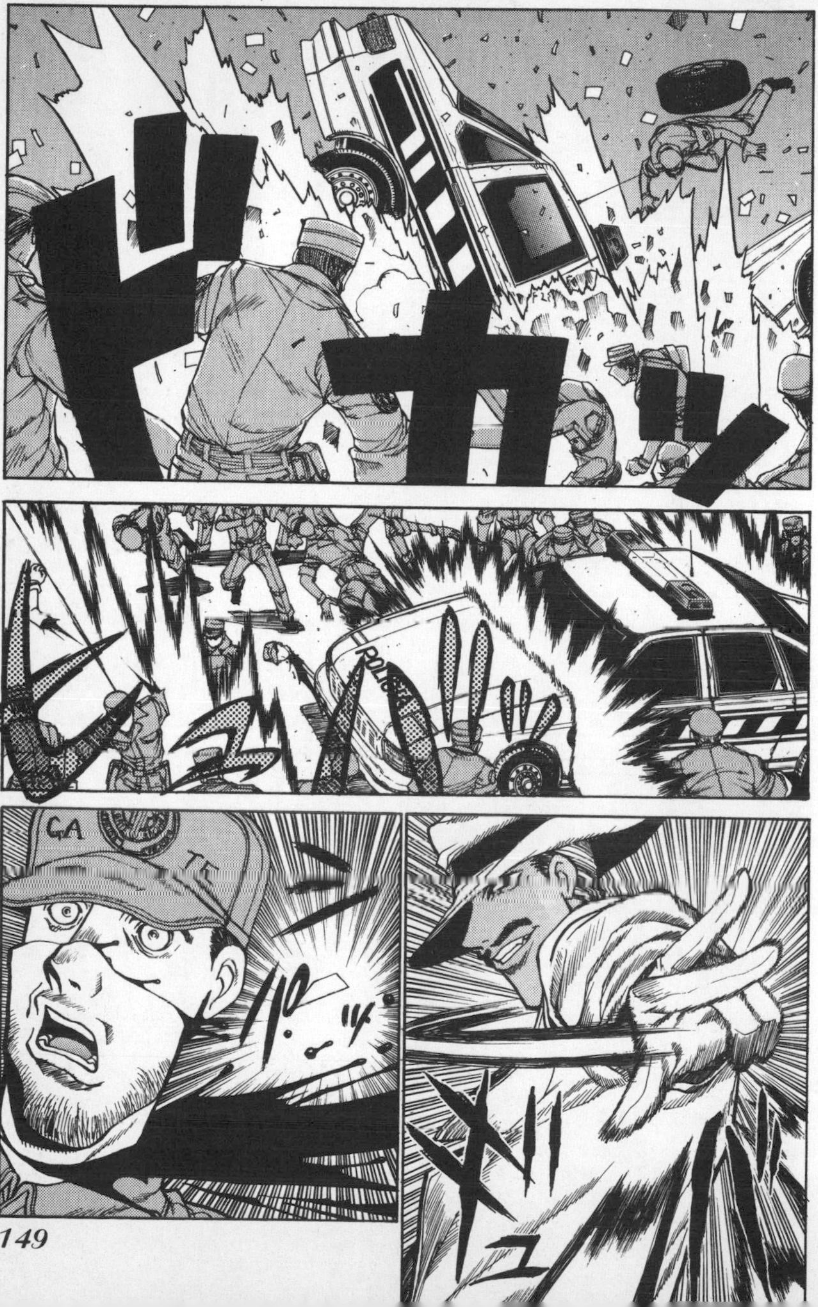
ドカッ

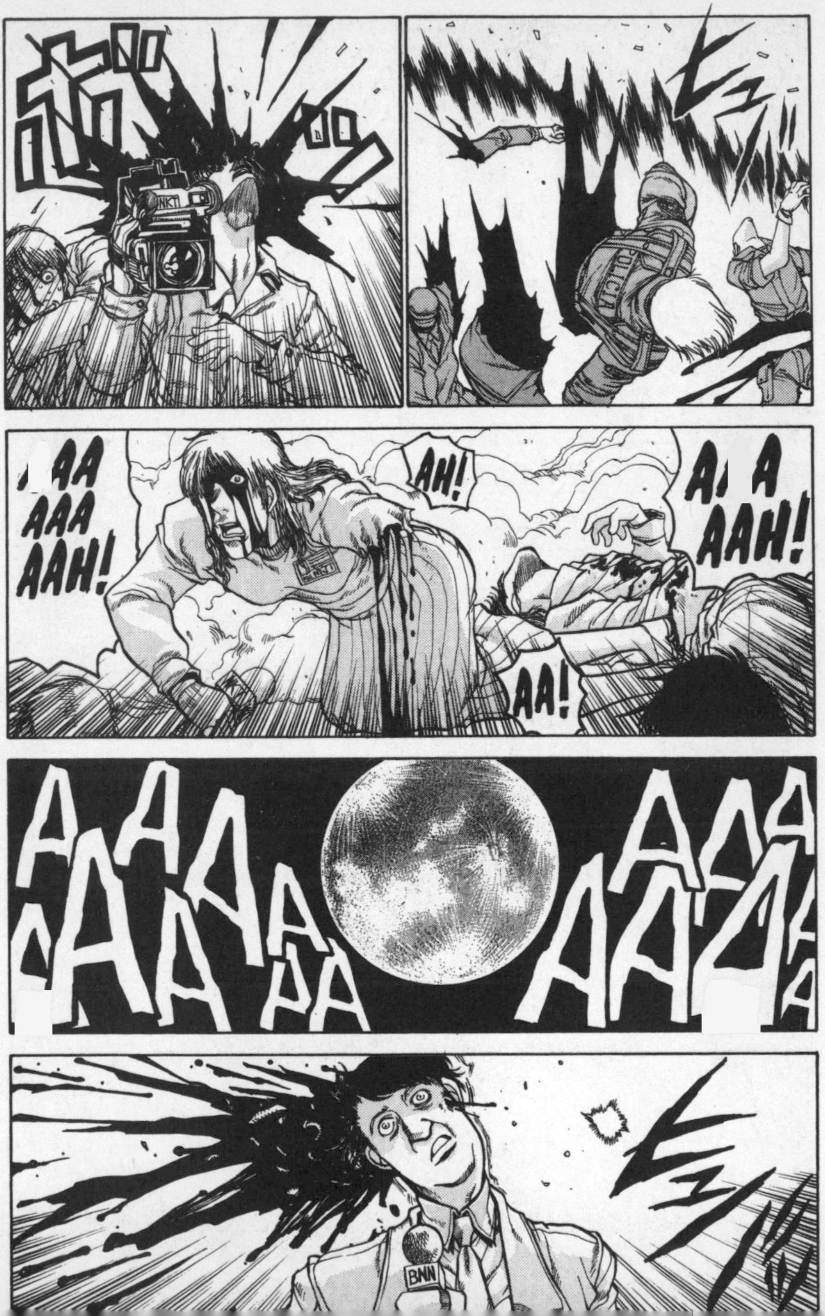
A A
AAH!
AA!
AH!
AA
AAA
AAH!

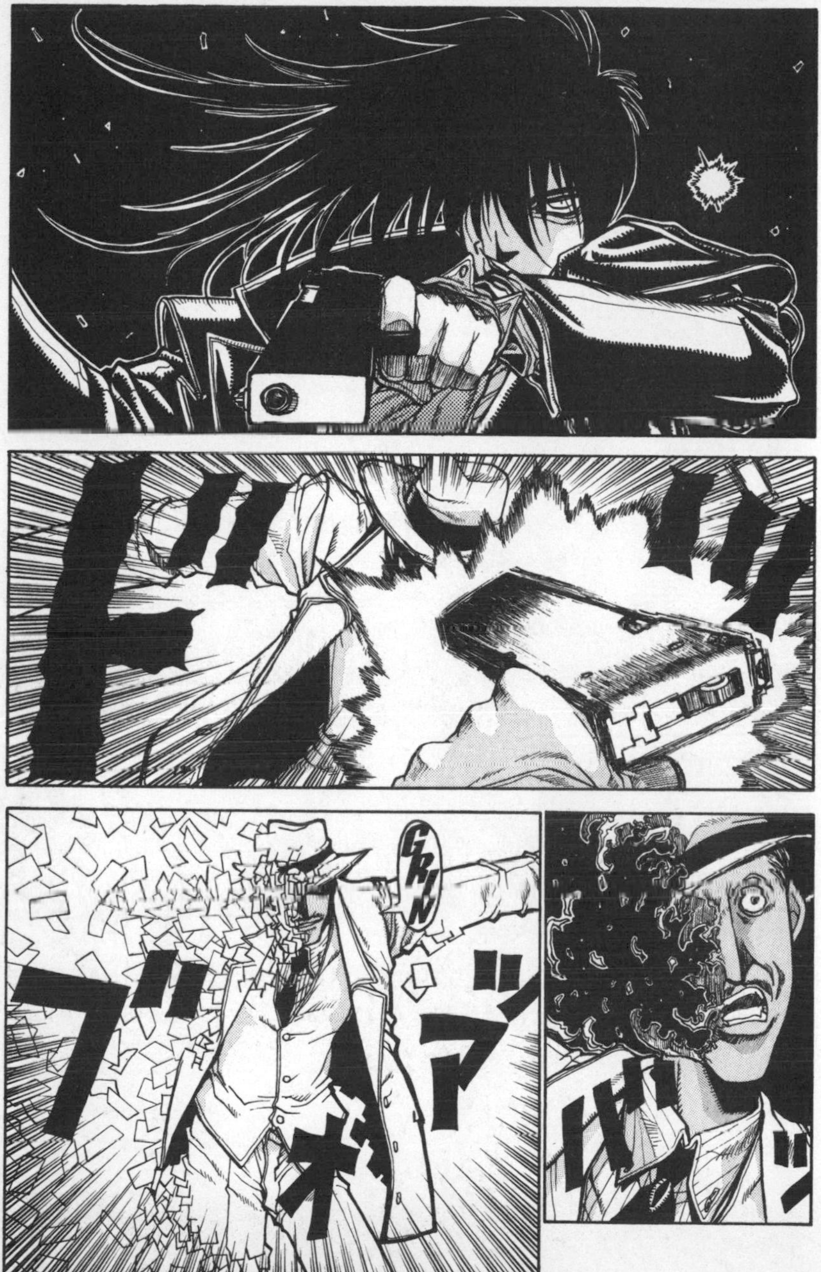
GRIN

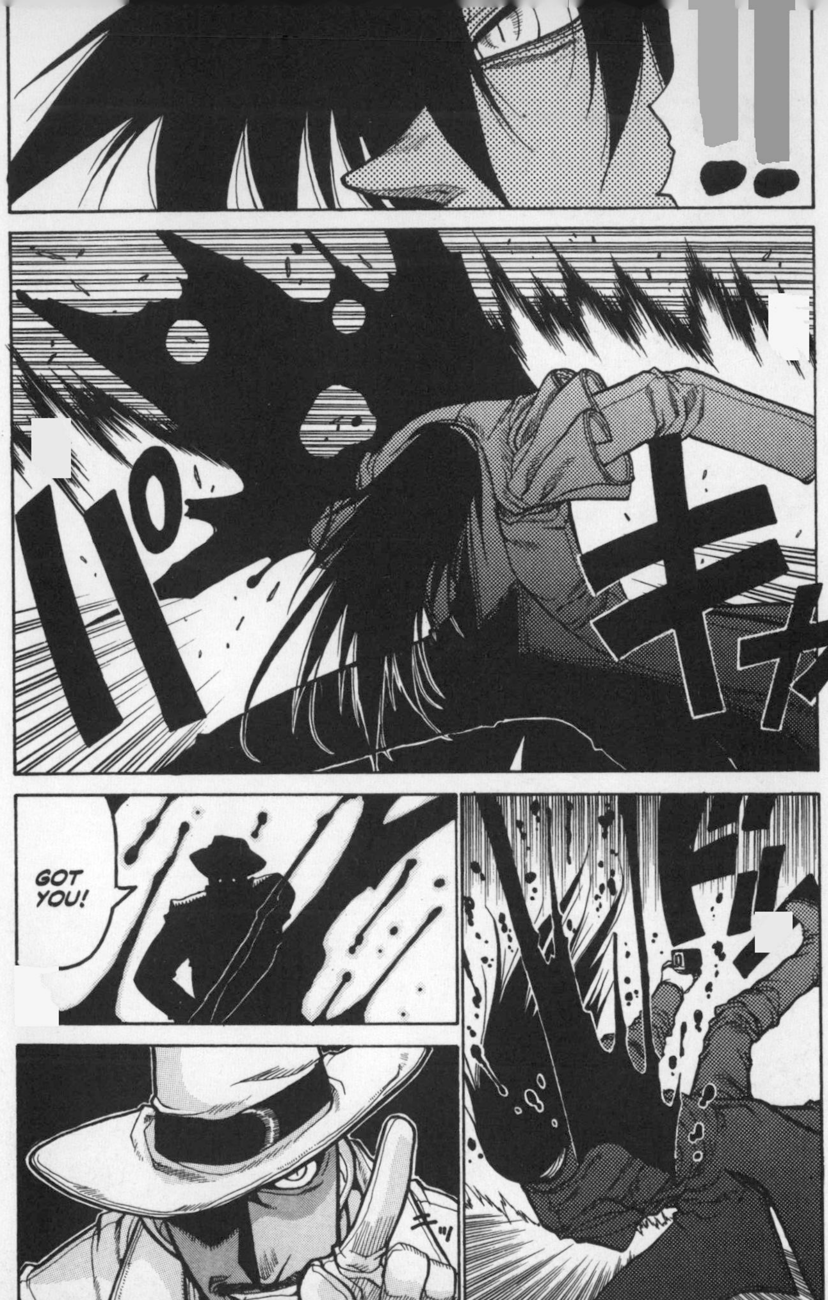
GOT YOU!

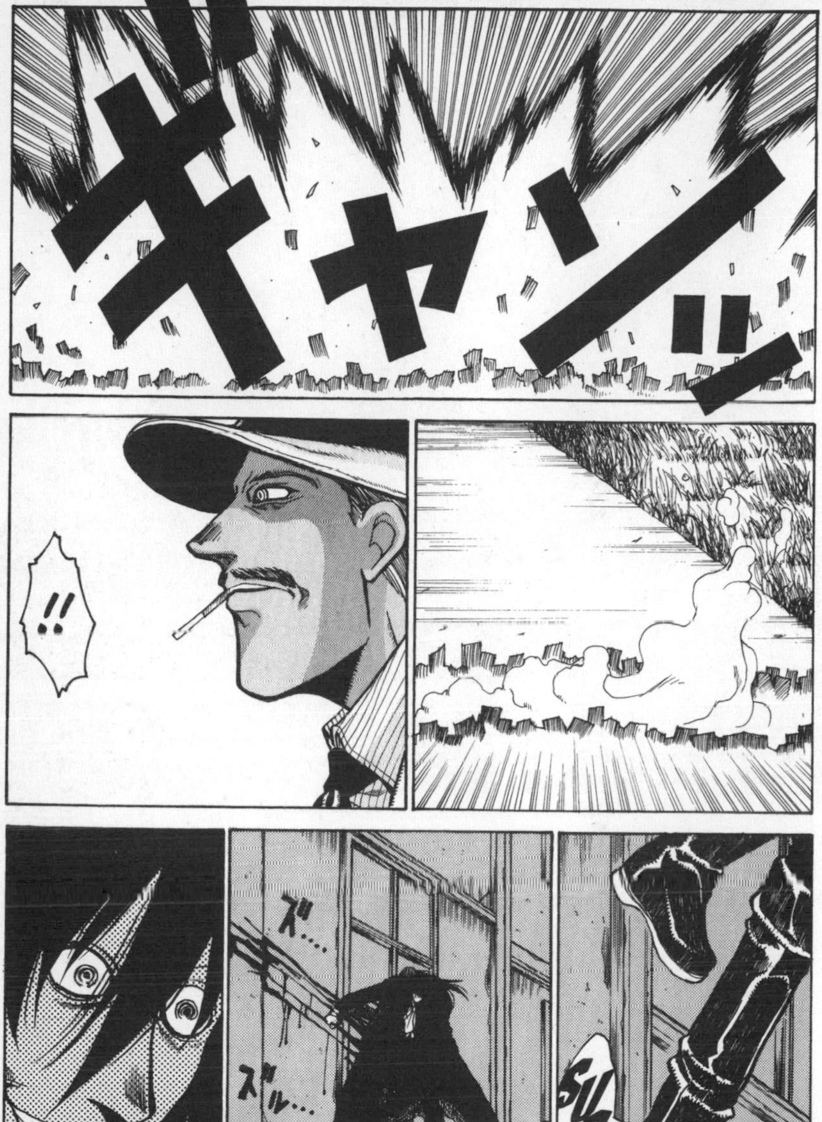
ギャンッ
!!
SUSAA
ズ…
ズル…

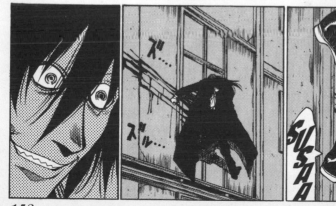

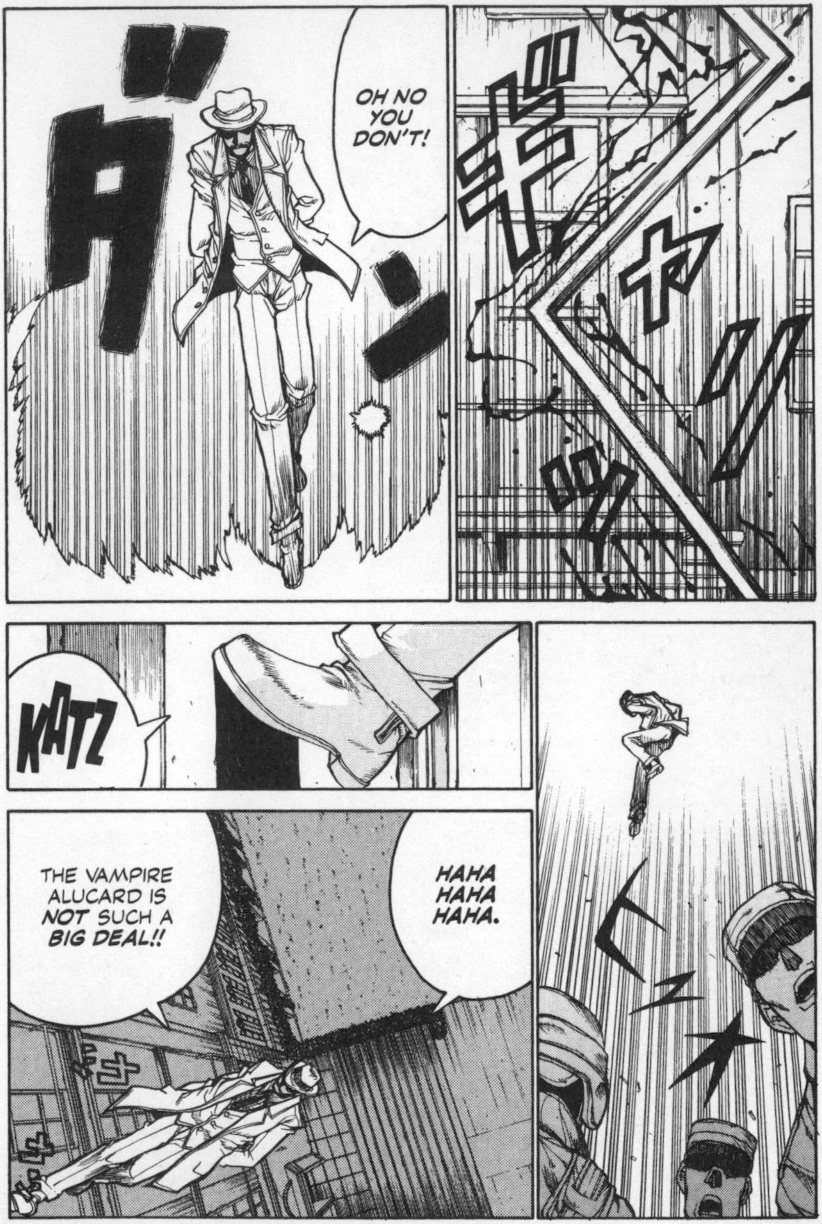
OH NO YOU DON'T!
ダン
KATZ
HAHA HAHA HAHA.
THE VAMPIRE ALUCARD IS NOT SUCH A BIG DEAL!!

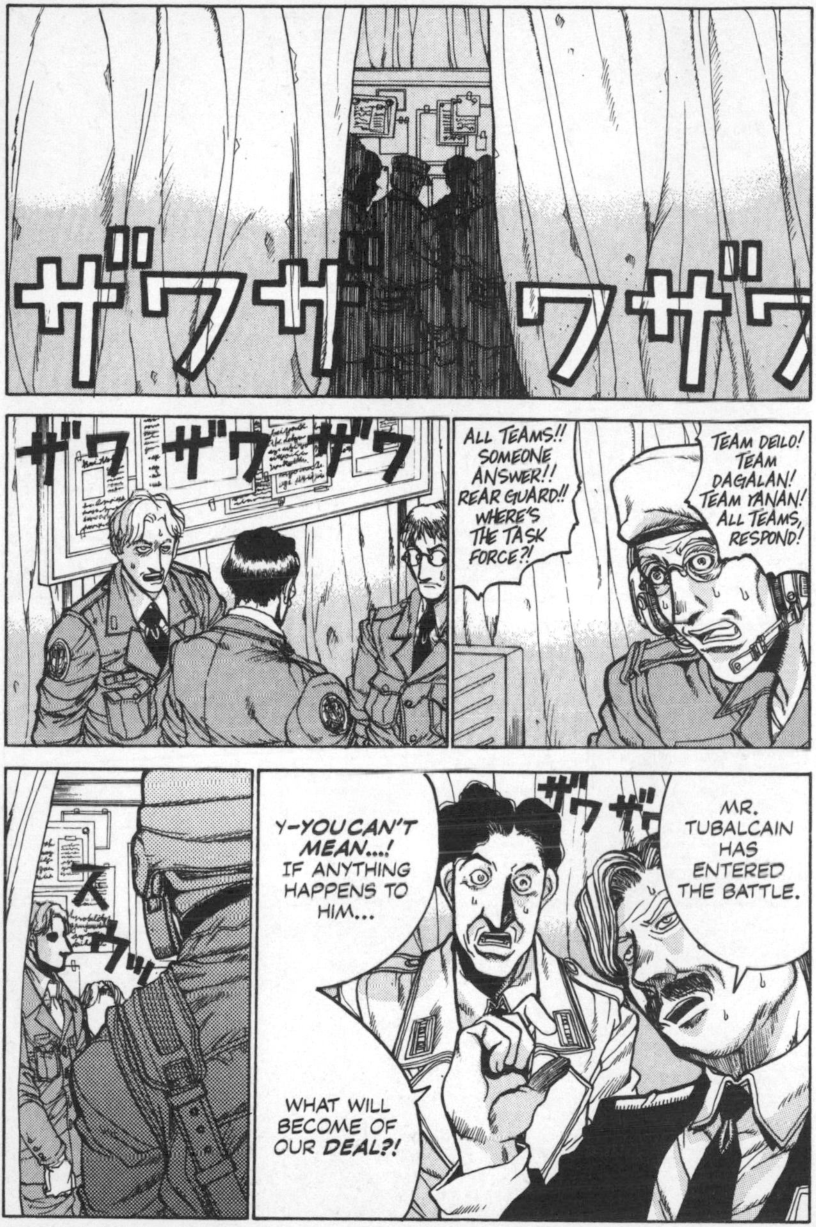
ザワザワザワ
TEAM DEILO! TEAM DAGALAN! TEAM YANAN! ALL TEAMS, RESPOND!
ALL TEAMS!! SOMEONE ANSWER!! REAR GUARD!! WHERE'S THE TASK FORCE?!
ザワザワザワ
MR. TUBALCAIN HAS ENTERED THE BATTLE.
ザワザワ
Y-*YOU CAN'T MEAN*...! IF ANYTHING HAPPENS TO HIM...
WHAT WILL BECOME OF OUR *DEAL?!*
スウッ

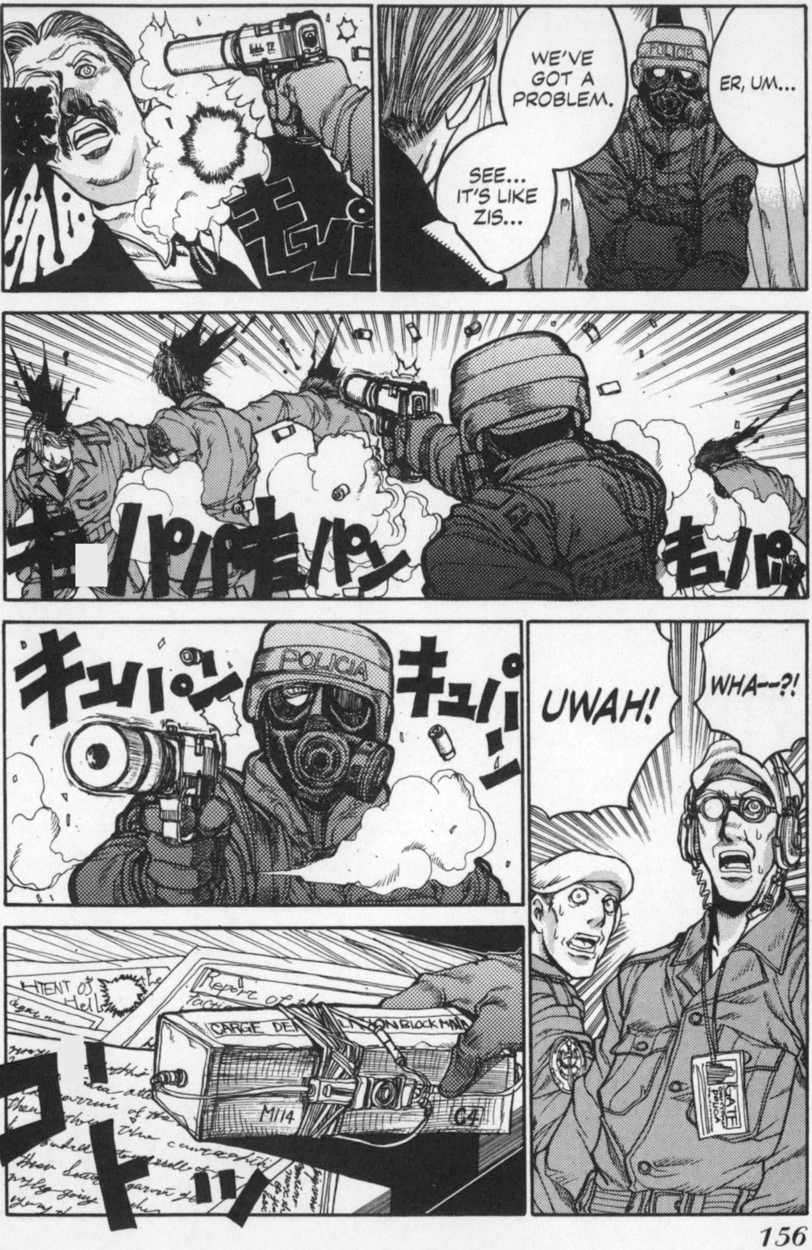
ER, UM...
WE'VE GOT A PROBLEM.
SEE... IT'S LIKE ZIS...
WHA--?!
UWAH!
POLICIA
M114
C4

カッ カッ
WHAT THE HELL'S GOING ON?!
POLICIA
AREN'T REINFORCEMENTS HERE YET?! THE GUY'S A MONSTER!
カッ カッ
WE'VE LOST CONTACT WITH TEAM DEILO!
WE CAN'T DO THIS!
ザッザッ
ザッザッ
HALT
ザッ ザッザッ
ドッ

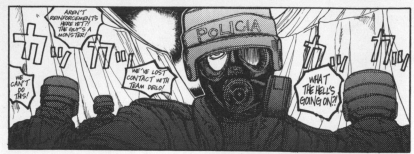

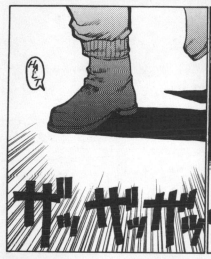

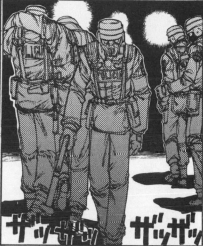

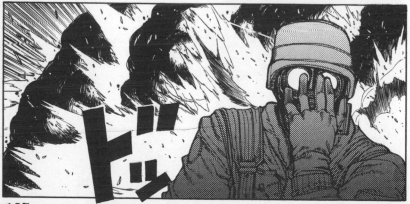

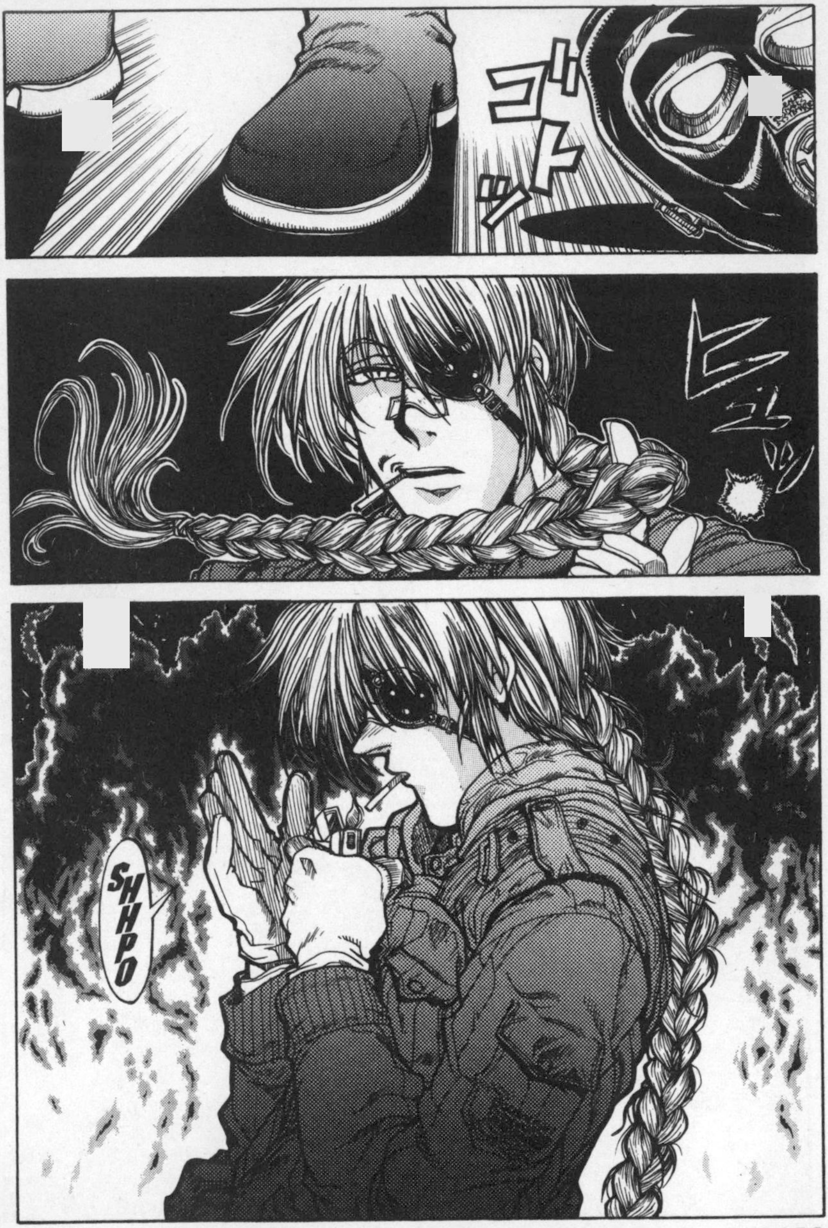
ゴトッ
SHHPO

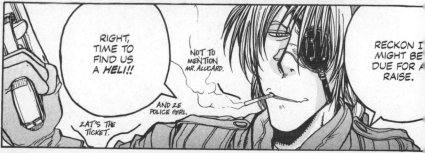

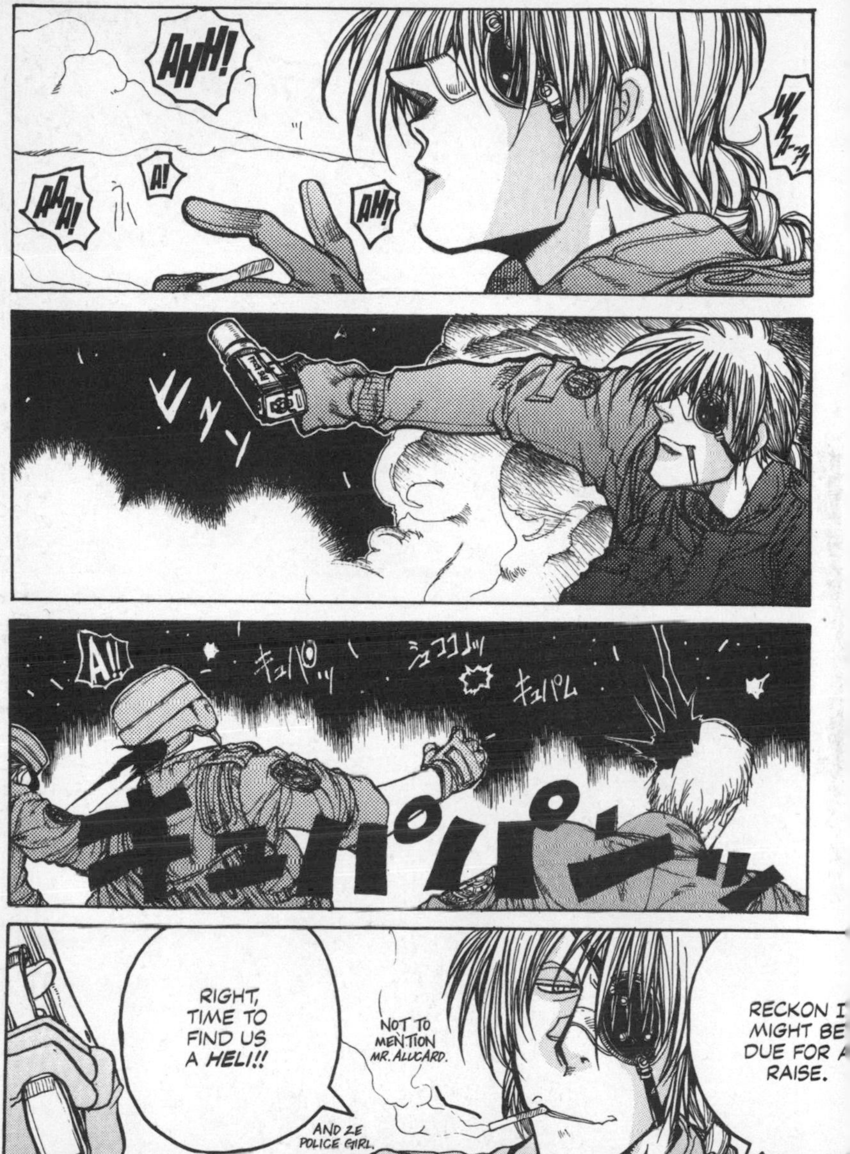
AHH!
AH!
A!
AAA!
A!!
RECKON I MIGHT BE DUE FOR A RAISE.
NOT TO MENTION MR. ALUCARD.
RIGHT, TIME TO FIND US A *HELI*!!
AND ZE POLICE GIRL.
ZAT'S THE TICKET.

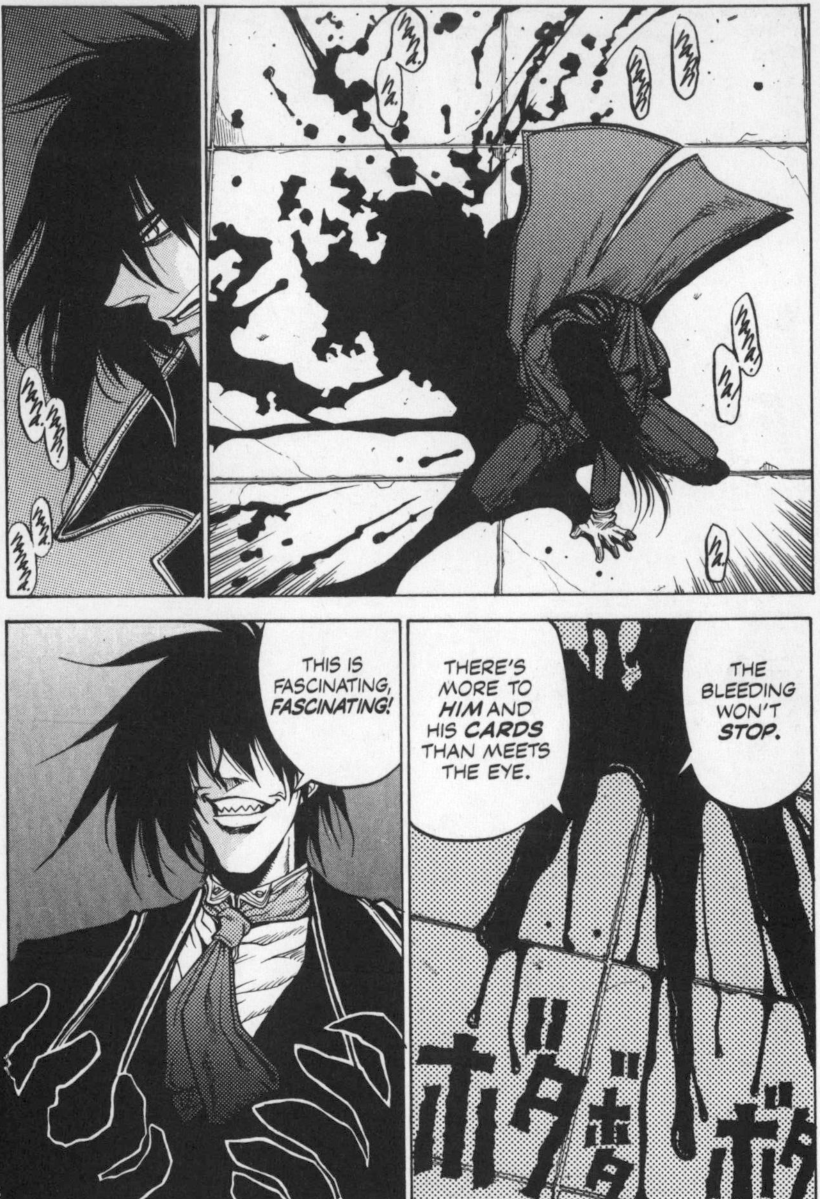
THE BLEEDING WON'T STOP.
THERE'S MORE TO HIM AND HIS CARDS THAN MEETS THE EYE.
ボタ
ボタ
ホタ
THIS IS FASCINATING, FASCINATING!

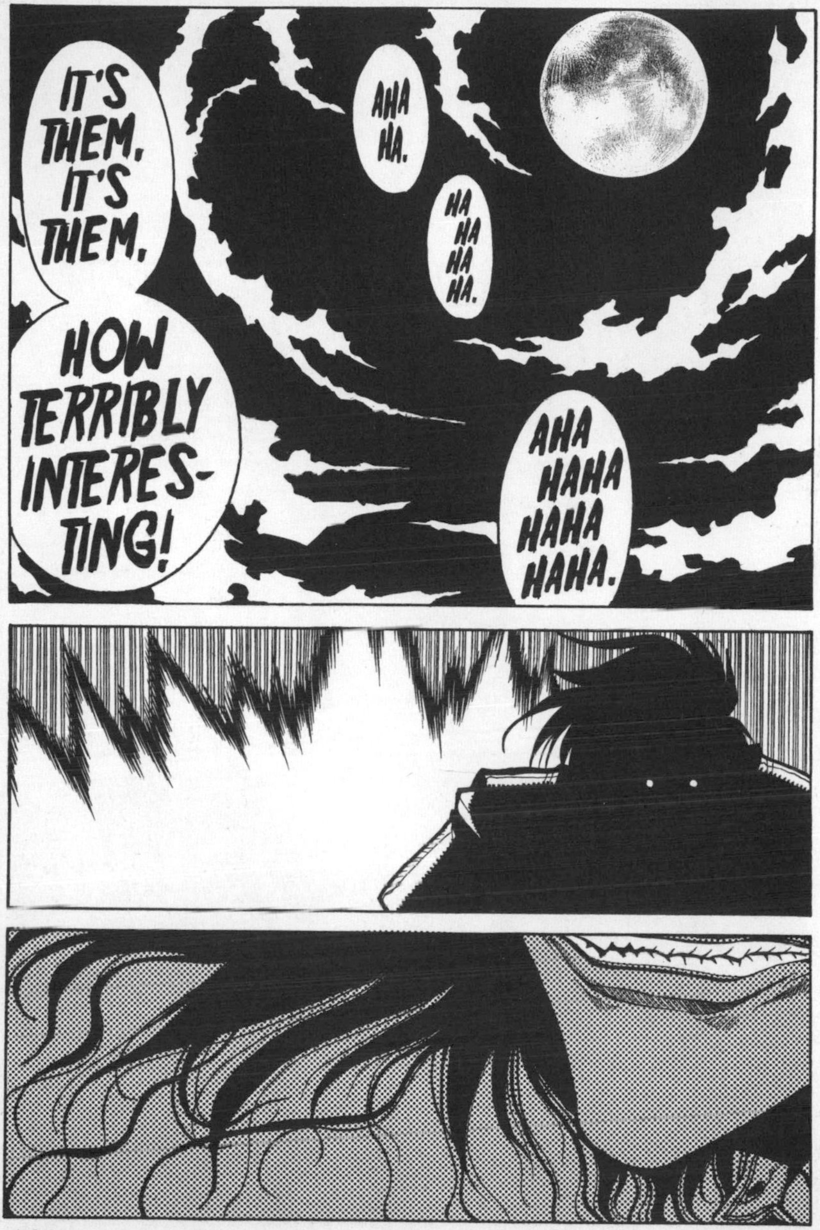
AHA HA.
HA HA HA HA.
AHA HAHA HAHA HAHA.
IT'S THEM. IT'S THEM.
HOW TERRIBLY INTERES-TING!

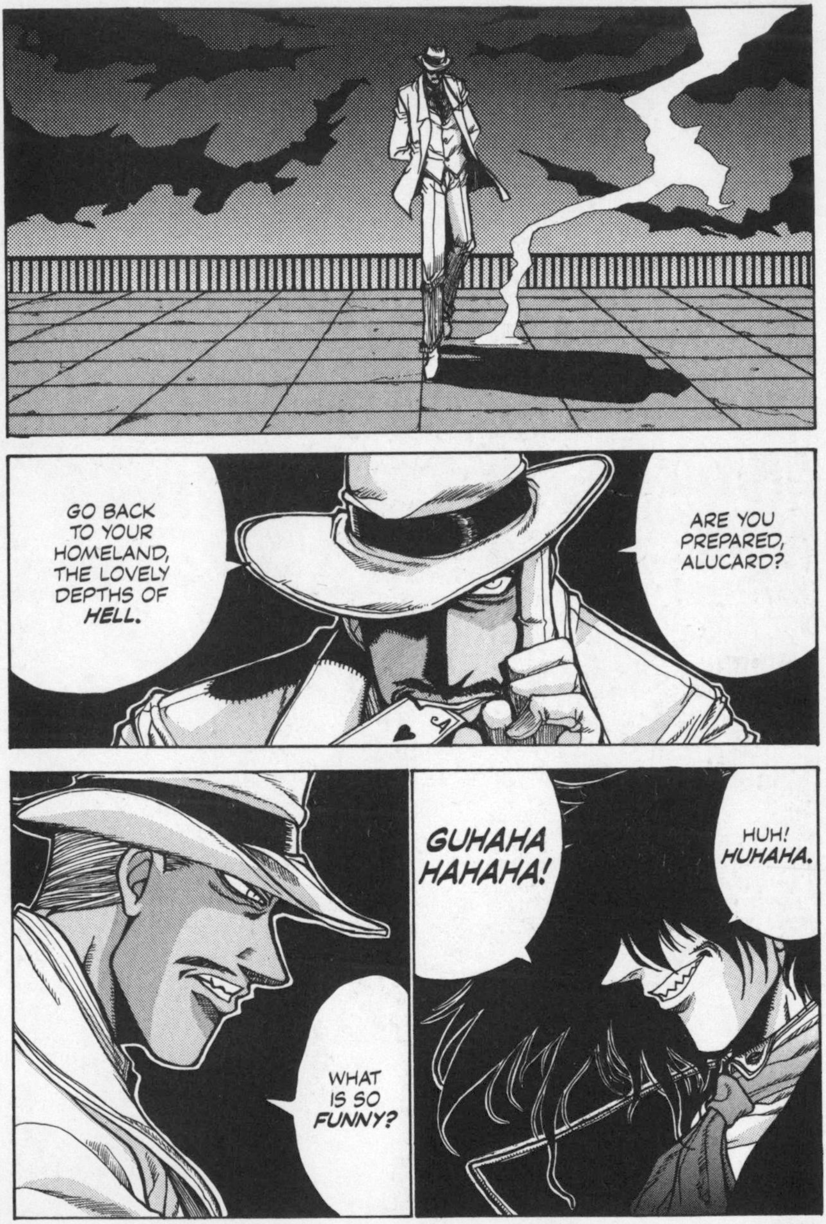
ARE YOU PREPARED, ALUCARD?
GO BACK TO YOUR HOMELAND, THE LOVELY DEPTHS OF *HELL*.
HUH! *HUHAHA.*
GUHAHA HAHAHA!
WHAT IS SO *FUNNY?*

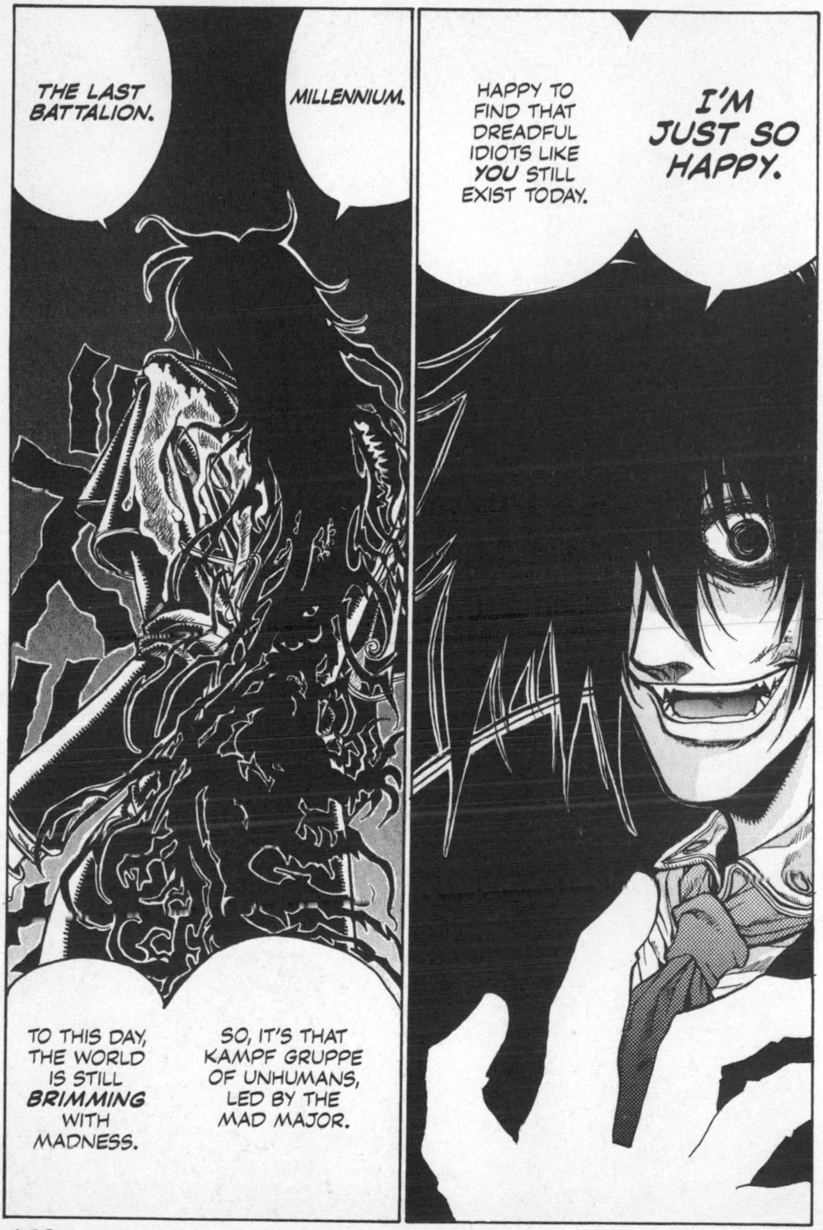
I'M JUST SO HAPPY.
HAPPY TO FIND THAT DREADFUL IDIOTS LIKE YOU STILL EXIST TODAY.
MILLENNIUM.
THE LAST BATTALION.
SO, IT'S THAT KAMPF GRUPPE OF UNHUMANS, LED BY THE MAD MAJOR.
TO THIS DAY, THE WORLD IS STILL BRIMMING WITH MADNESS.

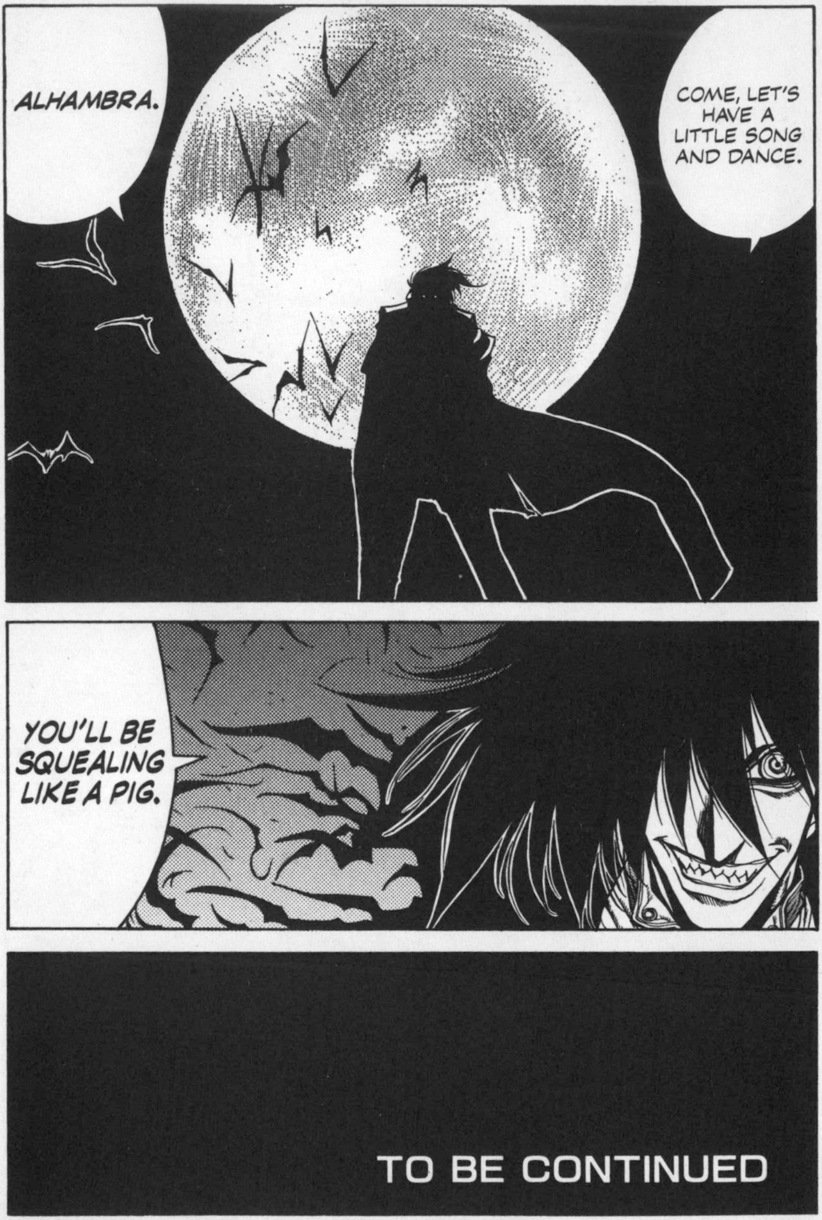
COME, LET'S HAVE A LITTLE SONG AND DANCE.
ALHAMBRA.
YOU'LL BE SQUEALING LIKE A PIG.
TO BE CONTINUED

ORDER 6 / END

HELLSING VOLUME 3 / END

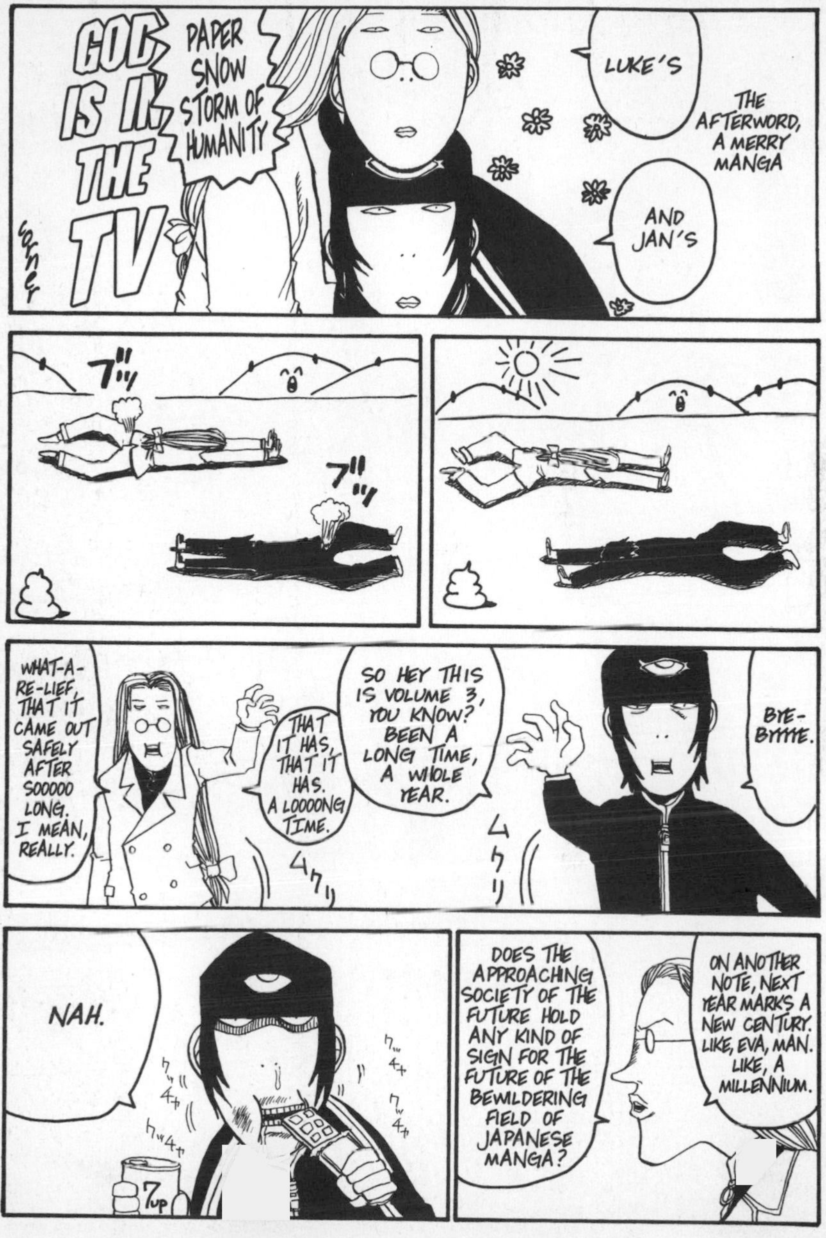

LUKE'S
THE AFTERWORD, A MERRY MANGA
AND JAN'S
PAPER SNOW STORM OF HUMANITY
GOD IS IN THE TV
corner
ブッ
ブッ
BYE-BYYYE.
SO HEY THIS IS VOLUME 3, YOU KNOW? BEEN A LONG TIME, A WHOLE YEAR.
THAT IT HAS, THAT IT HAS. A LOOOONG TIME.
WHAT-A-RE-LIEF, THAT IT CAME OUT SAFELY AFTER SOOOOO LONG. I MEAN, REALLY.
ムクリ
ムクリ
ON ANOTHER NOTE, NEXT YEAR MARKS A NEW CENTURY. LIKE, EVA, MAN. LIKE, A MILLENNIUM.
DOES THE APPROACHING SOCIETY OF THE FUTURE HOLD ANY KIND OF SIGN FOR THE FUTURE OF THE BEWILDERING FIELD OF JAPANESE MANGA?
NAH.
7up

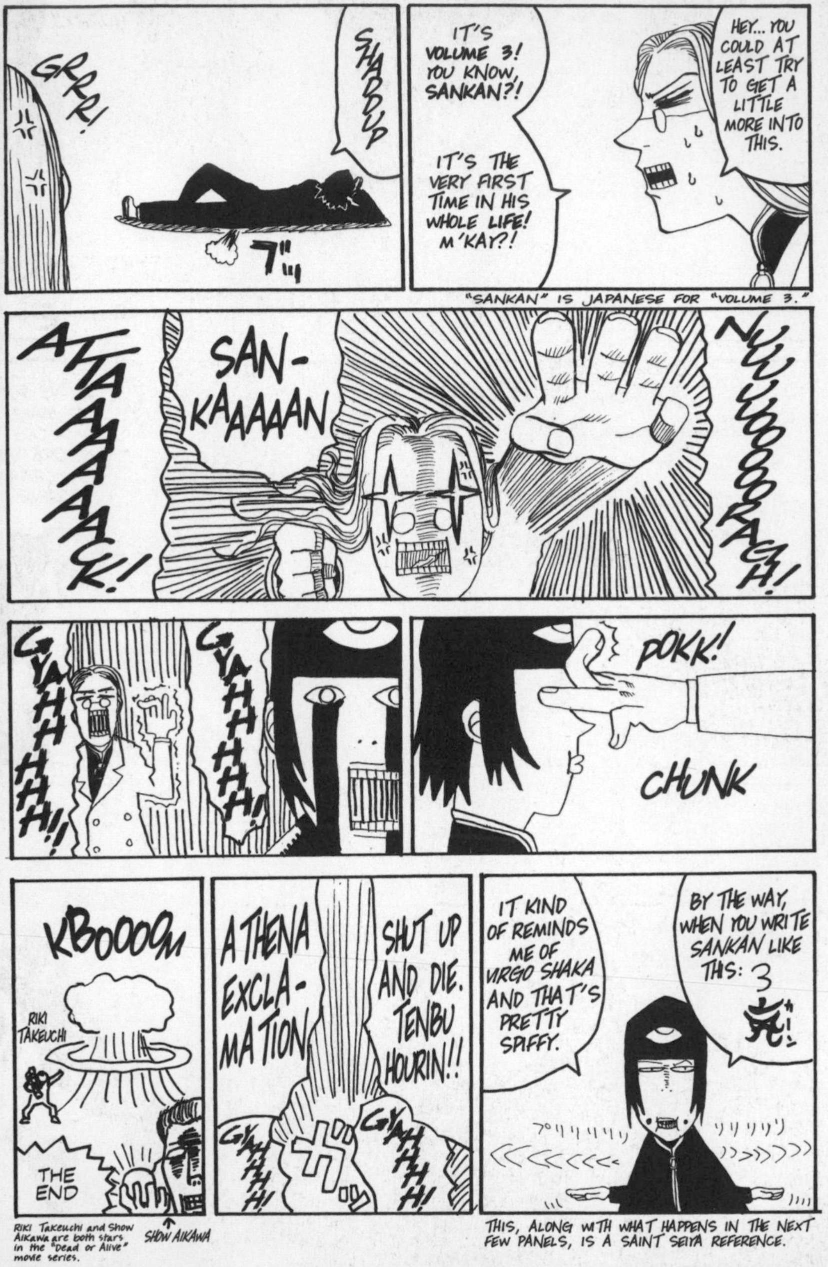
HEY... YOU COULD AT LEAST TRY TO GET A LITTLE MORE INTO THIS.
IT'S VOLUME 3! YOU KNOW, SANKAN?!
IT'S THE VERY FIRST TIME IN HIS WHOLE LIFE! M'KAY?!
SHADDUP
GRRR!
NUUUUOOOORAGH!
SAN-KAAAAAN
ATTAAAAAACK!
POKK!
CHUNK
GYAHHHHHH!
GYAHHHHHH!!
BY THE WAY, WHEN YOU WRITE SANKAN LIKE THIS: 3 巻
IT KIND OF REMINDS ME OF VIRGIO SHAKA AND THAT'S PRETTY SPIFFY.
SHUT UP AND DIE. TENBU HOURIN!!
ATHENA EXCLAMATION
GYAHHHH!
GYAHHHH!
KBOOOOM
RIKI TAKEUCHI
THE END
SHOW AIKAWA

"SANKAN" IS JAPANESE FOR "VOLUME 3."

THIS, ALONG WITH WHAT HAPPENS IN THE NEXT FEW PANELS, IS A SAINT SEIYA REFERENCE.

Riki Takeuchi and Show Aikawa are both stars in the "Dead or Alive" movie series.

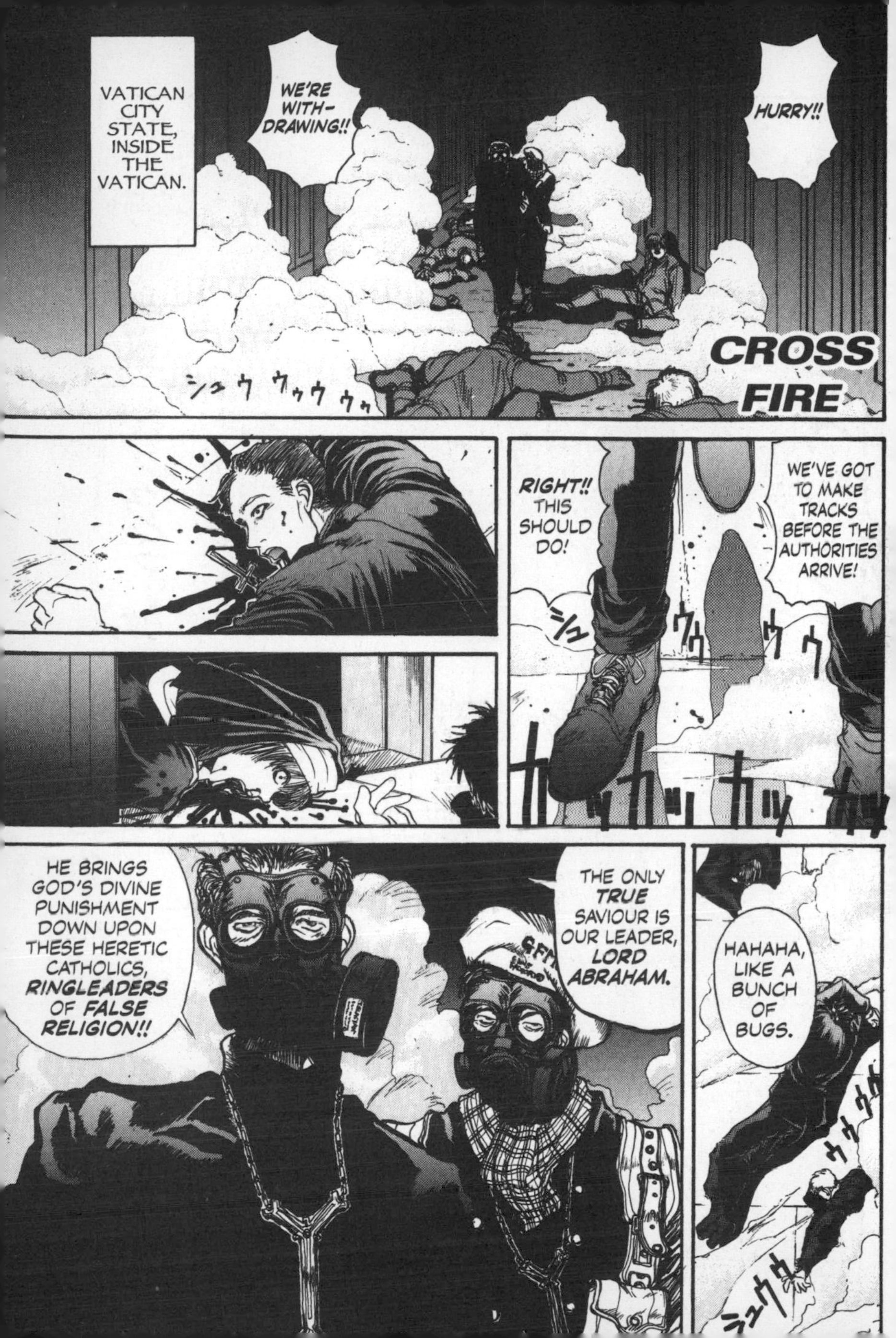
HURRY!!
WE'RE WITH-DRAWING!!
VATICAN CITY STATE, INSIDE THE VATICAN.
シュウ ウゥウ ウゥ
CROSS FIRE
WE'VE GOT TO MAKE TRACKS BEFORE THE AUTHORITIES ARRIVE!
RIGHT!! THIS SHOULD DO!
シュウウウウ
カッカッカッカッ
HAHAHA, LIKE A BUNCH OF BUGS.
THE ONLY TRUE SAVIOUR IS OUR LEADER, LORD ABRAHAM.
HE BRINGS GOD'S DIVINE PUNISHMENT DOWN UPON THESE HERETIC CATHOLICS, RINGLEADERS OF FALSE RELIGION!!

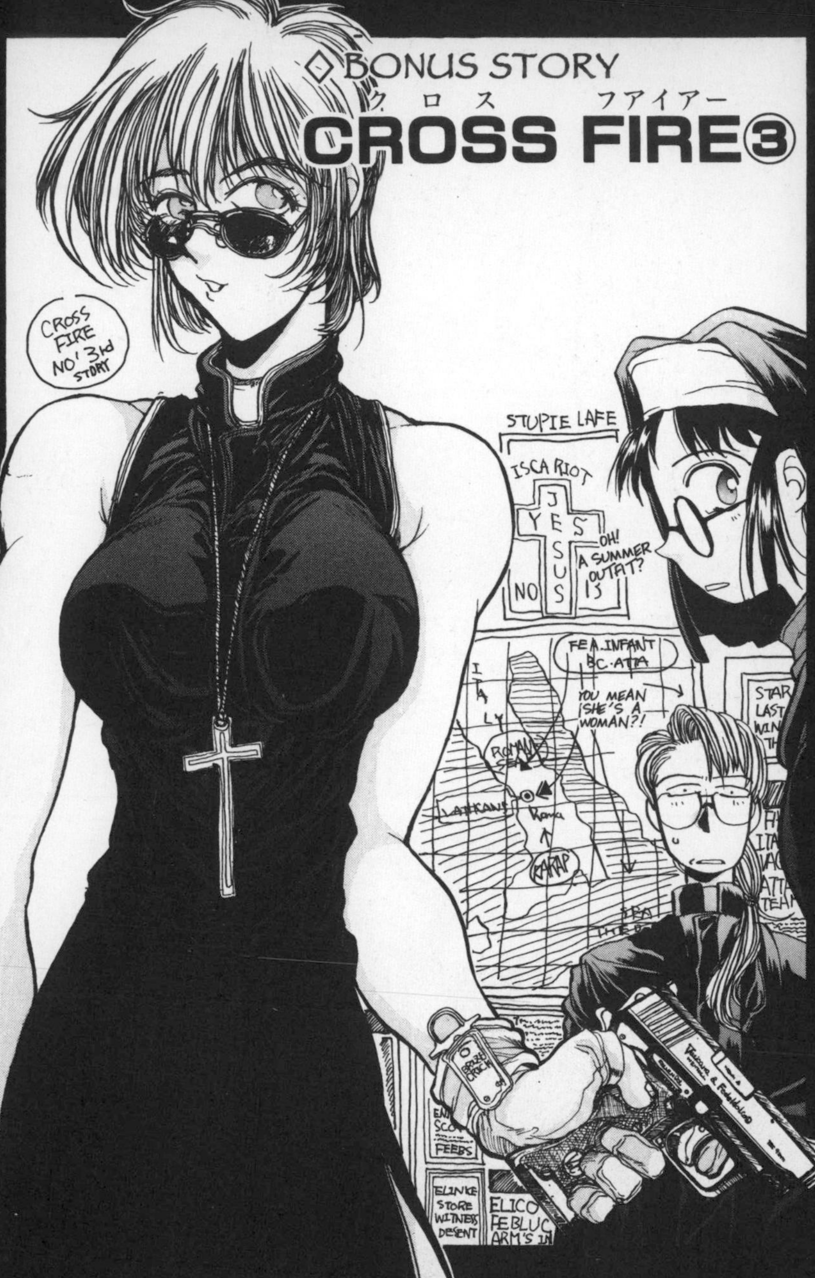
BONUS STORY
クロス ファイアー
CROSS FIRE③
CROSS FIRE NO' 3rd STORY
STUPIE LAFE
ISCA RIOT
J YES SUS
NO 13
OH! A SUMMER OUTFIT?
FE A. INFANT BC. ATIA
YOU MEAN SHE'S A WOMAN?!
ROMAN SEA
LATERANE
KARAP
FEEBS
ELINKE STORE WITNESS DESENT
ELICO FEBLUC ARM'S IN

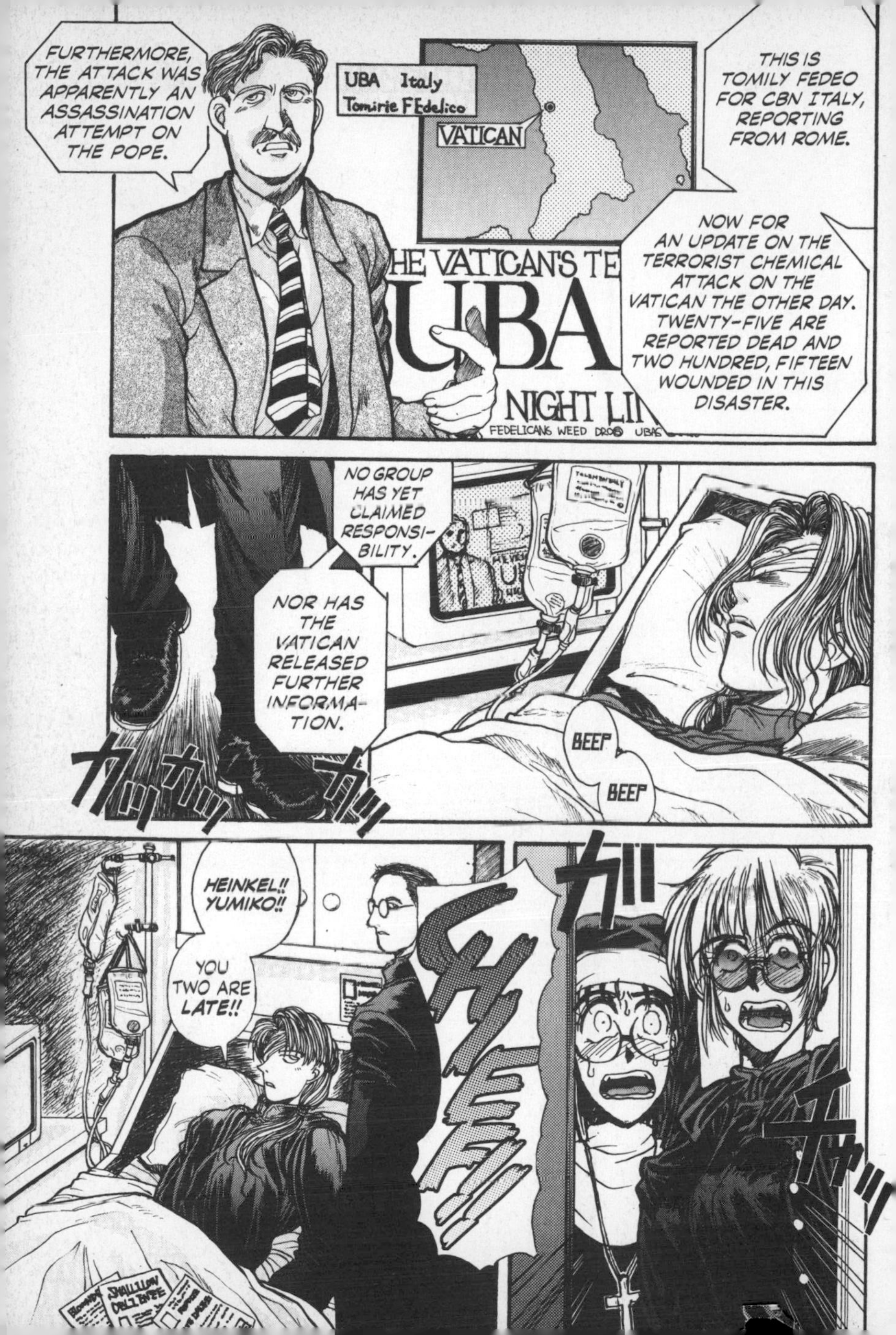
THIS IS TOMILY FEDEO FOR CBN ITALY, REPORTING FROM ROME.
NOW FOR AN UPDATE ON THE TERRORIST CHEMICAL ATTACK ON THE VATICAN THE OTHER DAY. TWENTY-FIVE ARE REPORTED DEAD AND TWO HUNDRED, FIFTEEN WOUNDED IN THIS DISASTER.
UBA Italy
Tomirie FEdelico
VATICAN
FURTHERMORE, THE ATTACK WAS APPARENTLY AN ASSASSINATION ATTEMPT ON THE POPE.
HE VATICAN'S TE
UBA
NIGHT LI
NO GROUP HAS YET CLAIMED RESPONSI-BILITY.
NOR HAS THE VATICAN RELEASED FURTHER INFORMA-TION.
BEEP
BEEP
HEINKEL!! YUMIKO!!
YOU TWO ARE LATE!!

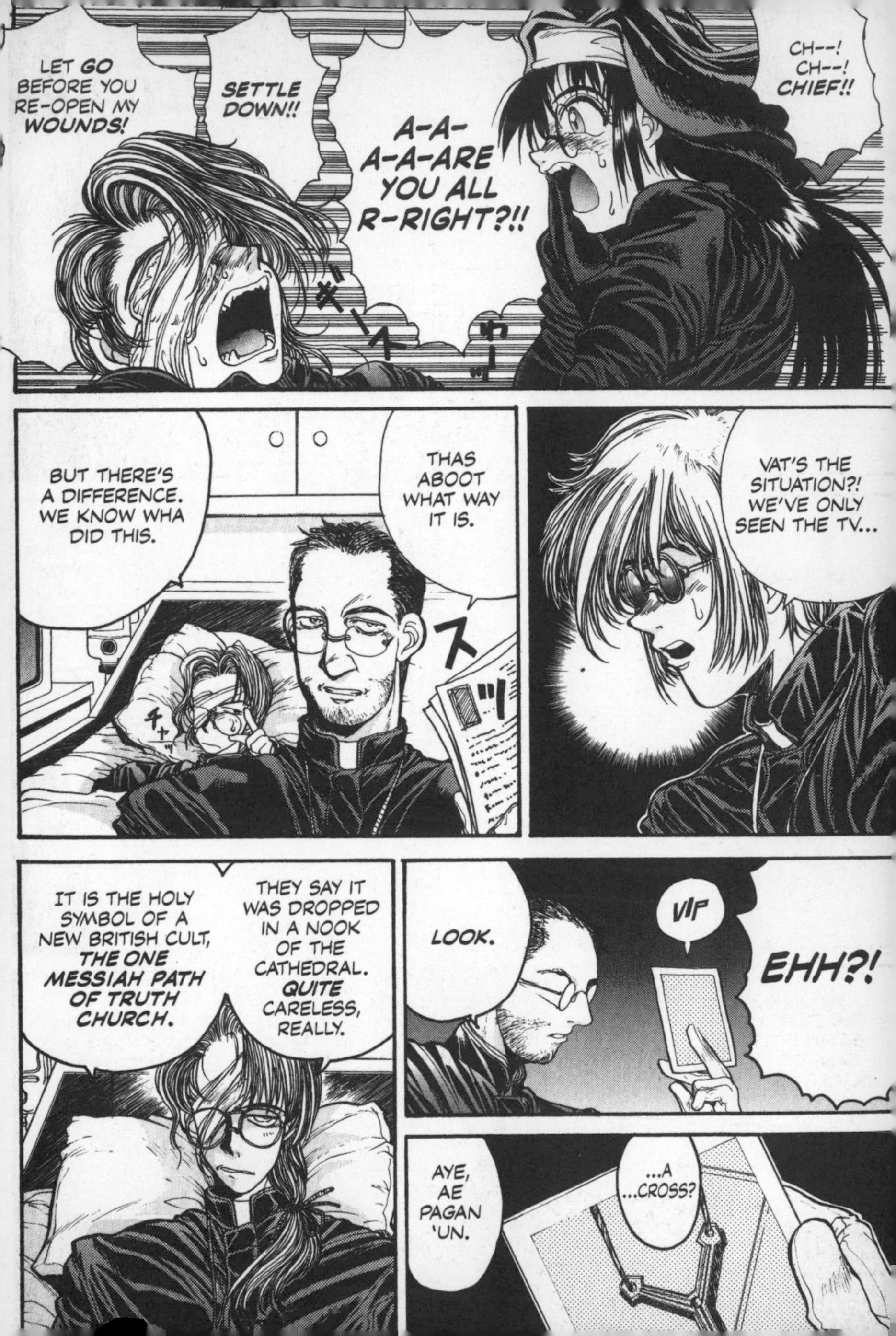
CH--! CH--! CHIEF!!
A-A-A-A-ARE YOU ALL R-RIGHT?!!
SETTLE DOWN!!
LET GO BEFORE YOU RE-OPEN MY WOUNDS!
VAT'S THE SITUATION?! WE'VE ONLY SEEN THE TV...
THAS ABOOT WHAT WAY IT IS.
BUT THERE'S A DIFFERENCE. WE KNOW WHA DID THIS.
EHH?!
VIP
LOOK.
...A ...CROSS?
AYE, AE PAGAN 'UN.
THEY SAY IT WAS DROPPED IN A NOOK OF THE CATHEDRAL. QUITE CARELESS, REALLY.
IT IS THE HOLY SYMBOL OF A NEW BRITISH CULT, THE ONE MESSIAH PATH OF TRUTH CHURCH.

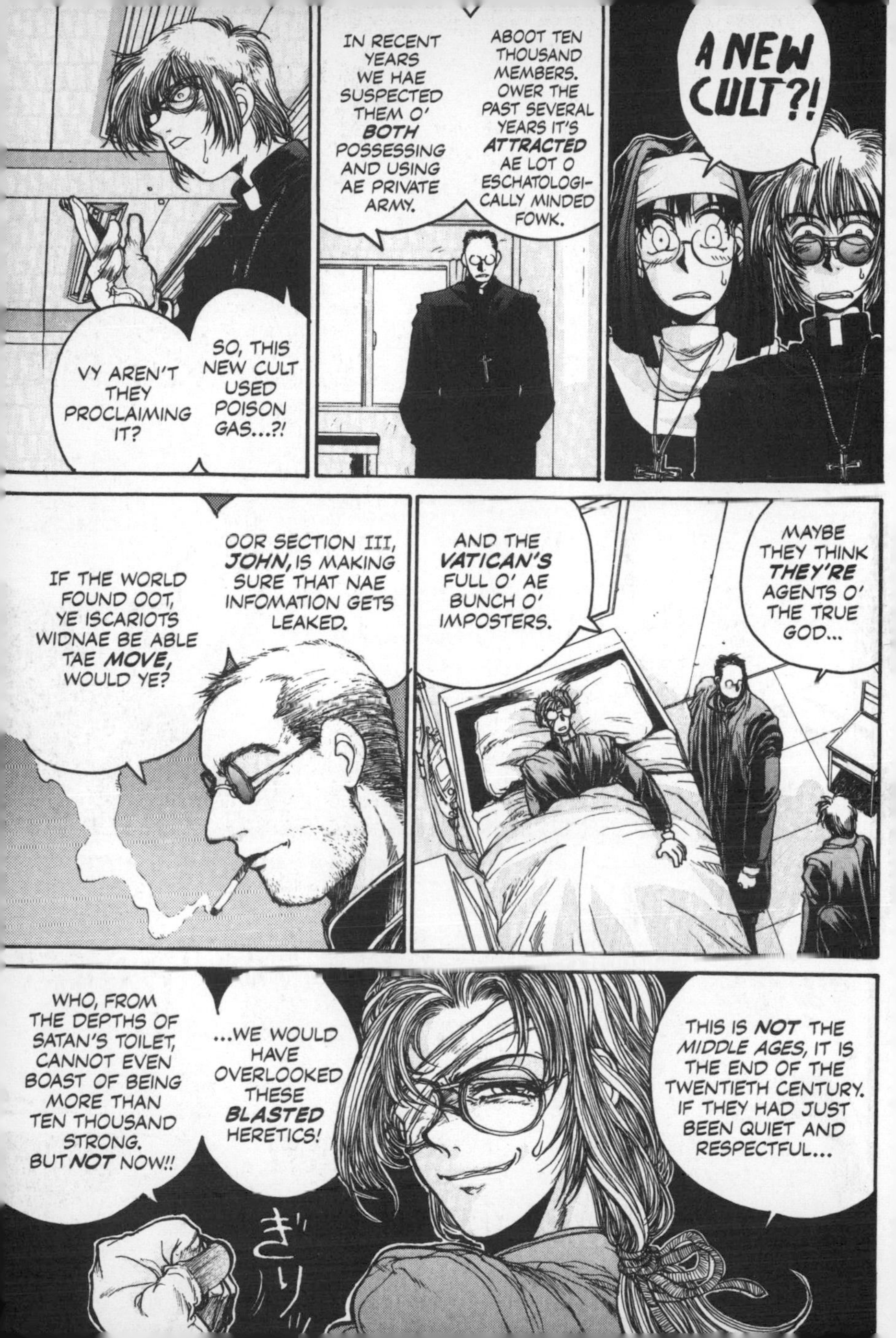
A NEW CULT?!
ABOOT TEN THOUSAND MEMBERS. OWER THE PAST SEVERAL YEARS IT'S *ATTRACTED* AE LOT O ESCHATOLOGICALLY MINDED FOWK.
IN RECENT YEARS WE HAE SUSPECTED THEM O' *BOTH* POSSESSING AND USING AE PRIVATE ARMY.
SO, THIS NEW CULT USED POISON GAS...?!
VY AREN'T THEY PROCLAIMING IT?
MAYBE THEY THINK *THEY'RE* AGENTS O' THE TRUE GOD...
AND THE *VATICAN'S* FULL O' AE BUNCH O' IMPOSTERS.
OOR SECTION III, *JOHN,* IS MAKING SURE THAT NAE INFOMATION GETS LEAKED.
IF THE WORLD FOUND OOT, YE ISCARIOTS WIDNAE BE ABLE TAE *MOVE,* WOULD YE?
THIS IS *NOT* THE *MIDDLE AGES,* IT IS THE END OF THE TWENTIETH CENTURY. IF THEY HAD JUST BEEN QUIET AND RESPECTFUL...
...WE WOULD HAVE OVERLOOKED THESE *BLASTED* HERETICS!
WHO, FROM THE DEPTHS OF SATAN'S TOILET, CANNOT EVEN BOAST OF BEING MORE THAN TEN THOUSAND STRONG. BUT *NOT* NOW!!
ぎり

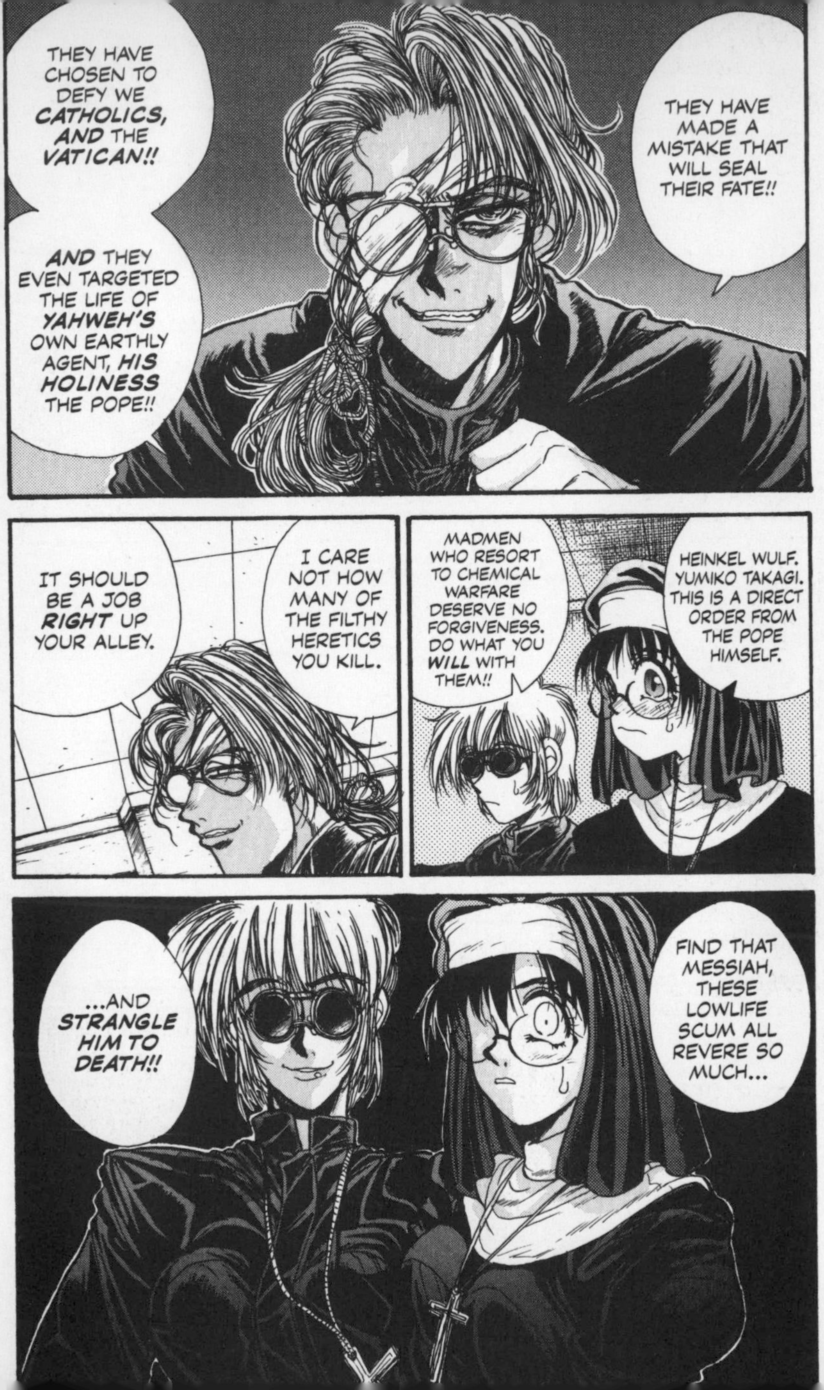
THEY HAVE MADE A MISTAKE THAT WILL SEAL THEIR FATE!!
THEY HAVE CHOSEN TO DEFY WE CATHOLICS, AND THE VATICAN!!
AND THEY EVEN TARGETED THE LIFE OF YAHWEH'S OWN EARTHLY AGENT, HIS HOLINESS THE POPE!!
HEINKEL WULF. YUMIKO TAKAGI. THIS IS A DIRECT ORDER FROM THE POPE HIMSELF.
MADMEN WHO RESORT TO CHEMICAL WARFARE DESERVE NO FORGIVENESS. DO WHAT YOU WILL WITH THEM!!
I CARE NOT HOW MANY OF THE FILTHY HERETICS YOU KILL.
IT SHOULD BE A JOB RIGHT UP YOUR ALLEY.
FIND THAT MESSIAH, THESE LOWLIFE SCUM ALL REVERE SO MUCH...
...AND STRANGLE HIM TO DEATH!!

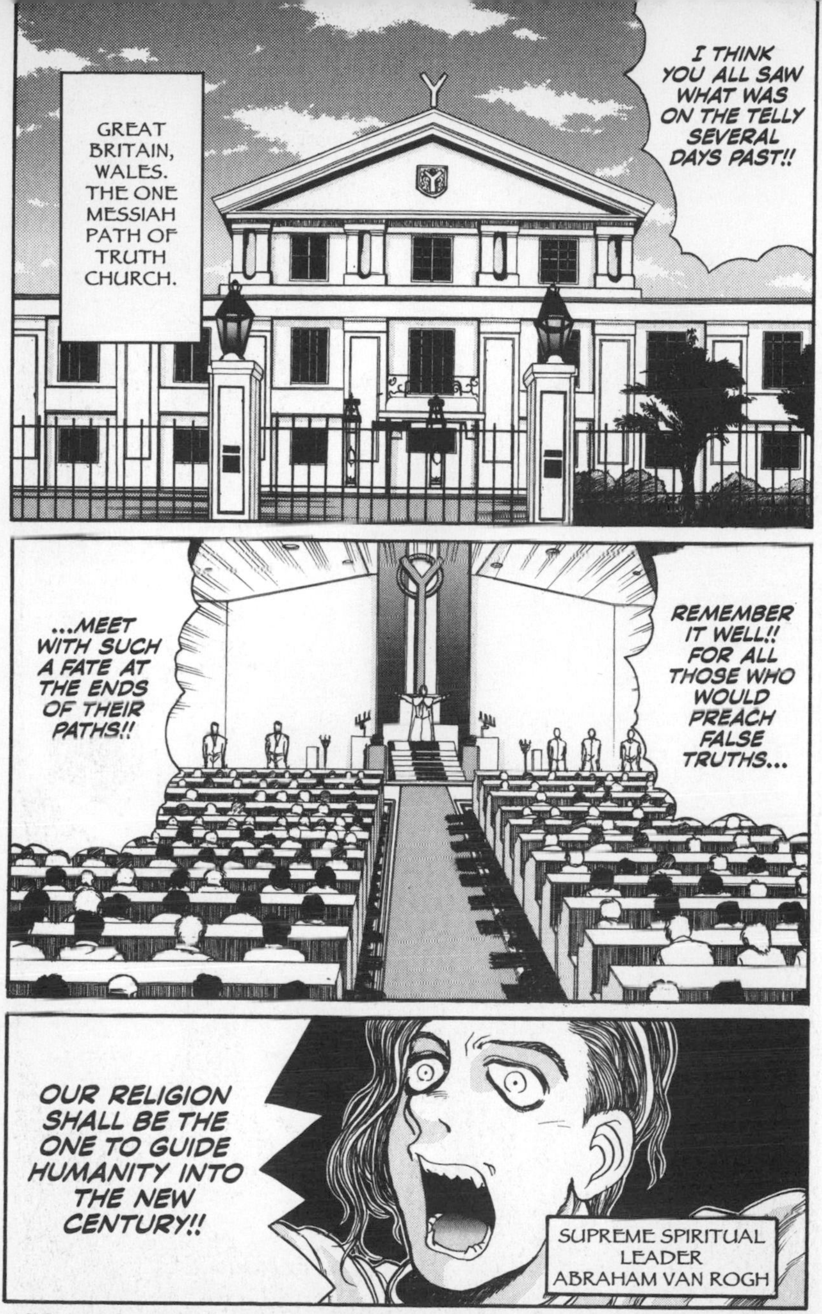

I THINK YOU ALL SAW WHAT WAS ON THE TELLY SEVERAL DAYS PAST!!
GREAT BRITAIN, WALES. THE ONE MESSIAH PATH OF TRUTH CHURCH.
REMEMBER IT WELL!! FOR ALL THOSE WHO WOULD PREACH FALSE TRUTHS...
...MEET WITH SUCH A FATE AT THE ENDS OF THEIR PATHS!!
OUR RELIGION SHALL BE THE ONE TO GUIDE HUMANITY INTO THE NEW CENTURY!!
SUPREME SPIRITUAL LEADER ABRAHAM VAN ROGH

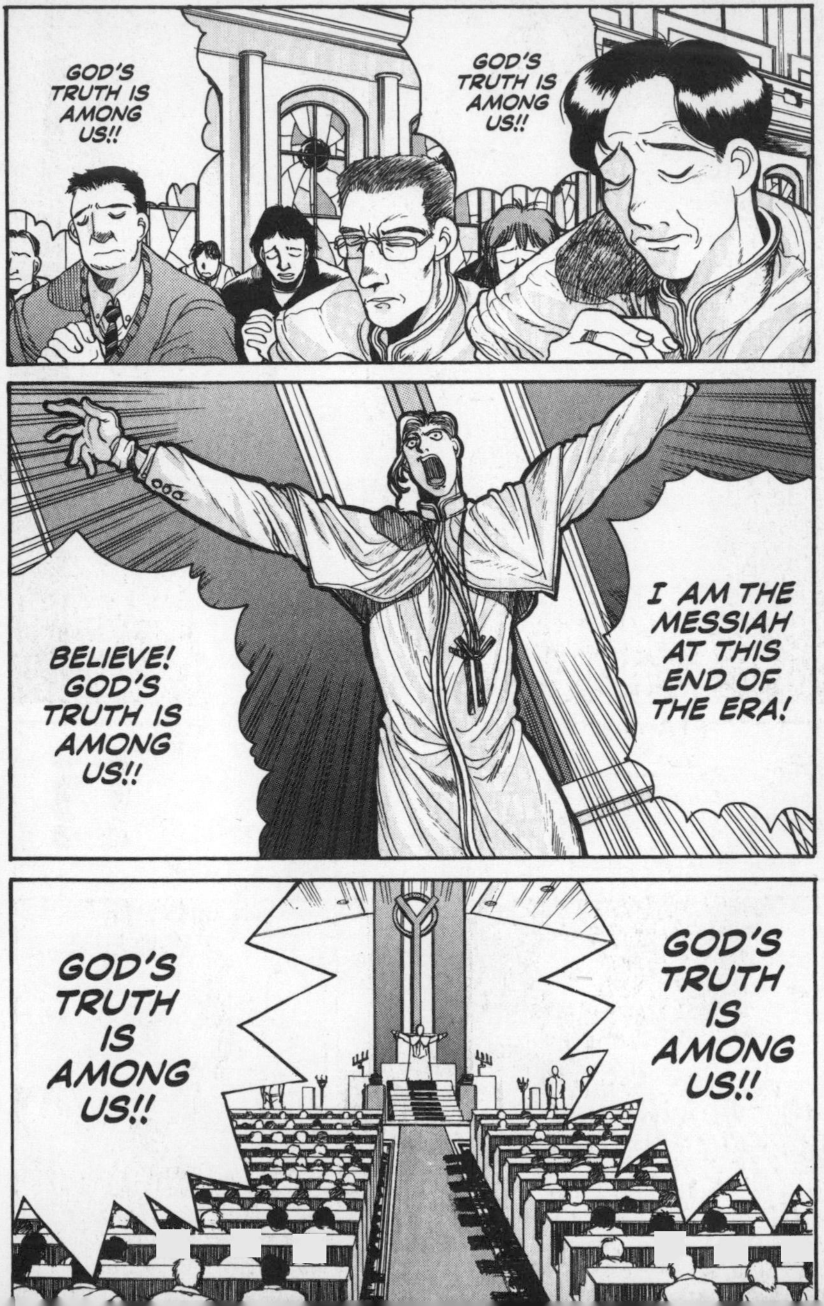
GOD'S TRUTH IS AMONG US!!
GOD'S TRUTH IS AMONG US!!
I AM THE MESSIAH AT THIS END OF THE ERA!
BELIEVE! GOD'S TRUTH IS AMONG US!!
GOD'S TRUTH IS AMONG US!!
GOD'S TRUTH IS AMONG US!!

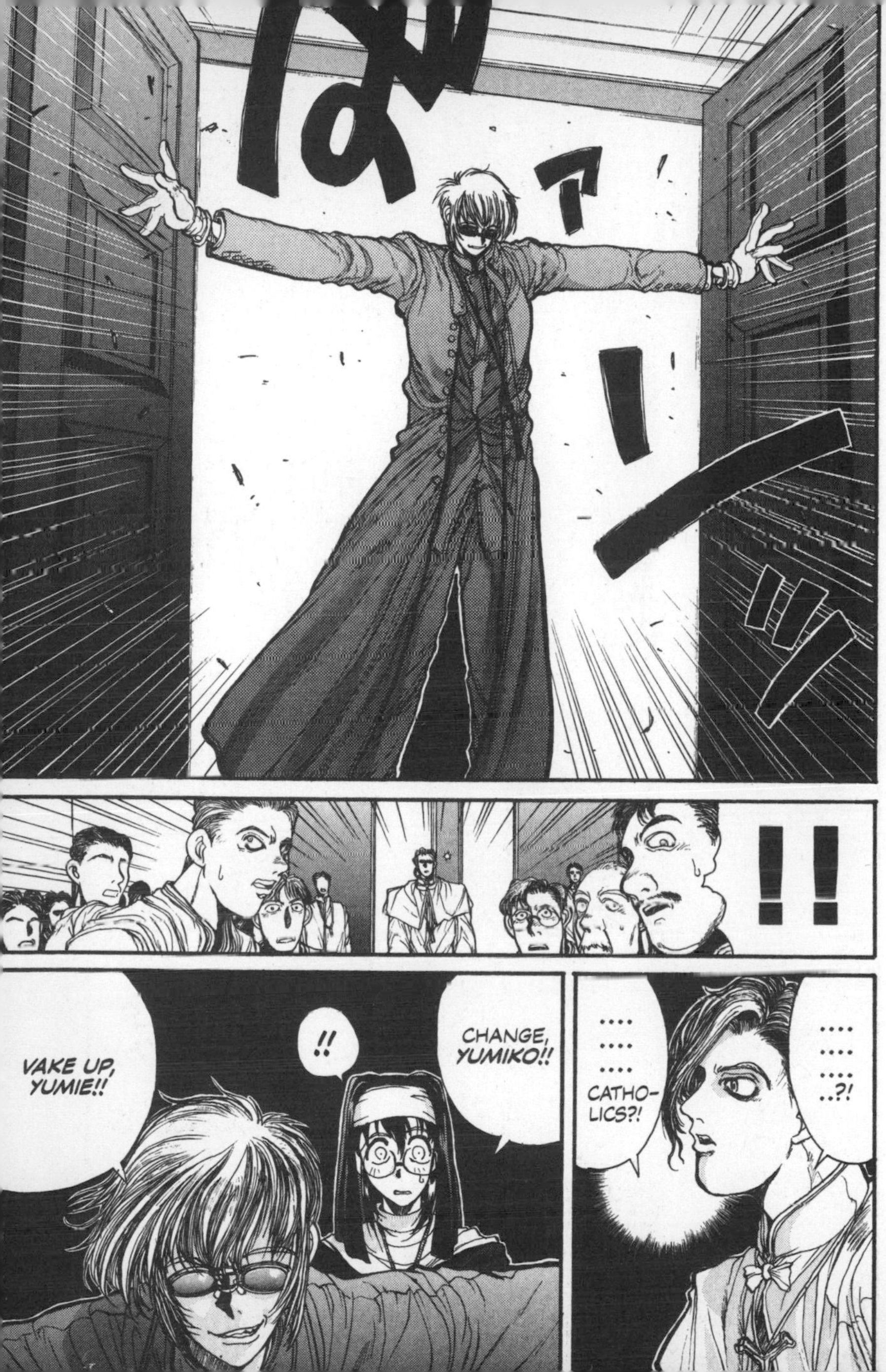
ばアーーッ
!!
....
....
....
..?!
....
....
....
CATHOLICS?!
CHANGE, YUMIKO!!
!!
VAKE UP, YUMIE!!

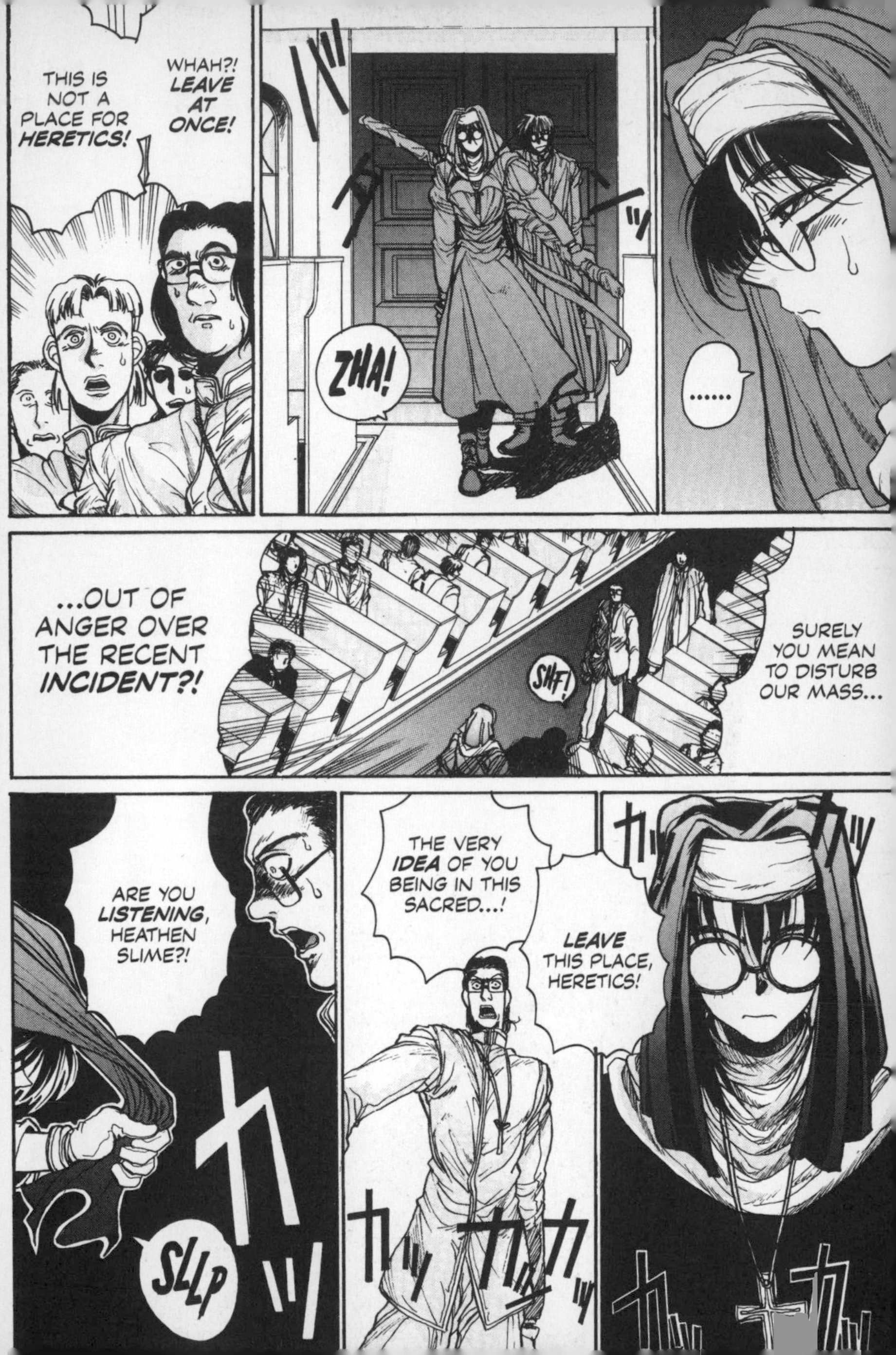

......
ZHA!
WHAH?! LEAVE AT ONCE!
THIS IS NOT A PLACE FOR HERETICS!
SURELY YOU MEAN TO DISTURB OUR MASS...
SHF!
...OUT OF ANGER OVER THE RECENT INCIDENT?!
THE VERY IDEA OF YOU BEING IN THIS SACRED...!
LEAVE THIS PLACE, HERETICS!
ARE YOU LISTENING, HEATHEN SLIME?!
SLLP

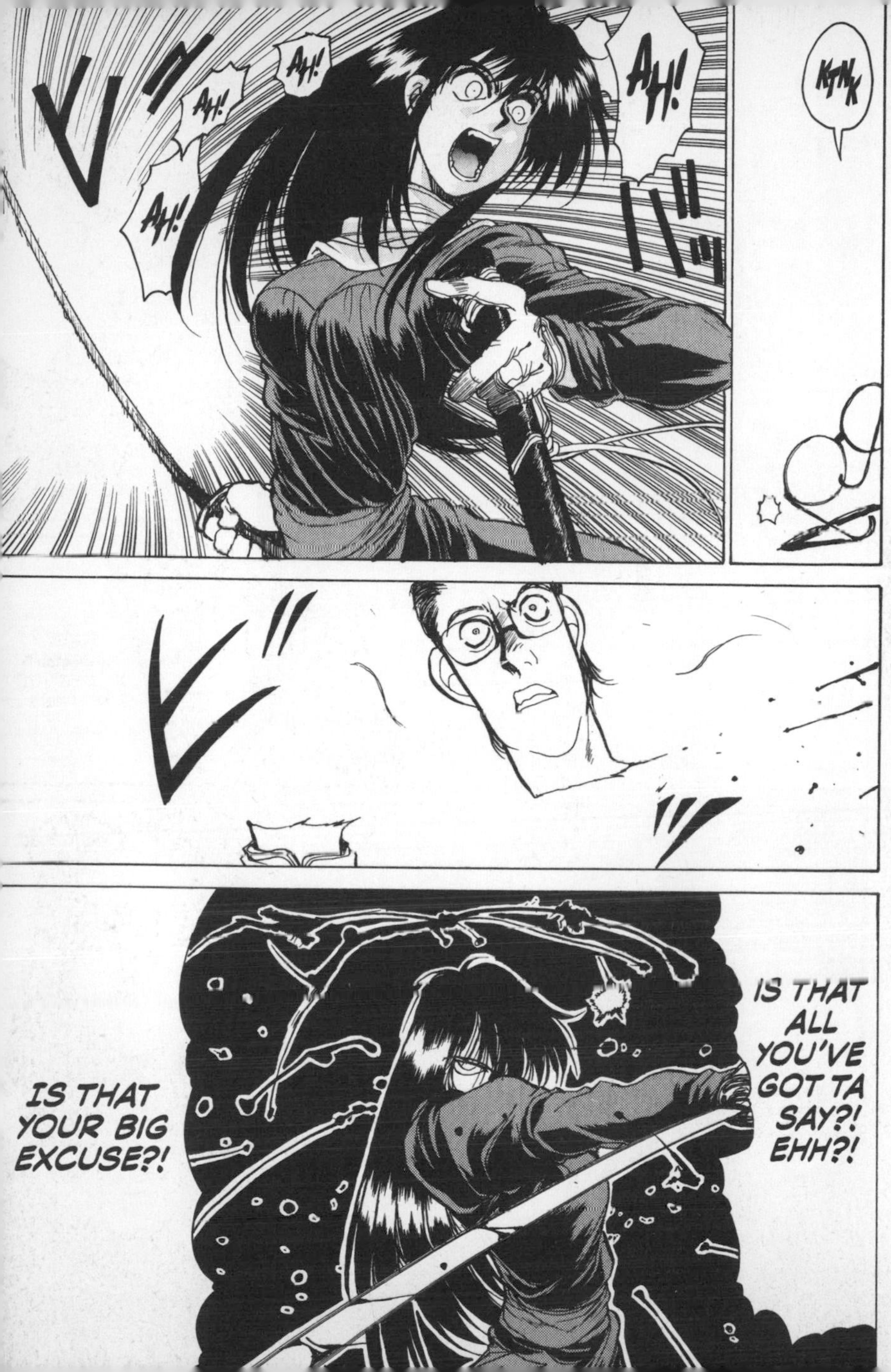
KTNK
AH!
AH!
AH!
AH!
IS THAT ALL YOU'VE GOT TA SAY?! EHH?!
IS THAT YOUR BIG EXCUSE?!

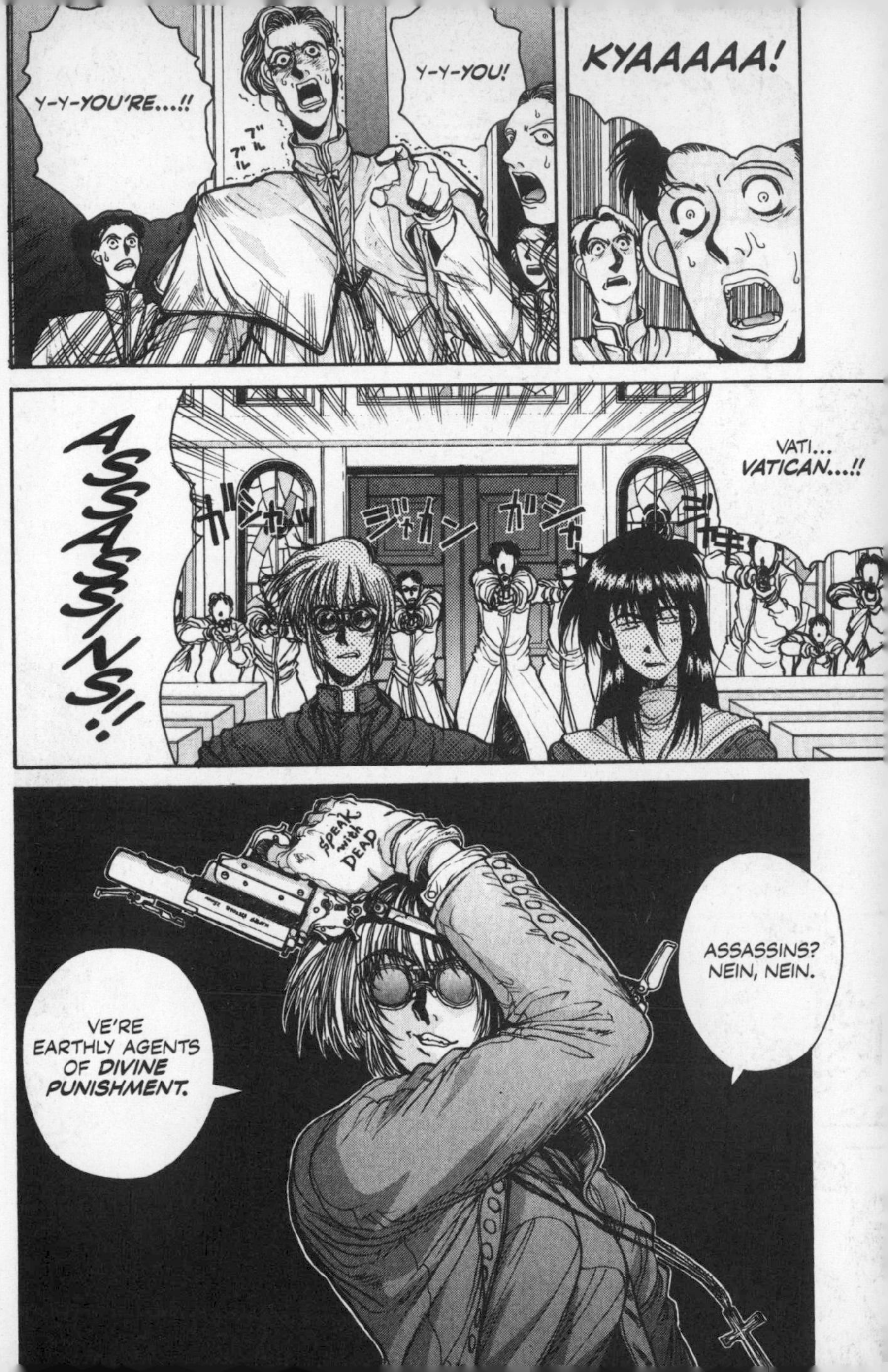
KYAAAAA!
Y-Y-YOU!
ブル ブル
Y-Y-YOU'RE...!!
VATI... VATICAN...!!
ジャキ
ガシャ
ジャカン
ガシャッ
ASSASSINS!!
SPEAK with DEAD
ASSASSINS? NEIN, NEIN.
VE'RE EARTHLY AGENTS OF DIVINE PUNISHMENT.

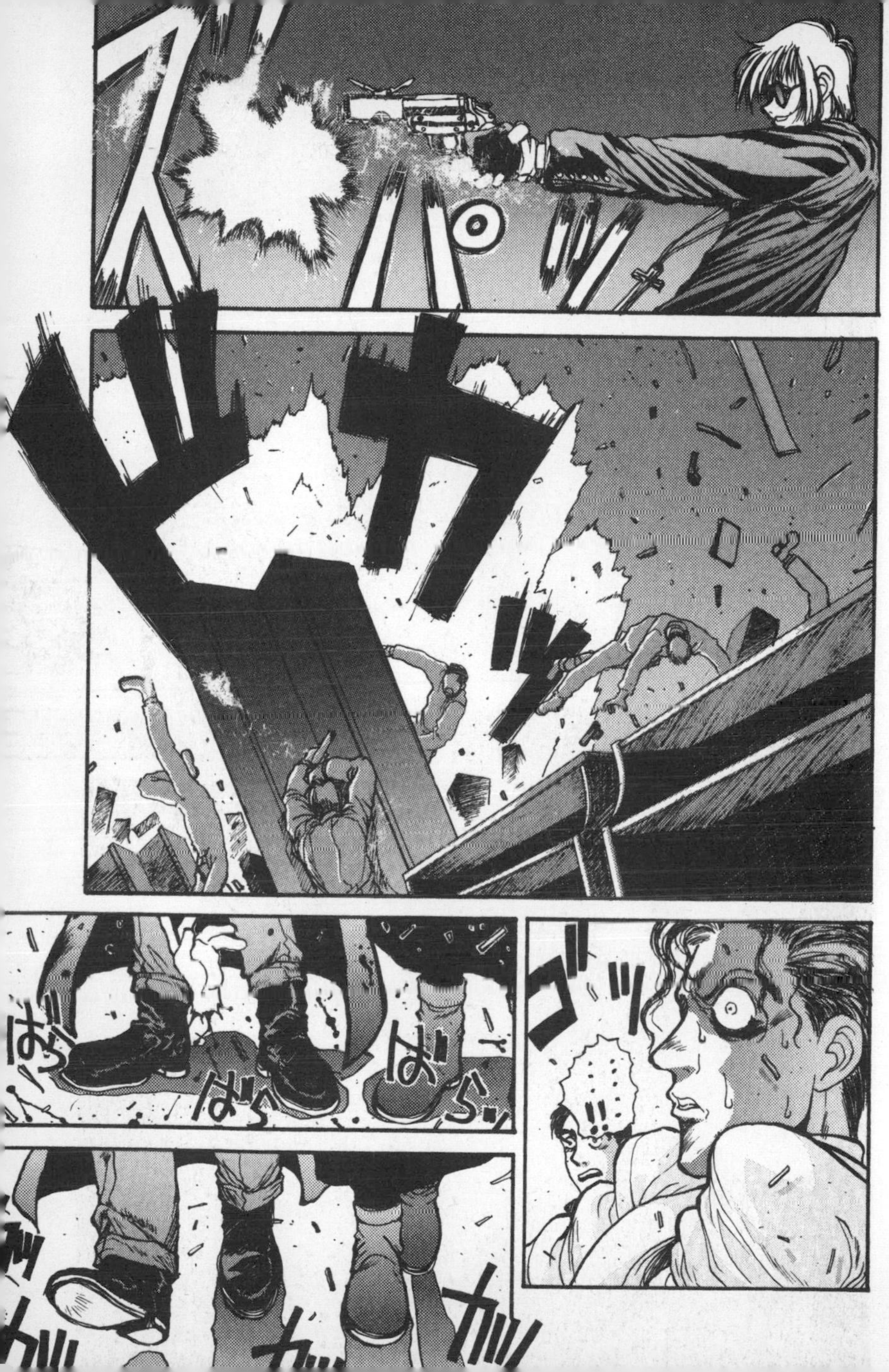
ズパッ
ドカッ
ゴッ
!!
ばら
ばら
ばら

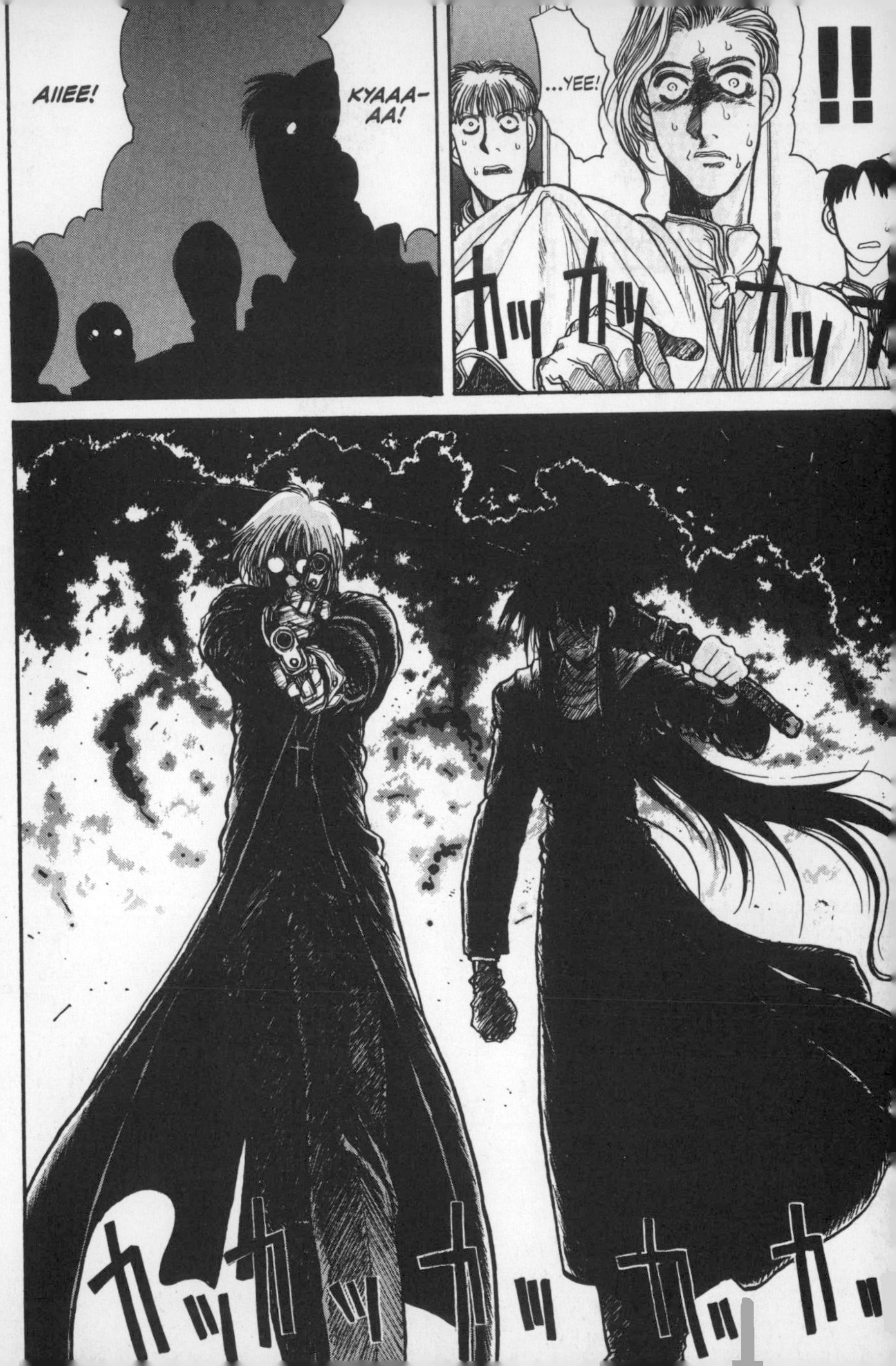
...YEE!
!!
KYAAAA-AA!
AIIEE!

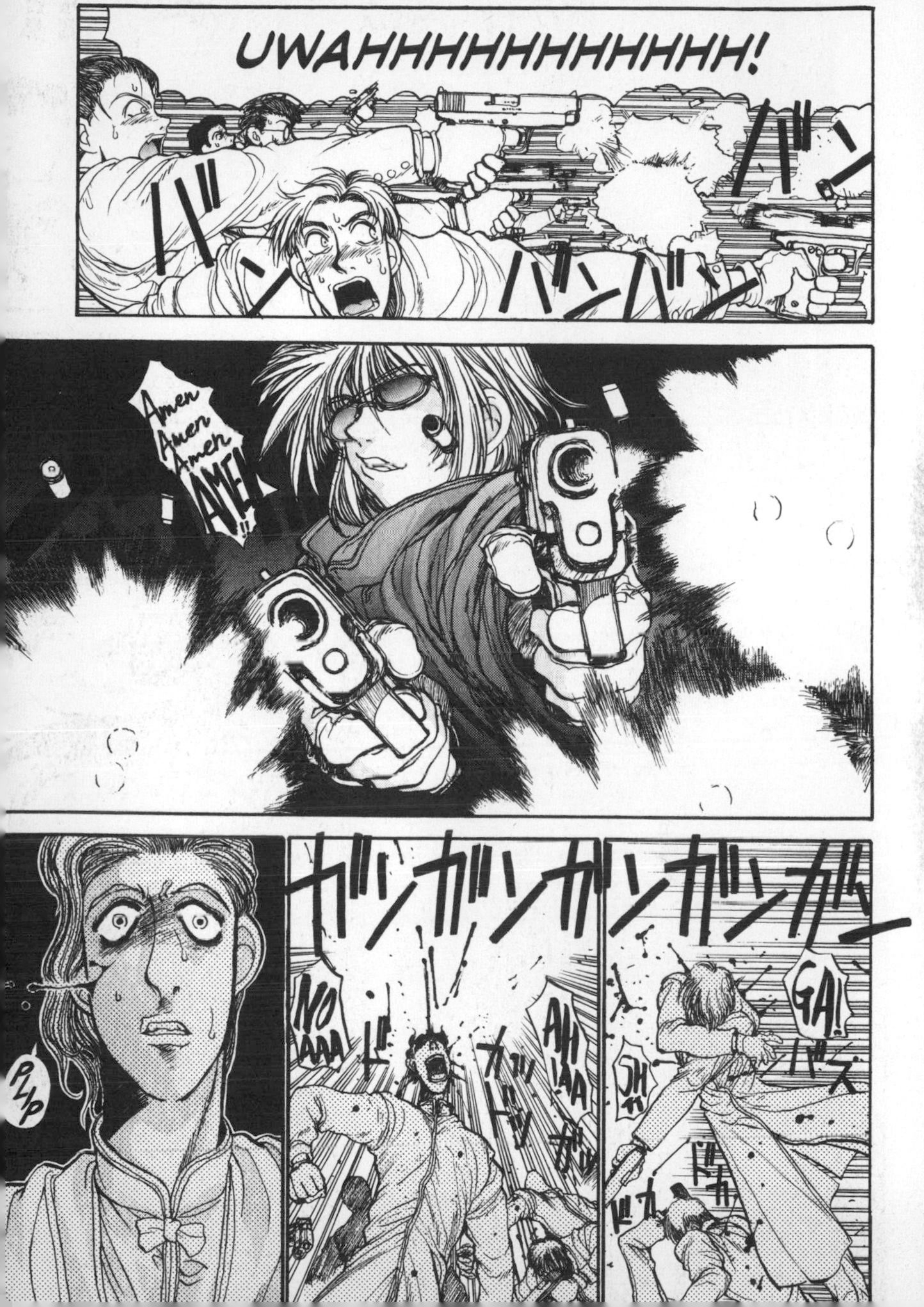

UWAHHHHHHHHHHH!
Amen Amen Amen AMEN!!
GA!
SH
AH !AA
NO AAA
PLIP

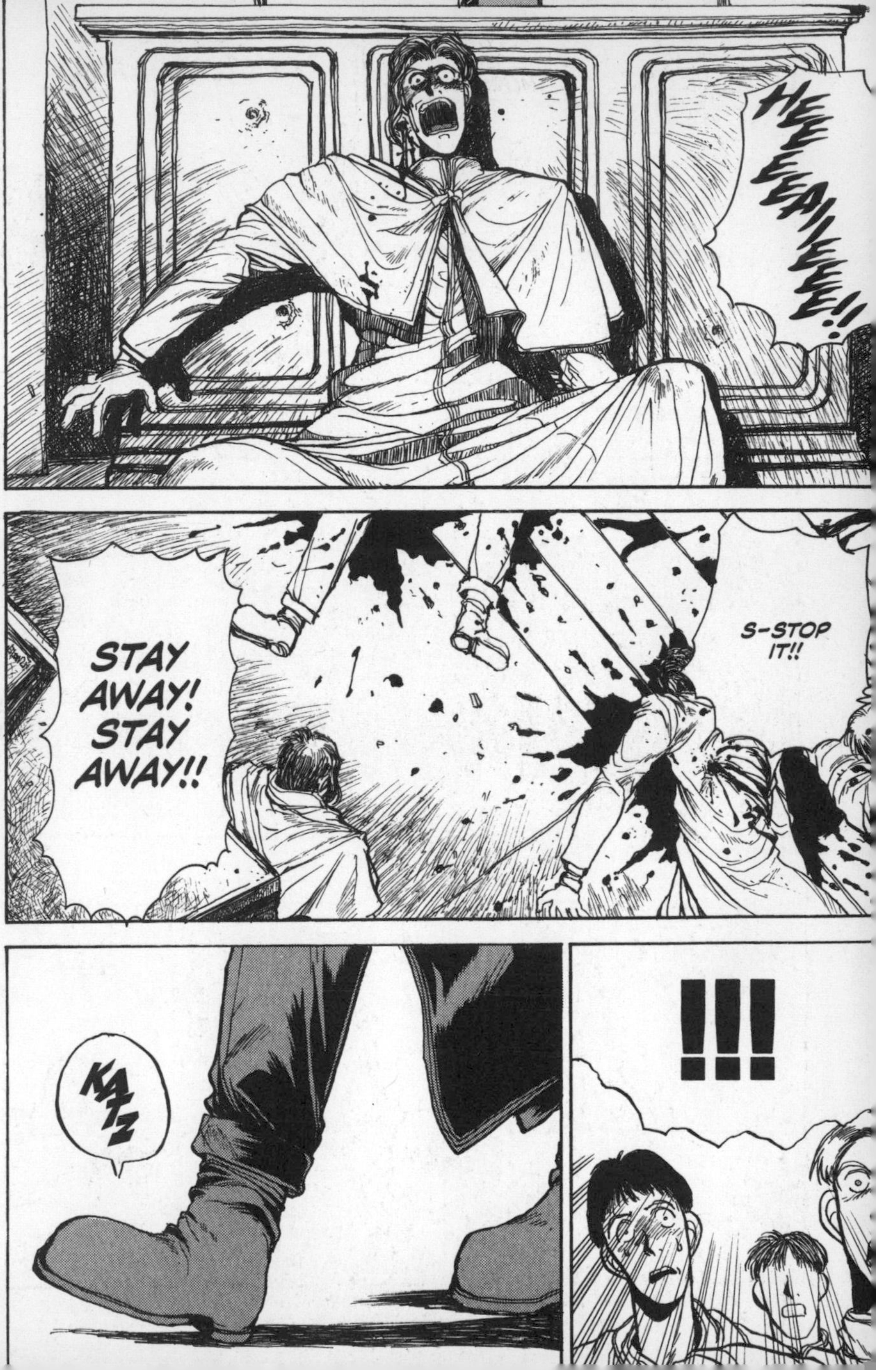
HEEEEAIEEEEE!!
S-STOP IT!!
STAY AWAY! STAY AWAY!!
!!!
KATZ

BLOODY MURDERERS!!
THAT'S RIGHT! MURDERERS!!
LEAVE! GO HOME, VATICAN ASSASSINS!
PROTECT THE MESSIAH!
ばッ
WE WON'T SUBMIT TO THE VATICAN'S RELIGIOUS PERSECU- TION!
GET OUT OF HERE, KILLERS!!
THE TRUTH IS AMONG US!!
GOD'S TRUTH IS AMONG
GOD'S TRUTH IS AMONG US!!
GOD'S TRUTH IS AMONG US!!
GRIN

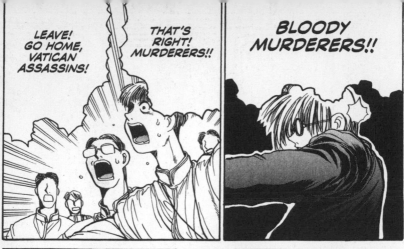

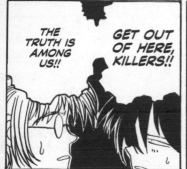

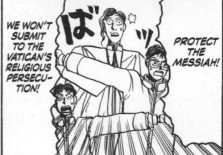

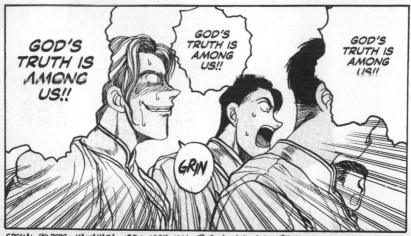

SPECIAL HELPERS: KAWAHARA, YABU, NISHI-KUN, TAYAMA, AND ANDY THANK YOU SO MUCH. IT'S HARD TO KEEP IT STRAIGHT WHO HELPED WITH WHAT NOW, SO MUCH HAS GONE ON.

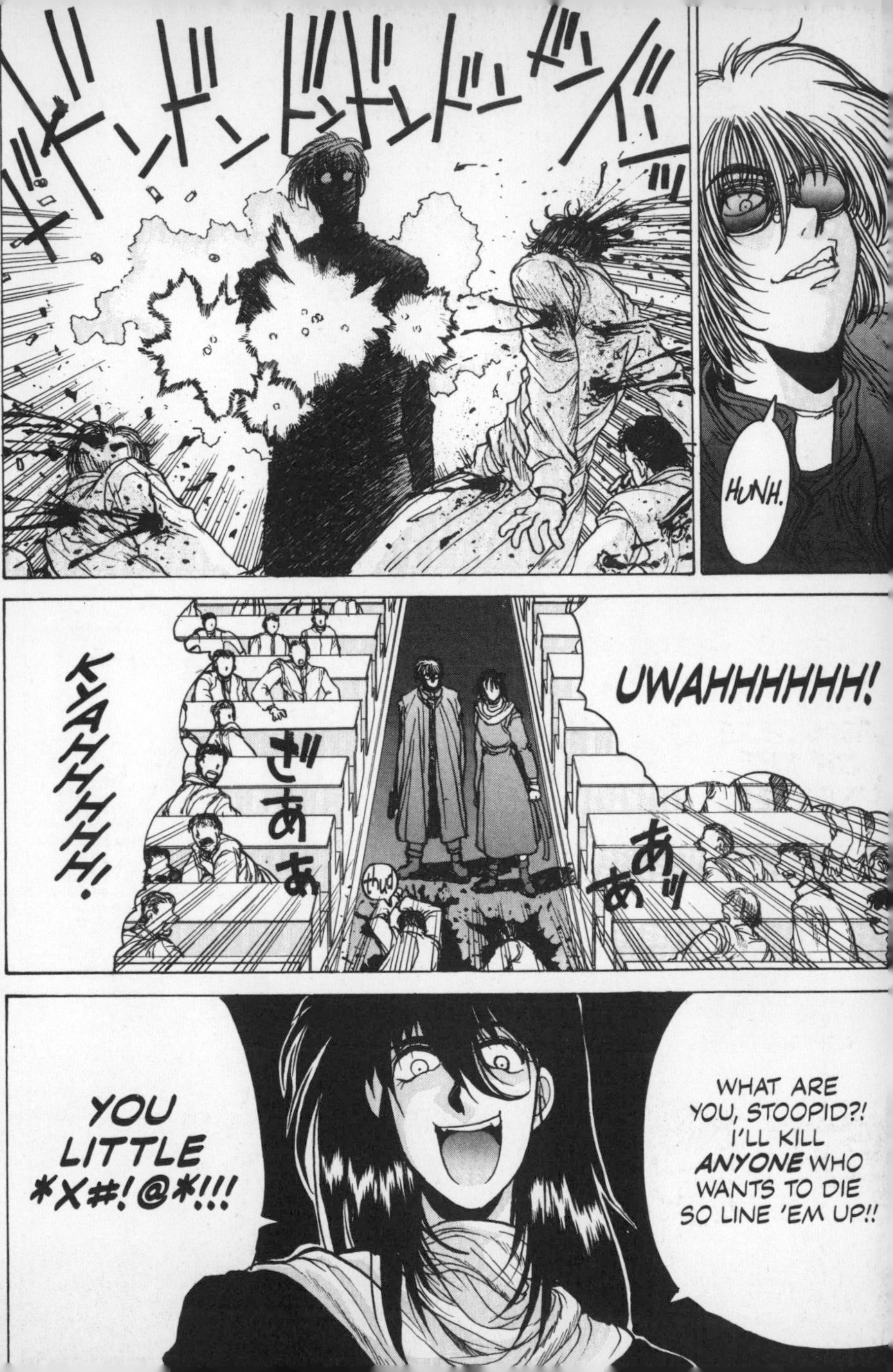
HUNH.
UWAHHHHHH!
あぁッ
ざぁぁ
thud
KYAHHHHHH!
WHAT ARE YOU, STOOPID?! I'LL KILL ANYONE WHO WANTS TO DIE SO LINE 'EM UP!!
YOU LITTLE *X#!@*!!!

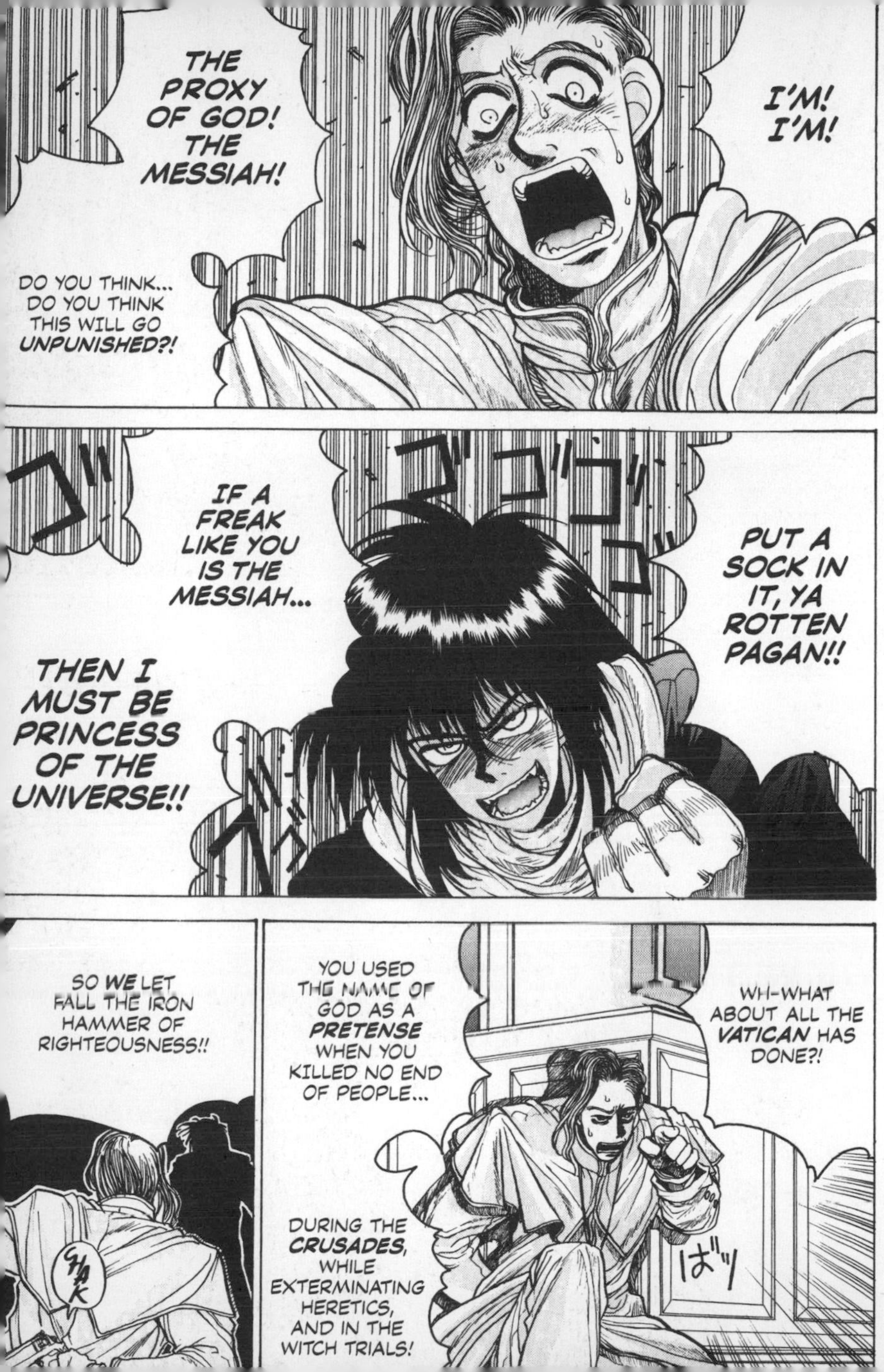
I'M! I'M!
THE PROXY OF GOD! THE MESSIAH!
DO YOU THINK... DO YOU THINK THIS WILL GO UNPUNISHED?!
ゴゴゴゴ
PUT A SOCK IN IT, YA ROTTEN PAGAN!!
IF A FREAK LIKE YOU IS THE MESSIAH...
ゴ
THEN I MUST BE PRINCESS OF THE UNIVERSE!!
WH-WHAT ABOUT ALL THE VATICAN HAS DONE?!
YOU USED THE NAME OF GOD AS A PRETENSE WHEN YOU KILLED NO END OF PEOPLE...
DURING THE CRUSADES, WHILE EXTERMINATING HERETICS, AND IN THE WITCH TRIALS!
ばッ
SO WE LET FALL THE IRON HAMMER OF RIGHTEOUSNESS!!
GHAK

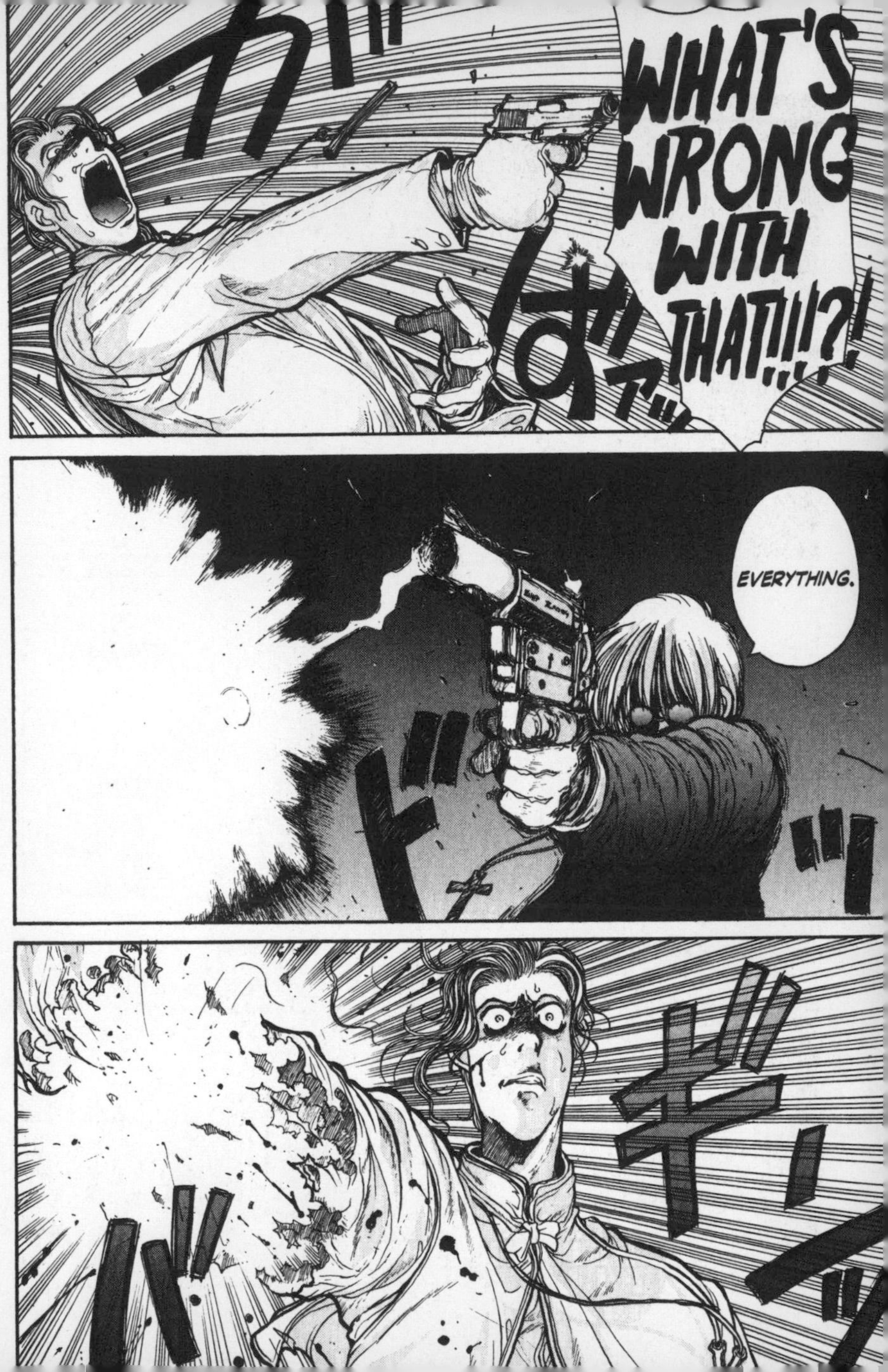
WHAT'S WRONG WITH THAT!!!?!
EVERYTHING.

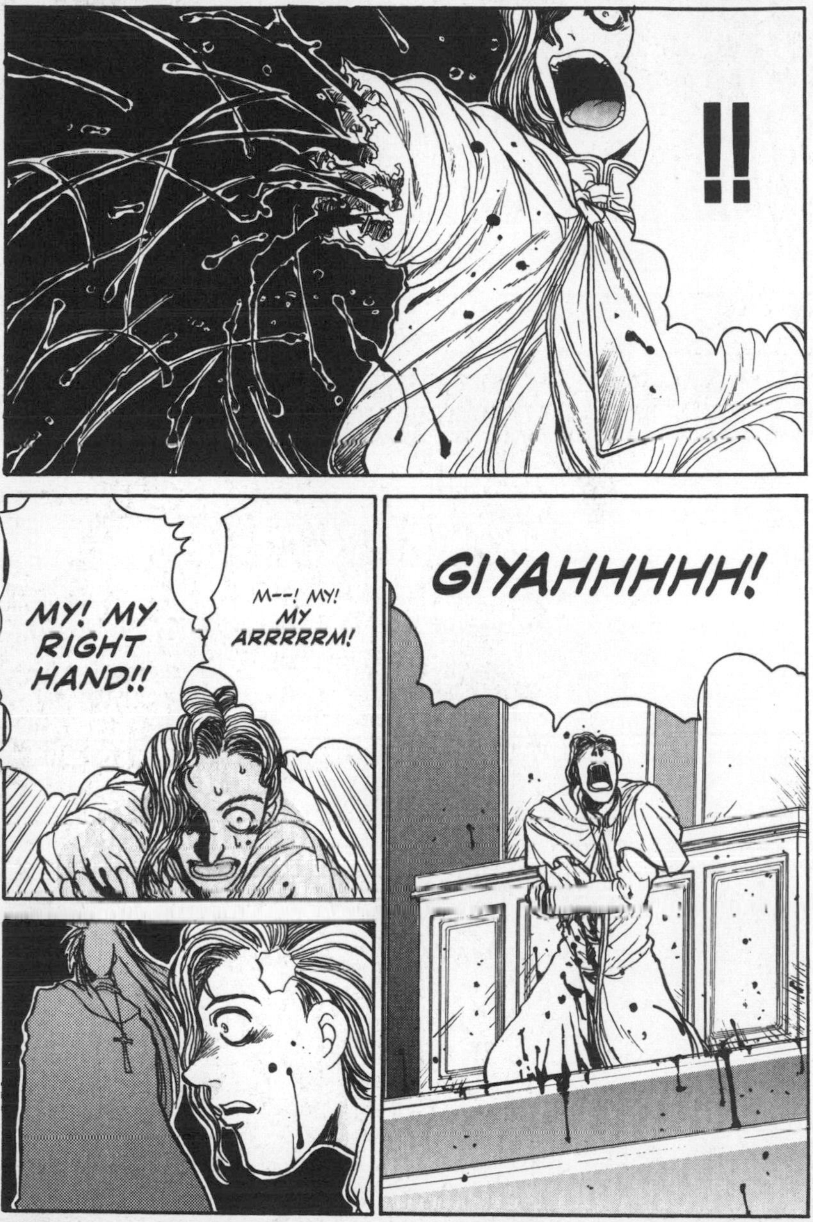
!!
GIYAHHHHH!
M--! MY! MY ARRRRRM!
MY! MY RIGHT HAND!!

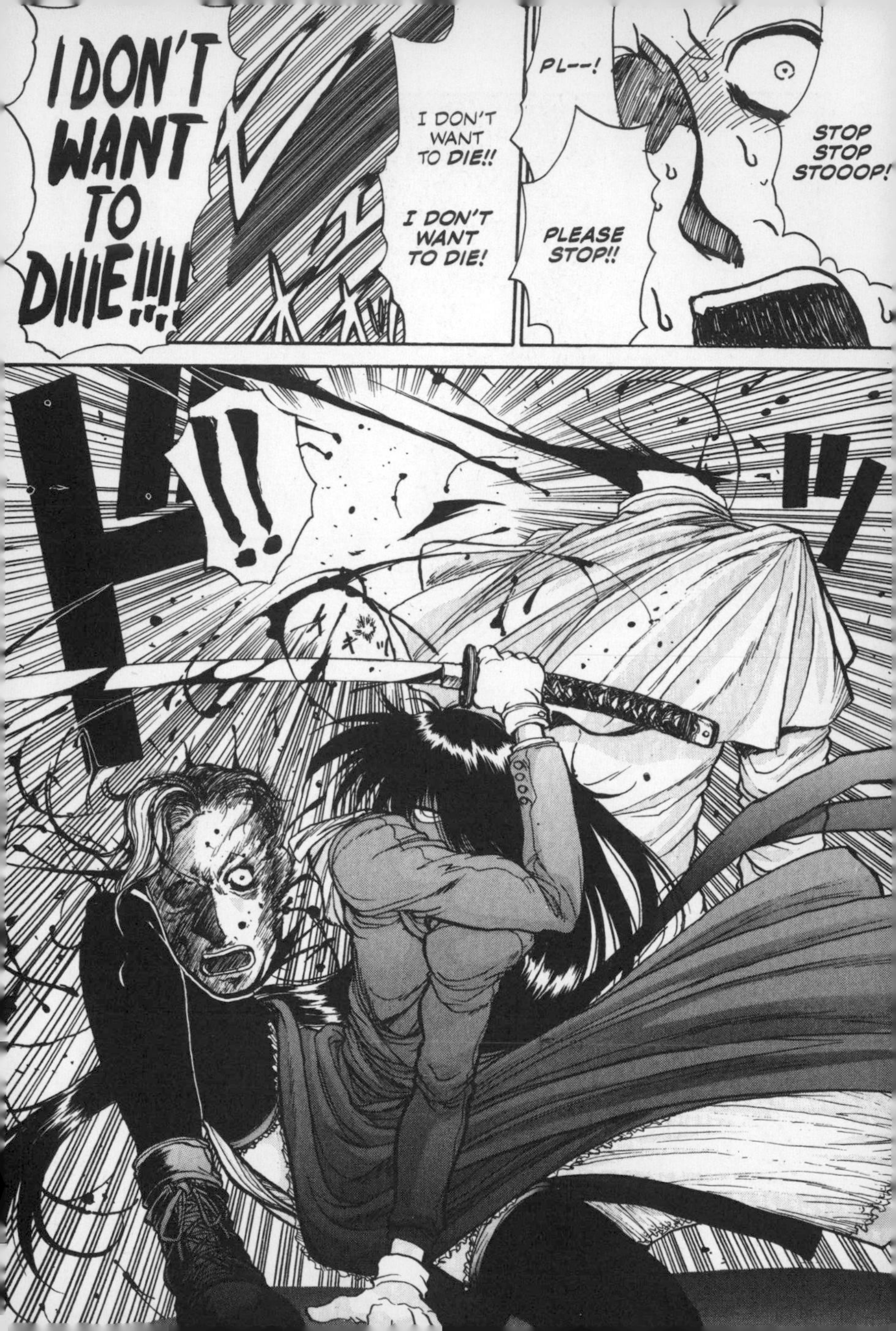
STOP STOP STOOOP!
PL--!
PLEASE STOP!!
I DON'T WANT TO DIE!!
I DON'T WANT TO DIE!
I DON'T WANT TO DIIIE!!!!

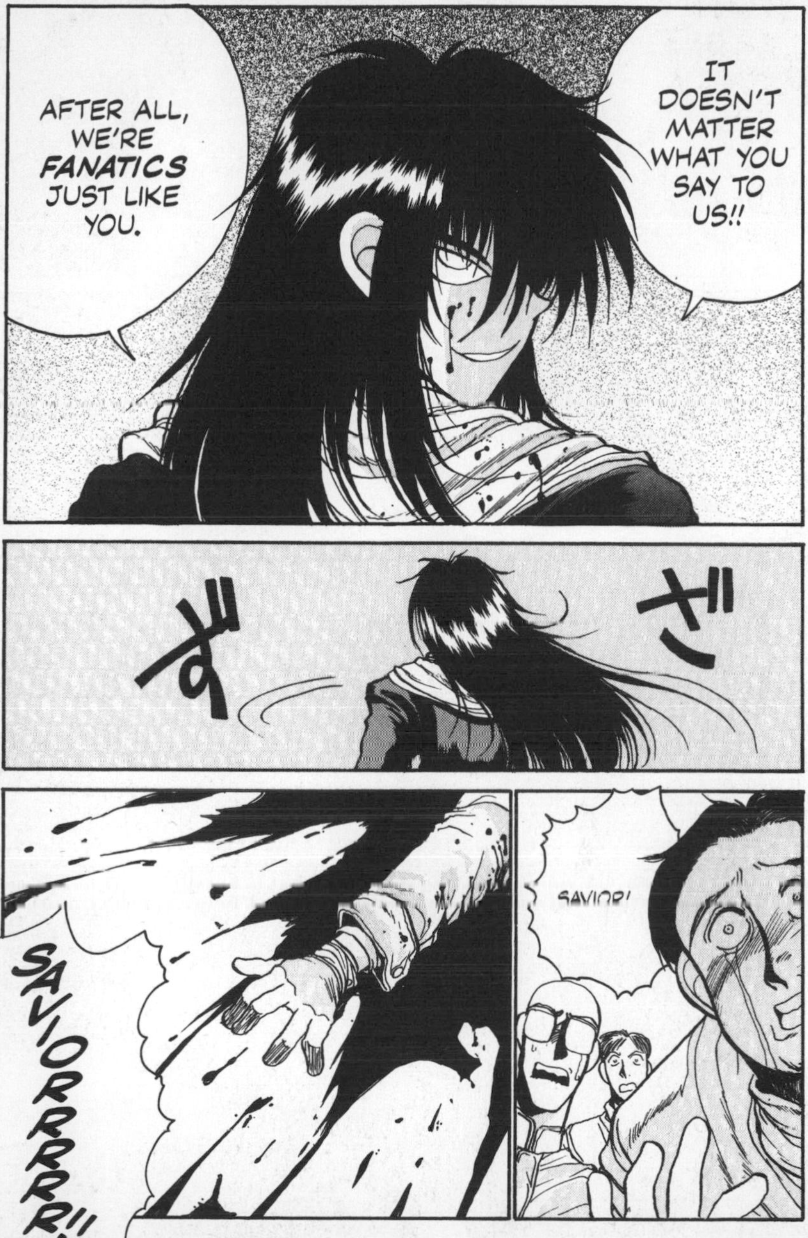
IT DOESN'T MATTER WHAT YOU SAY TO US!!
AFTER ALL, WE'RE *FANATICS* JUST LIKE YOU.
ざ
ず
SAVIOR!
SAVIORRRRR!!

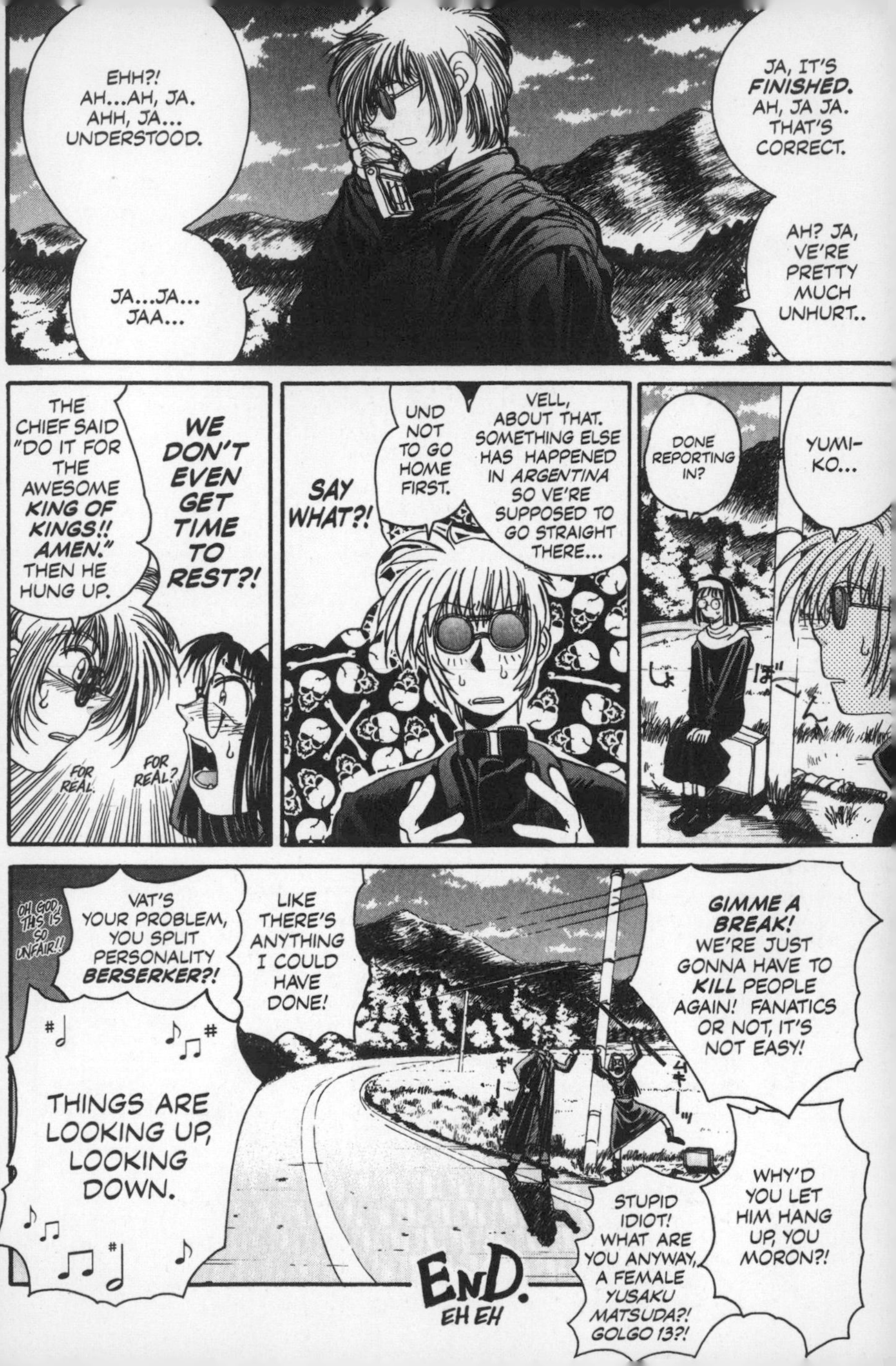

JA, IT'S **FINISHED.** AH, JA JA. THAT'S CORRECT.
AH? JA, VE'RE PRETTY MUCH UNHURT..
EHH?! AH...AH, JA. AHH, JA... UNDERSTOOD.
JA...JA... JAA...
YUMI-KO...
DONE REPORTING IN?
VELL, ABOUT THAT. SOMETHING ELSE HAS HAPPENED IN *ARGENTINA* SO VE'RE SUPPOSED TO GO STRAIGHT THERE...
UND NOT TO GO HOME FIRST.
SAY WHAT?!
WE DON'T EVEN GET TIME TO REST?!
THE CHIEF SAID "DO IT FOR THE AWESOME **KING OF KINGS!! AMEN."** THEN HE HUNG UP.
FOR REAL?
FOR REAL.
GIMME A BREAK! WE'RE JUST GONNA HAVE TO **KILL** PEOPLE AGAIN! FANATICS OR NOT, IT'S NOT EASY!
WHY'D YOU LET HIM HANG UP, YOU MORON?!
STUPID IDIOT! WHAT ARE YOU ANYWAY, A FEMALE *YUSAKU MATSUDA?! GOLGO 13?!*
LIKE THERE'S ANYTHING I COULD HAVE DONE!
VAT'S YOUR PROBLEM, YOU SPLIT PERSONALITY **BERSERKER?!**
OH GOD, THIS IS SO UNFAIR!!
THINGS ARE LOOKING UP, LOOKING DOWN.
END. EH EH

■ "SURPRISE!! BALLS TO THE SKY?!" (A GREETING I MADE UP) GOOD EVENING... THIS IS KOHTA HIRANO. AND SO, THIS IS VOLUME 3! IT'S TRUE, IT'S BEEN A YEAR SINCE THE LAST VOLUME CAME OUT. NOT A GOOD THING. VERY NOT. Y'KNOW? EXTREMELY NOT. BUT A WIDE RANGE OF THINGS HAVE HAPPENED THIS PAST YEAR. NOT!! NOTHING HAPPENED AT ALL. THE ONLY WORK I DID WAS DRAWING MANGA, READING MANGA, WATCHING ANIME, PLAYING GAMES, AND OTHER THAN THAT JUST CONVERTING FOOD INTO POOP!! OH, AND PLAYING WITH MYSELF. HUMANS ARE SUPPOSED TO HAVE MORE MEANINGFUL LIVES THAN THIS!! (CRIES OUT LOUD) KIDDING.

■ AND SO SINCE I'M ONCE AGAIN DOING WHATEVER I PLEASE WITH THE STORY I'M HAPPY THAT SOOOOOO MANY PEOPLE ARE STILL READING IT. IT'S ONE SPACED OUT MANGA. "LIKE THAT OLD SHOW THE FLYING HOUSE?" NO, NOT LIKE THAT.

■ I WONDER WHAT SPELL I'D HAVE TO CHANT TO MAKE MEGUMI FROM UROTSUKIDOJI APPEAR?

CHARACTER DESCRIPTIONS

■ **THE MAJOR** — A VILLAIN STRAIGHT OUT OF MY ADULT MATERIAL. (BEEN A LONG TIME...) ON THE OUTSIDE HE LOOKS LIKE AN OTAKU. SAME GOES FOR THE INSIDE. WITHIN HIS HEART LIES A MYSTERIOUS OTAKU. IT'S BEEN FIVE YEARS SINCE I LAST DREW HIM, AND HIS FACE SEEMS TO HAVE GROWN.

■ **THE CAPTAIN** — A SOLDIER STRAIGHT OUT OF MY ADULT MATERIAL. A TALLLL SHIFTY ROUGHNECK WITH A MAUSER IN ONE HAND. A REAL HELL'S ANGEL. KIDDING. HE'S THE TROUBLESOME KIND OF GUY WHO'LL BRING DOWN THE WHOLE NEIGHBORHOOD IF YOU TAKE YOUR EYES OFF HIM.

■ **THE PROFESSOR** — ANOTHER CHARACTER FROM MY ADULT MATERIAL THAT I ARRANGED A BIT TO USE WITH THE OTHERS. THIS GANG OF THREE IS OUT FOR A WAR OF VENGEANCE. GET A GRIP, ME!

CROSS FIRE PART 3 → NICKNAMED TWIN KILLERS.

THAT'S ABOUT HOW IT FEELS. IS IT OVERDONE? YOU THINK? WELL WHAT DO YOU KNOW?! JUST KIDDING. SORRY... WHEN I DREW IT, I WAS PRETTY CAUGHT UP IN STUFF IN THE NEWS LIKE AUM SO I WASN'T FEELING TOO SUBTLE.

KENTARO MIURA'S MANGA EPIC

Presented uncensored in its
original Japanese format

emanga.com

VOLUME 1: 1-59307-020-9....$13.95

AVAILABLE AT YOUR LOCAL COMICS SHOP OR BOOKSTORE
To find a comics shop in your area, call 1-888-266-4226.
For more information or to order direct visit darkhorse.com or call 1-800-862-0052

darkhorse.com

STOP

This is the back of the book!

This manga collection is translated into English but oriented in right-to-left reading format at the creator's request, maintaining the artwork's visual orientation as originally published in Japan. If you've never read manga in this way before, take a look at the diagram below to give yourself an idea of how to go about it. Basically, you'll be starting in the upper right corner and will read each balloon and panel moving right to left. It may take some getting used to, but you should get the hang of it very quickly. Have fun!

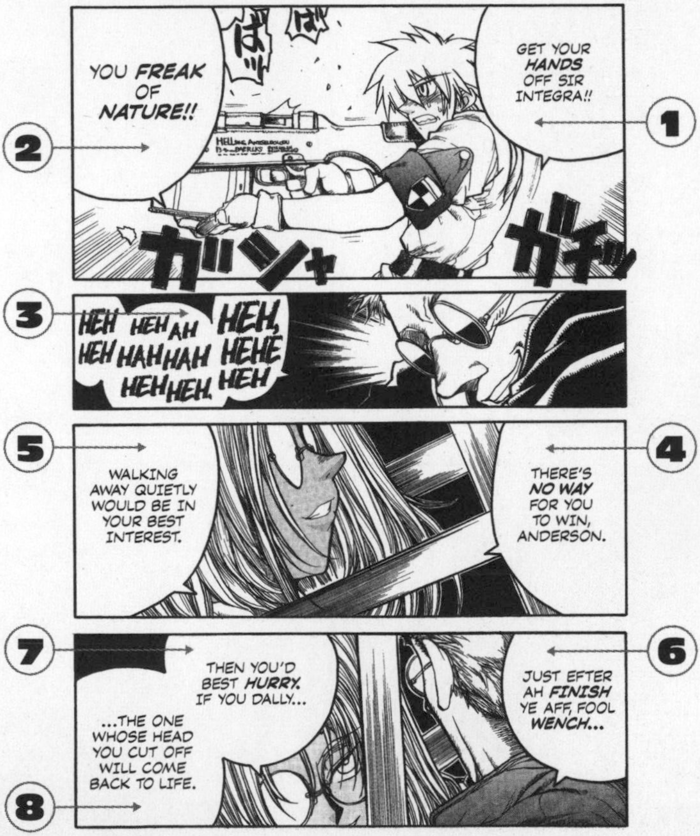
1
GET YOUR HANDS OFF SIR INTEGRA!!
2
YOU FREAK OF NATURE!!
3
HEH, HEHE HEH
HEH HAH AH HAH HEH HEH.
HEH HEH
4
THERE'S NO WAY FOR YOU TO WIN, ANDERSON.
5
WALKING AWAY QUIETLY WOULD BE IN YOUR BEST INTEREST.
6
JUST EFTER AH FINISH YE AFF, FOOL WENCH...
7
THEN YOU'D BEST HURRY. IF YOU DALLY...
8
...THE ONE WHOSE HEAD YOU CUT OFF WILL COME BACK TO LIFE.